SEVEN HEXES

ALSO BY ELIZABETH K. KING

THE HORRIFIC FAIRY TALES SERIES
Rotting Beauty
Beast By Day
The Little Sea Monster
Seven Hexes
Ghoul Girl (forthcoming)

Don't Go Into the Woods (novella)

SEVEN HEXES

HORRIFIC FAIRY TALES BOOK 4

ELIZABETH K. KING

This is a work of fiction. All of the characters, organizations, and events portrayed in this novel are either products of the author's imagination or are used fictitiously.

SEVEN HEXES

Published in the United States by Elizabeth King. For inquiries, please visit the author's website: www.elizabethkking.com

Cover Art by Miblart.

Map by Saumya Singh (@Saumyasvision/Inkarnate).

The text for this book was set in EB Garamond.

ISBN 979-8-9987153-0-3 (hardcover)

ISBN 979-8-9987153-1-0 (paperback)

ISBN 979-8-9888121-9-7 (ebook)

First Edition, May 2025.

For Lady

CONTENTS

AUTHOR'S NOTE

As this is the fourth book in the series, the story contains references to characters, places, events, and elements from the previous three books. In the back of this book, you will find a glossary that may be helpful if you are having trouble remembering some of these elements.

The glossary is spoiler-free for *Seven Hexes*. It is intended that you can reference it from the very first chapter of this book without being spoiled for anything later in the story. However, it will contain spoilers for the first three books: *Rotting Beauty*, *Beast By Day*, and *The Little Sea Monster*.

MOUNTAIN KINGDOM

Briar's Castle

FOREST KINGDOM

Old Castle

Black Forest

Glen Castle

GLEN KINGDOM

Snow's Castle

MARINER KINGDOM

DESERT KINGDOM

THE FIVE KINGDOMS

1

HEXED

ANSEL SCOWLED AT THE rising moon overhead, just visible through the naked branches of an aspen tree. Stuffing his hands into his pockets, he dropped his gaze, watching his breath mist the frigid air. *Late*, he thought furiously, *of course they're late.* While Ansel stood out here alone, at dusk. With only the trees for company.

And with a witch prowling these woods.

Ansel wasn't too concerned about the witch. It was very unlikely he'd run into her here. Not when she'd spent the past several months evading him. But even still, danger lurked in these woods, and that was why Ansel was here. Waiting in the cold. Watching the forest darken around him.

Ansel was at home in the woods. His father had raised him and his sister on the road, doing whatever simple work he could find—hunting, trapping, chopping wood. So Ansel had no reason to fear the woods, even in the dim light of the gloaming. It was familiar for him. And yet, the longer he stood there—the longer he waited—the stranger the woods became. The near-dark made monsters of the gnarled trees and ghosts of the whistling wind. When a raven *cawed* overhead, taking flight, Ansel jumped.

A raven, he told himself. *Only a raven.* But ravens at dusk were a bad omen. Everyone knew that.

He glanced up and saw, with a shiver prickling down his back, that the raven had landed on a thick, crooked branch above him. The ashy black of the raven was nearly lost against the backdrop of the tree's dark canopy. The raven blinked a pale, beady eye at Ansel, cocking its head in a most uncanny way.

Then another raven landed on the same branch, and another, and another. Ansel swallowed, looking away.

When he looked again a minute later, a dozen ravens perched in the tree above him. Staring down. Rustling their wings.

A great swooping sensation tugged at Ansel's middle. Perhaps it was a premonition. Because a second later, the rustle of wings became a great, flapping clatter.

The ravens burst from the tree and enveloped him.

Only half a shout escaped Ansel. The rest of it was battered back down his throat. The ravens swept around him in a storm of black wings and sharp beaks. They were only ravens, and probably startled by something. Ansel knew this, but still, he panicked. He lifted his hands to his head, trying to swat the creatures away, which only encouraged their frenzy. The tips of their wings knotted in his curly hair, and their talons raked his neck.

Ansel began to run blindly, arms raised about his head. He was in such a panic that he didn't notice when the birds swept away from him, spiraling up into the air. He kept running, shaking his head furiously, with no thought to where he was going—

Suddenly, something large loomed before him. Something that gave a shrill *whinny* and reared on its hind legs. Ansel scrambled back to avoid raised hooves, but his boot slipped over a slick patch of mud. He wheeled his arms wildly, trying to keep his balance, but he fell hard, rolling onto his back.

"Careful, there! Are you all right?"

Ansel blinked, stunned and bruised. The ground was cold and unforgiving, the packed mud a poor cushion beneath him. He pushed himself upright, peeling a large, dead maple leaf off his cheek. Dazed, he looked up.

A horse stood in the road. It stamped its foot and gave a nervous toss of its head, but it seemed calm enough now. Likely due to its rider, who sat astride the horse, soothing it with a gentle hand upon its neck. He was a young man, hazy in the dying light and further obscured by Ansel's swimmy vision. Ansel waited until he could make out the rider's floppy brown hair, fair skin, and narrow shoulders. All matching a description that had been given to him.

"Demetri?" Ansel said, wincing as he climbed to his feet.

"Yes." The young man, Demetri, frowned at Ansel. Then realization dawned on his face. "Ansel?"

"Yes."

"Oh, of course." Demetri's frown deepened, wrinkling his forehead. "Is everything all right?" He cast a glance down the road. "You were running—"

"It was nothing." Ansel's face grew warm. He suddenly resented Demetri's presence here even more than he already did.

"Just a flock of birds. Startled me." His voice dropped to a mutter, his cheeks positively burning. "That's all."

"Oh, good." To his credit, Demetri only sounded relieved. He did not laugh or crack a joke at Ansel's expense. "I was worried something had happened. Or that something was chasing you." He said "something" with undisguised apprehension. Ansel guessed that in Demetri's line of work, he'd seen a lot of *somethings*—some of them probably horrifying.

"Well, now we know everything's all right," came another voice, "might I get an introduction?"

Ansel glanced past Demetri, only now realizing there was another horse behind him. The young woman leaning out from her saddle lifted a hand in greeting. She was roughly the same age as Demetri, and her fitted jacket and trousers revealed a small but athletic frame.

"I'm sorry." Demetri twisted around in his saddle. "Ansel, this is my partner, Sabine."

The monster-hunting duo, Ansel thought. He, too, raised a hand in greeting. "Hello. I'm Ansel."

"And I'm Demetri," Demetri added belatedly.

Ansel stared at him. "Yes. I know."

Now Demetri was the one who flushed. "Just wanted to make a proper introduction." He fiddled with the cuff of his coat sleeve. The coat was posh if somewhat old-fashioned, a mid-length, black riding coat, flaring slightly from the waist. His tall boots were very fine too, well-oiled leather with silver buckles. Outdoor wear, to be sure, but richer garb than Ansel's worn boots and patched breeches.

Demetri gave an uncertain cough, looking down at Ansel. "Where's your horse?"

Ansel raised an eyebrow. First a "proper" introduction, and now he assumed everyone rode a horse? Ansel barely knew how to ride, and only because of the short time he'd spent as a guardsman in the Mariner Kingdom. Like most hunters and woodsmen, he preferred to travel on foot. He knew how to disguise his trail and keep quiet amongst the trees; he couldn't control the noise or movements of a horse.

But evidently, this Demetri was used to finer folk. Ansel wasn't sure what to make of that. He didn't really know anything about Demetri, except for what Prince Garrett had told him. And that was very little.

It had been nearly a year since Ansel had seen Prince Garrett, when they'd worked together to save Garrett's brother, Gryphon. (Of course, the predicament Gryphon had been in was partly Ansel's fault, but that was neither here nor there.) Ansel was still hunting the witch he'd faced then, Adela. When he'd realized he was closing in on Adela's trail—and in Garrett's kingdom, no less—he sent the prince an update via telegram.

He hadn't expected Garrett to send anyone to join him. But here Ansel was, meeting with this pair of monster hunters who worked for the crown. Apparently, they were investigating something in these parts as well, and Garrett thought their investigation might be linked to Adela. So he'd let Ansel know the two would join him, and Ansel found himself wishing he hadn't telegrammed the prince after all.

Ansel liked Prince Garrett. He did. But he was used to working alone. He worked faster on his own. And he didn't know anything about this Demetri—except that he traveled on horseback.

5

Demetri looked down at him with an expectant air—waiting for an answer to his question, Ansel realized. "I don't have a horse," Ansel said, stuffing his hands into the pockets of his baggy brown coat.

"Oh. Well, er—you could ride with one of us...?"

"I'm fine walking." Ansel tried to conceal his annoyance, but he was afraid some of it snuck into his tone. He gestured up the road. "The village isn't far. Less than a mile. It's just hard to find because it's set back from the road, and the wood is overgrown 'round here."

"Right." Demetri shifted his grip on his reins. "If you're sure you're all right, then..."

"I am." To demonstrate this, Ansel turned and started down the road, gesturing for the others to follow. He didn't look back to see if they did; he just listened for the soft, slow clopping of their horses' hooves trailing behind him.

He couldn't walk fast enough to stay ahead of the horses, of course. Not in the growing dark. The woods *were* overgrown, gangly poplar trees curving over the road, creating a brambly tunnel. The poplars were scrawnier than ever in the winter, their branches bare, but evergreen yews and southern oaks grew here too, their thick boughs tangling and blocking out the daylight. Ansel was forced to slow his pace to keep from stumbling, and gradually, he fell back to walk abreast of the mounted Demetri.

And Demetri, apparently, liked to chatter. A lot. He went on and on, first about Ansel's sister, Isabelle, whom he'd met over a year ago at her home in the northern part of the kingdom. From what Ansel gathered, they'd only known each other for a few days, but you wouldn't know it, as much as Demetri talked about her. Then he changed tack and started talking about the

Mariner Kingdom—evidently, he knew Ansel had spent some time there, and evidently, he had as well. Before he got too far into this topic of conversation, Ansel interrupted and said, "So, I understand Prince Garrett thought we might be after the same thing. Shall we get down to business?"

"Oh." Demetri's tone was tinged with surprise. "Right now? I thought we might discuss everything at the inn...over supper, perhaps..."

Ansel schooled his expression. Truthfully, once they got to the inn, Ansel hoped to eat quickly—preferably alone—and get up to bed. He didn't say that, though. He didn't say anything. His silence was expectant, and after a moment, Demetri cleared his throat and said, "Right, well, we can start now. I suppose. What did Garrett tell you about our investigation?"

"Not much," Ansel admitted. "Just that you're looking into some 'weird' things happening around here. And that he thought it might be connected to the witch I'm hunting. Adela."

"Well." Demetri shifted in his saddle. "I don't know if it's anything to do with your witch. It's tough to say if it's even supernatural."

"I don't know." Sabine pitched her voice loudly enough to be heard from behind them. "I wouldn't say there's anything natural about spontaneous combustion."

Ansel jerked around. "What now?"

"That was the first occurrence, as near as we can tell," Demetri explained. "But we didn't actually witness it. It happened in another village a little way from here—Harmut? So we only heard the story secondhand, but. Some of the witnesses were quite credible."

"The man was a logger." Sabine's grave tone seemed to deepen the gloom of the woods. "He just sat down to dinner in a tavern, and then, without warning—"

"Spontaneous combustion," said Demetri. "People said it was like his blood had begun to boil. He turned all red and splotchy, and then...flames."

Ansel shrugged off a shiver, imagining the shocking death.

"Then there were the spiders," Sabine said.

"Spiders?"

"A whole granary full of them." Hearing a tremor in Demetri's voice, Ansel looked up. The young man had gone pale. Well, paler. "Grain attracts pests, of course, but not usually full-grown spiders. Spiders the size of a man's fist."

"And there was no grain left," Sabine added. "Not in the bags, not in the stores—it was like the grain had turned *into* spiders. Overnight."

Ansel eyed Demetri. "Are you all right?"

"I don't like spiders," Demetri confessed.

"They can't hurt you. Well, not usually. Not much."

"Trust me," Sabine drawled. "He has good reason not to like them."

"We've seen things," Demetri said.

Ansel shrugged. "I'll take your word for it." He pushed aside a branch sticking out into the road, thinking all of this through. "Did this happen in the same village as the man who burst into flame?"

"Yes, the same village. We stayed there one night—the spiders happened the day after we arrived. Then a few days later, there was the snakes."

"Also the same village," Sabine said. "All the wells in the town suddenly overflowed with snakes. They were literally spilling out of the wells."

"Do these incidents sound like witchcraft?" Demetri inquired. "Could it be Adela?"

"Could it be? Yes." Ansel's tone was distracted, his mind divided between these strange happenings and watching for the turn-off for the village. "Any of those things could be a hex of some kind. The real question would be why."

"Does there have to be a why?" Sabine asked. "Seems like the sort of thing a witch might get a kick out of."

"Well, yes." Ansel slowed his pace as he recognized a particularly grotesque yew tree, squat and twisted. "But Adela has been on the run for a while now, and she takes great care to lie low. So why hang around torturing villagers?"

"You don't think it was her, then."

"I think if it was her," Ansel said absently, "she must have had a good reason to do those things. Something beyond petty fun for herself."

"Perhaps she has it out for someone in the village?" Demetri suggested.

"Maybe." Ansel rubbed two fingers over his forehead. "It just seems...I don't know." He let out a heavy breath. "I feel like I'm missing something. Or forgetting something. There has to be more going on."

They continued up the road for another minute, then made the turn-off. Ansel already smelled woodsmoke from the village, the crisply cold air laden with the heavy scent. Their pace slowed even more as the horses struggled to navigate the woods along a worn deer path. Ansel flinched at a flurry of wings, but it was

9

no raven this time. Only an owl, hooting as it swooped from one tree to another. Even though he wasn't alone anymore, Ansel still felt jumpy, unsettled by the shadowy woods.

It wasn't just the growing dark or the ravens. It was *these* woods. It was this place. It had been many years since Ansel spent time here, but the memories from that time were still fresh. Unwelcome, unpleasant memories.

Luckily, they were only in the woods a few minutes longer. Then they were out. There was no real transition, no thinning of the trees or clearing overhead. One minute, they were snarled in the thick of the woods, and the next, they were free of it, emerging into open air beneath the sky. The glade before them housed the village of Lise, a cluster of small, square buildings lit by standing gear-bulb lanterns lining the streets. The lanterns were lit but hardly needed; Ansel was surprised to see how light it still was. The last of the sun still glared a burnt-orange, just visible on the western horizon. It had seemed so much darker in the woods.

They started into the town. The first few buildings they passed were residential, small homes with pointed roofs and windows framed in wooden shutters. Most of the doors were hung with evergreen boughs and holly in celebration of the coming winter holidays. It wasn't long before the homes gave way to businesses, shop fronts preparing to close for the night. Ansel spotted an opening in the streets and pointed. "The inn's just ahead, on the corner of the village square."

"Oh, good," Demetri said with relief. "We've already got two rooms booked, so everything should be ready. Personally, I'm ready for a hot meal and..."

Ansel tuned out the young man, letting him natter on. It may have been earlier than he thought, but the day was fading fast. The sky was darkest on the left, twilight's hazy gray sliding into night's inky black. Wisps of cloud dotted the sky, making it even murkier. As Ansel watched, one of those wisps seemed to grow, breaking away from the rest of the clouds, growing blacker and larger in the sky.

"...honey butter," Demetri was saying. "That's my favorite. Then you don't have to choose—"

"Demetri," Ansel interrupted, pointing again—not at the square this time, but at the sky. "Do you see that?"

The rogue cloud was still drifting, churning, moving towards the village with increasing speed. And Ansel realized it was not a cloud at all. It was a *flock*. More ravens, he worried, but this was a massive amount of ravens. And as they grew closer, he realized there was something strange about the way they flapped their wings, quick and frenzied, and something strange about their chirping call, sharper and higher than a raven's deep-throated caw—

They were not ravens.

They were bats.

It was a massive colony of bats, descending upon the town with targeted fury. Moving as one and heading right for—

"Duck!" someone in the town square screamed.

Ansel dove to the ground just in time, his palms scraping over the gritty street. The army of bats shot by him, dipping down into the town square. He heard Demetri swear as he hastened out of his saddle, toppling to the ground. The bats screeched as they flapped past, arcing into the air, ignoring the shrieks of the villagers. Ansel glanced up and saw a second swarm barreling into

11

the square. Like the first, it moved as a single entity, smashing through a shop window and sending shards of glass flying.

"This isn't normal!" Sabine cried. She, too, had climbed down from her saddle and crouched low to the ground. "Bats don't attack like this!"

She was right. Bats didn't even move like this. This couldn't be natural.

This was witchcraft.

"Someone's behind this." Ansel wheeled around to face Demetri. "Someone's doing this. We have to—"

"Ansel, look out!" Demetri shouted.

Still on his knees, Ansel spun around.

Just as the swarm of bats shot straight for him, smothering him in a cloud of wings and claws.

2

MARKED

J ESINE WAS NOT AWARE of the bats. A mile outside the village of Lise, she sat beneath the gnarled branches of a barren hickory tree. No, not barren. Dormant. Asleep for the winter, conserving its energy. Protecting itself against the harsh cold.

And perhaps, protecting something else. Concealing something else.

Jesine settled herself, arraying the folds of her gray wool skirt around her and sliding back the hood of her olive-green coat. Her hair was braided and loosely bound behind her head, and the cold bit at the bare nape of her neck. But she ignored it, evening out her breathing. Inhaling deeply, exhaling softly. Each breath like a whisper.

She removed the glove from her right hand, then the one from her left. Closing her eyes, she leaned forward and placed her hands upon the ground. She stretched her fingers wide, as close to the base of the tree as possible, feeling the knobby roots beneath the earth. Once she felt in-tune with her own breath, she spread her focus out, concentrating on the *feel* of that bumpy earth beneath her fingers, on the curves of each root.

She focused on her breath. She focused on the roots. She imagined them twining together, her breath and the roots.

Then she spread her focus in a third direction, reaching for the link inside her. It was delicate yet supple, like a fine, silvery chain. One end resided within her, settled in her center. Jesine felt along the chain for the other end, unseen, hundreds of miles away. Lost to the distance.

Perhaps too much distance. Jesine gritted her teeth, briefly losing touch with her breath. *Where are you, Kel?* she wondered. Granted, it was probably for the best Kel wasn't here. She wouldn't approve of what Jesine was doing. But she wasn't here, and she couldn't refuse Jesine's pull at her magic. Their agreement forbid that.

The distance made things difficult, though. Jesine worried what else might be wrong. That delicate chain inside her seemed more and more delicate lately, each pull for magic harder and harder. *Was* it just the distance? Was Kel traveling, moving further north? Or was it something else?

Jesine drew in another breath, feeling along the chain. And then, finally, a trickle. A trickle of power, flowing along each link. Flowing through Jesine. Flowing through her touch, into the roots beneath her. Delving into the earth.

But there was nothing there. Oh, there was magic. Pockets of it buried alongside the roots. But no more than usual, no more than what lay beneath any other tree. Jesine's frustration gave way to disappointment as she released her magic, letting it disperse back into the earth. She sat back and blew out another breath. This one not so soft and even.

Her father's voice echoed inside her head, and she remembered the sound of it, the cadence, even though she hadn't heard it in over four years. *This task is our family's duty, Jesine, and your legacy. Bad witches outnumber us fifty to one, but that just makes what we do more important. We guard stores of unimaginable power, and if any bad witch ever got to it, that would be the end. For us. For everyone. Maybe for the entire world.*

Jesine sniffed. That was all well and good, but how was she supposed to protect anything if she didn't know where it was?

Wearily, she climbed to her feet, steadying herself against the hickory tree. Even that small bit of magic had strained her. She ran a hand over her head, clutching at her long, tousled hair behind her neck.

Maybe this search of hers was fruitless. What was there to protect, after all? There hadn't been any witches in these parts for several years. Most of the ones who had threatened the land during her father's time were dead. Maybe all of them were dead. Maybe—like Kel insisted—there was no reason for her to be here.

Of course, she had her own reasons for searching for that power. Beyond her family's "duty."

Still leaning into the tree, Jesine sniffed again, this time from the cold. Her gloves were on the ground, and her fingers had grown numb. The sun was sinking fast beyond the trees; if she hadn't been in this position, high on a hill above the woods, she wouldn't have been able to see it. *I'd better head home*, she thought, defeated. It was only going to get colder.

That was when she felt it. An icy prickle at the back of her neck.

Jesine stilled. This cold creeping up on her was not born from the plunging temperatures. This cold was more nebulous, sinister. It was a hand sliding up her spine, a whisper in her ear—

Jesine straightened and whipped around.

There was nothing there.

There never was.

Jesine wiped a tired hand across her forehead. Then she reached down to retrieve her gloves. Once she'd tugged them on, she started down the hill, carefully navigating the rugged land in her heeled boots.

She'd just reached the bottom of the hill when she heard the screams.

Jesine stopped again. For a moment, she wondered if she'd imagined that high-pitched shriek, but then she heard another one. Then another, and another, scream piled over scream. They were very distant, but unmistakable. Screams from multiple people.

Jesine frowned, perplexed. Who would be out in the woods so close to dark, so many people together...?

And then she realized. The village. Lise lay to the west, less than a mile away.

Jesine wavered. *It's none of my business*, a part of her said. A large part of her. Perhaps that was callous, given the access to power she had. But though witches like herself could help others freely, her father had discouraged going out of her way to do so. A good witch first had to protect herself—that was what he'd taught her. Since most common folk didn't make any distinction between "good" and "bad" witches. Still, she couldn't banish the guilt surging up in her as she turned away, angling north. Starting up the path that would take her home.

She was still weighing that guilt against her own self-preservation when something else reached her—something far more disturbing than the screams. Something she felt rather than heard.

It was like a punch to the gut, stealing her breath. An invisible force washing over her, leaving a static spark in the air. And a peculiar smell...loamy and damp, but *charged*. Like the smell of oncoming rain. It was not an unfamiliar feeling, but never had she felt it like this before. So sudden. So potent. So violent.

Magic. A lot of it. Dark magic.

Dread pooled in Jesine's gut. Dark magic. Bad witches. She closed her eyes, wishing she could close her mind as easily. Witches were here. They were back. Whether it was the same ones as before or different witches, it made no difference. Jesine knew why they were here.

Had she closed herself to this truth? There had been a couple of times over the last few weeks when she thought she'd felt something. A whisper of magic. But that was all it was. Whispers, soft and distant, easy to dismiss. Easy to convince herself she'd imagined it.

Well, she hadn't imagined this onslaught of power. This was real, and close by. And she didn't have to think very hard to guess where it came from. The use of such powerful magic at the same time screams overtook the village of Lise was no coincidence.

She turned and headed for the village, racing through the trees.

She reached Lise in less than ten minutes, breathless and clammy. At the tree line, she leaned around a broad oak to peer at the village outskirts. The screams and shouts were clearer here, but she couldn't see anything amiss. The houses were quiet and still, smoke curling up from their chimneys. Warily, Jesine crept out of the trees.

She hadn't taken three steps when something dark and massive appeared in the sky, a vast shadow sweeping over the town. It was a noisy shadow, flapping and screeching as it wove through the air.

Birds, Jesine thought, following the sinuous black wave as it dipped below the buildings. No, not birds. *Bats*.

Jesine picked up her pace, hurrying through the village, turning corner after corner until she reached the trouble. It was the town square, bordered by businesses built from pale gray stone and cedar-brown brick. Only now, those businesses were wrecked—windows shattered, walls gouged, doors splintered and hanging off their hinges. The square itself was relatively empty, the only visible people peering around corners and hiding beneath stalls and carts. But screams could be heard from inside the buildings, and the source of them was apparent.

Bats. Swarms of them, Jesine saw, several different swarms. But each one moved as a single entity, mammoth creatures of darkness bombarding the village. They smashed through windows and barreled down chimneys, and when they found a person out in the open, they attacked with teeth and talons. Jesine spotted a woman—a dead woman—slumped against a storefront. Blood streaked her cheeks, trickling from jagged gashes in her skin.

Many people feared bats, but that was irrational. Bats didn't attack people. Not like this. These were not normal bats. They weren't acting of their own accord.

This was a hex. A powerful, sophisticated one.

Jesine flinched as another swarm crashed through the windows on her left. She retreated a few steps and crouched down, trying to make herself less of a target. She could try and use magic to stop the bats, but that wasn't really a viable solution. Given the state of her magic lately, she wouldn't be able to summon enough to counter this hex. She could help the individual people here, but on her own, she could only do so much.

No, she needed to find the source of the hex—the witch sustaining the spell. And stop them.

They probably weren't in the village. They didn't need to see the village or the bats to work the hex. But they wouldn't be far. No matter how powerful the caster, or how many of them there were, they wouldn't be able to sustain the hex from too far away.

Jesine bent even lower as she closed her eyes, reaching inside herself. Not for that delicate chain—she didn't need her own magic to do this. To trace this hex, all she had to do was feel for it. Dark magic felt like a disturbance in the earth, a black rot she could follow to its source. Pulsating power, stolen magic, ripped from the land—

There. Jesine lifted her head like a bloodhound scenting the air. On her right, north of the square—north of the town.

Now she just had to get there.

She raised herself up, thinking to scurry through the back streets around the square, but she didn't even reach her full height before a swarm of bats dove straight at her. Jesine dove too, throwing herself around the corner. The swarm rushed past her, mostly; as Jesine pushed herself up, she discovered a bat tangled in her hair, its flapping and writhing pulling at her braid. She reached back, trying to slap it away. The little creature clawed at her hand, drawing blood. Annoyed, Jesine gripped the furry little menace and ripped it out of her hair.

She pulled it around to look at it. It glared at her with red eyes and hissed.

Jesine hissed back, released it, and managed a little spark from her fingertips, shocking it. *Oh, yes,* Jesine thought, *now I manage some magic.*

The bat screeched, tumbled in the air, and swooped away.

The swarm ricocheted into the air again, swerving around, arcing back towards the square. Jesine waited them out, then hurried down the block. She kept an eye on the bats as she crisscrossed through the streets, making her way to the northern end of the village. As she left the square behind, she picked up her pace, nearly running, casting one last glance behind her to make sure she was clear of the bats—

She rounded a corner and crashed into someone so hard that she lost her footing. She barely caught herself on hands and knees before she could fall flat on her face.

"Sorry," she gasped, lifting her skirt as she hastened back to her feet. "I'm sorry—"

But the person she'd run into, a young man, was also apologizing, speaking over her. "Sorry, sorry, my fault—"

Jesine dusted her coat off, looking north again. "Are you all right?"

"I'm fine, are *you* all right—"

"Yes, fine." Jesine turned away. "Sorry—"

"No, I'm—wait...you—"

"Sorry, I have to go." Without another glance, she hurried off, scampering down the village streets. The ruckus in the town—the screeching of the bats, the screams of the villagers, the explosions of brick and glass—all diminished as she neared the outskirts, glimpsing the tangled forest ahead. She stopped and closed her eyes, making sure she was on the right trail. Feeling out the rotten scent of dark magic.

Yes. This was the way.

She plunged into the twisted woods.

The full dark of night hadn't fallen over the village, but in these woods, it had. Jesine grimaced, forced to move more slowly than she wanted, pushing back jutting branches and climbing over mossy logs. Jesine was comfortable in the woods, even at night, but she usually had a lantern. She was just thinking of summoning her own light when she felt it again—a pulse of magic so strong and close, she could practically feel it beneath her feet, reverberating within the ground.

She pushed ahead further, and then she saw the light.

It was a warm, flickering gleam, casting dancing shadows over the woods. Breathing quietly, Jesine inched forward. The light illuminated a dip in the land before her, the forest floor descending sharply. Below was a rocky hollow, and in its center, a large fire burned, giving off that wavering light.

And circling the fire were two figures, cloaked and hooded, pale arms stretched out to their sides.

Jesine's breath stuttered in her throat. One of the figures wore a dark cloak, and the other a light-colored one. They moved sinuously, rhythmically, as though in a dance. They circled clockwise around the fire, making three complete turns, then turned to move the other way, each step slow and precise. They both held a smudging bundle in each hand, giving off faint wisps of smoke.

The fire was their focal point. They centered their power upon it and drew on its energy. Jesine bit her lip. If she could put the fire out, that would probably end the hex. Even if she only dampened it for a moment, that might be enough. But how to do it? Bringing enough wind or rain would be difficult; it would require a lot of magic and strength from her. She could strike at the fire directly, siphon off its energy, but she'd need to get closer for that—

A burst of sparks sputtered off the fire, shooting towards one of the figures—the one wearing a dark cloak. Before it reached the figure, the sparks blackened, smoldering into embers, and from those ashes, a scrap of parchment formed. The cloaked figure caught the parchment, pausing to read it while her fellow continued circling the fire.

After a moment, the dark-cloaked figure clenched her fist around the parchment, crumpling it in her hand. Jesine thought she said something to the other figure, but she was too far away to hear. Then the dark-cloaked figure moved off, away from the fire, melting into the shadows at the far end of the hollow.

The other figure—this one in a cream-colored cloak—continued to circle the fire on her own. *This is it*, Jesine thought. She had a better chance of sneaking close with only the one witch there. And with only one sustaining the hex, it would be easier to disrupt it.

Jesine cast her gaze around, looking for a way down into the hollow. The land sloped more gradually and shallowly on her right, and a large boulder at the base of the slope would provide some cover. Pulling her own hood over her head—her red hair would stand out in the darkness—Jesine crept down the slope. When she reached the boulder at the bottom, she pressed her back against it, easing herself around.

She twisted her head to peek over her shoulder.

But the cloaked figure was gone.

Jesine frowned. The fire still burned but—like the first witch—the second had gone. Hesitantly, Jesine turned, searching the hollow from left to right. Her gaze lingered on every crevice, pierced every shadow.

Nothing. The hollow was empty.

Jesine took a cautious step forward, out into the open. Then another.

"You shouldn't be here."

Heart lurching in her chest, Jesine spun around.

A woman stood before her, her cream-colored cloak bright in the darkness. She snatched Jesine's wrist, holding her in place. Her grip was surprisingly strong, and Jesine's eyes watered in pain.

"It's not time for you yet." The woman's voice was cool and unruffled. Jesine couldn't make out her face, but the long hair spilling out from her hood was a deep, burnished gold. "But no matter. I can deal with you."

She yanked at Jesine, pulling her close. Jesine was too startled to resist, stumbling, barely staying on her feet. The woman clasped Jesine's hand between both of her own, and in that instant, Jesine glimpsed the woman's eyes within the dark cove of her hood.

They were completely white, like the eyes of a blind woman. But Jesine knew she wasn't blind.

She was a witch. Channeling enormous power.

The witch squeezed Jesine's hand and uttered a single word. "*Victus.*"

Jesine's hand went icy cold, as though she'd plunged it into a frozen river. It was a cold that burned, sinking straight through her skin. She twisted away, trying to free herself, and when she couldn't, she collapsed to her knees. The cold solidified in the center of her palm, and then—it was gone.

The witch released her. Jesine slumped forward, boneless. Her entire body trembled, as though still caught in the grips of that awful cold. A faint wind rustled past her, and in that wind, Jesine heard a voice.

Jesine...Jesine...

"What did you do to me?" Jesine croaked.

The witch stood over her. Jesine could barely lift her head, but she could see the witch's pointy-toed boots, colored the same cream as her cloak.

"I've marked you," the witch said. "For *him*."

Jesine heard these words like a fish caught in a net. "Him who?"

"You know who," said the witch. "You've known for many years. Jesine."

The witch moved away, her boots crunching over dead leaves. As they vanished from Jesine's line of sight, Jesine clutched at her own wrist. She opened her hand and looked at it.

A large, black splotch marred her palm like an ugly bruise.

I've marked you. For him.

Jesine shook so badly, she thought her heart would stop beating.

She'd been marked. For that cold presence that had haunted her for years. For that whisper of a breath she often felt at the back of her neck, that icy hand that crept up her spine.

She'd been marked for the darkness. For the one who ruled over bad witches. The one who stole their souls.

And she couldn't escape.

3

COVEN

ANSEL SQUEEZED HIS EYES shut and tried to shield himself as the bats descended upon him like a black funnel cloud. It was like before, with the ravens, only ten times worse. Those ravens had been startled into flying at him; these bats were intent on his destruction. Ansel fell to his knees, a strangled cry stuck in his throat, as the bats scratched at his neck, his hands, the bits of his face he couldn't cover. Their furiously flapping wings sounded in his ears like a thunderstorm, beating at him, beating at him, *beating* at him—

And then, with shrill screeching, they rose into the air, leaving him. Ansel didn't understand why until he peeked his eyes open and saw a long, thin blade swiping the air, piercing some of the bats and forcing the others away.

"Ansel!" It was Demetri brandishing the blade. "Are you all right?" He swiped his blade again, once, twice, cutting bats down in rapid succession and with deadly precision. As the last of the bats took to the air, circling away, Demetri scanned the square.

"Bats don't act like this," he observed, in a surprisingly matter-of-fact tone.

"You're joking," Ansel said dryly. He scowled as he took in the cuts on the backs of his hands and winced as he felt another stinging, shallow gash along the side of his neck.

"Let me guess. Witches?"

"Has to be."

"Why, though? Why attack the town?"

"Can we worry about that later?" Ansel asked. "Maybe when we're not—*run!*"

A swarm of bats smashed through the nearest building, breaking apart brick like it was nothing. Plumes of grit and dust burst into the air from the crumbling rubble. Ansel and Demetri ran for the nearest shelter, ducking beneath a window overhang. Demetri hefted his rapier. "So what do we do? How do we stop this?"

"Find what—or who—is sustaining the hex," said Ansel.

"Easier said than done," Demetri noted. Then he swore. Ansel followed his line of sight and saw Sabine trying to help two women get to safety as bats bombarded them. "Stay here," Demetri ordered, and then he took off, charging with his blade raised.

Ansel did not take orders, least of all from someone he barely knew. He crouched, poised, ready to spring into a run after Demetri.

Then Ansel saw him. Directly across the square, standing in front of a tall red-bricked bank, was a man. He stood amidst the chaos, bats whirling around him, glass windows shattering behind him, villagers running past him. And yet, unlike everyone else, he stood still, hands calmly clasped behind his back.

And he stared straight at Ansel.

Ansel stared back and took a step forward. The man cut an eerie figure, untouched by the violence in the square. He was lean and dark, dressed impeccably in a three-piece suit and matching bowler hat. But what caught Ansel's attention, what rooted him to the spot, was the man's intense, dead-eyed gaze. He stared at Ansel for a long moment, and then a smile flickered across his face. A mirthless smile.

Someone ran headlong into Ansel, smacking his shoulder so hard, he spun around. Ansel wobbled but managed to keep his balance. As soon as he did, he whirled back, looking for the dead-eyed man.

But he was gone.

Ansel lurched forward, scanning the square for any sign of the man. He ducked as another wave of bats careened towards him, then he dodged another fleeing villager. And then—

There. Exiting the square at the northeast corner. The man had turned away, but Ansel was sure it was him. Not just because he recognized the bowler hat, but because of the man's calm, unhurried gait. He wasn't running from the square, like so many of the panicked villagers. He was just leaving. As though his business here was done.

He had to be involved in this. He had to be a witch.

Ansel picked up his pace as he tore across the square, evading villagers and bats alike. He managed to keep his eyes on the man until he vanished down a side street. When Ansel reached the edge of the square, he took the same street, running even faster. He watched the man round a corner, and Ansel dashed after him, throwing himself around the same corner—

—where he crashed right into someone. This time, he completely lost his footing, falling back onto his rear. The jolt of the hard landing reverberated up through him, and he winced, moving tenderly as he climbed to his feet.

"Sorry," gasped the person he'd run into. It was not the man he'd been chasing, but a young woman. "I'm sorry—"

Ansel apologized too, the words coming instinctively. "Sorry, sorry, my fault—"

"Are you all right?"

"I'm fine." Ansel stood stiffly and glimpsed a pale face, half-hidden by a curtain of long red hair. "Are *you* all right?"

"Yes, fine." The girl was already turning away. No doubt she'd just fled the square. "Sorry—"

"No, I'm—" Ansel broke off. He stepped to the left, trying to get a clearer look at the girl. There was something about that long red hair, something about her *voice*. Something that pulled at his memory. "Wait." Ansel lifted a hand towards her. "You—"

"Sorry, I have to go." And before Ansel could stop her, the girl took off, hurrying around another corner, vanishing from sight.

It was only then Ansel remembered the man he'd been chasing. The witch. Ansel turned left and right, looking for any sign of the man. But he was gone. He took a few minutes to search several side streets, just in case, but this proved fruitless. In the time it had taken Ansel to run into that girl, the man had disappeared.

Gritting his teeth, Ansel headed back to the square. He'd be better off there, helping the villagers, than searching blindly through the village streets. Besides, he'd left Demetri and Sabine. When he arrived back at the square, he paused, trying to sight his companions, trying to get a sense of where he could help best.

He watched a barrage of bats smash through the wooden door of a building on his right, and he heard the screams of people sheltering inside.

"Ansel!" someone called. Ansel turned and spotted Demetri and Sabine on his right, about twenty paces away. He started towards them, trying to hug the buildings lining the square. But before he'd gone more than a few steps, the bats attacked again.

They came at him like before. A flash of black out of the corner of his eye was his only warning, and then they were on him. Ansel ducked his head, lifting his hands to cover his face, slapping the bats away. But there were too many of them, clawing at him, scraping his skin with their teeth—

Then a shot rang out, loud enough to break through the bats' frenzied flapping and high-pitched shrieks. They took flight even more quickly than the first time, driven off by the gunfire. Ansel sagged in relief, but only for a second.

Then a scorching pain broke through his relief. The pain radiated down his arm, all the way to the tips of his fingers, which went numb. Ansel gasped a strangled gasp. "What—agh—" Ansel doubled over. His arm felt like a searing, white-hot poker. He looked down and saw, in disbelief, a ragged tear in his coat. "Someone shot me!"

"Oh, stones. It was an accident!" Demetri ran towards him. "I'm so sorry."

Ansel gaped at him. "You shot me!"

Tentative fingers gripped his elbow. Ansel hissed in pain as Sabine peered at his arm. "Just a graze, I think," she said.

"Just a—" Ansel gulped in another breath. The frosty air burned his throat. He wheeled away from Sabine, back to Demetri. "You *shot* me!" He felt suddenly flushed, heat suffusing his whole body. And yet he was shaking, violent tremors rattling through him.

"Ansel—" Demetri frowned in concern. "Ansel?"

Ansel tried to swear at him, but the young man was growing blurry. In fact, everything was growing blurry. His rattling body swayed. The last thing he heard, as darkness swept over him, was Sabine calling his name.

Then he passed out.

Ansel sucked in a breath as Sabine held his bared arm, her fingers dangerously close to his wound. She'd cut away part of his sleeve to examine it. "Yes, it's just a graze," she said. "Didn't even tear the skin. But there's a nasty burn. It must hurt."

"Only when I breathe," Ansel said acidly.

Sabine flicked him a wry smile. "I'll patch it up for you."

Trying to distract himself, Ansel looked around. He sat on a barstool inside the inn in Lise, the place where they had booked rooms. By the time Ansel had been roused from unconsciousness, the bats had gone. According to Demetri, they'd left as suddenly as they'd come, lifting into the air and flying away from the town. Despite sitting on the corner of the village square, the inn hadn't taken too much damage. Currently, many villagers were taking refuge here in the common room. The high, vaulted ceiling and large paned windows probably gave the place a spacious look, but right now, packed with people, it felt small. Every table, chair, and bench was occupied, as were all the barstools lining the curved, rustic counter where Ansel sat.

Ansel's gaze landed on Demetri across the room. He stood by some windows—a couple of which were broken—talking to some of the villagers. Demetri happened to glance aside as he spoke, and when he saw Ansel watching him, he flinched, averting his gaze.

"He should've stuck to his sword," Ansel grumbled.

"Rapier," Sabine corrected.

"Whatever."

Sabine placed a cloth bandage over Ansel's wound. The bandage was laced with antiseptic, and the stringent, chemical smell stung his nostrils. And it stung his arm.

"He's normally a very good shot." Sabine's tone was neutral. "I think his aim was just obscured. By the bats, you know. He probably couldn't quite see you beneath them."

Which is why he shouldn't have shot at all, Ansel thought. Though if he hadn't, the bats probably would've scratched his eyes out. But Ansel admitted that only grudgingly.

Once Sabine finished patching him up, Ansel shrugged his arm into his coat as gently as possible. Demetri made his way over to them, his face abashed.

"Ansel, I'm so sorry," he said as soon as he reached the bar. "Are you all right?"

"Fine," Ansel said gruffly. He was, really, and he knew Demetri hadn't shot him on purpose. Still, he didn't feel very warmly towards the man.

"Well, the good news is, the inn took minimal damage," Demetri told him. "The innkeeper said we can still stay here. Why don't you head up to bed and get some rest, and we'll make sure a meal is sent up to you?"

Ansel thought of the men Demetri had been speaking to. The conversation had looked intense, and he was fairly sure none of those men were the innkeeper. "And what are you going to do?"

"What?"

Ansel nodded across the room. "Who were you talking to?"

"Oh." Demetri glanced back. "Well—those men were just outside the village when the attack occurred. They're woodcutters, they were coming into Lise for an evening drink. They said they saw a plume of smoke out in the woods, not far from here." Demetri shrugged. "It could be nothing, but the woodcutters thought it was odd, given how close it was to town. Most travelers would have just come in to Lise, and anyone living out there would probably be further out."

That was true, Ansel thought. Woodsmen typically lived in the woods because they didn't want to be close to other people. "So you're going to check it out?"

"Like I said, it's probably nothing. But it's not far from here, so I thought we could investigate." Demetri looked at Sabine, making a halfhearted gesture towards her. Indicating that by "we," he meant him and Sabine.

"I'm coming with you," Ansel said.

"No," Demetri protested. "You should get some rest—"

"I'm fine." Ansel shoved himself off the barstool. "Just a graze, right, Sabine?"

Sabine looked dubious. "Yes. But you fainted—"

"I'm fine." Ansel looked from her to Demetri. "Look, if there is something out there—anything witch-related—you'll need me. You might not know what you're looking at, or how to deal with it."

Demetri relented, and they three set out together. Demetri insisted on riding horseback—it would be quicker; they didn't want to be out in the woods too late after dark. Ansel also suspected Demetri didn't want him, Ansel, walking and fainting again. So they rode out of town, Ansel, humiliatingly, sitting behind Demetri's saddle, holding onto his waist.

It was full dark when they left the village behind, Sabine's bright white lantern their only light against the deep-blue night sky. They entered the forest at a northeast angle, following the directions the woodcutters had given Demetri. It was even darker within the woods, black as pitch, though the trees were sparse here, bony aspens and bare poplars spaced out across a floor of dead leaves and half-buried stones.

"If I understood right, we should be coming up on the source of the smoke about here," Demetri murmured. They had been riding for only a few minutes. Up ahead, the forest seemed to darken, growing thicker, tangled, wild. Hulking shapes loomed in the black, rock formations carving jutting hills into the woods. This was the direction that man had gone, Ansel realized, that dead-eyed man in the bowler hat. The one he'd seen in the village square. He'd been angling out of town at the same northeast angle. He could've been coming to this very spot.

As Sabine slowed her horse, she raised her lantern, moving it from side to side as she surveyed the murky landscape. Ansel gave a subtle shake of his wrist, jostling the wooden stake up his sleeve into his hand. It was a fairy-wood stake, taken from the tree of a fairy. It was a rare thing, difficult to find, but it was the only weapon a witch could not manipulate with magic—and the only weapon that could incapacitate a witch for sure.

Sabine drew in a rough breath, the sound just audible in the quiet night.

"What is it?" Demetri asked tensely.

"I thought I saw something." Sabine's voice was steady, but her tone was uncertain. "Up there." She pointed to a sharp rise in the land, thickly covered in evergreens.

It took them a moment to find a way up the rise. The face of it was nearly sheer, but after riding around it, they found a walkable path. Leaving the horses below, they climbed up the rise, slow and careful in the dark. Sabine led the way, armed with lantern and pistol, and Ansel followed her, clutching his fairy-wood stake. Demetri brought up the rear.

Ansel's grip tightened on his stake as they ascended the rise, but nothing jumped out at them. The trees cast long shadows in the small light of the lantern, but as they ventured between the trees, looking in every direction, they found nothing.

"Well, if there was someone here, they're gone now," Demetri murmured. "I suppose they could have done, in the time it took us to get up here."

"What exactly did you see, Sabine?" Ansel asked.

"It wasn't much. Just a flash of color, I suppose. Red, I think."

A flash of red. Unbidden, a memory rose to the surface of Ansel's mind, a recent memory. The girl he'd seen earlier, the girl with long red hair. The one he'd run into just off the square. She, too, had taken off in this direction. But she'd just been fleeing the attack in the square. Ansel remembered how strangely familiar she'd seemed. But he couldn't recapture the feeling. He couldn't source the memory behind that familiarity. If he did know her from somewhere, he couldn't place it now.

"Ansel?" Sabine prompted him. "Are you coming?"

Ansel shook himself, realizing Demetri had already gone, taking the lantern and starting back down the rise. "Coming," he said. A low wind stirred up, blowing through the trees, and Ansel adjusted the scarf around his neck before heading down too.

They reached the bottom of the rise just in time for Ansel to see Demetri disappear into the darkness, the white shimmer of the lantern eaten up by the gloom. Ansel didn't understand where he'd gone until Demetri called, "Ansel. You'd better come see this."

Ansel ventured forward, Sabine at his side. The lantern light reappeared, a gleaming halo framing Demetri's face. There was a narrow hollow here, Ansel realized, framed on one side by the rise and by towering boulders on the other. Demetri had slipped in through the slim opening between these two sides. Ansel followed him through, into the hollow.

A telling scene lay before them. The remnants of a fire circle, a heap of scorched wood and black ash. Tendrils of smoke curled up from the smoldering remains.

"This was probably the source of that smoke." Sabine toed the charred pile of wood with her boot. "There are tiny little bones mixed in here. Animal bones, I'd guess. Does that mean anything to you, Ansel?"

Ansel crouched to peer into the remains. "They could be anything, but I bet they're bat bones. That would have given them the element they needed to control the bats." He sniffed at the smoke spiraling from the embers. He couldn't name the exact herbs used here, but he knew the deep, sharp scent of certain malevolent herbs when he smelled them. They prickled his nose. "This was definitely the work of a witch."

But could it have been the dead-eyed man Ansel saw? A hex like this would have required a witch's presence here to maintain the fire. The witch responsible couldn't have been at the square, watching the attack unfold.

"And what about this?" Demetri bent and picked something up. He held it alongside the lantern, letting the light fall over it.

Ansel stepped forward. The bound bundle Demetri held was made up of several different things, some of which Ansel recognized: certain flowers, their petals a dark violet, the color of a bruise. More of the herbs used in the fire. Coal-black feathers, probably from a crow. Leaves from a specific kind of tree. The entire bundle was bound with moss, and smeared red with blood.

"Here's another one—" Demetri bent again to retrieve a bundle from the ground. "And another—"

"And one here." Sabine also bent down.

Ansel caught his breath.

"What is it?" Demetri asked.

A branch snapped in the distance, and Ansel swallowed. "Well. A single witch would only need one or two of these bundles, at most, to work a spell. They might hold one in each hand, see. That there are four or more here suggest..."

"More than one witch?" Sabine guessed.

"More than one witch." Ansel nodded. "If Adela is here, she's not working alone. We're dealing with a coven."

4

GUTTED

ANSEL SPENT THE NEXT day in bed at the inn. Demetri and Sabine spent the day helping the town with recovery efforts—which was good for their investigation, said Demetri, because it gave them a chance to interview the villagers. Demetri, of course, was also the one who insisted Ansel stay at the inn and rest. Ansel wasn't sure if Demetri really believed Ansel's wound was severe enough to warrant bedrest, or if he just felt guilty for shooting him in the first place.

But by the next morning, bedrest was over. Ansel woke to a knock on his door and found Demetri on the other side, his fair face pasty in the low, unflattering light of the gear-bulb fixtures in the corridor. Apparently, a woman who lived in the nearby woods was missing—she'd had an appointment in town yesterday and never turned up—so Demetri and Sabine were going out to her cottage to check on her.

"You don't have to come," Demetri hastened, "if you need more rest. Sabine and I can handle it."

"No, I'll come." As much as a (petty) part of Ansel would have liked to milk Demetri's guilt, he was more than ready to get out of the inn. He was dying of boredom. But... "Why are *we* doing this? I mean, is there anything strange to her disappearance?"

Demetri seemed to understand that by "strange," Ansel meant "witchy." The young man rubbed a hand behind his neck and replied, "Not so far as we know. But the villagers are really spooked right now. Understandably. Sabine and I spoke with many of them yesterday, so they know why we're here, and that we work for the crown. So when the matter of the missing woman came up, well—"

"They wanted us to go look for her," Ansel filled in, "in case witches are involved."

They met downstairs a half hour later. While Sabine picked up some provisions for lunch, Ansel and Demetri loitered in the foyer. The alcove was furnished with cushioned cane chairs and a long chaise, but they both stood. Ansel leaned against the wood-paneled wall in the corner, staring out a smudged window, watching villagers pass on the street. He spotted a troop of men dressed in forest-green march by and couldn't help but notice they didn't look very happy.

"They're the village watch," said Demetri. He, too, stared out the window. "They're rather riled up after the attack on the town. Talking about 'rooting out these witches' themselves."

Ansel stifled a groan. In his experience, villagers didn't know much about hunting witches. In his experience, *no one* knew much about hunting witches. Most of what he'd picked up over the years had been hard-earned and hard-won.

"So." As though reading his mind, Demetri asked, "How did you get into witch hunting?"

Ansel flicked his gaze up. "How did you get into monster hunting?"

"Garrett." Demetri's tone was rueful. He tugged at the bottom of his black waistcoat, as though uncomfortable. "I don't know that I'm really suited to it."

"Didn't you help Prince Garrett with those corpse creatures in the Mountain Kingdom? And you hunted mermaids, too?"

"Yes, well, I stumbled into those situations," Demetri said wryly. "I didn't seek them out. But now I do. Officially, I work for the crown, so sometimes Garrett sends me places. Gives me tips about weird things he's heard of."

"What did you do before?"

"Oh, a little of this, a little of that." For some reason, Demetri's cheeks went pink. When he noticed Ansel staring, he added, "I was a courier for a bit. And a stable hand before that. Just, erm, picked up what jobs I could."

"What did your parents do?"

"Oh. Well." Demetri tugged at his waistcoat again. "They're dead."

"Oh. I'm sorry."

Demetri stopped tugging at his waistcoat, letting his riding coat fall forward. "It was a long time ago." But he turned away, standing in profile as he gazed out the window a little more intently than necessary.

Ansel eyed him. He should be friendly, he thought belatedly. He should try. The problem was, Ansel had never had many friends. It was hard when one lived on the road as he did. But also...well, Ansel wasn't *un*friendly, exactly. He just seemed to rub people the wrong way. He always had. He didn't know why.

Even his own father hadn't liked much about him.

Crossing his arms over his chest, Ansel said, "The first time I encountered a witch, I was eleven. She wanted to cook me and Isabelle. But we killed her instead."

Demetri's eyes widened. "She wanted to cook you? How did you manage to kill her?"

"We tossed her in her own oven."

"Oh." Demetri looked impressed. "Yes. I suppose that would do it."

Ansel leaned back, bouncing slightly on the balls of his feet. "What did Prince Garrett tell you about me? About me being a witch hunter, I mean."

"Hmm. Not much. Just that you were there in the Black Forest when he first came across Adela. And that you've been hunting her ever since."

Ansel gazed down at the floor. So Garrett hadn't said anything about Ansel's history with *her*. Delphine. The evil queen of the Mariner Kingdom. The one who'd killed her own stepdaughters, including Garrett's betrothed, Princess Snow. He wondered if he should mention it now...but...

But what did it matter? Delphine was locked up for good. It was painful enough Garrett knew his history with her. Painful enough that they shared a history with her. Even more than Garrett knew.

Sabine emerged from the common room with their provisions, and they exited the inn, setting out on foot. The missing woman's cottage was only a few leagues outside the village. They should reach it before lunchtime, Ansel thought, so long as nothing went wrong.

Nothing went wrong on their way to the cottage. But once they arrived, lunch was the last thing on Ansel's mind. It was hard to think about eating, faced with what they found.

Ansel had always believed nothing was more terrifying than a witch. Even as a child, long before he'd met a real witch, he'd been terrified just by the idea of them. Now, as he gazed down into a hollowed-out body cavity, he thought he might be wrong. Because whatever had killed this woman—whatever had divested her of her insides—had to be worse than a witch.

Shaking off a shudder, Ansel stepped back from the corpse. She'd been left here in this cottage on a table, as though for an autopsy. But it wasn't that kind of table. This was a dining table, simple and rustic, a swirling petal design etched into the gray wood. Now a grotesque mockery of domestic life, considering what had been done to this woman.

It occurred to Ansel that whatever had done this could still be nearby. He turned slowly, uneasily, eyes darting from corner to corner. But nothing jumped out at him. Nothing stirred. The house seemed empty and cold, despite the candles lit in sconces on the wall. It was nearly as cold as the sunless winter day outside. As though death had leeched all the warmth from the walls.

There was something...a peculiar odor in the air. A cloying stench, almost sweet. But foul too. A bit like rotting fruit. Ansel wrinkled his nose.

Perhaps it was just the corpse.

The door rasped open behind him, scraping against the floorboards, and Ansel jumped, but it was only Demetri. "Sabine's going to keep watch outside," he said. "Do we—" He broke off, going stock-still as his gaze fell upon the corpse.

"Gruesome, isn't it?" Ansel remarked.

"No." Demetri sounded strained. "I mean, yes, it is, but—I think I know what did this. I've seen it before. Or rather, a friend of mine did."

"What? Where?"

"In the Mariner Kingdom. When the sea witch tried to open a portal on the summer solstice, she sent *something* to attack a submarine in the bay. As a distraction. Briar—Princess Briar—was the only one strong and fast enough to fight the monster."

"Princess Briar." Ansel arched an eyebrow. "The one who's part-monster herself?"

"Yes." Demetri ran a hand over his mouth. "I wasn't there when the creature attacked, but I saw the corpses it left behind. They looked like this woman. Hollowed-out husks, all their insides missing. Just like this."

"So we're not just dealing with witches, then."

"No." Demetri tore his gaze from the corpse, looking at Ansel. "We're dealing with a demon."

Ansel blew out a breath. "You said the sea witch sent one to attack. So is it possible Adela and her coven are using this one? That it's working for them, I mean?"

"I think it would have to be. From what I understand, they have to be summoned by witchcraft."

Ansel scrubbed a hand through his cropped curls. He took another long, hard look at the body on the table, stifling an urge to gag. "Witches can inflict a lot of horror with their magic," he said. "I've seen a man choke on his own teeth. I've seen a woman's eyes burn in their sockets. But this—"

A long, slow *cre-e-e-ak* cut through his words. Like a door swinging open.

Ansel fell silent. That was not the front door. It remained shut. He and Demetri exchanged a cautious look before turning towards the back of the house.

There was another door there, leading to another part of the house. Another room. That door, too, was shut. Ansel scanned the strip of space beneath the door, but he saw nothing. No flutter of movement, no shifting light. Only darkness.

Nodding for Ansel to follow, Demetri crept forward, one hand on the pistol at his waist. He stilled two steps from the door as a creaky board shifted beneath his weight, and Ansel followed suit, listening. When nothing happened—no sound, no movement—they started forward again. Ansel stepped over the creaky board as Demetri reached the door and slipped his pistol from its holster. He looked at Ansel.

Ansel gripped the hilt of his long hunting knife. He nodded at Demetri.

Demetri nodded back.

Then he kicked the door open.

A long, keening screech echoed into the dark room. Demetri yelped and stumbled back, stomping on Ansel's toes with his boot. Ansel swore, hopping on one foot.

Then Demetri released a shaky laugh.

"What is so funny?" Ansel winced as he put his foot down. "What was that?"

"It's only a cat." Demetri eased the door open and went inside.

Ansel followed, squinting. There was only one small window, too small to cast much light through the formless shadows in the room. A pair of yellow eyes stared at them from one gloomy corner. As the shadows behind those eyes shifted, Ansel spotted the flick of a cat's tail.

"We must have scared it to death," Demetri said.

"It scared you to death."

"Yes, it did." Demetri ventured further into the room, and the cat leapt up from the floor. It sprang into a ramshackle rocking chair, and from there, onto the windowsill. By the muted light, Ansel saw it was a black cat.

"There's a back door here." Demetri peered around the rocking chair. "It looks like—"

"Wait!" Ansel cried, and he dove forward, tackling Demetri. They both tumbled into the rocking chair, which toppled over, crashing into the floor. The cat screeched again. Ansel's bony shoulder banged into the floor with a bruising *thump*, and his boots tangled in the base of the chair.

Demetri huffed and groaned as he crawled onto his knees. He had landed smack onto the rocking chair and flipped over it, landing flat on his back. The fall must have knocked the breath out of him, because he stared wordlessly at Ansel, heaving deep breaths. Then he said, "What—the hell—was that?"

"You can thank me later." Ansel felt at his tender shoulder with careful fingers. "You nearly walked right into a hex-trap."

He gestured, indicating the spot just inside the back door. Demetri turned, his eyes running over a carved stone at the doorway. There was a second stone below the windowsill, Ansel noted, and a third just past the rocking chair—or where the rocking chair had been.

"What's a hex-trap?" asked Demetri.

"Quite what it sounds like. A witch can leave a hex as a trap for someone to walk into." Ansel climbed to his feet. "It takes three runed stones to set and hold the trap." He kicked the closest stone out of the way, sending it rolling across the room.

Demetri rose to his feet. "Just like that? That's all it takes to break it?"

"The trap is only effective if the stones are within a certain distance of each other. About five feet or so."

"That's convenient."

"But that's only if you catch it before the hex is activated," Ansel warned. "After that, it gets trickier. Especially if you're alone and distracted by whatever hex you've walked into."

Demetri bent and picked up one of the stones, though he looked to Ansel and waited for his nod before doing so. It was quite small—the smaller the better for the witch, Ansel knew, because they were less noticeable—but they had to be large enough to accurately etch a rune onto. "What does the symbol mean?" Demetri asked.

"Hell if I know. The better question is, who left it there. And when. And why."

"That's three questions." Demetri pushed open the back door. "There are footprints out here. In the mud."

"That seems a little careless."

"It does." Demetri holstered his pistol, his hand straying to the hilt of his rapier instead. "But I'm going to follow them. I need to check in with Sabine anyway. Coming?"

"You go ahead. I want to take a closer look around here, see if we've missed anything."

Demetri vanished out into the cold, and Ansel returned to the main room alone. Alone except for the corpse on the table. He had avoided looking at her face—*really* looking at it—but he looked now, and what he saw chilled him to the bone. The woman's face was a grisly mask, her lips stretched wide, frozen in her last screams.

Ansel's heart gave a wrench. He reached out and closed her eyes, murmuring a quiet prayer for the dead.

"So sentimental, Ansel."

Ansel whipped around. His hand went at once to his knife—a habit he had never been able to break—but he stopped short of touching it.

A knife in his hands was a weapon for any witch. And that was what stood before him. A witch.

Adela.

"I was beginning to think you'd lost my trail for good," she said, in that nauseatingly girlish voice of hers.

"Wouldn't you have liked that," said Ansel.

"Oh, not this time." Adela wore the midnight-blue cloak Ansel had first seen her in. It was a pretension, he thought. Or maybe she was being ironic. No one wore cloaks anymore, not cloaks like that. He was surprised she didn't also wear a pointed hat, like the witches in the stories did.

"So I take it that was your hex-trap in the back room?" Ansel eased a step to the side.

Adela's smile faltered. The barest hint of annoyance flashed over her face.

Ansel smiled grimly. "What did it do, anyway? I have to admit, I'm curious."

"Then you should have stepped into it."

"So that was your whole plan?" Ansel's hand itched for the fairy-wood stake up his sleeve. "Lure me here, hope I'd walk into your trap? Must've been one hell of a hex to risk me finding you."

An ugly sneer crossed Adela's face. "I think you overestimate yourself."

"I don't." Ansel stepped sideways again—inching towards the door. Cutting off her closest means of escape. "You led me on a merry chase through the old Forest Kingdom long enough. Why do that if you weren't worried about me following you? Or were you just taking a holiday, touring every dingy village in the Black Forest?"

Adela glowered, but the unease in her eyes cut the sting of it. Her gaze twitched from him to the front door, then back again.

"And I can't imagine what you were doing in the western mountains," Ansel continued, "except trying to find a miracle pass through them. Or how about in Brisa? You left there in a hurry when I turned up."

"You think you're something special," Adela spat, "because you and your brat sister killed a witch? Henrietta was an imbecile who let her appetites get the best of her. Believe me, killing her was no great feat."

Ansel's stomach flipped, her words unbalancing him. "You knew her? What—how do you know about that?" Senses and images flashed through his mind. The putrid scent of searing flesh. Sickeningly sweet poison, burning the back of his tongue. And that witch, that woman, her eyes white all the way through, her skin cracking like dried parchment—

Adela sprinted for the door.

Ansel cursed, slipping his stake into his hand and hurling it after her. But he was distracted—damn it, that's why she'd said that about him and Isabelle, just to distract him—and his throw, too wild, missed. The tip of the stake merely snagged Adela's cloak. She ripped it free and burst through the front door, dashing outside. Ansel followed, a rush of wintry air hitting him as he stepped over the threshold—

And found himself in jet-black darkness.

"What the..." He faltered, spinning around. In the complete darkness, he couldn't see the doorway, couldn't see the house. It couldn't be night yet. Could it? No, he knew it wasn't. They'd left the inn about mid-morning and reached the cottage a couple of hours later. He hadn't been in there for more than half an hour. Could there have been an eclipse...?

A peal of high laughter tinkled out behind him.

Adela. Ansel whirled around again, expecting to find her right behind him, but she wasn't there. Nothing was. The dark was so absolute that he couldn't see anything. Not the trees, not a light in the sky. Well, it was cloudy, after all. But Adela sounded so close he should have been able to see her. And why hadn't she run? Why was she still here?

"Is something wrong, Ansel?" Adela purred.

Ansel swiped his arm out in front of him. The tips of his fingers brushed soft wool. Her cloak? Another peal of laughter echoed through the air, *right there*, right in front of him, but he still couldn't see her. He lunged for her, taking two steps—

—and tripped over something small, hard, and uneven. A small stone, it felt like.

A small stone.

"Oh, stones," Ansel whispered.

"Stones is right." Adela's voice crackled with glee. "I'm sorry, I forgot to mention. That hex-trap in the back room wasn't the only one. In fact, I set this one out here while you and that princeling were bumbling around in there. Have you figured out what it does?"

Ansel felt as though his ribcage had caved in on him, dread making a hollow of his insides. Just like the corpse of that woman. Slowly, he held his hands up in front of his face, inches away.

He could smell them. He could smell the cold, and the leather of his knife hilt, and even some of the pepper off the dried plums he'd eaten earlier.

But he couldn't see them. He couldn't see his hands right in front of his face. No matter how furiously he blinked, no matter how long he stared.

He was blind.

"Oh, dear." Adela's voice was rife with amusement. "How are you going to catch me now, little hunter?"

"You know I can still hear you, right?" Ansel snapped, but inside, he was tumbling apart. Blind. He was *blind*. He couldn't see his hands in front of his face, couldn't see the woods around him, couldn't see the witch standing paces away—

The hex-marker. He had to find the hex-marker. Whatever object she'd used to bind the trap, whatever baby's finger bone or bird's spleen, he had to find it, he had to burn it—that would break the hex. But how could he find anything when he couldn't see, especially with her watching him, fumbling around...

"Well, I'm afraid I can't stay," Adela said. "I have business elsewhere. But don't worry." Ansel *heard* the wicked smile in her voice. "I'm not going to leave you alone."

"Have another witch friend nearby?" Ansel asked, but he wasn't really paying attention. He drew the toe of his boot through the ground, searching for something, hoping to hit the hex-marker.

"Not a witch. This friend is not quite human."

Ansel's breath tangled in his chest.

"And I'm afraid he's not the best company," Adela went on. "He's a bit...well, you saw what he did to the woman in that house. He's a little overzealous."

Ansel felt as though his veins had turned to ice. *The woman in that house.* He could see her clearly in his mind's eye, the terror imprinted on her face, her torso cracked open, completely divested of all her insides...

"But then, he's not from around here. His origins are *otherworldly*, you see. So he's not familiar with the local customs. Still, I'm sure you can provide plenty of entertainment for him, don't you think?" Adela asked.

Ansel fought with everything in him not to show fear on his face, but it built inside him. Shutting out his ability to think, to move—

"So I suppose this is goodbye for now." Adela's voice was already fading into the distance. "Or perhaps, goodbye for always." She let out one last ringing laugh.

And then, there was only silence.

And darkness.

5

BEWILDERED

J ESINE WOKE WITH A start. The residue of bad dreams clung
to her like cobwebs in a dusty corner. She sat curled up in her
lumpy chair before the hearth, but the fire had gone out. Hours
ago, judging by the stale, smoky scent in the room. A glacial cold
hung in the air, and Jesine shivered as she pushed herself upright,
tugging her brown plaid shawl up around her shoulders. She'd
fallen asleep in an awkward position, and now, her neck felt stiff
and achy. She rubbed at it as the last of her nightmares washed
over her, refusing to be forgotten.

*Running in the darkness. Racing through the woods. Trees clos-
ing in around her. Red-hot flames lighting up the night sky—*

*She wasn't going to get there in time. She would be too late. Too
late to save...*

Ansel.

She had been dreaming of Ansel, Jesine realized. Of that horrible night. The last night she'd seen him. She hadn't thought of

that night in years, or she'd tried not to. Yet now she dreamt of it, dreamt of him. But why?

Then she remembered. She'd heard his voice a couple of days ago. Or thought she had. It couldn't have really been him. In her distracted, distressed state, she'd heard a voice in the woods and ascribed it to someone she knew, someone buried in her memories. She'd been in such a hurry, panicking as she fled—

The hollow.

The hollow in the woods, where she'd spied those two witches. Where one of them had marked her for a terrible fate.

Jesine shuddered, though this time, the shiver had nothing to do with how cold her house was. And though she hated to do so—though her stomach seethed and her heart sank—she peeled open her hand to look at the mark burned into her palm. It was a compulsion; she had to look at it. Because somehow, *not* looking was even worse.

"Burned" was the right word, though it did not look like a burn. It looked like a splotchy bruise, black and uneven. But there was no better word for the touch of dark magic. It was like an infection, sunk into her skin.

What was it? What had that witch done to her?

Jesine glanced at the book on the low table before her. It was a massively thick tome, the pages filmy and crinkled with age. One of her father's old books on magic, a book that had been in her family for generations. There were more of them upstairs, but Jesine hadn't even managed to get through this one. All day yesterday, and late into the night, she'd flipped through the pages, looking for something to explain this mark on her palm. But she'd been in such a state—not to mention exhausted—that the words had begun to swim on the page, blurring and running into each other. She couldn't make sense of anything.

And then she'd fallen asleep, here in this chair. In the early hours of the morning. So exhausted, even her anxiety could not keep her awake.

It seemed she'd slept the day away, she thought, casting her gaze around her cottage. It was a squat structure with low ceilings and only a few small windows. A dim interior, even on the sunniest day. Right now, it was dimmer than usual, the rustic kitchen and long dining table swathed in shadow. All she could really make out was the stone hearth before her, the dingy rug on the floor, the motheaten chaise opposite her.

She tried to remember everything that witch had said to her. The golden-haired witch in her cream-colored cloak. She'd said something like... *"You shouldn't be here. It's not time for you yet."* And what did that mean, Jesine wondered? It was like the witch knew who she was—

But of course she did. She'd called Jesine by name. *"I've marked you. For him. You know who. You've known for many years. Jesine."*

Jesine feared she did know. And if she was right...

The thought terrified her.

She sighed, slumping in her chair. She wished Kel was here. Kel was her fairy, bound to her for the last four years. She was the source of Jesine's magic, or rather, she was her access to magic. Jesine wished she was here because maybe, she might know something about this mark. But she also just wanted to see Kel. To take comfort in her presence.

Jesine had inherited Kel. She'd been her father's fairy before she was Jesine's, before her father died. And before that, she'd been bonded to Jesine's grandmother. Which meant Jesine had known Kel for her entire life, since she was old enough to remember anything. Kel would have scoffed to hear herself described as nursemaid, but Jesine had often thought of her that way. A strange, fickle, prickly nursemaid who had no tact or compassion and said the weirdest things.

But she'd been all Jesine had, aside from her father. And she'd barely had him. Her father had always had more important things to do than raise a child. He'd made that perfectly clear.

Yes, in many ways, Kel had been more of a parent to Jesine than her own father. And she dearly wanted her now. To help figure this out. But Kel had not wanted to come back here. She hadn't wanted Jesine to come back here. They had argued about it before Jesine left. And so far, her fairy had not followed her. In fact, if her tenuous magic lately was any indication, she was moving farther away from Jesine, in the opposite direction.

Jesine glanced up at the clock on the mantel above the hearth. She could hear its steady *tick-tick-tick*. And by the dusty gray light filtering through the windows, she could just make out the time. It wasn't as late as she'd thought, only just after noon. Yet it was so dark in here. Obviously, the day outside was overcast, but it felt too dark for that. And growing darker by the minute—

Suddenly, the temperature in the room seemed to plummet, the chill becoming icy cold. The shadowy dimness intensified into total darkness, as though a black cloak had fallen over the house, blocking out the windows.

And a low rumbling began to build, rattling the floorboards.

A fearful puff of air escaped Jesine. It misted before her, the fog of her breath visible in the absolute darkness. It was the *only* thing visible in the darkness, and somehow, it served to remind Jesine how alone she was here. How vulnerable.

The rumbling built, escaping the floorboards, filling the space around her. Literally *filling* it, blocking out the air, blocking out all other sound, like the *tick-tick-tick* of the clock. The rumbling enveloped Jesine until it solidified into a voice. A voice that echoed through her.

Jesine...

The voice was warped and dissonant. In that voice, the sound of her own name scratched at her skin, carving each letter in blood.

Jesine...

Jesine wanted to cry out, but she had no voice of her own anymore. She wanted to cover her ears, but she couldn't move. Her body was like wood, stiff and unyielding. Her body wasn't hers.

Jesine...come, my child...

Jesine clenched her lips together so tightly, she could feel the veins in her mouth straining. As the rumbling voice filled her, the darkness went even darker and the cold turned even colder. It was the cold of death, the frost that filled a cemetery on a frigid, foggy night. It was the darkness of a grave, damp, musty earth packed in tight. She sensed a presence in that darkness, a presence she knew well.

She'd known it for many years. Just like that witch had said.

It was that prickle at the back of her neck. That hand sliding up her spine. That cold breath in her ear.

But never had she known it like this. Never this physical darkness, overtaking her. It was everywhere, *he* was everywhere. All around. Stealing through her.

Jesine's molars bit into the sides of her tongue.

Jesine...you are mine...

She felt that tingling at the back of her neck. That breath ghosting over her skin. The whisper of clammy fingertips, reaching for her—

With a sharp breath, Jesine whipped around.

And the darkness lifted, cloudy daylight sifting through the windows once again.

Jesine let out a long, shaky breath. This time, it did not mist before her. The icy chill in the room abated, though it was still cold. But not preternaturally cold. Jesine let out another breath, practically choking on it. She should build up the fire again, she thought, but she sagged in her chair, slack and somehow empty without that voice slithering through her.

Was this what that golden-haired witch had meant? When she said she'd marked Jesine *for him?* That dark presence had haunted her for years, but this had felt so much worse. So much closer, so much more real. Jesine clutched at her wrist. What had that witch done to her?

A rustling drew Jesine's attention. She turned her head and saw another reason for the awful cold in the house.

The window in her kitchen was open.

And something was rustling just outside it.

Jesine swallowed. She found herself torn between the mad desire to dash out into the woods and the childlike desire to stay rooted to the spot. To draw the wool blanket at her feet over her head and pretend that if she couldn't see anything, nothing could see her.

She didn't have time to decide what to do. In that moment, a raven swung in through the square window, squawking out a single *caw*.

Jesine shot straight up, relief flooding through her. "Bastian! Where have you been?"

The raven—Bastian—perched on her wooden kitchen counter and let out another *caw*. He hopped once, twice, in half a circle. Until Jesine noticed the sliver of parchment tied to his foot.

Jesine's heart stilled. "Where did you get that?"

The raven let out another *caw*, and Jesine jumped up to face him. He fixed her with one beady eye and hopped again, rather impatiently.

Jesine approached the raven with trepidation. Not because of the raven itself. No, it was the note she eyed suspiciously, even as she moved closer, drawn to that little piece of parchment. As she stepped within reach of him, the raven bobbed his head and pecked at her palm, with the air of chiding her for taking so long. Jesine slapped his beak away and snatched at the parchment.

It was indeed a note, tightly rolled. Pulling the edges taut, Jesine squinted in the scant light and read the words scrawled there in dark, messy ink—

Witching hour, tonight.

That was it. Except, next to the words, was a sinister red blot.

Jesine stared at it. *Witching hour.* Superstitious nonsense called midnight the witching hour, but it was actually whenever the moon was highest in the sky. Tonight, that would be a little after sunset.

Nonplussed, Jesine flipped the scroll over. It was blank on that side, she knew it was. And yet, as soon as she pulled it taut again, patches of ink began to appear right before her eyes. The words came in bits and pieces, a loop of a *g* here, the curve of an *o* there. Jesine began reading the words before they were all clear, so that the meaning came to her as the last of the words appeared.

It was ingredients for a spell. Jesine knew the spell. She knew what it did.

And now she knew what that crimson blot on the front was.

Jesine looked up at the raven accusingly. "This is dark magic! Where did you get this?"

But the raven only ruffled his feathers, turning away from her. Annoyed? Or flustered? Jesine could only guess. She glared at him a moment longer. She could speak to the raven, and he understood her. She was sure of that. But he had no real way of speaking back. No way to explain further.

Jesine let out a long sigh, dropping the parchment onto the table in front of her. A mark she couldn't escape. A darkness haunting her. And now, mysterious messages popping up from mysterious sources.

It was all too much. Jesine raked both hands through her hair, mussing it thoroughly. She told the raven, "I need some air. I'm going for a walk."

She dressed in a simple brown dress, belted at the waist, and her olive-green coat, taking care to secure all the buttons up the front, all the way up to her neck. Outside, the day was pale and cheerless. Jesine's little cottage was huddled deep within the woods, surrounded by vast oaks and tangled aspens, with only a small clearing for a yard in front, covered in scrubby winter grass and patches of gold and brown leaves. The bits of sky she glimpsed through the treetops were overcast, the sun blotted out by thick clouds. A dreary day, but Jesine didn't mind such weather. She kind of liked it.

The bitter cold, she liked less. A wispy wind slipped through the trees, its low, soothing whisper rising into a high-pitched wail. Jesine gathered her hair back into a loose braid to keep it from her face, then shoved her hands into the pockets of her coat as she started up again, crunching through the forest. She circled along a path she knew well, one that led to the nearby road.

She turned off before she reached the road, heading back towards her house. She'd had plans to map out more of the land today, she remembered, to continue her search beneath the earth and trees. But she couldn't imagine concentrating on such work now, important as it was. It would have to wait.

"Jesine? Oh, Jesine! I'm glad I ran into you!"

Jesine started, yanked out of her thoughts. She looked around and realized she was only a few minutes from home. Blinking, she glanced over her shoulder.

There was a girl behind her, coming from the same direction Jesine had, from the road. Her smiling, plump-cheeked face was framed by a mop of bouncy, ash-brown curls. Jesine knew her. She'd known her since they were little girls.

"Saskia." Jesine tried to summon her own smile, but it did not come easily. She didn't smile much to begin with, and trying to make herself do so felt physically difficult. "What are you doing out here?"

"I have your usual supplies." Saskia held up a canvas bag. "The shipment came early this month."

"Oh. Right." Jesine shrugged a shoulder, indicating the girl should follow her. Saskia worked as a barmaid at the inn in

Lise and regularly procured some spices and herbs that Jesine couldn't get locally. Jesine paid Saskia in return, of course, though not always in coin. Sometimes, Saskia took a protective charm or a bundle of cleansing herbs instead. Jesine did not think the barmaid really believed in them—like many of the villagers, Saskia was familiar with the rumors of Jesine being a witch. But she didn't actually believe it.

Saskia chatted amiably as she followed Jesine back to her cottage. She was one of the very few people Jesine had ever let inside her home, and as such, one of the very few people who could find her home. The magical wards set about Jesine's house kept most people from wandering too close.

Saskia took her payment in coin this time, laughing when Jesine offered her another charm. "Oh, you should be careful, Jesine. We've got witch hunters staying at the inn right now." She laughed again at the startled look on Jesine's face. "I'm only teasing you. Well, it's hardly surprising, is it, after that mad attack on the town! I wasn't there, thank the stars. It was my day off."

The barmaid left a few minutes later, still prattling on. Jesine waved her off from the porch, wrapping her coat tightly about her. She wondered if there really were witch hunters in Lise. She wasn't sure if Saskia had been joking or not.

She was about to go back inside when a keening cry broke through the air. This time, it was not the cry of the wind, but of a living creature. Jesine's eyes searched the bare-limbed trees and tall green pines. Sure enough, a dark shape swooped overhead, perching upon the frail branch of a white aspen.

"Bastian!" Jesine called. "What are you doing?"

The raven fluffed his feathers in a discontented way. He soared onto another branch on another tree, some ways further on. Then he hopped to the next tree.

Jesine huffed. "You want me to follow you?"

He cocked his head as though to say, *What do you think?*

"All right," she grumbled. "Lead the way."

She trotted down her porch steps, following the raven. Bastian flew from tree to tree, stopping now and then to fix her with his gaze, hopping impatiently as he waited for her to catch up. They wended through the trees for about ten minutes before Jesine stopped, leaning against a stout oak to catch her breath. "Bastian." She hunched over and sucked in air. "Where are you taking me? What's going on?" She looked up.

The raven was gone.

Jesine straightened, her arm falling to her side. She scanned the wood, scouring every branch, but Bastian was nowhere to be seen. He'd vanished without a sound, leaving Jesine alone. Before she could try and remember every curse she knew, Jesine's gaze snagged on something through the trees. Not Bastian, not any kind of creature. It looked like—a structure. A low, sloping roof. A shed or cabin, perhaps?

Warily, Jesine closed in on the building, her boots sifting through piles of pine needles. The closer she got, the more the structure emerged from the twisted woods. It was truly nestled within the trees; the forest seemed about to swallow it up, claiming it for the wild. And yet Jesine saw, as she stepped past a copse of squat yew trees, there were lights on inside. Low, flickering lights. As though someone lived here.

Jesine frowned. A cottage not far from her own, and yet, she didn't think she'd seen it before. How strange. It was brick and stone, pale-gray stone and the ocher brick mined from the quarries near here. Patches of moss dotted the back wall. As she circled the cottage, coming around the side of it, a voice called out from nearby.

"Who's there?"

Something inside Jesine stilled.

She knew that voice. Didn't she? She thought she'd heard it two days ago. But it couldn't be...

Moving quickly but quietly, Jesine inched forward, coming around the front of the cottage. She peered out.

Standing there, a few paces from the front door, was someone Jesine thought she'd never see again.

It was Ansel.

6

BLINDSIDED

ANSEL STOOD, SHIVERING, LISTENING in the darkness. Fighting off fear, fighting to stay in control. He listened, but all he heard were branches, creaking as the wind winnowed through the woods. For all he knew, Adela was still there watching him, but there was no use trying to engage with her. It wasn't like she would help him, after all. Still, it was hard to shrug off the feeling of eyes on him as he bent down to the ground, and harder still not to think that those eyes might belong to someone...or something...else.

He blew out a long, low breath. He couldn't panic. He just had to find the hex-marker. Crouching low to the ground, he reached out, feeling through a layer of dead leaves blanketing the forest floor. The leaves were clumped together with cold mud, and soon his fingers were damp and stinging, but he kept searching, turning in slow circles, praying he would not trod on whatever object bound this hex...

A loud *whump* sounded out behind him, wood smacking against wood.

Ansel snapped his head up, realizing at once what the noise was.

It was the cottage door slamming shut. Which might not have been so odd, except there was no wind at the moment.

"Who's there?" Ansel asked, his voice ragged.

Silence was his only answer. Silence, and...what was that scent on the air? Rank but sickeningly sweet. Like something rotting...

"Is someone there?" he repeated.

This time, he heard something. A kind of whispering, like something moving through the leaves carpeting the ground. Something moving closer.

"Who's there?" he asked a third time. "Answer me!"

But there was no answer. Ansel whirled around, but that was useless. The darkness behind him was as absolute as the darkness in front of him.

And then, a most peculiar sound. A kind of *snatch-snatch*. He caught a whiff of something acrid, something burning, and then—

The darkness lifted.

The first thing Ansel's vision lit on was something bright and blazing, but small. Tiny, flickering flames. They seemed to hover in front of him, and then, as he watched, the flames fell to the ground, smoldering out.

Ansel gazed at the embers. He realized he was looking at the charred remains of...something. But whatever those remains had been, they were too damaged to make out now.

"A bundle of crow's feet," said a voice. A very soft, close voice. "That was the hex-marker."

Ansel whipped his head up. Someone stood before him, not two paces away. Of course. The flames he'd glimpsed, the burning hex-marker, had not been hovering in the air. It had been held by someone. Someone who had found and burnt the hex-marker, freeing him from Adela's trap. Someone who came into focus now. Ansel took in long red hair, bound in a messy braid, an olive-green coat, knee-length and fitted at the waist, and a face that was—

Familiar?

"You!" Ansel shook his head. "It's you!"

The girl standing before him looked uncertain. No, worse than that. She looked like a deer caught in a hunter's crosshairs. There was a fixed, almost frightened look in her almond-shaped eyes, and Ansel realized he had startled her. Of course he had, shouting like an idiot.

"Sorry." He held up both hands in a "no-harm-meant" pose. "That was rude. I just meant—I know you, don't I? You're the girl I ran into the other day. Back in Lise? When those bats attacked?"

The fearful look in the girl's eyes melted. "That was you. It *was* you..." She spoke in the same soft voice, and just like before, it tugged at Ansel's memory.

Her soft voice. That red hair. Ansel stared—much more intently than was polite, he was sure, but this barely registered. He took in the girl's face. It was a leaner, sharper face than he remembered, but there were other familiar things. The slightly upturned nose, and those eyes—a beautiful shade that looked brown at first, but closer up, they were hazel, flecked with green...

"I know you," he said, dumbstruck. "Don't I? You're—" He racked his memory, searching for a name he'd long forgotten. Weirdly, it came to him at once. "Jesine. It's Jesine, isn't it?"

The girl—Jesine? It had to be her—stared back at him, just as openly as he did. But the expression in her eyes shuttered. Becoming mysterious and unreadable.

Ansel placed a hand on his chest. "You probably don't remember me. I'm—"

"Ansel," Jesine finished. "Yes. I remember."

A laugh escaped Ansel. It was an uneasy, yet relieved sound. The strangest sensation blossomed in his chest. Like he'd been looking for something, something very dear to him, and finally found it. Like he'd been looking for *her*.

But that didn't make sense. Ansel barely knew this girl. Jesine. She'd been a friend of his, he recalled, when he'd lived in the area. Six years ago. Even back then, Ansel hadn't made friends easily, but he'd had one friend here. Jesine. He remembered playing with her, running through the woods, splashing through shallow streams, laughing and talking. He remembered...

Not much else. Well, it was six years ago. He was surprised he'd recognized her at all.

"So." Ansel noticed the silence stretching between them, and how awkward it was becoming. "Er. You still live here, then?"

Jesine fiddled with a button on her green coat. Her skirt beneath the coat was a deep brown, and she seemed to blend into the woods behind her. "I do now. We moved away for a bit. My father and I. But I'm back."

"Your father." Ansel frowned, trying to remember her father. But he didn't think he'd ever met the man. "And how is he doing these days?"

Jesine blinked owlishly. "He's dead."

"Oh. I—I'm sorry."

"It's all right." Her soft voice went even softer.

Feeling more awkward than ever, Ansel dropped his gaze. His eyes alighted on the charred hex-marker on the ground. "The hex-marker. You found it. You burned it!" Astonished, he asked, "But how did you know? How do you know about hex-traps?"

"Oh. Well." Jesine continued to fiddle with her button, twisting from side to side. "There used to be a lot of witches around here. Some years back. My father knew a bit about them, and he—he taught me some things. To defend myself, you know," she added hastily. "Like I said. They used to be common around these parts. I thought they were all gone now."

"The one who set this trap is new to the area. And I don't think she's working alone," Ansel said. "Well, I'm glad your father taught you about hex-traps. You saved me." He ran a nervous hand over the base of his neck. "That hex blinded me. Literally."

Jesine half-looked about to say something, but then a voice sounded in the distance. Calling out to Ansel. *Demetri*, Ansel thought. He'd completely forgotten about Demetri and Sabine. Thank the stars they were all right.

Jesine glanced over her shoulder. "I'd better go."

"Oh. Right. Er, do you live close by? It's just, with that witch about—" *And the demon*, he thought, wondering if he should warn her about that too. He didn't want to scare her, but...

"Oh, yes," Jesine said. "I'm quite close."

"Well. All right. It was nice seeing you. And...just be careful, won't you?"

Jesine smiled at him. It was a tight, quick smile. The sort you gave someone after an awkward exchange. And yet—was it his imagination?—there seemed something more to her expression. A kind of sad, lingering look. A look that wanted to say more but couldn't.

"I'll be careful," Jesine promised, turning to go. Her steps were swift and measured as she walked away, vanishing into the wood. Ansel had the strangest feeling she might have started running as soon as she was out of sight.

"Friend of yours?"

Ansel jumped, spinning around. He hadn't even heard Demetri and Sabine coming up behind him. But there Demetri stood, an expectant look on his face.

"What?" Ansel said stupidly.

"That girl that was here. Is she a friend of yours?"

"I don't really know."

Demetri gave him a strange look. "Well, what was she doing here?"

"Saving my life."

"What!"

Ansel looked into the woods one last time. But though Jesine had gone, the strange sensation in his chest hadn't. Instead, it intensified as he gazed into the trees, Jesine's tousled red hair bright in his mind's eye. Stirring something inside him.

"Ansel?" Demetri persisted. "What happened?"

Ansel turned to face Demetri and Sabine, and explained what had happened: Adela turning up, the hex-trap she'd left, robbing him of his sight. And Jesine burning the hex-marker. Setting him free.

"Hmm," Sabine mused. "Did this Jesine say what she was doing out here?"

"No. Well, she said she lives nearby."

Demetri and Sabine exchanged a quick look. "Any reason to think she might have been lying?" Demetri asked carefully.

"What? No." Ansel shook his head more vehemently than he meant to. "Of course not."

"Right, sorry." Demetri shrugged. "I suppose she is a friend, then."

The three of them decided to head out. They wanted plenty of time to get back to Lise before dark, and the sun set early this time of year, so close to the winter solstice. The daylight, already stunted by clusters of gray clouds, dimmed by the minute, leeching the color out of the woods. As they tramped back through the forest, Demetri bemoaned his decision to follow those footsteps from the cottage. "The witch probably set the trail deliberately, to lead us away."

"Hmm," Ansel agreed, but he wasn't really listening. His mind was still back there, outside that cottage, fixated by red hair.

He had nearly forgotten her until now. Jesine. Or had he? He was sure he had not thought of her once in the last six years, and yet, seeing her again, all of it came back so easily. What little there was. He hadn't spent that much time with her, he recalled. He hadn't known her that well. So why did he feel so strange, so out of sorts? Why had seeing her again touched him so deeply?

Ansel shook his head, trying to let these thoughts go. He thought again of Adela, going over everything she'd said. Trying to glean anything he might have missed, anything she'd given away. There had been one strange thing, he thought.

"Why did she call you princeling?" he asked.

Demetri jerked his head up. "What?"

"Adela. When she mentioned us exploring that cottage, she called you a 'princeling.'"

"Oh." It was hard to tell by the low light of the gloomy forest, but Ansel thought a flush suffused Demetri's cheeks. "Er. Before I was a monster hunter—and before I was a courier and a stable hand—I was a prince."

"*What?*"

"Of the Glen Kingdom."

Ansel was stunned. "You're related to Prince Garrett?"

"Oh, no." Demetri waved a hand. "It's kind of a long story, but. I'm from a different line. The last of that line, actually. My family ruled before Garrett's. So I'm not really a prince anymore. I'm sure Garrett would have his father grant me a title if I wanted it, but. Well, I'm done with that life. Just want to move on."

He said all of this very quickly. The explanation had the air of something rehearsed—not because it was made up, but because he'd said it many times before. And no wonder, Ansel thought sourly. Most people, like himself, would need some kind of explanation about why one would prefer to be a stable hand to a prince. He cast a sideways glance at Sabine. She quirked a small smile in return, giving the barest shake of her head.

Ansel turned away. This was the problem with rich people. The titles and nobility did something to their brains. "So you just *chose* to be a commoner. Instead of a prince."

"Well—yes." Demetri sounded puzzled by Ansel's hostility. "I suppose."

I knew there was something wrong with him, Ansel thought in annoyance.

They continued in silence for another few minutes, winding a path through the trees. Ansel's gaze was on the forest floor, tracking the heels of Demetri's boots just ahead of him.

"So that friend of yours back there," Sabine said, startling Ansel. "Is she just a friend, then?"

Without lifting his gaze, Ansel frowned. "What do you mean?"

"You said you used to know her. How close were you?"

Ansel took in Sabine's expression—her arched eyebrow, the slight twist to her lips—and realized what she meant. "We were just friends." The reply came out more curtly than he intended. "I mean. It was several years ago. We were just children."

"Ah."

Ansel rolled his shoulders. He didn't know why he felt so discomfited, why Sabine's question unsettled him so. There was no reason it should. But it did. The suggestion of some kind of romance, with anyone, always needled him a little. Not because he was entirely closed off to it, but, well—he just didn't have time for such things. That kind of relationship wasn't for him.

It never could be. He'd learned that the hard way.

It was already growing dark by the time they returned to Lise, the village lights winking through the pine trees. Ansel found his mood fading like the sun, the day's events wearing on him. He trumped into the inn behind Demetri, his gaze downcast, ready to collapse into his bed—

Demetri came to a sudden stop. So sudden, Ansel bumped right into him. He scowled, opening his mouth to demand what Demetri was doing.

But then he saw what Demetri had seen. And Ansel gaped.

At the center of the common room, Prince Garrett stood up from a large, round table. Grinning, he spread his arms wide. "There you all are! I thought you'd never get back!"

———◄O►———

Prince Garrett, it transpired, had arrived in Lise earlier that day. Shortly after arranging for Ansel and Demetri to meet, Garrett had decided he, too, would join them here in the southern woods. "Truth be told, I've been going mad at home," he said by way of explanation. "I haven't been on a proper venture in months. So I figured, why not join you all?"

Ansel, tapping his fingers against the sticky tabletop, eyed the prince sidelong. Then he ran his gaze over the dark-haired girl sitting opposite them at the round table—Gemma, Prince Garrett's sharpshooter and tracker—and over the tall, scarred young man slouching at the table beside them—Klaus, Garrett's newest recruit. (And formerly one of Ansel's captors, but that was bygones.) Though Gemma and Klaus were both soldiers in Prince Garrett's company, neither was dressed in uniform. Instead, they dressed as civilians in drab hunting coats and scarves.

Ansel didn't know much about a prince's life—*Demetri would know better*, he thought snidely—but only two guards on a "venture" seemed strange. From what he'd heard about Garrett's father, the king was a more practical man than his son. Ansel would've thought he'd insist on more than two soldiers to accompany the prince.

Prince Garrett leaned back in his chair and said something else, but the words were lost in their noisy surroundings.

"What?" Ansel frowned. "I can barely hear myself think in here."

Garrett glanced around, as though just noticing the crowd. The inn's common room was packed from corner to corner, the air filled with drunken, raucous laughter and smelling of ale and smoke from the old-fashioned fireplace. But Garrett didn't seem to mind any of it. In fact, he gave the room a fond smile, then leaned forward to repeat himself. "I said, are you all right? You look a bit..." He gestured vaguely.

Ansel merely raised an eyebrow, waiting for Garrett to finish.

"...grumpy," Garrett said with an air of apology.

"Just tired," Ansel said shortly. Which was true. His wounded arm was throbbing too, the muscle sore and his skin uncomfortably warm beneath his sleeve. But he didn't want to get into that with Prince Garrett.

"You don't have to stay up with us."

"I'm fine." Ansel realized his sour tone indicated otherwise. Truthfully—whatever the reason—Ansel was relieved Prince Garrett had joined them. He trusted Garrett. And with him here, maybe Ansel wouldn't have to spend so much time with Demetri.

As if triggered by his thoughts, Sabine—who sat on Ansel's left—pushed back her chair and said, "I'll be back, Your Highness. I'm going to see what's keeping Demetri with those drinks."

"*Sabine,*" Garrett hissed. He widened his eyes dramatically.

Sabine's expression suggested she thought he might be insane. "What?"

Gemma drawled, "He wants us to dispense with the titles, Sabine."

"Oh. Why is that, again?"

"I'm undercover," Garrett said eagerly. "As far as anyone here in Lise is concerned, Demetri is in charge of this expedition." He thumbed a finger at Gemma. "That's why I only brought two guards. I'm just a humble witch hunter, working alongside Demetri."

Ansel coughed unconvincingly, trying to hide a snort. Much like Demetri, Garrett was dressed for the outdoors in riding boots and breeches. But also like Demetri, his garb was quite a bit finer than anything Ansel was used to. The long overcoat slung over the back of Garrett's chair was lined with fur, and his tan waistcoat sported gleaming buttons and a matching watch chain. *Humble* witch hunter indeed. Perhaps in some ways, princes were all the same.

"Right," Sabine said. "Well, whoever you are, I'm going to help Demetri with the drinks."

Ansel watched her go until she disappeared into the crowd. Then he turned back to Garrett and said, a bit bluntly, "What's wrong with your friend?"

"Who?" Garrett looked taken aback. "Sabine?"

"No." Ansel jerked his head at the bar. "Him. Demetri." He resisted adding *Prince* Demetri.

"What do you mean, what's wrong with him?" Garrett twisted around to face the bar. Ansel turned to look too. Through the crowd, he spotted the former prince wedged between two, much larger men. Even at this distance, Ansel could see Demetri's cheeks were pink, and not, Ansel thought, because it was warm in the room. He rather thought it had more to do with the curly-haired barmaid he was speaking to. The very pretty, curly-haired barmaid.

Ansel considered how to answer Garrett's question. He settled on, "He talks to himself."

Garrett pulled his gaze from the bar. "What? No, he doesn't."

"He does. I've seen him at it."

"Well, a lot of people talk to themselves."

"Not like this," said Ansel. "It was weird."

Garrett bristled. "Look. He's had a tough time, all right? I mean, he's doing much better, but. He lost someone this past summer. Someone he cared about. A girl."

Ansel's gaze wandered in Demetri's direction again, just in time to see him stumble at the crowded bar, nearly knocking his chin into the countertop—right in front of the pretty barmaid. "Yes. He seems very torn up."

"We all grieve in different ways," said Garrett. "Just give him a chance. You hardly know him. He's a good man, and a solid hunter."

Ansel bit back the urge to say, *But not a particularly good shot.* Instead he said, "Well, if the stories are even half-true, I believe you. Corpse people. Mermaids."

"Man-eating mermaids," Garrett supplied.

"It's almost nice to hunt regular witches."

"'Nice' isn't quite the word I'd use."

"Yes." Ansel eyed Garrett cannily. "I suppose you have even more reason to hate witches than I do."

"It's an easy thing to forget about me, I know." Garrett's tone was light, but it sounded forced.

"Not really." Ansel's stomach gave an uncomfortable flip. "I never forget. What she did to you. And to Snow."

Princess Snow. She was what ultimately connected Ansel and Prince Garrett. Ansel had worked in the Mariner Kingdom as

75

a palace guard during the time when Snow's evil stepmother reigned. As such, Ansel had witnessed some fairly despicable things. Up until the point when the queen ordered him to do a despicable thing.

Kill Princess Snow.

He had chosen to disobey those orders and help Snow escape instead. Not that it mattered, in the end. Snow had still died. Killed by her stepmother, the witch Delphine.

Sabine returned with drinks for Ansel and Garrett. She slid the mugs towards them, then headed back to wait for the rest with Demetri. As Garrett inhaled happily from his mug, Ansel lifted his and took a deep drink. He nearly choked on the strong taste of nuts and spices, sputtering. "What is this?"

"Mulled wine," Garrett enthused. "Festive, isn't it?"

"Festive?"

"The winter solstice! St. Liara's Day! The Festival of Gifts! They're all coming up in the next couple of weeks."

"And you celebrate...all of those?" Ansel asked. Most people celebrated the Festival of Gifts, though the original meaning of the holiday had gotten a bit lost. But St. Liara's Day was the winter celebration in the Church of the Saints. Ansel didn't think the royal family adhered to that old faith.

"I celebrate everything." Garrett frowned. "Though maybe not, so much, the Festival of Gifts. After meeting real fairies, I feel a little strange celebrating holidays devoted to worshipping them."

"I mean, no one really does anymore. It's just...the gifts."

"I just love everything about this time of year." Garrett beamed. "The lights, the gifts, the food, the evergreens—"

"Mmm."

"Are you sure you're all right?" Garrett pressed.

"I'm fine. Just—" Ansel chanced a glance at the prince. Perhaps it was his open expression, the real concern in his eyes. But Ansel said, "It was just today. When we were out. I ran into an old friend of mine. Someone I used to know."

"An old friend?" Garrett echoed. "Does that mean you've been here before?"

"Yes. Six years ago. She was just a friend. I mean, we were children. I don't remember much about her. But for some reason, that's bothering me." Ansel shrugged. "It's not surprising I don't remember much. Everything around here got a little complicated, and Isabelle and I moved on. So."

Everything got complicated. That was putting it mildly, Ansel thought. The truth was, his friendship with Jesine was the only good memory he had of his time here. Small and fleeting as that memory was. He and Isabelle had only stayed so long because they'd been waiting for their father to return. It had been months before they'd finally accepted he wasn't coming back.

It had taken a witch nearly cooking them in an oven. Ansel still remembered Isabelle's face after they'd escaped the burning house, her cheeks stained with soot. He remembered her trembling voice. *Ansel, he's not coming back. I don't think he's coming b-back. We can't stay here forever. Especially now. We have to go.*

"Hang on." Garrett's brow furrowed. "Six years ago. Wasn't that about the time that witch tried to—er, eat you and Isabelle?"

Ansel hadn't realized the prince knew about that. "Yes. That happened here. I mean, not in Lise, but around here."

"You don't think what's happening now, with Adela, could have anything to do with that, do you?"

"I don't see how. So far as I know, that witch was working on her own. And she's dead now." *Although, Adela knew her*, Ansel thought, remembering what she'd said today. Adela knew the witch's name. *Henrietta*. But she hadn't seemed to think much of her either, so he doubted they had any affiliation. Certainly not one that mattered, now Henrietta was dead.

"I certainly hope not," Garrett fretted. "Witches, I can deal with. But someone who wants to eat me? That's going a little far."

"Didn't your Princess Briar try to eat my sister?"

Garrett waved a hand. "That was all a misunderstanding."

"If you say so." Ansel took a cautious sip of his wine. It wasn't too bad, once you got used to the strong, sweet taste. "I'm surprised you didn't bring her. Princess Briar. I understand she's...formidable." And the only one who'd bested a demon, according to Demetri.

"Well." Garrett tugged at his necktie. "She's rather busy at the moment. With her own work. I didn't want to bother her." He dropped his gaze, rubbing a finger over a burn spot on the table.

Ansel watched the prince shrewdly. Perhaps he was just projecting, he thought. But Ansel had the feeling he wasn't the only one troubled by a girl.

7

OVERHEARD

J ESINE LAY IN BED, staring up at the low ceiling. She'd climbed up to her loft as soon as she'd gotten home, but so far, sleep eluded her. Her thoughts swirled round and round, going over what had happened this afternoon, out in the woods.

That cottage. The hex-trap.

Ansel.

Ansel, back again. After all this time. She'd thought she would never see him again. And not only was he here, but it seemed he was tangled up with witches. Again.

She rolled onto her side to face the wall. Maybe he wasn't involved with witches, she thought, gnawing at her bottom lip. She cast her mind back, trying to remember what he'd said. He'd known about hex-traps, but that didn't mean anything. Anyone who'd run in with a witch before might know about them. Jesine didn't even know whose cottage that was, or what Ansel was doing there.

But Ansel had also known about the witch herself. *"The one who set this trap is new to the area. And I don't think she's working alone."*

So perhaps he was mixed up in whatever these witches were doing here. But how, and why? Jesine wished she had asked him, but then, she wasn't sure how she could have done that without arousing suspicion. And besides...

She wasn't sure how she could have done that when her head was spinning. Spinning at the sight of Ansel. Right there. Before her.

She was surprised she'd managed to say anything at all.

Jesine closed her eyes. Truthfully, it wasn't the things Ansel had said about that witch that had been burned into her brain. It was everything else he'd said.

You probably don't remember me.

She could never have forgotten him. Not considering what she felt for him. Not considering everything he'd meant to her.

But she was surprised he remembered her at all.

A squawking from below got Jesine's attention, alerting her to Bastian's arrival. The raven hadn't come back with her earlier. She sat up, swinging her legs over the edge of the bed and smoothing out her rumpled dress. It had grown late, she realized. The only light shining through the window at the front of the house was moonlight, the clouds having cleared out. She lit a candle and carried it downstairs with her where, by the flickering flame, she spotted Bastian. The raven perched on her long table, hopping around in a circle, ruffling his feathers in an agitated way.

Before him was the sliver of parchment he'd delivered. The note with the spell and message that read, *Witching hour, tonight.*

Jesine glanced at the clock on her mantel.

It was almost that time.

But should she complete the spell? Bastian seemed to think she should, but he was a raven. She still had no idea who'd sent it to her or why. What if, Jesine thought, with a spike of anxiety, the golden-haired witch sent it? The same one who'd marked her? What if this was a trap?

She had very little time to consider. Cursing, she flew into action before she could think about what she was doing and began assembling the ingredients for the spell. A lock of her own hair, bright, orangey red. Fresh earth from the ground, easily obtained. The feather of a crow or raven—Jesine didn't typically store these, but she did have a few spare feathers Bastian had dropped. A pinch of a protective herb blend, its scent dark and smoky; Jesine was comforted to throw that into the spell. And the next ingredient—

The lifeblood of a living creature.

Jesine eyed the raven.

Bastian let out a squawk of protest.

Shaking her head, Jesine pulled a jar of spiders out of her cabinet. They were barely large enough to maintain a spell of this like, but one should suffice. She pulled a spider, wriggling, from the jar and tossed it into a stone bowl with the rest of the ingredients. Then she immediately set the bowl's contents alight with a match struck against the table. She turned her eyes from the spider's frantic, writhing death throes. *Dark magic,* she thought in disgust.

The final ingredient was the message itself. The parchment with the blot of human blood on it.

Jesine held it over the stone bowl and hesitated.

This really could be a trap. This was an eavesdropping spell, one usually sent between allied witches. Jesine knew the spell but had never used it before. She'd never had any witchy allies to communicate with. So far as she knew, she still had none.

But there were witches in the area who had already moved against her. And if she used this spell, once she was there—wherever "there" was—she could be pulled in. Rooted. Caught in a snare.

Trapped.

Jesine closed her eyes, directed her energy inward, and focused. Not on her magic—this was not magic. Or perhaps it was only a magic of her own kind.

She focused inward until everything went quiet.

And in a moment, she had her answer.

Trust it.

She dropped the parchment into the stone bowl.

The wavering flames leapt and crackled. For a split-second, the smoke spiraling up from the bowl turned a bright, blazing blue, and a caustic stench prickled Jesine's nose. Then Jesine felt a *tug* at her middle, like she'd been grabbed around the waist and yanked from where she stood. Everything tilted sideways, the room before her spun, and then—

She was somewhere else.

Slightly nauseated, Jesine blinked. Once, twice, three times. She thought maybe she was going to faint before she realized her vision wasn't going dark—she was *in* the dark.

This wasn't comforting, considering the uncertain circumstances that had brought her here. Fighting off alarm, Jesine rooted herself in her surroundings, taking in as much as she could. In the distance, she heard a long, thin *cre-e-e-a-k* followed by a soft *thud-thud-th-thud*. The sounds repeated over and over again—an unlatched or broken window perhaps, stirring in the wind? And the air held a slightly musty smell, like old, damp wood sitting in an airless space. She swept her gaze from side to side, and slowly, her eyes began to adjust.

It wasn't total darkness, not really. A shaft of moonlight beamed in from somewhere, its scant gleam illuminating decrepit wooden floorboards. So, inside, then. That made sense. It wasn't quite cold enough to be outside, though it *was* cold. Cold and quiet and still in a way that felt...dead. As though she sat in the heart of the underworld.

Shadows shifted around her. Jesine looked left and realized she was not alone.

A woman sat upon a long, low chest. Her legs were tucked beneath her, and her full, layered skirts spread around her like a protective circle. Jesine thought she might have light-colored hair, for something of it glistened in the gloom. The golden-haired witch? Jesine wondered, with an unpleasant shiver. But in the darkness, she couldn't tell.

The woman's glistening head turned then—towards Jesine. It was impossible to tell, wrapped in shadow as she was, but Jesine could have sworn the woman was looking right at her.

A chill touched Jesine's heart. That should have been impossible. No one should be able to see her, not even the one who had invited her here.

And Jesine had no idea if this woman had invited her here.

A loud *thunk* sounded out, startling Jesine. A door blew open, letting in a blast of frigid air. No, the door had not blown open. It had been shoved open by a dark figure who hustled inside.

"Stones, it's colder than the rotten Mountain Kingdom out there. Actually, it's just as cold in here." The voice was sleek and posh, and before Jesine could decide if she recognized it, light flashed to life in the darkness. A ball of flame shot past Jesine into an empty fireplace behind her. Despite the lack of kindling, flames spread along the hearth, bringing warmth and light into the room. "Why the hell are you lot sitting in the dark? Bit creepy, isn't it."

"It's just the two of us," said the woman sitting on the chest.

"Well, that explains it. You two are a bit creepy."

But Jesine barely heard this last comment. For as she looked at the woman sitting on the chest, she jumped, her heart tripping in her chest.

It *was* the golden-haired witch.

Jesine clenched her palm reflexively. She reminded herself that no one could see her, and indeed, the golden-haired witch gave no indication that she was aware of Jesine's presence. Nervously, Jesine looked at her head-on, taking her in more fully. Her burnished-gold hair wasn't the only lovely thing about her. She was stunningly beautiful, from her fair, flawless complexion to the long lashes framing her eyes. In place of the hooded cloak she'd donned before, she wore a cream-colored cashmere coat, very fine and expensive.

"*She* isn't here yet," the golden-haired woman said.

The man who had just come in clucked his tongue as he shrugged out of his heavy overcoat. "Late, is she? Shocking." Now that she could see him, Jesine knew they had not met before. He was a lean man with golden-brown skin and dark, piercing eyes. Like his female counterpart, he was quite attractive. There was such a sense of *style* to him, from his fashionable fur-lined hat to his emerald-green silk tie, knotted to look like an old-fashioned cravat.

The woman's mouth thinned. "It means nothing good."

"I dunno. If something ill has befallen dear Adela, I would have to say some good is come."

"Except, we need four for the spell. And the time we have to work is running short."

"She'll be here," the man said carelessly. He leaned against the peeling mantel over the fireplace, crossing his arms over his chest. "It's not like you to worry so much, Malina."

Jesine eyed the golden-haired woman appraisingly. So now she had a name to put to the witch who'd marked her: Malina.

Malina's expression was humorless. "You don't know me as well as you think you do."

"Oh, come now. We've been friends for a couple of centuries, at least—"

"We've *known* each other for a couple of centuries. Not the same thing."

The man put on a fiendish smile. "A couple of centuries. Yet you're still beautiful as ever, darling. In fact, you haven't aged a day."

"But you have," Malina replied.

A dark look flitted over the man's face. He reached up to adjust the fur-lined hat over his head, but not before Jesine caught a glimpse of a white lock of hair on his head.

Somewhere from the darkness on the far side of the room, a low, deep chuckle floated out of the shadows. Revealing the presence of a third witch.

Jesine's heart stilled.

That sound—that *laugh*—scratched at her mind, awakening old memories. But unlike when she'd seen Ansel, these were not pleasant memories. These memories were like digging into the scar tissue of an old wound.

She knew that laugh. She knew the third witch.

Before she could dwell on it, the door burst open again. This time, it was a woman who rushed in, slamming the door shut behind her. Judging by her dark-blue cloak, Jesine thought she was the other witch she'd seen in the hollow two nights ago. The woman yanked back her hood, revealing a face that was not nearly as attractive as her fellow witches. There was too much of a pinched, twisted look about her. Her blue eyes were squinty and small, her upturned nose a little too long.

"Adela," Malina said without moving from her seat, "I hope you realize you're late."

"Late? *Late?*" The witch, Adela, practically snarled, her lips drawing back from her teeth. "Forget late! I barely escaped our little witch hunter this afternoon. Do you know he has a fairy-wood stake? And I've just discovered he isn't alone anymore. *Prince Garrett* arrived in Lise this afternoon, accompanied by royal guards!"

"You're joking." The man in the fur-lined hat looked delighted. "He's here already? Well, that makes our job easier, doesn't it?"

"He wasn't supposed to be here yet!" Adela snapped. "You said that—that—creature from hell would bring him here, Castel. Yet here he is, before news about a gutted corpse could have traveled across the kingdom!"

The man—she had called him Castel—looked unruffled. He didn't straighten from his casual pose, slouched beside the fire. "I'm hardly an expert," he said, "but from what I've heard of the prince, he's something of an adventurer. Perhaps he was bored and decided to join Ansel for fun."

Jesine gave another start. *Ansel.* So he *was* mixed up in this after all. But why? Was he the "witch hunter" they had mentioned? Surely not. Yes, he'd killed one witch six years ago, but he'd only been eleven years old. What had Ansel been up to during all this time?

"Or perhaps the prince came for revenge." Malina ran an appraising gaze over Adela. "You did try to kill his brother, after all."

The glare Adela threw her was pure venom. "You've done as much and worse to his brother, so perhaps he's here to take vengeance against *you.*"

"I don't know why you're so rattled, dear Adela," said Castel. "Did Prince Garrett see you?"

"No, but—"

"And as for Ansel and his fairy-wood stake, what did you really have to fear? Considering the back-up you had."

"Back-up," Adela scoffed. "Back-up I can hardly control! It takes all the skill I possess to direct that creature and make it do what I want."

Castel lifted a shoulder in an indolent shrug. "The sea witch never had trouble controlling them."

"Yes, well, she was stark raving mad," Adela retorted. "Half-demon herself, if even a tenth of the rumors about her were true."

"Oh, they were. And yes, she was quite mad. But…" Castel's casual shrug this time was deliberately insulting. "She controlled them."

"And you summoned the creature." Adela fixed Castel with another poisonous glare. "So you've done your part. Why are you still here, again?"

"You know why."

Another rush of *déjà vu* swept over Jesine, unsettling her to the point of dizziness. She closed her eyes, trying to ground herself. She only wished she could close her ears so easily.

That *voice*. Oh, yes, she knew it. She had no trouble placing it.

There was a slow, deep, grating sound in the darkness on her right, old wood scraping over old wood as a rickety chair was pushed back, barely visible in the shadows. Jesine watched, her heart in her throat, as a dark figure unfolded from that chair, turned to face them, and took three steps forward. Emerging into the light cast by the fire.

Jesine gazed into a face she hoped she would never see again.

That face was a little different now. Oh, at first glance, it was the same. Rich-brown complexion, penetrating eyes, sharply angled jaw. But Jesine was used to seeing that face creased with mirth, full of mischievous laughter, a broad grin dimpling those cheeks.

But not anymore. Now, those penetrating eyes were dead. No light or laughter lurked within them. As his gaze landed on the other witches, a smile did cross his face, but there was no real humor in it. He was like a ghoul, mimicking a movement he'd seen before with no real feeling beneath it.

Yes, Jesine knew this man. This witch. His name was Harper.

"He's here for the same reason you are," Harper continued, stepping further into the light. He wore a three-piece suit, the garb not nearly as stylish as Castel's, but well-put together. Serviceable rather than stylish. "Because we need four for the spell. Once that's done, well. You're free to go, and so is he."

"I only wonder at his motives," Adela said through gritted teeth.

"I don't," Harper said indifferently. "No more than I wonder at yours."

"I want that hunter dead," Adela spat. "But so far as I can tell, Castel isn't getting anything out of this arrangement."

"That's because you don't know what I want, dear." Castel's voice was as blasé as ever, yet there was an ominous undercurrent to it now. Bearing a warning. He twirled a finger to point at the golden-haired witch, Malina. "I don't hear you questioning her motives. Too afraid of her, are you?"

"Of course not." Adela narrowed her eyes at Malina. "Perhaps I *should* ask after your motives, dear sister. Given the things you've been up to in the past few centuries, one might wonder where your allegiances lie. I'm half-surprised you aren't sporting a white lock of hair like Castel here."

"Hardly." Malina's voice was as smooth and cold as a layer of ice across a frozen pond. "And I'm here for the same reason you are. Revenge."

"Against whom? Prince Garrett? Don't tell me you're still after that ridiculous—"

"Enough." Harper's curt, passionless voice cut through them. "We don't have time for this bickering."

"Yes." Malina rose to her feet gracefully. "The moon will soon descend. We need to get to work."

Harper didn't move, but the other witches did. They moved towards him as though he were a magnet, drawing them in. He had always been that way, Jesine thought faintly. Magnetic. Charming, though in a blunt, mean way. Impossible not to like, even though he wasn't always particularly likable. No one would have ever called him a "nice" person.

Jesine had not always been nice either.

She couldn't tear her eyes from his face as the others moved, forming a four-pointed circle with Harper at the head. Jesine stared into his dead-eyed face, and years of fear rush through her. Even though he couldn't see her—his eyes never flicked her way—she felt exposed, standing there. Small and exposed.

Harper slipped a small compass out of his pocket and flipped it open. He consulted it briefly and took two steps to the right, then flipped the compass shut again.

"Really?" Castel's voice bore a note of disapproval. He and the others aligned themselves according to Harper—aligning themselves with the corners of the world, Jesine realized. North, south, east, and west. "The whole point is to use the moon, you know."

"I'm not going out there," Harper said tonelessly. "It's bloody freezing."

"It doesn't matter." Malina tilted her head back, and the others followed suit. They stood evenly spaced, two paces apart from each other. Enough to hold something at the center of their circle, like the fire they'd used in the hollow. But they placed nothing there—no sacrifice, no scrying bone, nothing to focus their work.

This had to be a summoning, then.

Harper began the incantation. Adela joined in, and then Castel, and finally Malina. Jesine recognized the beginnings of it, the opening to any summoning, but the longer they went on, the more convoluted their spell became. They spoke in parts, yet their voices blended like one, nuanced and resonant. Jesine knew she did not imagine it when the flames in the grate jumped and sizzled, and she did not imagine it a few minutes later when the fire shuddered and dimmed, the flames growing so small, Jesine thought they would go out.

The temperature in the room dropped, the air turning staler and colder. As though the magic at its center drew all the life—dilapidated and neglected as it was—from the room. Jesine feared her own warmth, her own spirit, would be sucked in.

Then the fire sputtered and died, plunging the room into darkness, and the incantation was at an end.

The silence was so weighted, Jesine could feel it pressing down on her. In the darkness, she felt sure there were eyes on her, seeing her, spying her. After a few seconds, the silence was broken by a heavy, terrible breath. Then another, and another, and each one seemed louder, closer. Jesine wanted to move, to leave this old house, leave this place—

Then the light returned, the fire roaring to life in the hearth. Jesine choked on a breath. There was no one or nothing near her, no eyes turned on her. The four witches still stood in the center of the room, only now, they stood around something.

Someone. A person. A rather small person. A woman dressed in little more than a rag.

Castel spoke, breaking through the quiet. "Welcome, Your Majesty." His voice held a sardonic ring.

"Hardly that," was the small woman's reply. "Anymore." She took a step forward, pushing Castel aside. It was not a hard push, but a firm one. The regal gesture of someone who expected to be obeyed. Even though the woman was so tiny, her long, dark hair as ragged as her garb.

The woman looked past Castel—right at Jesine. Her blue eyes gleamed like brilliant gem stones.

She said, "Are you aware someone is spying on you?"

Jesine had no time to react. There was a blow, a physical *blow*, like a battering ram crashing into her chest. Her surroundings fell away, the witches, the fire, the ramshackle house. All of it vanished into darkness. Jesine had one, quick glimpse of her own house, her table and her stone bowl, before she collapsed onto the floor, sinking into unconsciousness.

8

AMBUSHED

G ARRETT WATCHED ANSEL WEAVE through the crowded room, then start up the staircase to the second floor.
The hunter was obviously exhausted, and Garrett had finally
convinced him to head up to bed. Garrett knew Ansel wasn't
a particularly sociable person, but he'd seemed more truculent
than usual.

Demetri and Sabine returned with the rest of their drinks.
Demetri's cheeks were still very pink, and he didn't quite meet
Garrett's gaze as he said, "It's very hot in here."

"Yes," Garrett agreed tactfully, though not without amusement. "A bit."

"Where's Ansel?" Sabine asked.

"He went up to bed."

"Probably best he gets some rest." Sabine sipped at her mug.
"Since Demetri shot him and all."

"*What?*"

"I grazed him." Demetri's cheeks were bright red now. "A bit. And it was an accident. Obviously. I was aiming for the bats."

Garrett cleared his throat. "Perhaps you should fill me in on everything I've missed. Because it seems more than I realized." He sipped at his wine. "Your initial telegram only said weird things were happening around here. And Ansel said he'd tracked Adela..."

"Well." Demetri shifted in his seat. The low light in the tap-room cast a muted glare across half of his face, giving him a strange, spectral look. "We didn't know, at first, if it was witches doing everything. But I didn't know what else it could be." He paused. "More to the point, Sabine didn't know."

Garrett looked at Sabine. She was something of an expert in the supernatural.

"Well, I had it narrowed down," Sabine said defensively. "I'd ruled out were-wolves, changelings, fairies, trolls—"

"There are no such things as trolls," Garrett interrupted.

Sabine looked crestfallen. "Really?"

"I know," Garrett said glumly. "Ogres are real, though."

"What are they like?"

"Pretty much like a troll."

Demetri added, "She'd also ruled out goblins, corpse crea-tures, djinn, ghouls, and gremlins."

"There's no such thing as a ghoul either."

"No offense, Your High—er, Garrett," said Sabine, "but that shows what you know."

"You're joking."

"She's not," said Demetri. "Anyway. Once we met up with Ansel, we found evidence of witchcraft fairly quickly." He launched into a recap of their last few days, relating the attack from the bats, the remnants of the hex they'd discovered, Ansel's encounter with Adela, the corpse she'd left behind—and what had killed her.

A demon. Like the one Briar had seen in the Mariner Kingdom.

Garrett met this particular news with part-trepidation, part-excitement. On the one hand, knowing what this demon could do to a person was more than a little terrifying. On the other hand, Garrett was the sort of person who lived for "more than a little terrifying." It meant he had plenty of reason to stay here and investigate rather than go back home.

And he really needed a distraction from home.

They all discussed these events a little longer, then Gemma retired for bed; she would relieve Klaus from guard duty early in the morning. But Demetri was eager for a second cup of wine, nearly jumping up out of his chair to fetch another round.

Garrett was only too willing to join him. He didn't want to think about his problems at home, or witches and demons, anymore tonight. He would drink some wine, he decided, catch up with Demetri, and then retire early enough to get a good night's sleep.

But that was not what happened. What happened was, after their second round, Demetri went back to the bar and returned with something stronger than wine. Garrett politely declined, but Demetri downed his glass in about five minutes, and a second one in less time than that. By the end of the hour, he was quite drunk, though evidently, that didn't impede his skill with the violin. Given that he joined the piano player in the corner in a rousing rendition of a well-known winter carol, much to the enthusiasm of everyone in the common room.

Garrett sat and watched his friend, slack-jawed. A few minutes later, Sabine joined him, sinking into a chair. "He's quite good, isn't he?" She nodded at Demetri as his bow zipped furiously back and forth across his violin. "I've told him if he tires of investigating, he could become a traveling fiddler."

Garrett snapped his jaw shut. "How could you let this happen?"

"Let what happen?"

"This—him—" He waved a hand in Demetri's general direction. "His getting drunk like this!"

Sabine's answering look was almost disdainful. "I didn't realize I was meant to be his mum."

Garrett raised an eyebrow at her.

Sabine coughed. "Well, you said to dispense with your title. Sire."

Garrett waved a dismissive hand. "It's fine."

"And so is Demetri. Just because he drinks a little now and then—"

"A little?"

"Just because he gets properly smashed now and then," Sabine amended, "doesn't mean he's not all right."

"Well. I suppose if it really is only now and then..."

"It is. I promise. He's not getting sloshed every night or at every tavern we stay at."

Demetri finished off his carol with a mad flourish of his bow and grinned, lifting his violin high in the air to the applause of everyone in the room. The crowd roared for more. As Demetri placed his fiddle under his chin to oblige, Garrett watched him, noting his flushed face and rumpled hair. He recalled what Ansel had said—*He talks to himself*—and asked quietly, "Is he really all right, Sabine?"

Sabine opened her mouth, then paused.

"What?" Garrett prompted.

"It's nothing, really. It's just, grief, you know. It does strange things to a person."

"Yes," Garrett murmured, and the pang he felt at her words seemed oddly fresh. "I know."

If Sabine noticed anything off in his response, she didn't say so. She probably hadn't noticed, he thought. Sabine had only joined the guard about eight months ago and left to work with Demetri shortly after. She probably knew about Garrett's past—his betrothal to Princess Snow, her subsequent death—but she hadn't known him when he was at his worst. She hadn't known the prince who'd quested for danger and death a little too eagerly.

The prince that Snow's stepmother, Delphine, had turned him into.

———◆———

Garrett trampled down the stairs at the inn the next morning, the wooden steps groaning beneath his pounding boots. It was already mid-morning. After their late night, they'd all had a bit of a lie-in. Garrett, who was usually an early riser, was starving.

"Hey. Garrett."

Garrett stopped on the stairs, cringing. He knew without turning who had called down to him. The only one of his guards who took so easily to dropping his title: Klaus. That wasn't the reason for his displeasure, though. It was because he knew what Klaus wanted. But Garrett wiped his expression clean as he looked up. "Yes?"

In reply, Klaus held up a small, dark bottle and a syringe.

"Oh, right," said Garrett. "I'd forgotten."

He had not forgotten. Of course he had not forgotten.

He jogged back up the steps and followed Klaus back into his room. Garrett removed his tan sack coat and rolled up his sleeve, his eyes tracking Klaus's movements as he inserted the syringe into the bottle.

"You really should have brought Roy for this, you know," Klaus said.

But Garrett had not wanted any physicians on this trip. Not even Roy, who was only a medic. "You seem to know what you're doing." Striving for a nonchalant tone, Garrett added, "You know, maybe we should ration it out. Wait another few days?"

Klaus eyed him knowingly. "Roy said not to do that."

Damn. So Roy was onto him. "It's just, since the supply is getting low…"

Klaus held the syringe up, flicking it once. "Thatcher is confident he'll find an anti-venom before that."

Garrett bit his tongue on the obvious reply. That Thatcher had already had over a year to figure that out. That even after consulting with specialists from the Desert Kingdom and sending envoys to Queen Laurel in the Mountain Kingdom, he had yet to do so.

As soon as Klaus was done, Garrett snatched up his coat and hurried down to the common room. Despite the clouds in the sky outside, the common room was brighter than it had been last night, and somehow airier too. The rustic tables, benches, and chairs littering the room were mostly empty now, as was the sticky, spotted bar at the back of the room. That was where Demetri sat, perched on a barstool, eating his breakfast. Garrett slid onto the seat next to him, noting how bleary-eyed his friend looked.

"Late night?" Garrett asked as he slid into a chair across from his friend.

"You should know," Demetri groused.

"Not really," Garrett disagreed. "When I went up to bed around midnight, you didn't look to be retiring anytime soon." He tipped his head down the bar. "Where's your friend, by the way?"

"You mean Saskia? The barmaid?" When Garrett nodded, Demetri said, "Funny you should mention her. I saw her when I first came down this morning, she was on her way out. But she told me something she'd heard from some laborers last night—yesterday, while they were working in a quarry north of here, a geyser of *blood* erupted from the ground."

"Really?" Garrett tapped his fingers against the bar, a thrill of excitement flooding through him. "Sounds worth checking out."

"I figured you'd say that." Demetri buttered his last slice of toast. "Also, I was thinking. Perhaps you should telegram Briar."

"What?" The grin on Garrett's face vanished. "Why? What for?"

Demetri turned a confused expression on him. "Because of the demon. I mean, even with her abilities, Briar barely survived that thing. It nearly cleaved her in two. Surely she told you about it?"

"Of course." Briar had been much more blasé about the whole thing than Demetri was, but then, that was Briar. Garrett's throat tightened as he thought about her, and he didn't speak until he could manage a casual tone. "But I don't think we need to bring her into this. Anyway, this story your Saskia told you—"

"She's not *my* Saskia—"

"—another hex, do you think? This would make, what? Five?"

"Could be," Demetri mused. "You never know, though. People exaggerate sometimes. It might not be supernatural at all."

Garrett gave a mock-sigh. "I don't know how Sabine puts up with you, Demetri. Such a killjoy."

They decided to leave Ansel behind so he could get some more rest, and Klaus as well, since he'd been up most of the night. The rest of them headed out after Garrett ate breakfast. The quarry was a good way outside of Lise, through a long, thick stretch of tangled wood that was not easy to travel on horseback. It might have been faster on foot, Garrett thought, for by the time they reached the quarry, emerging out along a ridge, the soft daylight was already fading, the shrouded sun low in the sky.

The quarry was empty. It was a vast pit, ledges upon ledges of dark-gray rock carved out of the earth. It had obviously been in use for a long time; the topmost ledges were discolored with erosion and dotted with young, scraggly trees. Evergreen pines lined the western and northern edges of the quarry, tall and uniform in their appearance along the horizon, while the southern end was bordered by the knotted, wild forest they had emerged from.

As Garrett stood at the edge and looked down into the quarry, he frowned. He saw nothing like a geyser of blood anywhere. But then Gemma said, "There," and Garrett turned, following the tracker's keen eyes towards the far end of the pit.

It was not a geyser, and difficult to see in the weakening daylight. But there, near the north end of the quarry, was a thick crimson pool.

Gemma scouted their surroundings as Garrett, Demetri, and Sabine climbed down into the quarry. When they reached the bottom, and the edge of the pool, they stopped and stared at the congealing liquid. Now that they were closer, Garrett could see the blood was still coming up—not in a spewing geyser, but bubbling out of a fissure in the ground. The pool had spread to about eight feet across, staining the rocky floor.

Sabine crouched low to the ground and reached out, dipping two fingers into the liquid. Garrett watched avidly as she rubbed her fingers together. "I don't think this is blood."

"What? What is it, then?"

"I'm not sure." Sabine lifted her hand towards Garrett and Demetri. Her fingers were stained a dusty red and dirtied with some kind of sediment.

"No, I see what you mean," Demetri said. "The color's not quite right."

"No." Garrett leaned back, absurdly disappointed.

"Well, we should collect a sample," said Sabine. "There's a laboratory in one of the other villages. Instold, or something like that? I mean, if the quarry workers have never seen it before, it's still something strange."

That perked Garrett's spirits up.

Once Sabine had obtained a sample, they rejoined Gemma atop the ridge and set out back to Lise. Their return journey was even slower than before. The woodland was mired in mud, and in the growing dark, they had to tread carefully to keep the horses safe. Luckily, about halfway back, Gemma found them an easier path. It twisted around at first, but eventually led into a scanter, more open wood, the trees lofty but spaced out along the forest floor.

Garrett let out a long breath and watched it mist the frosty air in front of him. The cold was brutal this year; this far south, they didn't usually get much snow. But he felt this year might be different. *Just so long as it doesn't snow now*, he thought. Twilight was already upon them, tinting the woods in ghostly shades of blue and gray. Snow would only slow them down more. Garrett was ready to get back to the inn and sit down for a hot meal.

Like a silent ghost in the deep-blue darkness, Gemma appeared at Garrett's side. Her dark hair was smartly braided back from her face, and she wore a hunter's cap pulled down over her ears. "Sire," she said in a low voice, "someone is watching us from those trees up ahead."

Garrett stiffened. Sabine rode in front of him, and he followed Gemma's line of sight by the white gleam of Sabine's lantern. "That thick cluster there?" he muttered. "Slightly to the right?"

She gave an almost imperceptible nod. "With that big, dying oak at the front."

"Any idea who?"

"No." Gemma flexed her gloved fingers. "Only, it's definitely a person."

"As opposed to...?"

"A demon." She slanted her eyes towards him. "Or a were-wolf. Or a rotting corpse monster—"

"All right, all right. But it could be a witch."

"I suppose so. Then again, it might just be a curious villager."

"Out alone? In the dark?"

"Everyone's a little stupid now and then," Gemma said bluntly. Coming from her, it was just an honest observation. "Want me to circle around, get a closer look?"

"Yes. But be careful. Signal us with one of your birdcalls if everything is all right."

"And if everything is not?"

"Er—scream or something."

The look Gemma sent him was unamused. "I don't scream. But I'll shout a warning, nice and loud."

"You do that."

She dropped back, and when Garrett tossed a surreptitious glance over his shoulder a minute later, she had vanished into the shadowy murk of the wood.

They continued forward, making their way toward the trees Gemma had indicated. The sky grew darker but clearer overhead, the clouds giving way to the moon and stars. Maybe that was why the air felt sharper to Garrett, sharp with cold, sharp with tension. He felt his thigh muscles tightening and forced himself to relax before his horse misunderstood and took off at a gallop.

He felt eyes on him and his heart somersaulted in his chest, but then he realized it was only Demetri, staring at him with a hard, knowing look. He mouthed, *Trouble?*

Maybe, Garrett mouthed back, tossing a nod at the trees up ahead.

Demetri cast an edgy look in Sabine's direction, but Garrett didn't want to risk warning her and drawing the suspicion of the watcher. Sabine was close enough to pull back quickly if she needed to. Besides, they should have that signal from Gemma soon enough...

A branch snapped behind Garrett, and he flinched. Any moment now...that dying beast of an oak was less than twenty paces from them—

Any time now, Gemma, Garrett thought.

But he heard no birdcall and certainly no scream. Shout. At fifteen paces, Garrett pulled his horse to a stop, raising his voice. "I think a cinch on my saddle is loose," he said casually. "If we could just hold up a moment—"

"Yes, please do," said a high, girlish voice. "I'm here to roll out the welcome mat, after all."

Garrett froze, clutching his reins. Every hair on the nape of his neck rose as a tall figure stepped out from behind the dying oak, a figure wreathed in a halo of light cast by the lantern she carried. He didn't need to see her face to know who it was, but she pulled back the hood of her midnight-blue cloak, revealing rosy cheeks and eyes as dark as an endless abyss.

"Hello again, prince," Adela said. "Remember me?"

"How could I forget?" Garrett shrugged off a shudder, remembering the jagged, choking sensation of needles in his throat. "You did try to kill my brother, after all."

Adela released a tinkling laugh. "Oh, don't take that too personally. My interest in your brother was purely professional. That curse of his was rather intriguing. Did he ever figure out how to break it?"

"No idea," Garrett said.

"You don't keep in touch? And after all you went through to save him."

"I don't think you're here to talk about my brother."

"No." The false geniality vanished from Adela's face. "I'm not." She raised her arm to one side, fist closed, and made a sharp *tugging* motion.

Garrett's heart skidded in his chest, and out of the corner of his eye, he saw Demetri reach for his pistol. But nothing happened—no attack came.

Instead, Gemma stumbled out of the trees on their left.

Garrett sucked in a breath. Adela gave another sharp tug of her arm, and Gemma lurched forward, as though Adela had her on an invisible leash.

"Let her go," Garrett said tensely.

"Oh, I'm not going to hurt her." Adela cast a speculative look at Gemma. "Much."

"What the hell do you want?" Garrett demanded.

"It's not about what I want, Your Highness." Adela tugged again, and Gemma came closer, within Adela's circle of light. Another tug, and Gemma's knees hit the ground, her spine ramrod straight. Her hunter's cap was gone, her dark hair mussed, pulling free of her braid. Her jaw was clenched so tight, Garrett could see the muscles straining in her face.

"I'm following someone else's agenda," Adela said. "Truthfully, I work best that way." A shadow crossed her face. "Certainly it's better than running all over the earth, trying to avoid that hunter."

"Yes, well, just because you've stopped moving doesn't mean Ansel has. Your little hex-trap didn't stop him for long."

"You aren't listening, Prince Garrett." Adela's voice was smooth, almost pleasant. It made Garrett feel like there was a spider crawling across his back. "I'm not here alone. I have some friends very nearby. And one of them *really* wants to see you."

105

"Yes, but your friends aren't here now," Garrett pointed out. "So I'm not sure what's to stop one of my friends putting a bullet in your head."

"That's not a very nice thing to say." Adela pouted. "When I could crush this girl's head like a grape." The witch tightened her fist. Gemma tensed even more, a little gasp escaping her lips. Her eyes bulged in her face.

Garrett's heart raced, galloping like a steed. "I *will* kill you."

"But will your bullets reach me before I blast her head wide open? Before her brain starts oozing out of her ears?"

Dark, thick blood trickled from Gemma's nose, dribbling down her lips, staining them black. She swayed, barely upright, a vein pulsing starkly in her temple.

"It's an interesting challenge." Adela's eyes glittered, hungry for blood. "One I might even risk my life for. The question is, will you risk her life for it?"

Gemma swayed again. As Garrett watched, her eyes began to roll back in her head.

"Stop it," he growled.

Adela laughed again, but the ugly expression on her face didn't alter. It was a frightening juxtaposition, that girlish laugh from that bloodthirsty glare. "That's what I thought. Now order your people back, prince. A good five hundred paces. And believe me, I'll know when they get there."

"Garrett—" Demetri started.

"Do it," Garrett ordered. "Go. Both of you, now."

He heard Sabine let out a low curse, but Demetri gestured and they fell back. Garrett didn't turn to watch. His eyes were still trained on Gemma, whose face had gone sallow. He waited tensely, every muscle knotting more by the second. He waited until he couldn't hear the others' horses anymore, until the only light left to see by was Adela's own lantern.

Then—finally—Adela let out a satisfied breath. "There we go."

"What do you want?" Garrett repeated.

"I already told you, prince. I have a dear friend who very much wants to see you."

"Let Gemma go first," he commanded, "and then I'll go wherever you want."

"Of course you will. You won't have any choice."

Before Garrett could think what that meant, Adela flexed open her fingers. Gemma dropped like a sack of stones, falling onto her face. And before Garrett could even think about dismounting to check on her, Adela flung an arm out towards him.

He had no time to defend himself. There was a bright flash of light and a sharp crack against his skull, like the butt of a pistol slamming into his temple.

Then everything went dark.

9

BOTHERED

J ESINE DIDN'T KNOW WHAT else to do but go back to the cottage where she'd found Ansel. After her eavesdropping spell ended so abruptly, she woke hours later, on the floor of her house, with a ringing headache. She then spent another sleepless night pacing in front of her hearth, half-expecting that coven of witches to come barging into her house. That shouldn't have been possible—she had her magical wards set, the ones that kept most people from finding her place.

But these weren't most people. These were witches. And it shouldn't have been possible for them to detect her within the eavesdropping spell.

Yet one of them had.

But the night faded into hazy daylight, and no one barged into her house, witch or otherwise. Jesine finally collapsed onto her bed and slept, and when she woke again, it was well past noon.

She went over in her head what she'd heard last night, eavesdropping on the coven, but it wasn't much. Nothing to give her insight into what they wanted—they hadn't trusted each other enough to speak of that. And nothing to give her any clue about this blasted mark on her palm.

So she decided to return to that cottage where Ansel had been caught in the hex-trap. It wasn't far from her house, and if witches had been there, they might have left some clue behind. It meant delaying her search another day, but that was probably for the best. If those witches were looking for the same power she was, better not to draw attention to it by delving into the earth.

It was another dreary day, the sky blanketed in a thick layer of clouds, the air bitterly cold. Jesine dressed in a thick, stiff skirt and a fitted jacket, then piled on her coat, hood, and gloves for warmth. Bastian was nowhere to be found, and as she set out from her house, she struggled to remember the way to the cottage without him. She spotted a few landmarks she recalled and eventually found her way. She had just glimpsed the slope of the cottage roof through the trees when something caught her gaze out of the corner of her eye.

A bird, soaring through the woods. Out into a vast stretch of open sky.

Curious, Jesine turned. She couldn't say why. Something was nagging at her memory, catching her in the snare of years gone by. Turning her back on the cottage, she ventured through the woods, her steps careful and quiet. She kept going until the forest thinned, giving way to a broad, grassy glade.

Jesine caught her breath. She stood right at the edge of the tree line, half-hidden in the shadows of towering pine trees. For a moment, she thought she'd gone back in time.

Because she remembered this glade. She hadn't realized it was so close to that cottage, but she remembered it. She remembered meeting someone here, someone dear to her. Six years ago.

And that someone was here now, standing in the glade.

It was Ansel.

Jesine watched him turn in a slow circle, standing in profile to her. She took in the lines of his silhouette: the slope of his long nose, his chiseled cheekbones, his square chin. The round face was the same in a way, yet also different. Older. Less baby-faced, more defined. His shoulders were broader too, his frame less gangly, though even now, at seventeen, he was compact, of medium height and build.

Suddenly, she realized he was looking right at her. Peering suspiciously into the gnarled boughs of the trees.

"Who's there?" he called, his voice harder than she remembered. Jesine was struck by the same idea she'd had when she saw Harper—that Ansel was so different from the boy she'd known. Not in appearance, but in demeanor. In attitude. Out in the middle of the glade, beneath the fading daylight, Ansel looked tense and guarded, his body tightly coiled. In that moment, he looked not at all like the carefree, somewhat shy boy she remembered.

"Is someone there?" Ansel repeated, taking a step towards her.

Jesine hesitated, then pushed past the trees, stepping out into the glade.

"Oh. Jesine." Ansel relaxed, his face smoothing out. "I was hoping I'd run into you."

A pathetic little surge of hope rose inside Jesine. She shoved it down, feeling self-conscious. As though Ansel could read her feelings on her face. "You were?" She took a few more steps, closing the distance between them.

"Yes, I—er—" Ansel ran a hand through his short, tightly curled hair. "I wanted to warn you. When I saw you here yesterday, I forgot to mention—it's not just witches in the area. They have some kind of fell creature working for them—some call it a demon. It moves fast and kills quite gruesomely." A grimace came over his face. "Anyway. I realized I should have said something. I mean, I don't want to scare you, but if you often walk these woods alone…"

"Thank you," Jesine said awkwardly. This demon must have been the "back-up" the witches had mentioned last night. "And you didn't scare me."

"Oh. Good."

Silence fell between them. A gentle wind blustered through the glade, rippling through the short, green-gray winter grass. Jesine scrambled for something to say. "So, er…what are you doing out here? Or—are you staying nearby?"

"I'm staying in Lise," Ansel said, "at the inn." He cast his gaze around the clearing. "Truthfully, I was bored. My companions left me at the inn today to rest, but I was going mad, cooped up all day. So I thought I'd come back here and see if we missed anything yesterday. I seem to have got turned around though. I was looking for that cottage—"

"It's just through the woods." Jesine pointed across the glade. "That way. It's not far."

"Oh." Ansel turned to look. "I was close, then. Actually, I came across this clearing here, and I…got distracted. I'm not sure why. Something about this place seems familiar, I suppose."

A lump grew in Jesine's throat. Yes, it would be familiar, she thought. Even if he didn't remember why.

"Anyway," Ansel said, "I just wanted to look over that cottage again. There was a woman killed there—probably the woman who lived there. Did you know her?"

"No." In fact, Jesine had never seen that cottage before. Never known it was there. She was still puzzled by that, considering how long she'd lived in this area. True, she hadn't been here the past few years, but that cottage wouldn't have been built so recently. It was obviously older than that.

"Well, it seems she was killed by that demon creature. But we didn't have much time to look around here yesterday, and…" Ansel trailed off, looking pensive. "It just seems strange. I mean, I don't have any clue what these witches are up to, but even still. I just wonder, why that cottage? Why that woman?"

"Oh, the woman was nothing special. Wrong place, wrong time, is all."

Ansel and Jesine whirled around.

A figure stood at the edge of the woods. He wore a slender, simple topcoat over a three-piece suit, emphasizing his lean frame. The brown bowler hat that topped his head matched his waistcoat. His dark eyes fixed on the pair of them unerringly, even in the gloomy gray daylight.

Jesine's heart leapt in her chest.

It was Harper.

"This place was chosen out of familiarity, nothing more." Harper strolled out into the glade, coming towards them. His steps were languid, deliberately nonthreatening. "In point of fact, that cottage was my house, many years ago. I was born there, or so I'm told."

That's why I never knew it was there. The thought pierced through Jesine's shock. A witch's house would have been cloaked and warded, like her own house was. She shivered to think that Harper and his family had lived so close.

"Never liked the place much though." He stopped and stood, some fifteen paces from them. "See, my father wasn't exactly a kind man. Something Jesine here and I had in common." He bent his gaze on her, his lips curving into a crude semblance of a smile. But then his gaze flipped in Ansel's direction. "And from what I hear, something you share with us too, Ansel."

Jesine darted a glance at Ansel. His face was like a stone. When he spoke, his voice was tight but unafraid. "I'm sorry. I don't think we've been introduced."

"Not formally, no." Harper inclined his head, putting a hand to the brim of his hat. "But I've heard all about you. Ansel, the famous witch hunter." Harper lifted his head soon enough for Jesine to see a shadow flit over his face. "As it happens, I've wanted to meet you for a long time. A very long time."

Jesine looked at Harper, but his gaze was still fixed on Ansel. Was that true, what he said? That he was interested in Ansel? Like the rest of the witches, Harper's motives weren't clear, but Jesine assumed he was here for her. That he wanted something from her, just like he had before. All those years ago, when he'd sought to use her to get what he wanted. What his coven wanted.

Perhaps getting to Ansel, she realized, was his way of getting to her. Could Harper know what Ansel was to her? The time she had known Harper and the time she had known Ansel did overlap a little, but so far as she knew, they had never crossed paths. She had certainly never mentioned Ansel to Harper. She never would have, even before she'd realized she couldn't trust Harper.

As if sensing her attention, Harper's gaze turned from Ansel to Jesine. "And you." His tone was casual, as though it hadn't been years since he'd seen her. "I came here looking to catch a prince. Instead I find you. Little Jes. All grown up now." He used that old nickname for her, pronouncing her name as it should be, with a hard *s* that sounded more like a *z*. "Say now, Jes. Was that you last night? Spying on us?" Harper spread his arms wide. "You know you don't have to hide like that. You're welcome to join us any time."

Heat rushed through Jesine, uncomfortable, unwelcome heat. She resisted the urge to look at Ansel, but she must have flinched in his direction because Harper said, "Oh, no worries, Jes. I won't fill your friend here in on all your deep, dark secrets."

But Ansel seemed to have barely heard this. He balled his hands into fists at his side. "I saw you," he said. "In the town square. When the bats attacked. Who are you?"

"You'll find out soon enough," Harper said. "Though you might wish you didn't."

Ansel didn't look concerned, and that concerned Jesine. Harper was so disarming, so unassuming; it was easy to underestimate him. Plenty of people had. But this, here, just talking to him...Ansel was in far more danger than he realized.

"Is that so?" Ansel said coolly. "Because in my experience, one witch is much like another."

Harper laughed at that. It was so like his old laugh that it made Jesine ache to hear it. Just a booming laugh from a handsome man. Still, she could hear the difference. Just like his eyes, Harper's laugh was empty. And there was a small, pathetic part of her that was sad to hear it. A part of her that wondered what had happened to take all his joy.

"You don't really mean that." Harper removed his hat, spinning it around on one hand. "Your experience with Delphine, surely, must have been unlike any other. I've never met a witch with such a particularity for cutting out people's hearts. I heard she got fairly creative with her methods." He looked curiously at Ansel. "Is it true she sometimes *eats* them?"

"Don't you eat fairy hearts or something?"

"I drink fairy blood, and only for the magic. I don't enjoy it. But a human heart..." Harper shuddered, popping his hat back onto his head. "That I can't imagine."

Jesine tried to tune out their chatter. Tune out all distractions. The wind winnowing through the glade and biting at her nose, the birds gliding overhead, chirping and calling to one another as dusk fell. She reached inside herself for that link, that delicate silver chain. She reached for magic. If she could strike at Harper, just long enough for them to get away...

Come on, she thought, and she didn't like how frantic she felt. *Come on.* She began to draw power from that chain, a little bit at a time. But it was slow, too slow...

"Even if Delphine did eat human hearts," Ansel was saying, "it still wouldn't be anything special. See, the first witch I met tried to cook and eat me."

"Yes." Harper's tone darkened. "I heard about that. But I thought Jesine was the first witch you met."

Startled, Jesine lost her grip on her magic.

Ansel, too, seemed caught off-guard. "Wh-what?"

"Oh, I see." Harper gave a little chuckle. "She didn't tell you *anything*, did she? What she is? Well, no need to worry. She's a 'good witch,' you see." His voice dripped with mockery. "But she wasn't always so pure and good. She dabbled a little, didn't you, Jes? She flirted with the dark side." He smiled viciously at Ansel. "And I mean that literally."

Jesine faced Harper down. She would not, could not, look at Ansel. Instead, she reached again for the link inside her, pulling at her magic.

And then, everything went wrong.

The chain linking her to her fairy vanished. A wave of darkness swept over it, a black curtain, hiding it from sight. Dimly, Jesine registered the sudden cold in the air, an icy cold seeping through her bones. But she barely had time to notice it. Because Jesine began to choke on the darkness as it welled inside her, pressing all the air from her lungs, filling up her throat—

And then a deep rumbling awoke inside her. *Inside her.* Not from the floor, like before, not from beneath her feet—*inside her.*

Terror gripped Jesine, making her rigid. She felt it like a physical thing. The fingertips that had ghosted over her neck, the hand that had stretched towards her, now gripped her from the inside. Cold fingers, wrapping around her spine. Holding her firm.

And the owner of that hand, that *voice*, spoke inside her.

Jesine...

I am here.

The darkness erupted.

It poured from her, a tarry blackness. She tasted it as it pooled in her mouth, felt her cheeks grow sticky as it bled from her eyes. Someone cried out, and someone was laughing, but Jesine couldn't see because the darkness rolled out like a tidal wave, crashing over the glade, dousing everything in shadow—

She couldn't move. Her body was not her own. She was nothing but bits of flesh and bone and blood, crudely stitched together. A vessel for the darkness.

A vessel for *him*.

Jesine...come with me...

And then the darkness broke apart. Like ash spewing from a volcano, it settled, dark flecks hanging suspended in the air. For just a moment.

And then it was just gone.

The darkness was gone.

It was only her and Ansel, in the clearing in the woods. Kneeling in the dying grass beneath the slate-gray sky. Even the birds still trilled and twittered, somewhere back in the trees.

Ansel crouched before her, one hand on the side of his face. His wide, wild eyes told her she had not imagined what just happened. It was not a dream or a hallucination.

He had experienced it too.

"By the Gift..." Ansel's voice was a hoarse whisper. He dropped his hand to the ground as though to steady himself. "What was that?"

Jesine looked down. A streak of dirt stained her stiff skirt. Trembling, she dropped her gloved hands into her lap, squeezing them together. Her short, shallow breaths coalesced in the wintry air, mingling with Ansel's. For a moment, they sat in silence, absorbing the horror they'd just experienced.

Then someone began to laugh.

It was Harper. She had forgotten Harper.

Ansel shot straight up and spun around. Jesine, too, climbed to her feet as quickly as her unsteady limbs allowed.

Harper still stood before them.

"What the hell did you just do to us?" Ansel demanded.

"Me?" Harper held up his hands. "Wasn't me, boy. I didn't have to do anything." He laughed again, a revelatory sound. "I don't have to do *anything*. I can just sit back and watch!"

"What are you talking about? What do you mean!"

"I wouldn't want to spoil the surprise," Harper said. "And I really must be on my way. We're on a tight schedule, see. But I'll be seeing you two." Then he retreated into the trees, his laughter trailing behind him.

Ansel swore, turning away. He ran a shaking hand over his wan face, his cheekbones hollowed with shock. "What *was* that—that darkness—"

"You saw it?" Jesine whispered. She knew he had. But she needed to hear him say it, she needed to know what he saw. Jesine reached up to touch her face, tracing the contours of her nose and lips. She felt nothing, but...

Had Ansel seen it? Had that darkness actually poured out of her?

Was it still inside her?

"It was like a shadow," Ansel muttered, hunching in on himself. "But so, so dark. I don't know where it came from—"

A small, slim trickle of relief sluiced through Jesine. So he hadn't seen it come from her, then. Had it actually come from her, or had she only imagined that part?

"And then I heard this voice," Ansel murmured. "But not really a voice. A *feeling*. All around me—"

Jesine tensed. "What did it say?"

"My name." Ansel turned as though just now remembering she was there. His eyes found hers. "Ansel. Just that." He shivered. "It knew my name."

Jesine went cold all over. As though it had come again, bringing that preternatural chill. As though it had reached out to her from whatever dirty, far-off crevice it lurked in. She wrapped her arms around herself, hugging her body tight.

He had spoken to Ansel. He knew Ansel's name.

There could only be one explanation for that. There could be only one reason. This was her fault. She had brought this upon him.

"Was it you?" Ansel demanded.

Jesine snapped her head up. "What?"

"If it wasn't him, that witch..." He shoved a trembling hand through his hair. He trembled all over, Jesine noticed, and she wondered if his ashen face wasn't just from shock. What had he said, that his companions left him behind to rest? But why did he need rest? Was he injured, or ill?

"Ansel," she started, reaching towards him.

"No." Ansel jerked as though she'd burned him. Even though she hadn't actually come close to touching him. Suspicion and hostility warped his face; he looked nothing like the boy she'd once known. "*Was it you?* I thought he was lying when he said you were a witch, but—was he? That darkness, was that you?"

"Ansel, no, I didn't—"

"You're a witch," he accused. "You're—you—" But he broke off. For a moment, he went strangely still, closing his eyes.

Then he swayed on his feet.

"Ansel?" Jesine prompted, worried.

Ansel's eyes fluttered. "You're a witch," he repeated, his voice much weaker, his words slurring. Then his eyes rolled back in his head and he fainted, crumpling to the ground.

10

PREY

GARRETT WOKE TO A most unsettling noise. It was a deep, grinding sound, high-pitched and rough and rhythmic. Like something sliding back and forth—no, like something being cut. With a saw, perhaps? He could hear the resistance in it, a sharp edge meeting something tough and hard. Something not meant to be cut. It was an upsetting sound that he could somehow *feel* more than hear.

It woke instinctual terror in him.

He was someplace dark. That much was clear. Garrett squeezed his eyes shut to make sure he was awake, to ground himself in this new reality. He lay on his back, on a cold, hard, pitted surface. A little groan escaped his lips; his body felt stiff and sore. Most especially, his back throbbed, and though his muscles protested when he rolled over to prop himself up, his back thanked him for the reprieve.

Garrett let out a long, low breath as he tried to make out his surroundings. It was still dark, but he glimpsed a light ahead, somewhere. His vision was swimmy, blurring the light, making it seem brighter than it probably was.

He squeezed his eyes shut again and tried to think back. Where was he? And how did he get here? The last thing he remembered was...something upsetting. Something that made his stomach clench. Something that—combined with that persistent sawing sound—woke another thrill of fear inside him.

Gemma. *Gemma.* Bleeding from the nose, crumpled in the snow. Garrett, alone and unable to defend himself. Defend himself from—

Adela. The witch.

Garrett's heart gave an erratic skitter. That *sawing* noise. He sat up quickly, too quickly, and a wave of dizziness threatened to overtake him. Shaking it off, he looked over his shoulder. That way was more darkness, but also a distant light. It was not so distant as the light in the other direction, but it was a warmer, flickering light. Firelight.

Garrett looked around again. His vision had cleared a bit, his eyes adjusting to the darkness, and he saw the walls encasing him were stone. Rough and jagged, not man-made.

It was like...a cave. He was in a cave.

And he'd been taken by a witch.

That sawing sound. Sawing into something hard and resistant. Something like...bone.

He had to get out of here.

Stifling a grunt, Garrett climbed to his feet, steadying himself against the cave wall. He took a few uncertain steps. The ground beneath him was firm but damp, grassy ground patched over more rock. Probably still in the woods, then. Probably, the cave opening was close by.

Garrett glanced over his shoulder. There was no sign of Adela, aside from the firelight and that grinding sound. No sign that she knew he was awake. His whole body ached as though he'd been thrown from a horse. She must have dragged him here, he thought, at least part of the way—wherever here was. Still, he didn't seem severely injured. He could walk. Or run, if it came to that.

Tossing one more glance over his shoulder, Garrett took another step. Then another. He quickened his pace, wincing, but the more he moved, the less he hurt. He moved away from the firelight, away from that ominous sound, and towards that other source of light, brighter and hazier up ahead. The cave narrowed the closer he got, becoming a tunnel, and Garrett reached out to the sides of it, steadying himself as he moved—

Crash.

Garrett flinched. He looked down.

He'd kicked something in the tunnel. It was too dark to see what it was, but it gleamed like bronze or brass in the scant light. A pot or pitcher, he guessed, made of burnished metal. He'd kicked it, and it had crashed into the rocky wall, clattering loudly.

Garrett looked over his shoulder. He saw only darkness.

But.

The sawing sound had stopped.

Garrett held his breath. He knew he should move, but he felt rooted to the spot, waiting, listening. Maybe none of this was as sinister as he thought. Maybe it wasn't Adela back there at all. Maybe he'd gotten away from her somehow, or she'd dumped him, and some poor old woodsman had found him and brought him here—

"Dear princeling," a girlish voice crooned. "Where have you got to?"

Garrett's breath snagged in his throat. That was no woodsman.

That was Adela.

Her voice broke the spell holding him in place, and he lurched forward. He'd stood still long enough that his aches and pains had returned, making him stiff, and he moved awkwardly as he propelled himself down the tunnel, using his hands to push himself along the wall. He heard Adela laughing behind him, but the light up ahead was emerging, becoming brighter. It was the cave opening, the way out—

He stumbled forward and staggered free of the cave.

There he stopped again, disoriented. It had seemed so bright from inside the tunnel that he'd expected to step into daylight. But it was the night that encapsulated him and the surrounding forest. The light he'd seen was moonlight, gleaming white, piercing the treetops. A shaft of it shone down right outside the cave, like a gear-bulb lantern lighting the way.

Adela. Was still coming after him. Moonlight would hardly keep her away. Garrett shook himself as another of her tinkling laughs echoed out from the cave.

He ran.

He tore into the woods, away from the moonlight, into the darkness. That was not, perhaps, the best plan, as it soon grew so dark he couldn't see his hand in front of his face. But it was his only plan. He couldn't stay where he was, and even if he had light to see by—a lantern, a match—it would lead Adela straight to him.

So he ran blindly, tree branches scraping him, bramble tangling around his ankles. He tripped twice over something embedded in the forest floor, rocks or roots, but both times, he caught himself before he fell. He didn't stop to listen for Adela, didn't stop to consider where he was running to. The fact was, Adela had power she could use to find him without physically chasing him, and he didn't want to think about that. She also had a demon, he recalled. A demon that had already killed one woman by gorging on her insides...

He ran faster. All that mattered was he put some distance between himself and that cave.

He didn't know how long he ran. He ran until his lungs burned, until the ache in his back and legs intensified tenfold. He ran until his throat felt raw from the cold and his eyes stung, making them water.

He ran until he broke free of the tangled wood, emerging into a small clearing with a tiny, trickling stream. A rickety bridge crossed the stream, and beyond it lay an old, desolate cabin. It looked like a hunter's cabin, built from local lumber with only a few small windows punctuating the dark wood.

Garrett clutched at his knees and leaned over, wheezing. The tears on his face from his watering eyes felt frozen. He coughed once, twice, each one scarring his throat. Then he tried to go still and silent. Tried to listen.

He couldn't hear anything behind him. But somehow, he didn't think he would hear that demon coming.

His pulse jumped at the thought of the demon. He chanced a glance at the cabin ahead. It seemed too good to be true—well, really, it seemed damned creepy—but he had no idea where he was, and he had no weapons. That cabin could rectify one of those things.

His mind made up, Garrett straightened and staggered forward, across the arched little bridge and towards the cabin. The cabin had a wraparound porch, though it was even more decrepit than the little bridge. The porch steps bore his weight without snapping though, and the door looked stout enough. Perhaps too stout, if it was locked.

But when he tried the handle, the door swung open easily. Practically on its own. Far from comforted, Garrett braced himself and stepped inside.

It was just as dark in as it was out. Unwilling to shut the door behind him, Garrett stood in the entry and blinked, waiting for his eyes to adjust. Vague shapes took form around him—some furniture, he thought, chairs and tables and cabinets—and a glistening on the far wall that was probably a window or maybe a mirror. The space before him seemed wide and open, a single large room. Beyond that, it was too dark to make out anything.

He took an uncertain step. Then another. Expecting any minute for the floor to give out beneath him. He reached an arm out to feel along the wall, his fingers trailing over rough shards of unvarnished wood. He continued to move until his boot came down upon a different surface—pebbled and hard, not the same rickety wood from before. He looked down.

Something was scattered on the ground before him. Fear made his heart thunder in his chest, but when Garrett crouched down to feel at the stuff, he realized it was only ash. Cold ash. It was a fireplace before him, its last fire long dead.

He rose to his full height, and now he could make out a mantel set into the wall above the fireplace. He doubted there was any wood in here, but, with hope, he reached for the mantel, sliding his hand along it—

He knocked something onto the floor. A box of matches.

Garrett released a long exhale. He dug a match out of the box and struck it three times before it lit. Holding it up in front of his face, he looked around. The match's tiny light did not extend very far, nor did it burn for long before the flame bit at his fingers, but he glimpsed a rocking chair, the peeling wood floor, the door he'd left open to the cold—

—a pair of glowing red eyes—

Garrett's heart froze in his chest. In the same moment, the little flame burned his finger and he dropped the match, the light going out. Leaving him in the dark.

The tense knot in his gut intensified, tightening and twisting, making him sick with fear. His breath went so shallow that his chest began to hurt, and he tried to even it out, tried to *think*. Another match, he needed another match—he dug one out, knocking several onto the floor in his haste, and he struggled to strike it—

The flame flickered alight. He raised the match and looked to the door.

There was no one there. No eyes, red or otherwise, staring back at him.

Garrett moved his arm around, sweeping the rest of the room with his gaze. No eyes anywhere. No shapes even vaguely resembling a person or...creature...of any kind. He saw a long, low wooden chest, something that was probably a chair, a large paned window, and—

The match burned out, this time before the flames could lick his fingers. But before it did, Garrett swore he'd glimpsed another door in the far wall. Probably leading to another room. Maybe a room less bare than this one. Maybe a room with a better source of light. Maybe a room with a weapon.

He moved across the room. He found it ridiculously hard to step past the open front door, even though he wasn't anywhere near it. It was stupid, but he forced himself not to glance at it as he passed by, forced himself to keep moving. He tripped over a low step in the floor he hadn't seen before, and then, as he neared the interior door, he dug out another match and lit it. The door stood halfway open, and with only that small flame to see by, he pushed it the rest of the way open.

Behind the door was a tiny square bedroom. He saw that much before his light burned out. Garrett fumbled for a fourth match, lit it, and took in the simple bed in front of him. It was cot-like, an iron frame and a thin mattress, covered by a moth-eaten coverlet.

And on top of the bed, just lying there, was a gun. A pistol.

By the quivering light of his match, Garrett stared at the pistol, unable to comprehend it. He knew what he was seeing. He understood what it was. But it seemed wrong, somehow. Unlikely.

Too good to be true.

Unease prickled down his spine. He swept his arm around the room just before the match burned out, long enough to see he was alone. There was no one else there. Cursing, he dug out a fifth match, struck it alight, and looked again at the pistol.

Too good to be true. Worse, it felt like a trap. But…it was there. And he needed a weapon. And it wasn't *completely* impossible someone might have left a pistol here, Garrett reasoned, desperate to convince himself. He stepped into the room, reached down, and picked up the pistol.

It felt real. It felt solid.

It felt...strangely light.

"Now what good do you think that will do you, Gallant?"

Garrett swung his arm around so fast, he leveled the pistol at his target before he recognized the voice. Before he realized why it chilled him, turning his heart to ice.

By the light of his little match, he saw the face of the queen.

Queen Delphine.

Then his match burned out.

Pull the trigger, a voice in his head said, but he had forgotten what that meant. Much less how to do it. He was already convincing himself he had not seen what he thought when he heard her low, deep laugh in the darkness. And then, dread filling up his lungs, another light flickered to life.

Not a match this time. A lantern.

Held by the queen.

She stood in the doorway, blocking his only exit. She was so much smaller than Garrett, and she held no weapon like he did. For though the rest of his body shook, his arm held the pistol steady, aimed at her chest. Yet in that moment, it didn't matter one bit. He was frozen in shock.

It couldn't be her. It just couldn't be.

The queen. Delphine. Snow's stepmother.

The witch who had killed Snow.

"This isn't real," he whispered.

"Oh, but it is." Her voice was soft and terrifying. Insubstantial, in a way, like the shadows encircling them. "Very, very real."

"This is—Adela did something to me—"

"She knocked you out." Delphine gave a casual flick of her fingers. "And dragged you through the woods. But nothing more.

I'm sure she would have loved to do all sorts of things to you, but she didn't, per my instructions. She even let you go. Also per my instructions."

He couldn't make sense of this. She couldn't be here. It was impossible.

"You're locked up," he said. His voice sounded weird to his ears. Strangled and muffled. As though he was speaking underwater. As though he was drowning. "In that prison, in the middle of nowhere. It was built for you, there's no way you could have escaped—"

"Not on my own, no." She cocked her head. "I needed a little help. And it took a while to get that help, since it was so difficult to communicate with anyone outside those walls. But I managed it eventually. I just had to find the right individuals and properly motivate them."

Garrett tightened his grip on the pistol. It felt cold and smooth in his hand. It felt real. Unlike the woman before him. "It's not possible."

"Why don't you stop fighting what's right before your eyes and shoot already, Gallant?" she asked. "You know you want to. And, well, if I'm not real, you'll just shoot into the wall, won't you? So why not just *shoot?*"

Oh, stones. This was definitely a trap, he thought, licking his lips. He'd known it the moment he'd seen the pistol. But he held it in his hand, his finger on the trigger, and it would be so easy—

"What are you waiting for?" Her voice hardened. "Do it already. *Shoot* me, Garrett. Shoot—"

He squeezed the trigger.

Nothing happened.

He squeezed it again. The trigger clicked aimlessly.

Delphine let out a peal of laughter.

The gun wasn't loaded. That, Garrett thought, was why it felt so light. He dropped his arm to his side. Everything was beginning to feel fuzzy. The room around him spun, everything shrinking away. Everything fading. Even Delphine's laughter sounded muted and indistinct, and Garrett realized he was about to black out again. Reaching out, he grabbed a hold of one of the bedposts, steadying himself.

"Why?" he heard himself ask.

"Why what?" Delphine returned.

Good question. Garrett fought to stay there, to stay present. He forced himself to look at the queen, to focus on her, and that seemed to help. At least, it helped him stay conscious. It didn't help anything else. It didn't help dampen his fear or confusion. He felt cold, on the *inside*, as though his heart had stopped beating the moment he'd seen her and hadn't started up again. It just couldn't be her. Not this woman. Not this witch. No matter how long or hard he stared at her, it didn't feel real.

The last time he'd seen her, she'd been in prison. She'd been dressed in a shapeless rag, her hair long and lank, lines marking her face. The woman who stood before him now was different. This woman was dressed in rich satin and fur. This woman's face was unblemished, her lips bloodred, her dark hair lustrous and swept atop her head.

"The gun." He gestured uselessly with it. "You left it there. For me to find."

"Why, yes. I did."

"And Adela. You said she let me go because you told her to."

"You're not usually quite this dense, Gallant. Perhaps Adela used too much force when she knocked you out. Or are you just so stunned to see me that you can't think straight?"

Fury blazed inside Garrett, and he welcomed it. It steadied him, cleared his senses. "*Why?* Why play these games?"

"Do I need a reason?" The queen's eyes went hard, like twin sapphires. "You and your father took my kingdom from me, stripped me of everything, and tossed me in some backwater prison to be forgotten. I should love nothing more than to play games with you for the rest of your life. However short that might be."

"Is that a threat?"

"Not at all." Delphine's tone was nonchalant. "We both know you don't have long to live, Gallant. Thanks to that venom poisoning you. It's a shame, really." She sighed. "I would love to have years to torment you. But I estimate you have no more than a few weeks left. Sad."

Garrett fought not to react. "I think I have a little longer than that."

"Do you? Why? Because that's what your physicians told you? They lied to you, prince. They didn't want to frighten you, I'm sure. Or maybe it's because you feel just fine? Don't let that fool you. I think your health will decline quite quickly." Delphine's eyes danced at the thought of his pain and death. "Isn't that how it happened the first time?"

Garrett swallowed. He had no reason at all to believe her—this was Delphine, after all—but the fact was, he already suspected exactly what she was saying. He knew Thatcher and Roy had put a rosy spin on the situation. And she wasn't wrong about how quickly he could deteriorate—that was exactly how it happened before, when he'd first been poisoned by the corpse creature's bite.

"Of course..." Delphine took a step towards him, and Garrett couldn't help but back away. He couldn't contain a flinch when the queen reached up and laid a hand against the side of his face. "I could do something about that. If only to prolong our fun together. I could burn that venom right out of you. And even better—for me—it will be very painful."

Garrett's mouth was too dry to speak. And she didn't give him a chance to say anything.

Her fingertips dug into the side of his face, and then all he knew was pain.

It racked through him, paroxysms of agony arcing through his body. He felt like he was on fire, his blood had *become* fire, boiling in his veins. A horrid, keening scream came from somewhere, a scream so strident, he thought his eardrums would burst.

Then he realized he was the one screaming.

Distantly, he thought he knew this pain. Distantly, he felt its familiarity. Like a memory.

And then it ended. He didn't register it at first. The absence of pain. He didn't register it because he could still feel it, a throbbing residue left inside him. What he registered was everything else—the splintering wood floor beneath his cheek, the sour stink of vomit—oh. *His* vomit. He was lying in it.

Sound came back next. He heard Delphine. He heard her laughing. And he knew, with animal desperation, that he had to get out of here. He pushed himself onto trembling hands and knees and found he could not get further than that.

So he began to crawl.

Delphine didn't try to stop him. That only increased his terror. She didn't try to stop him, he thought, because she knew he couldn't get far.

He crawled. Slipping onto elbows, knees juddering, half-dragging himself, he made it into the front room of the cabin. And still her laughter trailed him, even as he reached the door and threw himself over the threshold—

He tumbled down the porch steps, head over knees, and landed in cold, sludgy mud. He was shaking so badly that he didn't feel like a part of his own body, and when he opened his eyes and saw Delphine standing on the porch, looming over him, he knew there was no escaping her.

No escape.

"Now I have all the time in the world to play my games with you, Gallant." She placed her hands on her hips, exultant in her victory. "Aren't you going to thank me?"

Garrett drew in a guttering breath. *Get up*, he told himself. He had to stand, face her on his feet. He couldn't lie here in the mud like a dog, he had to *get up*—

Bam!

Garrett blinked as Delphine rocked backwards.

Bam!

The queen reeled again, this time tumbling back, falling out of Garrett's line of sight. He stared up at the sky, trying to process what had just happened. Gunfire. That had been gunfire—someone had shot—

A face appeared, leaning over him, but it was not Delphine.

"Gemma," Garrett practically sobbed.

"C'mon." Gemma's face was chalky white, save for the dried blood staining her upper lip. But even that—what Adela had done to her—had not, apparently, affected her marksman's abilities. Garrett had never been happier to see anyone in his life, and he sagged against her gratefully as she got an arm under him, heaving him onto his feet.

"That won't have killed her." He twisted his head to look for the queen. He could never believe she'd be killed so easily.

"I know," Gemma said grimly. "That's why we have to go. Don't look."

They staggered together, Garrett quivering, Gemma struggling under his weight. But they grew steadier with every step, and soon they were running, running across the rickety bridge, out of the clearing, and into the overgrown wood. And as they stumbled through the darkness beneath the trees, Garrett swore he heard the queen's laughter trailing after them, lurking in the shadows of the forest.

11

BRUISED

ANSEL'S SHOULDER THROBBED, PAIN rolling through
him. That was the first thing he noticed as he clawed
his way back to consciousness. His senses returned slowly, his
eyesight clouded by fatigue and pain. Someone knelt beside him,
a figure that filled his vision. Something tickled his face, and he
realized it was hair. Long, coppery strands of hair, falling forward
to curtain him—

Jesine.

Ansel jerked away, trying to sit up. He didn't manage it. The
pain in his shoulder sharpened, and everything went fuzzy again,
another black wave of unconsciousness threatening to overtake
him.

His shoulder. The wound he'd taken when Demetri grazed
him. It was why they'd left him behind today to rest at the inn.
But the pain had been minimal when he'd set out for the cottage,
his arm only a little sore. It had begun to feel worse by the time

he'd reached the glade, but he'd done his best to ignore it. Until he couldn't.

And Jesine. And that witch. That witch had said Jesine—

Was also a witch.

Of course, Ansel had no reason to trust that other witch. He didn't even know the man's name. But that darkness that had washed over them...and now Jesine knelt right beside him. Pressing her fingertips against his chest, urging him back down.

"No." But Ansel couldn't fight her. Dizzying pain swept through him, no longer confined to his shoulder. The pain rushed through him like wildfire, sweat breaking out all over his body. He felt...bad. He felt sick. "How long..."

"You were only out a few minutes," Jesine answered, and Ansel saw the truth of her words over her shoulder. Dusk hadn't fallen yet, though it was well on its way. The woolly gray clouds that had cloaked the sky all day were shifting swiftly overhead, tireless gusts of wind herding them along.

"It's all right," Jesine murmured. "But you're not well. Are you injured?"

"Bullet grazed me." Ansel gulped a breath. She was still touching him, her gentle hands at odds with the fear making a mess of his insides. "Couple of days ago. But I'm—" He clenched his teeth as Jesine wrapped her hand around his arm, loosely, right below the wound. She couldn't have felt the injury through his coat, though perhaps she'd felt the edge of the bandage. He found himself watching with bated breath as her eyes fell shut, her face serene with concentration.

"You are a witch," Ansel breathed.

"Yes." Jesine's hand squeezed his arm.

Ansel's heart tripped, but before he could object, something *rushed* through him. It was the strangest sensation. Not unpleasant but unsettling, like a stream of cool water flooding his body, quenching the flames. When it reached the wound in his shoulder, there was a brief flare of pain, and then—

Relief. Blessed relief.

The pain was gone.

Ansel's breath stuck in his throat. He was afraid to move, afraid to reawaken the pain. But when he flexed his fingers and shifted his arm, there was nothing.

"What did you do?" His words came out harshly.

"I healed you," Jesine said in that soft voice of hers. He suddenly remembered that about her—how soft her voice was. She'd been a shy girl when he'd met her. Something of that shyness was missing in this young woman before him, but her voice was still soft. "Your wound is gone, Ansel."

"That's impossible."

"For a bad witch, yes. But not for a good witch."

"There's no such thing." The response was automatic.

"Of course there is. I couldn't have healed you otherwise. Bad witches aren't capable of it."

Ansel couldn't argue with that. She had healed him. Unless this was all an elaborate trick—and such a thing *could* be possible, a witch messing with his mind, making him see things and feel things. When it came to a witch, how could he trust his own mind?

A witch. A *witch*. He should have realized. He should have put it together. She'd known about hex-traps, known how to break one. Even if witches had been prevalent around here once, they knew how to work quietly and stay hidden. They kept the secrets of their trade, well, secret. It had taken a lot of research and personal experience on Ansel's part to learn about things like hex-traps.

Still, Jesine had freed him from that hex-trap. That would suggest she really was trying to help him. Unless that, too, was part of some game she and these witches were playing. Even the confrontation he had just witnessed might have been staged. To get him to trust Jesine.

Jesine watched him intently. Watching his thoughts and emotions play out over his face. Ansel struggled to wipe his expression clean. "What about that darkness?" he asked. "What was that?"

Jesine's face went blank. Wiping her own expression clean. But her eyes were troubled. "I...don't know. What it was."

"You're lying."

"No, I—" Jesine looked away, exhaling a breath. "I can't explain it. I can't."

Ansel gave her a hard stare. She was lying to him. She was lying to him, and that hurt, he realized. Which didn't make any sense. Feeling afraid of her, feeling wary, *that* made sense. But to be hurt by her?

He didn't know her well enough to be hurt by her. To feel hurt that she wouldn't trust him.

Jesine looked at him, her lips clamped shut. Then her eyes softened. She placed a hand on his forehead. Ansel flinched, but he didn't move fast enough to pull away. The pain in his shoulder was gone, but his exhaustion remained, making him slow.

"Don't," Ansel mumbled. "Whatever you're doing—"

"Shh," Jesine murmured. "You can trust me, Ansel."

"No." Ansel's eyes fluttered shut against his own volition. "I can't—"

"You can." Jesine's voice became a whisper, so soft, he thought he might have imagined her next words. "You trusted me once. You just don't remember."

Ansel was too exhausted to be confused. His fatigue settled over him like a pile of bricks.

Sleep pulled him under.

He dreamt. He dreamt his hands were burning. The skin of his palms was like parchment, curling and flaking into ash as he burned. He stared at his hands, stared into the flames, entranced by their brightness. He felt no pain.

Then he looked up, and the fire was everywhere. It filled his vision from corner to corner. Thick, dark smoke stung his eyes and clogged up his throat. He groped his way forward, waving his arms in front of him, stumbling step by step.

He could hear someone screaming in the fire. *Isabelle?* he thought wildly, fear for his sister filling up the little space left in his lungs. He remembered now; she was here too. The fear paralyzed him, nailing his feet to the burning, splintering floor. The screaming became louder, piercing the smoke, and then, through the flames, he saw her...

But it wasn't Isabelle. Her skin was brown like his sister's, her hair a similar mass of thick curls. Those curls smoldered and burned, turning to gray ash that flitted away on the wind. And when she lumbered towards him, he saw her face was like molten wax, the skin sagging right off the bone.

But it wasn't his sister. For the eyes in that waxy face, the eyes that fixed on him, were completely white.

It was the witch.

And Ansel's burning hands suddenly burst with agonizing pain.

Ansel knew this dream. He'd had it before. But what came next was not usually part of it. Something loomed in the darkness, taking shape before him. An inky black wing materialized, and then another. Between the wings, an eye blinked at him, round, beady, and piercing.

Ansel realized what it was.

A raven.

Another wing appeared. Another, and another. The eyes multiplied too, glinting like menacing stars in the dark. It was not one raven. It was a flock of them. They unfurled from the gloom like a many-winged beast, and then they scattered, feathered wings thrashing through the air.

And Ansel woke with a gasp.

It was dark around him, and cold, and both of those things made it difficult to distinguish his dreams from reality. He lay there for a moment, chilled in his own sweat, until he realized he wasn't alone.

"Thank the stars," said an aggravated voice. A familiar, aggravated voice. "I thought you were dead. Wasn't looking forward to explaining that to Garrett."

Ansel's eyes focused. He looked up into the face of Klaus. Klaus, too, had been left at the inn today. He'd insisted it was because he was off duty and not because he'd been left to babysit Ansel. Yet here he was.

"Klaus." Ansel pushed himself upright and realized he was on the ground, cold, stiff grass sticking to his damp clothes. Tall pines loomed out of the darkness, surrounding him on all sides, but in the distance. He lay in the middle of—

A clearing. The glade near the cottage. Where he'd come looking for answers.

Where he'd run into Jesine.

"There was someone here." Ansel rubbed the side of his face,
brushing off grass and dirt. It was fully dark now. Jesine claimed
to be a good witch, yet she'd left him here alone, easy prey for the
coven and their demon? "A girl. A witch. She—"

"Red hair?" Klaus interrupted. "Green coat?"

"I—yes. Did you—"

"She was just arrested. By the village watch."

"What!"

Klaus jerked a thumb over his shoulder, towards the woods
and the way back to Lise. "I saw them on my way here. They had
her locked up in a big iron cage on the back of a wagon. Said she
was a known witch, and they found her near here. Where that
dead woman was found."

An iron cage. Ansel rolled his eyes. That was folk superstition,
the idea that iron weakened witches. Their only real weakness
was wood from a fairy's tree, but most people didn't know that.
Iron wouldn't stop a witch, good or bad. So why, Ansel wondered, had Jesine allowed herself to be taken? Why hadn't she
used magic to escape?

"Come on." Klaus took Ansel by the arms and hauled him
to his feet. "I figured you'd come back here. You're fairly pre-
dictable."

Ansel shoved Klaus away. "What are they going to do with
her? The witch?"

Klaus shrugged, dusting off his gray breeches and adjusting
the thin scarf around his neck. "They said they'd hold her in the
town jail until sentencing. And it's not hard to guess what that

might be. I'm just glad she didn't do anything to you. Prince Garrett would never have let me hear the end of it. It's bad enough I let you sneak out of the inn."

"I knew you were babysitting me," Ansel grumbled, but there was no ire in his words. He stared into the woods, distracted. Disturbed by his own feelings. He should have been relieved she'd been arrested. But it wasn't relief he felt. No, it was something much more unsettled and uncertain.

His first instinct was to go after her. To see her set free. And he couldn't shake that.

She was arrested for being a witch, he thought, *and she is a witch*. Which she had lied about. Or, well, she hadn't lied, exactly. She just hadn't told him she was a witch. But why should she, he argued with himself. He barely knew her. So why did he feel so betrayed?

Why did he feel so worried?

"Sure you're all right?" Klaus drawled.

"I'm fine." And he was fine. Physically. Ansel took a step, testing out his limbs, making sure another wave of dizziness didn't sweep over him. He was still tired—he could have slept for several more hours, he thought, right there on the ground—but otherwise, he felt fine.

His shoulder, he remembered, clapping a hand to it. But just like before, there was no pain. The wound was gone. All that was left was a faint soreness, like the dull pain of an old bruise.

———◆———

It was over an hour past dusk by the time they reached Lise and arrived at the inn. Ansel was not surprised to find Sabine in the common room, returned from their trip out to the quarry. Her overcoat was balled up over the back of her chair, and the topmost buttons of her jacket were undone, exposing the collar of her linen shirt. She looked almost unwell, Ansel thought, a sheen of sweat glinting over her dark-brown face. But she leapt up from her table when she saw them, and Ansel realized she was not unwell, but anxious and stressed. "There you two are," she said. "The innkeeper said you'd gone out, but he didn't know where."

"Is something wrong?" Ansel asked. "Where is Prince Garrett?"

"Not here," Sabine said gravely. "Demetri's out looking for them with some of the village watch. He wanted me to stay here and get Klaus—"

"Why?" Klaus asked sharply. "What's happened? Where's Gemma?"

Sabine rubbed at her forehead. "I'm sorry. Let me back up." She looked up at him, her eyes red with exhaustion. "Demetri and I got back a little while ago. We were hoping they'd be here. Gemma and Garrett." She shook her head. "We ran into Adela in the woods."

Ansel went still. "When?"

"A little after dusk. We were on our way back from the quarry. Gemma was trying to scout around her, but Adela caught her, and she—I don't know what she did to her, only Gemma was bleeding from the nose, and she looked like her head was going to explode or something." Sabine looked chagrined. "Adela ordered us to leave him. Prince Garrett. We went back, of course, as soon as we could—but they were gone, Gemma and Garrett. And Adela."

143

Ansel shook his head. A little after dusk. Shortly after that witch had turned up in the glade. What had he said? *I came here looking to catch a prince.* "That must have been what he meant," he murmured.

"We wanted to keep looking, of course, but it was dark, and Demetri worried about the demon, so we came back here. We hoped they'd made it back too, but they weren't here. Demetri went out to search. That was nearly an hour ago. So far—"

The door to the inn burst open, interrupting Sabine. Demetri walked in...and with him, Prince Garrett.

"Demetri!" Sabine rushed towards them, Klaus on her heels. "You found him!"

"Where's Gemma?" Klaus demanded.

Ansel followed more slowly, taking in the look of the two young men. Prince Garrett, his face pallid and strangely slack, had an arm slung around Demetri. His fur-lined overcoat was soiled, though with what, Ansel couldn't tell. Dirt? Blood? He was conscious but slumped over, as though he could barely stand. Demetri seemed to bear most of his weight, the smaller man grimacing at the effort of doing so.

Something was wrong, Ansel thought, looking between the two of them. Something was very wrong.

"We found Gemma too," Demetri grunted, shifting awkwardly. His rumpled riding coat hung lopsided from his shoulders, the fabric bunched up beneath Garrett's heavy arm. "A couple of the village watchmen took her to see a physician the next street over."

Klaus jerked his head. "I'll check on her," he said shortly, and then he was gone, the door flying shut behind him. He didn't seem to notice this left Garrett without any guards, Ansel thought, though Garrett didn't seem to notice Klaus's departure either. In fact, he hadn't looked up once. The prince's eyes were bloodshot, his gaze numb. As he and Demetri came closer, Ansel caught a whiff of something foul. Then he saw the stain on Garrett's waistcoat and realized what it was. Stale vomit.

Yes, something was very wrong.

"Let me help," Ansel offered, taking Garrett's other arm.

"You should get some sleep," Demetri told Sabine. "Nothing to be done until the morning."

Ansel braced himself against the sour smell as he and Demetri prodded Garrett along to the staircase. "Are you sure he shouldn't see a physician as well?" Ansel asked.

"No." It was Garrett who answered. His voice was hoarse, as though he'd come down with a cold. "No doctor."

They got the prince into his room. It was spacious, Ansel noted, three times the size of his own room here at the inn, with a wider bed layered in thick quilts, a tall wardrobe, and a table large enough to seat four. There was also a private tub in the washroom, which Demetri filled so Garrett could wash himself off. He didn't take long, emerging a few minutes later with dripping hair and clean clothes, rumpled trousers and a loose shirt. With his hair damp like that, Ansel thought, it looked darker, dirty blond instead of its usual golden hue. Ansel and Demetri shared a concerned look as the prince collapsed onto his bed, tilting his head back until it rested against the wooden headboard.

"We'll let you get some sleep, then," Demetri said uncertainly.

"No." Garrett's eyes flew open, and for a moment, Ansel saw fear in them. "No. Not just yet."

Ansel had never seen Prince Garrett afraid before. It was...well, shocking. Unnerving. Because anything that could frighten someone like Garrett must be horrific indeed. Planting himself at the foot of Garrett's bed, Ansel folded his arms over his chest and asked, "What exactly happened out there?" A bit tactless perhaps, given how rough Garrett looked. But in Ansel's experience, it was best to get terrible things out right away.

"The queen," said Garrett. "It was the queen."

Demetri lowered himself into a hardbacked chair at Garrett's bedside. "You said that before, when we found you. What queen are you talking about?"

But Garrett didn't answer. He only looked at Ansel.

And Ansel knew.

"Impossible," he said.

"That's what I said." Garrett cleared his throat, though it did no good. By the sound of it, his throat had been scraped raw. As though he'd been screaming. "Saying it didn't make it real, though."

"You can't mean..." Demetri's eyes went wide. "Not the *queen?* Delphine?"

"Yes." Garrett closed his eyes. "That's the one."

"Not possible," was Demetri's swift response.

Something like a smile twitched at Garrett's lips, and he opened his eyes to look at his friend. "I understand." He almost sounded like the pleasant Garrett that Ansel had come to know. "It's the automatic reaction."

The queen. *The queen.* Delphine. She wasn't a queen anymore, of course, but Ansel understood Garrett referring to her that way. In Ansel's mind, she would always be *the queen.* She was the queen he had once served, though not very willingly. And not for very long.

And now she was here. Free. Ansel could not wrap his mind around it. "I helped build her prison myself. There was fairy-wood built into the walls. There's just no way—"

"All I know is, she said she had help." Garrett winced as he shifted atop his bed. "Other witches, I assume. Probably *these* witches. Adela and—"

"I saw another one tonight." Ansel rubbed a hand over his forehead, distracted by his growing dread. *Two*, he thought belatedly. He'd seen two witches tonight. But despite his own misgivings, he couldn't bring himself to mention Jesine. "I didn't know him. But he said he'd heard of me."

"So," Demetri said, "these witches probably helped the queen escape."

"Not possible," Ansel murmured again. But he was already reframing his reality, coming to accept it. Delphine was free. He knew they had built the best prison one could build to hold a witch, but he also knew what this particular witch was capable of. He'd witnessed Delphine's power—and her atrocities—firsthand.

Ansel felt a little sick. *Delphine. Free. Here.* This was far worse than he had imagined.

"And this coven we're dealing with," Demetri went on, "is led by her now."

Garrett looked at Ansel. Once again, Ansel saw fear in his eyes. Strangely though, after a moment, some of that fear dissipated. As though something he'd seen in Ansel had comforted him. Ansel couldn't imagine what, because all he could think Garrett might have seen was Ansel's own fear. Then again, perhaps that *was* comforting. Fear was a lonely thing but made a little less so when someone shared it. And Ansel did share it. In a way Demetri, or anyone else here, probably never could.

"What did she do to you?" Ansel asked quietly.

"I'm not really sure," Garrett said with a sigh. "But it was painful." The prince sank into his pillows, slouching down. He wore a hollow, hopeless expression as he contemplated whatever pain Delphine had visited upon him.

"Garrett," Demetri said, his voice firm, "I'm not going to let her get you. I won't."

"Thank you." Garrett let his eyes fall shut, and this time, he did not open them. "I think I'd like to sleep now."

Demetri nodded and stood. Ansel opened the door, and they stepped out into the corridor.

"What can she want?" Ansel asked once the door was shut behind them. "What can she possibly want?"

"To torture Garrett," Demetri said bleakly.

He was probably right, Ansel thought. Adela coming here, the demon murdering that woman, the weird hexes Demetri had investigated—including the bloody quarry, he realized, which explained how Adela had known where they were—it had likely all been about Garrett.

They had been lured here. And now they were caught.

"Well." Demetri rubbed a hand over his face. "I'm exhausted, but I'm also starving." He frowned at Ansel. "What about you? Did you get some rest today?"

Ansel didn't answer right away. He thought of Jesine, healing his arm and putting him to sleep in the glade. Leaving him there. Only, she hadn't left him, he realized. She'd been arrested by the village watch. She must have seen or heard them coming and tried to get away—otherwise, they would have found him too.

But she hadn't gotten away. She was here now, in Lise. Locked up in the village jail.

He hadn't wanted to mention her before. In connection with these other witches, with the queen. And he realized it was because he didn't believe it. He didn't believe Jesine was involved with their coven. He didn't believe she would help someone like Delphine escape.

It made no sense. He barely knew her. And he still couldn't get past the sting of betrayal at finding out she was a witch.

But he didn't believe she was a bad witch. She couldn't be.

"Demetri," Ansel said, "can you help me with something tomorrow? First thing in the morning—could you come with me to the town jail?"

12

NUMBERED

G ARRETT WOKE THE NEXT morning feeling strangely rested. Strangely, because he had been sure he would not sleep
a wink after Ansel and Demetri left his room last night. But he
had and, stranger still, if he'd dreamed, he did not remember it.

The light coming in through his window was dull and indistinct, just like the day before. Garrett rose and began to dress,
garbing himself in riding breeches and boots, shirt and waistcoat.
He had slept late, unusually, for the second day in a row. But
then, he hadn't even gotten to bed until well after midnight.
He didn't want to think why that was. He didn't want to think
about what happened last night. Or rather, he only wanted to
think about it with other people around. And only in a rational, practical, how-to-tackle-the-problem sort of way. Like Briar
would.

His fingers stumbled as he knotted his tie at his neck. Garrett's
heart physically hurt to think about Briar. He wanted, suddenly,
very much for her to be here. And yet when he recalled Demetri's

suggestion that they telegram her, he did not want to do that either. He felt simultaneously that she could fix everything, but also that her being here would make everything worse. Especially because...

"I could do something about that, if only to prolong our fun together. I could burn that poison right out of you."

"Now I have all the time in the world to play my games with you, Gallant. Aren't you going to thank me?"

Leaving his tie half-done, Garrett lowered himself onto the edge of his bed.

Had she really done it? And if she had...how would he know?

She couldn't have done it. Bad witches couldn't heal people. Not without suffering consequences, and he doubted Delphine was that desperate to "play games" with him. But then again, perhaps she could do it if her intention was just to harm him in the long run. Magic was about intention, after all.

Garrett sighed, rubbing at his eyes with two fingers. He didn't want to think about it. He didn't want to think about any of it.

Thankfully, at that moment, there was a sharp rap on his door. Sabine poked her head in, looking flustered. "Excuse me, Prince—er, that is—Garrett—but you're needed. Down at the town jailhouse."

"The jailhouse?" Garrett reached up to finish with his tie, then fastened a loose button at his wrist. "What for? What's going on?"

Sabine seemed bemused. "It's hard to explain. Or, well. It's a long story."

"Just give me the basics."

"All right, so..." Sabine pursed her lips. "Ansel has this, um. Friend. Who was arrested yesterday for being a witch."

Garrett sighed. "And given how cocksure the village watch is, I take it she's not really a witch."

"No, she is."

"Oh." Garrett blinked. "Er..."

"Anyway, Ansel went to see if he could get her released." Sabine looked thoughtful. "I'm not sure why she doesn't just get herself out. If she's a witch, I mean."

"So this girl...a *witch*...is a friend of Ansel's?"

"Yes. I think she's a good witch? Either way, Ansel seems to think she can help us figure out what's going on with the coven here, what they're up to and how to stop them."

Garrett frowned, still puzzled. "Ansel has a friend?"

Sabine shrugged.

Garrett suddenly remembered Ansel mentioning a girl the other day—someone he'd known when he'd lived here before, he recalled. Perhaps that was this "friend" of his. A *witch* friend. "So I need to go down to the jailhouse to...what?"

"Well, Demetri is down there now," Sabine explained, "with Ansel. They're trying to convince the village watch to release her, on account of Demetri being an agent of the crown and all, but the watch isn't keen. They don't seem to care who Demetri is. Your Highness." She said this last bit apologetically.

Garrett sighed again. "I see."

"I'm sorry, Prince Garrett."

"Don't be." Garrett reached for his dust-colored sack coat and swung it on. "Come with me, Sabine."

The jailhouse in Lise was not far, only across the square. Garrett strode inside, his boots thumping against the wooden floorboards. His steps were not loud enough to cut through the cacophony of raised voices—the voices of the village watch, the voices of Demetri and Ansel. Everyone stood gathered at the far end of the front room, to the left of a long corridor which, presumably, housed the jail cells. Once Garrett got closer, he picked out Ansel from the group. The witch hunter's eyes were cold with fury, his jaw tense and set. Demetri was beside him, red-faced, waving a piece of parchment about, though it was clenched so tightly in his fist that the royal seal was likely crushed.

"—official business of the crown—!"

"—no authority over these people—!"

"—not a witch, you've no proof—!"

"—cannot allow a threat like her to—!"

"Gentlemen," Garrett said loudly. No one took any notice. Clearing his throat, he tried again. "Gentlemen!"

Sabine, who'd followed Garrett inside, exchanged a wry glance with him. Then she put two fingers in her mouth and emitted the most high-pitched whistle Garrett had ever heard—right next to his ear.

Everyone in the jail fell silent, five heads turning in their direction.

Garrett placed a hand over his ear. "Ow."

"Sorry," said Sabine.

"No, no, that was brilliant. Thank you." Summoning his most amiable smile, Garrett stepped forward before anyone could start arguing again. "Gentlemen," he said, addressing the village watchmen, "please forgive my intrusion."

Three watchmen stood in the jailhouse, opposite Demetri. Two were behind a small beechwood desk—an older man with a thick gray beard, and behind him, a younger man with hair so blond, it was nearly white. The third man stood beside the desk, a man with hard eyes and a weathered face. Both the bearded man and hard-eyed man looked at Garrett with traces of apprehension, but the younger man said in a sullen tone, "What do you want?"

The hard-eyed man dropped his forehead into his hand, while the bearded man rounded on the young man, glaring. Garrett found these reactions a little weird, but he didn't allow his smile to falter.

"You've all met Demetri here, of course." Garrett gestured to Demetri, who attempted to smooth out the crinkled royal writ giving him his authority. "And I think you know he's here on business for the crown, investigating the activity of witches in the area. Unfortunately, we've misled you a bit. While it's true Demetri is an agent of the crown, *I* have the, ah, higher authority in this matter." Taking a deep breath, Garrett said, "You see, I am—"

"We know who you are," the bearded man said with resignation.

"You—what?"

"We know you're the crown prince," said the hard-eyed man.

"The what?" yelped the younger man. "No one told me!"

"How did you not know?" the hard-eyed man demanded.

"How did you know?" the younger man shot back.

"Yes, how *did* you?" Garrett was crestfallen. "Have you seen me before? Someone here has been to the capital, perhaps?"

"So far as I know, no one 'round here has seen you in person, Your Highness," the bearded man admitted. "But we all read the penny press papers, even in a village as remote as ours. You're in them quite a lot, and the stories sometimes include pictures."

"And here I thought my disguise was foolproof." Garrett sighed. "Foiled by the press!"

The hard-eyed man tossed a nod Demetri's way. "We know you too. What you've done, I mean, fighting corpses and sea monsters and what not."

"And yet," said Demetri, "you don't seem to feel I'm qualified to determine if this young woman is a threat." He pointed a finger behind him, and Garrett realized, for the first time, that the woman in question was present. Peering around Demetri, he spotted her—Ansel's witch friend, standing silently in the shadows of the first cell. Heavy iron manacles were locked around her wrists, and another manacle around her ankle chained her to the floor. She wore little expression on her face, watching the proceedings with alert eyes. She certainly didn't look dangerous or powerful. Her skirt was stained with mud, her jacket disheveled and wrinkled. Her hair, a fiery red, was bedraggled, escaping the tumbling braid she'd bound it in.

But Garrett knew very well that appearances could be deceiving. Especially for a witch.

"It has nothing to do with qualifications," the bearded man said. "This woman is a known witch, and she falls under our jurisdiction—" His eyes flew to Garrett.

Garrett smiled pleasantly. "Yes, she does, of course. But—loathe as I am to do this—I must remind you that, as crown prince, it is *my* authority that has the final say in this matter. Remote as your village is," he said, quoting the man's own words, "it is still a part of the Glen Kingdom."

"So you just want us to let a witch walk free?" the young man blurted out. Hastily, he added, "Ah—Your Highness."

"Well, yes." Garrett's tone was deceptively mild. "That is what I want."

"You don't even deny she's a witch," the hard-eyed man noted.

"What I know," Garrett said, locking eyes with the man and dropping his mild tone, "is that she has committed no crime, she is no danger to anyone, and she is essential to our investigation in this village. Consider her in my custody, if you must, but she *is* walking out of here with me today. I will hear no objections to that."

"And if she does cause harm to any innocent person," said the bearded man, "the crown will bear the burden of responsibility."

"You have our word," Garrett promised.

And that was that.

A few minutes later, Sabine, Demetri, Garrett, Ansel, and the witch—Jesine was her name—filed out of the jail and into the town square. Garrett squinted up at the sunless sky. "Stones," he muttered. "And I thought I was undercover!"

"Bit hard when you're so famous, isn't it," Demetri said dryly.

"Thank you, Prince Garrett," Ansel interjected. "For what you did. I know you didn't want to reveal yourself—"

Garrett waved a hand. "My only real motivation in staying hidden was to make the locals more receptive towards us. But that didn't help, so it really doesn't matter." He glanced back at the young woman trailing Ansel, who looked as though she wanted nothing more than to sneak away from them as soon as she could. "Will you join us for a late breakfast?" he asked her. "I was led to believe you might be of some help with these witches."

The girl, Jesine, snapped her head up at that. She didn't glare exactly, but the look she directed at him wasn't particularly friendly either.

"That is not why I stepped in back there." Garrett raised both hands in a gesture of peace. "Not at all. You don't owe me anything, Miss—Jesine? I'm sorry. We haven't been properly introduced."

"Jesine, Prince Garrett," Ansel said tersely. "Prince Garrett, Jesine."

"Really?" Demetri's tone was disapproving.

Ansel shrugged. "Sorry. I don't do formalities. I'm not a prince."

"Technically, neither am I," Demetri said.

As they neared the inn, they all slowed to a halt. "Look," Ansel said to Jesine, and Garrett couldn't help but notice the way Ansel looked at her but didn't *look* at her, his gaze hovering around her shoulder, "I'm not trying to pressure you into revealing anything you don't want to. But, well, I think whatever is going on here—with these witches—is more complicated than any of us realized, and, well. We could use your input."

Jesine hesitated. It hadn't really occurred to Garrett that she hadn't spoken a word until she opened her mouth and said, "All right." Her voice was incredibly soft, little more than a whisper.

"Wonderful," said Garrett.

They had breakfast brought up to Garrett's room to afford them some privacy. Round, rustic wooden trays filled with bowls of fruit, plates with eggs, rashers, and ham, a pile of pastries, and stacks of thick slices of toast with two different jams and a slab of butter. Not to mention a steaming pot of tea, for which Garrett was grateful. It was cold in his room—not cold enough to warrant lighting a fire in the grate, but just enough that a hot cup of spiced tea warmed him through.

For about ten minutes, they ate in silence. Garrett was starving, and judging by the way Jesine ate, he supposed they hadn't fed her in the jail. Once he'd finished off most of his iced tart, however, Garrett leaned back in his chair at the table and said, "So. Ansel. Jesine. How do you two know each other?"

He sensed it was a delicate question, and given the way Jesine and Ansel still did not quite look at each other—there were quick, darting glances, no more than that—he guessed he was right. He didn't want to pry, but he needed some background information to get started.

Ansel, perching on a stool in the corner, finished off his buttered toast and wiped his hands on his trousers. "I told you I lived around here about six years ago. With Isabelle. So Jesine and I knew each other." Ansel ran another quick, appraising eye over her. "I didn't know she was a witch."

Jesine shot him a hard look. She sat in an upholstered chair across the room from Ansel, about as far away as she could get, her plate and teacup set on a small side table near her.

"She's a good witch," Ansel added grudgingly. "Her father was as well, I think...?"

Jesine nodded.

"A good witch? Truly?" Demetri asked. He sat across the table from Garrett, where he'd already wolfed down a full plate of rashers and eggs with grilled tomatoes, plus a large cinnamon bun. Now he peered at Jesine with a fascinated expression. "With a fairy familiar and everything?"

Setting aside her napkin, Jesine nodded again, though she looked aggrieved. "Kel—my fairy—has been away for a while." Her voice was still soft, and she formed her words tentatively, almost awkwardly. As though she spoke so little, she didn't quite remember how. "That's why I couldn't use magic to escape last night. It's harder, when she's so far away. And after everything else..." Her eyes flicked in Ansel's direction again. "It was just too much. It left me weak."

Ansel leaned forward, hunching his shoulders. "After healing me, you mean."

"Yes."

"You could have said something." Ansel's tone was vaguely accusatory.

Jesine pointedly ignored this, sipping from her teacup.

"So, do you know anything about these witches?" Garrett tilted his chair back and crossed his arms over his chest. "I mean—I'm sorry, I don't know much about witch society—but I gather you don't run in the same circles."

"That one witch knew you," Ansel said.

"Who?" Garrett asked.

"The witch I saw yesterday. I saw him in the square too, when the bats attacked. By the sound of things, he's working with Adela and the others."

"His name is Harper," Jesine said, but then she wavered. She looked between Ansel and Garrett. Ducking her head, she said, "You really shouldn't."

"Shouldn't what?" Garrett asked calmly.

"Get involved in all this." Still evading their eyes, Jesine tucked a strand of blazing-red hair behind her ear. Then she clenched her hand into a fist, quickly dropping it down by her side. "It's too dangerous. This is witch business. I can handle it myself."

Garrett considered his answer for a moment, absently watching Demetri pile sugar into his second cup of tea. Then he said, "It's not that I don't believe you capable, Jesine, believe me. But

ELIZABETH K. KING

there really is nowhere I can run from this." The witch looked up at him, and he smiled bleakly. "You see—at least in part—this is about me."

"One of the witches," Ansel explained, "knows Garrett. They have quite a history."

"Not a pretty one either," Demetri added.

"It seems likely she's here for him," Ansel went on. "In fact, it tallies with the little we do know. Remember last night, that witch—Harper?—said something about catching a prince? He was talking about Garrett. One of the other witches did catch him and took him to Delphine—the witch that's after him."

Jesine still looked skeptical, but her forehead creased thoughtfully. After a moment, she looked at Garrett and said, "I heard them say something about you too. That they were surprised you were already here, but that it was good. Less work for them."

"When did you hear that?" Ansel asked.

"Two nights ago. I did a spell to eavesdrop on them. There were four of them." She frowned. "They did some kind of summoning spell and brought another witch to them. She was small, but somehow terrifying."

Garrett felt a chill that had nothing to do with the temperature in the room. He reached for the pot of tea anyway. "Delphine."

"So is this just about you, then?" Ansel asked as Garrett poured more tea into his cup. "The demon and all these hexes Demetri's been tracking...maybe even Adela coming here...was it all to lure you here?"

Garrett found the thought frightening, but it had already occurred. "It sort of seems like it." He stirred cream into his tea, the ritual oddly soothing.

"Why would all these witches help Delphine, though, just so she can mess with you?" Demetri mused. "Granted, I'm no expert. But I never got the sense witches would work together unless it benefited all of them."

"Tracks with what I know," Ansel admitted.

Garrett finished off the last of his tart, chewing slowly. When he finished, he said, "Maybe she just threatened them. She did say something about 'properly motivating' them."

Jesine straightened in her seat. "It sounded like they were all getting something out of this arrangement. And they all had a role to play. That one witch, Adela, was used to lure Ansel here—and one of the other witches knew how to summon the demon—"

"But then, what are they all getting out of it? What do they want?" Ansel prompted. "That witch Harper—you don't have any idea what he wants?" He spoke in a neutral, weirdly polite tone, avoiding Jesine's gaze again. The set of his shoulders had gone stiff. Garrett had the sense Ansel was working around a more direct question he wanted to ask.

Jesine did not look at him either. "That's why I think it's about more than just Prince Garrett. Dark witches have always had an interest in the land here."

"Witches like Harper, you mean? What do you mean, an *interest?*"

If possible, Jesine's gaze grew even warier. "I'm not sure. It's just something my father used to say." There was an edge to her voice, and Garrett couldn't help but feel she was being deliberately vague. "But I do know that, several years ago, Harper was part of a coven working in this area, and there was something here they were after. Something that would grant them a lot of power. They could be after the same thing now. That might even be Harper's role to play—he knows about what they're interested in."

"But you don't know about it?" Garrett prompted. "Or even what it is, exactly?"

Jesine dithered, then shook her head.

But you have some idea, he thought. Still, he wouldn't press the issue. Not when Jesine was already so unsure about working with them.

"Harper said something else," Ansel said. "That they were on a tight schedule."

"Well," Garrett said, troubled, "the winter solstice is coming up. Aren't there all sorts of things witches could use the solstice for? All sorts of powerful, bad things?"

"That's less than a week away," Demetri noted. "Could it have anything to do with these hexes after all, then? Perhaps they weren't just meant to lure you here, Garrett."

"How many have there been?" Ansel asked.

Demetri counted on his fingers. "The burning man, the spiders, the snakes, the bats, the bleeding quarry—well, if that was anything at all—"

"So four, maybe five," Ansel said bleakly. "Maybe."

"Why do you ask?" Demetri asked him.

Ansel exchanged a look with Jesine across the room. "It's just, there are some rather significant numbers when it comes to magic and witchcraft. Three. Twelve." He paused. "Seven."

"I don't like the sound of that," Demetri noted.

"So," Ansel said, "perhaps more hexes to come. Perhaps something spectacular happening in six days' time, on the solstice—"

"Spectacularly evil," Garrett corrected.

"—and we've no idea what," Demetri finished. "Or why."

They all contemplated this in silence for a moment. Then Garrett said, "Well. Happy holidays, everyone."

13

Affinity

A NSEL WASN'T SURPRISED THAT, shortly after their breakfast together, Jesine left, slipping quietly out of the inn. Yes, she had provided them with some information, but even then she hadn't seemed all that keen to help. How much of that had to do with Ansel and what had happened between them, that day in the glade—how much of it had to do with the accusatory way Ansel had spoken to her—he didn't know.

A part of him was disappointed when she left. A part of him was relieved. So the next day, when Prince Garrett asked him to go find Jesine, he didn't know what to feel.

"I'm not sure it's a good idea," Ansel hedged.

"Why not?" Garrett asked. "You think she's lying about being a good witch?"

The two of them sat in the common room, having breakfast. They sat at a small table in the corner, opposite the bar and beneath the staircase. It was a private, secluded, quiet spot, which Ansel appreciated. He wasn't in the mood for crowds and chatter this morning. Well, he was never in the mood for crowds and chatter.

Now Ansel watched Garrett as the prince spread a sweet-berry jam across his fruit scone. He had quite the sweet tooth, Ansel observed. He bit into his own piece of plain, buttered toast, chewed, and swallowed before answering. "No, I don't think she's lying about that." He contemplated another bite of his toast before adding, "But I do think she's hiding something."

Prince Garrett surprised him by saying, "I think so too. Which is all the more reason to track her down and talk to her."

"But why me? Why do you want me to do it?"

"Well, you're her friend, aren't you?" Garrett sipped at his tea. "She trusts you."

"I don't think she trusts me," Ansel muttered. "She never told me she was a witch, after all."

Prince Garrett studied him for a moment as he ate his scone. He ate slowly, clearly savoring each bite. Ansel had already wolfed down his toast. Finally, Garrett said, "What aren't you telling me?"

Ansel furrowed his brow. "Nothing."

"Well, who is this girl, then?"

"Don't you know. You met her yesterday."

"Yes. I meant, who is she to *you?*"

Ansel didn't answer, shoveling a bite of eggs into his mouth instead. He wasn't deliberately trying to keep Garrett in the dark. It was just that he, Ansel, in the dark. He wasn't sure what to say. How to explain.

He had nearly forgotten about Jesine until now. That wasn't so strange, given how fleetingly he'd known her and how long ago. But it felt different than that. It was like he'd buried Jesine deep down until any passing thought of her felt like a story he'd heard. About someone else, somewhere else. From someone else's life.

And maybe it was. Certainly, he was a much different person now than he had been back then. Back then, he had not abandoned his sister in a foolish attempt to protect her. Back then, he had not met Queen Delphine and her stepdaughters. Back then, Snow had not died, despite his attempts to save her.

Back then, he had not been so mistrustful of the world. And of himself.

Maybe that's all this was. This weird disconnect between his memories of Jesine and who he was now. Maybe it was just that so much had happened since then, so much had changed. But that didn't explain why he *felt* the way he did. Why he felt so strangely, so strongly, about Jesine.

He didn't know how to explain any of this. So all he said was, "I don't know what you mean."

"I mean," Garrett said delicately, "you two are just friends?"

Ansel slanted a glance at Garrett. "Yes."

"Not something more?"

"More like what?" When Garrett looked at him pointedly, Ansel said with a tinge of exasperation, "If you're suggesting some romantic notion...well. We were only eleven."

"Eleven-year-olds can fall in love."

Ansel shook his head. "No. We were just friends. I told you, I didn't know her for very long. And it couldn't have been more. It just couldn't."

"Why not?"

"I..." Ansel hesitated, laying a hand upon his cup of tea. "I'm not capable of that sort of thing."

"What do you mean? Romance doesn't interest you?"

Ansel recalled the exchange he'd had with Sabine just a few days ago. He remembered thinking that he didn't have time for romance. He told himself that all the time. He'd told himself that for so long, he usually believed it.

But the truth was much more complicated than that. The truth was, Ansel just wasn't suited to romance. To love like that. He'd accepted, many years ago, that it wasn't meant for him. Not because he didn't want it, not because it didn't interest him...but because it *wasn't for him.*

There was something...wrong...with him. Something he lacked. The ability to connect with others like everyone else did. That piece of a person's soul that knew instinctively how to talk to and empathize with and care for other people, especially in that way. That romantic sort of way.

"I'm just not capable of it," Ansel repeated. His face was blank—he made sure of that—but his tone was bleak. "I've got a heart of stone."

Garrett frowned. "I don't think that's true."

"More true than you know." Ansel cleared his throat. This conversation skirted dangerously close to something he never wanted to talk about with anyone, least of all Prince Garrett. "It's better this way. Trust me. I'm fine on my own."

Garrett eyed him a moment longer. Ansel concentrated on drinking his tea and finishing his eggs. Finally, the prince sighed and said, "Well, maybe you are fine on your own. But we aren't, not while we're dealing with these witches. We need Jesine's help."

"Prince Garrett," Ansel protested, "I don't even know how to find her. Where she lives or—"

"That's not a problem." Garrett jerked a thumb over his shoulder. "The barmaid, Saskia, knows where she lives. She can give you directions."

———◆◦◆———

The directions Saskia gave Ansel did not lead him to a house, but to a grove of poplar trees a few leagues outside the village. She had explained she always had trouble remembering exactly where Jesine's house was, but she remembered the grove, and she assured him he could find the house from there. "Especially if you know the woods," she'd added cheerfully. "But she might even be there, at the grove. She spends a lot of time there."

The grove was set apart from the wild woods surrounding it, a ring of spindly, pale-gray trees. Saskia said the grove had been planted hundreds of years ago. Ansel found it without much trouble, and now he stood within it, feeling strangely exposed. Three months from now, the trees would be thick and green and lush, enclosing the center of the grove from prying eyes. But now, with winter reigning, the trees were stark in their bareness, their flimsy, grasping branches both forbidding and pitiful.

Ansel stepped through the trees cautiously, but there was no one there. No Jesine. A part of him was relieved he wouldn't have to face her. Still, for a few minutes, Ansel waited in the cold, his breath practically turning to frost right before him. He stuffed his gloved hands into the pockets of his coat, and that was when he heard it—the long, mournful *caw* of a raven.

Ansel spun around. He spotted the raven at once, perched in the crook of a poplar's lowest branch. Ansel stared at the raven, and it stared back. Then he began to turn away, but the bird cawed again. Ansel looked and saw it had moved closer, shuffling onto the branch of another tree. Decidedly unnerved as he recalled the ravens that had flown at him, that first night in these woods, Ansel turned away, determined to ignore the bird.

The raven cawed a third time. And Ansel could not help it—he glanced over his shoulder.

The raven stood perched on a boulder just a few paces from him.

A chill slipped through Ansel, like icy fingers running down his spine. He turned and faced the raven head-on. "What do you want?"

He had not expected an answer. And he didn't get one, not really. But the way the raven cocked its head at him, ruffling its feathers in such an agitated way—there was something so *human* about the reaction. As though the raven was frustrated with him. It cawed again, then hopped off the boulder onto the ground. It hopped around a few more times, then launched into the air, soaring onto the nearest tree branch. From that perch, the raven turned to look at Ansel.

Ansel wondered if he was going mad. "You...want me to follow you?"

The raven ruffled its feathers with another *caw*.

Ansel rubbed a hand over his eyes. "I'm talking to a bird," he muttered. Not just any bird. A raven. Following a raven, an omen of bad luck, felt ill-advised. But he remembered the dream he'd had, his recurring nightmare. He remembered how ravens had invaded that dream, interrupting the nightmare. That did not feel like a bad omen. Rather the opposite.

"All right," he said aloud. "Lead on, I guess."

The raven glided onto another branch, a little further ahead. Ansel followed, tracking the bird as it soared from one tree to the next, out of the poplar grove, deep into the woods. The landscape became darker and thicker with towering pines and barren hickory trees, their twisted boughs casting shadows across the forest floor. The ground dipped, descending into a shallow ravine, the earth laden with dead leaves and clumps of roots. Ansel nearly tripped a couple of times as the raven picked up its pace, leading Ansel through the ravine until he was so lost, he had no idea how to get back to the grove.

"Hang on!" he called to the bird, cursing as he stubbed his toe against a rock. "Where are you—"

He stopped short, stumbling forward another step.

Out of the forest and onto a road.

"What..." Ansel looked left and saw the road winding into the distance. This was the main road leading back to the village. He looked right and saw—

Jesine.

She was headed down the road in the opposite direction, her back to him. But there was no mistaking her red hair, streaming behind her, or her olive-green coat, fitted at the waist by the cross-tied laces running down the back. Her distant figure was small on the road stretching before him, surrounded by gray-green pines on both sides.

"Jesine!" he called.

Jesine stopped dead. She went so still, he wondered if she was going to take off running down the road.

But she didn't. She turned to face him, her shoulders stiff with dread. Ansel knew the feeling. He, too, had gone still when he'd seen her, but on the inside. Because here were the feelings he was afraid to face. Here was the truth he was afraid of. The reason he'd felt so worried when he heard Jesine had been arrested. The reason he couldn't believe she was working with that coven. The reason he'd felt so betrayed by her—and the reason that now, looking at her, he couldn't hold that betrayal against her. Couldn't stay angry.

Because the truth was, when he looked at Jesine—when he looked into her gleaming hazel eyes, when he took in the graceful curve of her elbow and tracked the dusting of freckles across her face...

He felt something. Deep in his chest. Something that didn't match the memories in his head.

They were at odds. His heart and his head. And he didn't understand why.

It was maddening. He was both desperate to understand, and desperate to shut those feelings away. Because he *was* afraid of those feelings. He was afraid of the power they could hold over him. He knew very well the power of feelings. They could save a person—and they could doom a person.

"What are you doing here?" Jesine called. She carried a lantern in one hand, though it was off, the bulb inside unlit. It may have been another dismal, gray day, but it wasn't dusk yet. Though it would be soon.

"Looking for you." Ansel glanced back, puzzled, and saw the raven standing in the road beside him. It fixed him with its beady-eyed gaze. "I didn't think it would be so easy."

Jesine leveled a long, hard stare at the raven.

"You two know each other?" Ansel ventured.

Jesine looked at him. "He's my brother."

"Oh. Wait, what?"

"He's my brother," Jesine said. "He wasn't always a raven, of course."

"Of course." Ansel looked from her to the raven. "I didn't even know you had a brother."

"He's been this way as long as you've known me."

Suddenly, Ansel understood. "Someone hexed him. Who?"

Jesine's face shuttered. "I don't know for sure. Someone from Harper's old coven."

"The witches who were here six years ago?"

Jesine nodded. "It doesn't matter. Which of them did it. All that matters is I can't undo it. I spent years trying. Looking for some spell or magical remedy to help him. I traveled all over the Five Kingdoms, but I found nothing." There was a faraway cast to her eyes, but then she focused, fixing him with a direct look. The look was eerily reminiscent of her raven brother. "You can't be here, Ansel."

"Why not?"

"I'm surprised you'd want to be," Jesine said tightly. "After what happened a couple of days ago. Outside that cottage." She paused, then added, "You seemed rather...upset about it all."

Ansel sensed what she didn't say. That he'd been upset with *her*. Upset enough to accuse her of summoning that darkness, upset enough to lay some malevolent intention at her feet. Ansel spread his hands wide and said, "Yes, I was upset. I'm sorry about that. But you have to admit, that darkness was fairly upsetting."

Jesine watched him for a moment. There was a tense ring about her eyes, alighting her misgivings. But the longer she looked at him, the more her gaze softened.

"Look, I don't know what happened," Ansel went on. "I don't know what that was, that darkness. You wouldn't tell me before.

Will you tell me now?" When she didn't back away, he stepped forward, drawing closer. "Was it something you did? Or was it Harper? Just because he said he didn't do anything doesn't mean that's true. It could have been some spell he cast—"

"No, Ansel." Jesine's voice quavered. "I don't think so. It came from me."

The phrasing of this struck Ansel. She didn't say it was something she did, like a hex or a spell. She said it "came" from her. "Is this something to do with what Harper said? When he said you dabbled with dark magic?"

Jesine looked at him for a long moment. A brutal wind barreled past, and Ansel couldn't repress a shiver, the gust slicing through his coat. He watched the same wind whorl around Jesine, picking at her hair, sweeping up a flurry of leaves around her ankles.

"I knew Harper," Jesine said, starting back down the road, "before I knew you."

Ansel fell in beside her, mulling this over. There was something about the way she said it that made him wonder. He remembered what Harper had hinted at. *She flirted with the dark side for a while. And I mean that literally.*

"What was he to you?" he asked frankly.

Jesine released a slow breath, carefully controlled.

"I mean," Ansel said, "he's older than you."

Jesine turned a flat look on him.

"Well, he's a witch," Ansel hastened, "so of course he's older—"

"He's actually a new witch," Jesine said softly. "Like me. He's more or less the age he appears to be. But, yes, he's older than me. When I met him, I was eleven. He was sixteen or so." She rolled her eyes at the look on Ansel's face. "It wasn't like that. He was charming. A flirt. But it was never more than that. Not on his part anyway."

"But for you..."

"There was a time," she said, her voice softer than ever, "when I would have done anything he asked of me."

"Which was the point," Ansel said shrewdly. "Wasn't it?"

Jesine nodded. "I didn't know at first. That he was a witch. When I found out, he insisted it didn't matter. He said being a witch was a family obligation, that he wasn't interested in his coven or what they wanted. And I don't think he was completely lying about that. But he *was* trying to use me."

"Use you for what?"

"Remember what I told you and your friends yesterday?" Jesine asked. "That Harper's coven was after something around here? Whatever it was, he thought he could use me to get it. Maybe he thought my father knew where it was and I could find out for him. Maybe he just wanted to use me as leverage against my father. I don't know." She shrugged. "That's all his interest in me was."

She tried to play it off, Ansel thought, watching her sidelong. But there was misery beneath her words. Because Harper had hurt her? *No*, he thought, *because this is what she does.* He knew this somehow. He knew this was like her. To blame herself, to doubt herself. And it pained him. To see her do that now.

"You were just a child," Ansel pointed out. "Only eleven—"

Jesine offered him a weary smile. "I was eleven when I met you too. We didn't think we were children back then."

"No." And again, Ansel felt it. That strange disconnect between his head and his heart. His memories telling one story. His heart telling another, one that felt so real—but also so nebulous. "We were, though. Just children."

"It doesn't excuse what I did." Jesine stopped in the middle of the road. "What I almost did."

"Which was what?"

Jesine didn't answer at first. Ansel waited her out, shoving his hands into his pockets.

"When Harper's friendship with me didn't pay off the way his coven wanted it to," Jesine finally said, "they hexed my brother. They turned him into a raven to get to *me*." Jesine looked at him, and he saw the pain of this in her eyes.

"Get to you how?" Ansel asked quietly.

"Harper said he could help me. Help me break the hex. He pretended he didn't know who'd done it, of course, pretended he didn't know his coven was going to make a move against my family. But he said there was a way to turn my brother back. Only, he couldn't do it. I had to because I was his sister. We had a blood connection. And Harper said the spell needed that."

"He wanted you to do a spell?"

"Yes. This was before I was a witch, Ansel. My father was one, and I was destined to inherit his fairy when he died. But I hadn't actually made that choice yet. Good or bad. Light or dark."

"And the spell Harper wanted you to perform..."

"It was dark magic." Jesine's eyes fell shut, as though she couldn't bear to look at him. "Harper said only dark magic could undo the hex. Maybe he was right," she added bitterly, "since I haven't found a way to reverse it in six years."

"But you didn't do it," Ansel said, troubled. "You can't have done. I mean, once you become a bad witch, you can't become a good one."

"I didn't become a bad witch, Ansel. A bad witch is one who makes a deal with dark forces. That deal enables them to kill fairies without repercussions. That's how they get their magic." Jesine's chin trembled. "I never made such a deal. But I did participate in a ritual with Harper. A dark ritual."

Ansel almost didn't want to ask. "And what did this ritual entail?"

Jesine wrung her hands together. "I d-drank fairy blood. Blood that Harper obtained. I had nothing to do with killing the fairy, of course, but even so—what I did was..." A look of revulsion crossed her face. "But I was desperate. To save my brother."

"And the spell Harper wanted you to do—"

"I didn't do it. My father got there and stopped me before I could. Which is just as well, because I found out later it wouldn't have worked anyway."

"Well, then it's all right, isn't it? If you didn't do anything—"

"But I almost did, Ansel. And that ritual I took part in..." Jesine looked so small and brittle. Ansel hated to see her so. She wrung her hands, worrying at her right palm over and over. "That day, Ansel, I let darkness into me. And ever since, it's like—it's haunting me. It's like I'm tainted somehow—"

"Jesine." Without thinking, Ansel took Jesine's hands in his. She flinched but didn't pull away. "You're not tainted. You're a good witch. You took on your father's fairy. You never killed one of them, never made a deal—"

"But it wants me to make a deal. *He* wants me to—"

"But you haven't." Ansel didn't know who she meant by "he," but he suspected. Harper. "And you won't. I know you won't."

"You don't know. You don't know what it's like."

"Jesine—"

"That's why you have to leave." Jesine yanked away from him, stumbling slightly. Her glistening eyes were wide. "Don't you understand? That's why I'm telling you this, because if you stay—"

"If I stay near you, you mean," he said quietly.

"Please." Jesine drew in an uneven breath. "I don't want to see you hurt, Ansel. I can't."

"Why?" he pressed. Oh, how he hated that wretched look in her eyes. The tears trembling there. "Why does it matter what happens to me? You haven't known me in six years, Jesine. And we were only children. So why?"

Jesine gulped in another breath. A tear fell from her eyes, leaving a damp track on her cheek.

Then a long, ominous rumbling sounded out.

Ansel whipped around, heart pounding, thinking of that rumbling voice he'd heard in the darkness, in the glade with Jesine. But it wasn't the same. This rumbling had come from above. Thunder?

Jesine glanced up, looking confused. Ansel mirrored the gesture. It definitely sounded like thunder. But though the sky was smothered in clouds, they were dove-gray and nearly stagnant, not the dark, rolling clouds of a storm.

"That can't be thunder," Jesine murmured, echoing his thoughts. "But—"

She was interrupted by another blast of thunder, louder this time. Closer. Cracking through the air before tapering into a softer, menacing grumble.

Ansel and Jesine exchanged a worried look.

Then the sky broke open, and death rained down upon them.

14

Burned

J ESINE HEARD IT BEFORE she felt it. The air filled with a
strange hum, and then came the *pitter-patter* of raindrops,
splattering the leaf-strewn road. It was a hard, heavy rain, gathering quickly in puddles before them. Jesine stared down at a
clump of pine needles at her feet. They were suddenly streaked
with mud, and the mud was spreading, pooling, thin and run-
ny—

But it wasn't dark enough to be mud. It gleamed a deep bur-
gundy. And as Jesine lifted her eyes to the rain falling around her,
she realized...

It wasn't rain.

It was blood.

Ansel gasped in pain. "The rain. It *burned* me!"

Jesine opened her mouth to respond, uncomprehending, but
then a large drop of rain—no, blood—broke through the evergreen canopy overhead and landed on the back of her hand.

Jesine let out a small cry as a fiery pain erupted. The blood was like acid on her skin, making it sizzle and blister.

"Agh!" Ansel clapped a hand over his head as another fat drop fell from the sky, burning him. "What's—stones! *Stones!*"

The blood-rain fell faster now, thundering in Jesine's ears as it pounded against the road. Her scalp burned as though someone had set fire to her hair; she wrested her hood up over her head, stifling cries as more blood splashed onto her fingers

"Run!" Ansel took her by the hand. "*Run!*"

They ran. They left the road, dashing into the woods. But the trees were no shield against the burning blood gushing down from the sky. It was a pouring rain, turning the forest into a scene of carnage. Blood stained the dark foliage, crimson rivulets snaking down tree trunks and soaking the earth. It spattered stones and *drip-drip-dripped* from the leaves overhead. Jesine felt like she was fleeing a massacre, only there was nowhere to run. It was everywhere.

Ansel hauled her along as he tore through the trees, running blindly. Jesine tried to look around and figure out where they were, but every time she lifted her head, the blood-rain spattered her face, searing her skin. It didn't matter. The woods had become unrecognizable, covered in blood.

She gave up trying to orient herself and simply ran. Her hood kept falling back from her head, and every time she tried to tug it up again, her hands blistered. It was either her hands or her head, but she couldn't seem to protect either. Her hair grew slick with blood. It fell so thickly that she could barely see Ansel in front of her, and his hand grew slippery in hers—

And then she saw it. Out of pure, dumb luck. As a trickle of blood ran down her forehead, Jesine flinched, turning her head to flick it away—and glimpsed dark-gray brick through the trees on her right. The brick formed a looming shape, some kind of overhang built into the structure, protecting it from the rain. Even though she could barely see through the blood, a memory pulled at her, the sight of that brick face awakening some deep-seated instinct. *I know this place*, she thought. More importantly, it was shelter.

She yanked back on Ansel, pulling him in the opposite direction. He cried out as he nearly lost his hold on her, but she held fast, and he followed her as she sprinted for the brick ruin. That's what it was—a ruin, a burned-out shell of a cottage, but it was shelter, it would do—

More of the ruin became visible as they neared it, taking shape in the bloody darkness. A wrecked chimney, the tallest part that still stood. Piles of fallen brick around it. Half of the building had burned away, the gutted-out frame at the back all that was left.

"Wait," Ansel said, and for a moment, he slowed. He had recognized these ruins too, Jesine thought. But he let Jesine lead him forward, though Jesine thought he said something—something that sounded like, *"Not in there."*

They stumbled into the hollowed-out remains of the house. The wall supporting what was left of the chimney stood, but none of the ceiling was left. But then—blinking blood from her eyes—Jesine spotted some cover jutting out from the wall, a cylindrical structure built from the same brick. She lunged for it, inadvertently releasing Ansel's hand as she ducked beneath the overhang.

She scooted back against the wall, making room for Ansel, but he didn't move. She peered out, trying to wipe the blood from her face to look for him.

Ansel stood out in the open, the bloody onslaught raining down on him. He'd lifted both arms to shield his head, his face tight with pain. But he didn't move.

Jesine lurched forward, grabbed him by his blood-drenched sleeve, and yanked him down with her. For a moment, she feared he would pull away, but he ducked into the shelter behind her. Jesine shoved herself back, pressing her body into the wall. Ansel followed suit, though he had to turn sideways, fully facing her as he wedged one shoulder against the wall. But he was out of the rain, completely covered, and that was all that mattered.

Jesine let out a long breath. Her entire body trembled with pain and exhaustion. She had no idea how long they'd been running, but it felt like forever. She should assess the damage, she thought, see how badly they were hurt. But all she could do was sag in on herself, her limbs like jelly. She glimpsed Ansel's face in the gloom, covered in blood, like some kind of gruesome mask. She couldn't see the whites of his eyes, and she realized it was because they were screwed shut.

Jesine shut hers as well, letting her head fall back against the wall.

They sat like that for a long time, silent. Jesine listened as their breaths slowly evened out. She listened as the blood thundered down outside. She was soaked in it, but it didn't burn anymore. It hadn't burned through her clothes, and thank the stars for that, because her coat and skirt were stained through. So was her hair, as though she'd poured a load of crimson dye over it. But even the blood coating her hands and face didn't burn anymore; it had only burned when it first made contact. That was something.

She folded her coat back, trying to expose her cleaner sleeves beneath, the snug wool sleeves of her dress. She used those to wipe her face, clearing away as much of the blood as she could. Her skin was tender to the touch, but she felt no obvious burns. When she was done with her face, she wiped her hands against her dress beneath her coat. They felt the same, a bit tender, a bit raw. It was too dark to see in this tiny cavern, but she thought she felt raised welts running over the backs of her hands.

"Had to be another hex." Ansel's croak of a voice was sudden and startling in the dark. "Right?"

"Yes." Jesine hadn't processed it at the time, but she'd felt it, the hex. She'd felt that rush of magic wash over her, she'd scented it in the air. All in a split-second before the blood rained down.

Ansel was quiet another moment. Then he said, "Are you all right?"

"I think so. Are you?"

Ansel didn't answer. All she could hear was the soft, tattered sound of his breath.

"Ansel," she persisted, "are you hurt? Are you in pain?"

Ansel grunted. "Not really."

This was not a comforting answer. "Did it—your face, your hands, are they—"

"It's not that." His words were stiff and heavy in the dark. And close. So close. "It's just...this place."

And then she understood. *This place.* He had recognized it just as she had. And though Jesine had managed to shut out the dire memories, though she had managed to see the ruin only as their much-needed shelter, he could not.

He had almost died here. Of course he could not shut that out.

"I can't be here." His breaths grew harsher than ever. "I have to get out of here."

Jesine couldn't bear the distress in his voice. Before she could stop herself, before she could question it, she tugged at the sleeve of his coat. The thick wool was crusted with blood, already drying. In the darkness, she saw his eyes slant in her direction. He reached up to lay his hand over hers, clasping it to him. She thought of the black mark on her palm, but it was so easy to ignore in the darkness. So easy to pretend it wasn't there. And though she knew she shouldn't, Jesine squeezed Ansel's arm, trying to send solace through her touch.

Ansel squeezed her back. He let out a shaky breath.

He scooted closer towards her.

Jesine held her breath. *This is all right*, she told herself. She was only comforting him. He needed that right now. But oh, he was so, so close in this tiny, cramped space, and when he moved like that, shifting closer, his knee sank into the concave curve of her hip. Her hand and his, still entwined, became trapped between their bodies, between his shoulder and her chest—

He gazed into her eyes. She gazed back. Was it just her imagination, or had it grown lighter around them? For she could see the fine details of his face—the jut of his cheekbones, the strong square of his jaw. A reddish welt marred the dark skin there, slightly raised. Where the blood-rain had burned him.

She was only comforting him. That was all she could do.

And yet it would be so easy to just—

She reached out with her left hand and cupped his chin. Pressing a featherlight thumb against the welt. Ansel flinched, but instead of pulling back, he leaned into her touch. Their breaths passed between them like they needed each other to survive. Their lips hovering so close...

It would be so easy...

But when Ansel leaned in, his eyes falling shut, Jesine's apprehension returned. Another long buried memory resurfaced. In her mind's eye, she saw Ansel in this same place, but he was different. Younger. No welt scarring his jaw, his face softer and rounder. Ansel the boy, his eyes closed as they were now. But not closed in anticipation, expecting a kiss.

Closed forever. And it was all her fault.

"No," Jesine whispered, and she did the only thing she could with nowhere to go. She ducked her head as low as she could. Ansel's chin knocked into the top of her head, and a startled noise escaped him.

"Jesine?" She felt him draw back the little that he could. And when Jesine lifted her head, she glimpsed the opening and realized it *was* lighter out there. She couldn't hear the rain anymore, beating down against their shelter. Rather unceremoniously, she pushed Ansel back and scrambled over him, crawling out from beneath their shelter to emerge into the light.

It wasn't much light. It was the soft gray of oncoming dusk. Jesine scanned the trees, looking over what should have been a blood-soaked forest. But the blood was quickly evaporating, much more quickly than normal rainwater. It dried up before her eyes, pools of blood sinking into the ground and leaving no trace.

"It's stopped." The words were Ansel's. He climbed out of the ruins behind her. "It's gone."

She could feel his eyes on her, but Jesine evaded him, turning to frown at the spot they'd sheltered in. Such a strangely shaped structure, cylindrical, sticking straight out of the wall. It must have been...

An oven, she thought. It was the remains of a massive, crematory oven.

Jesine shuddered. No wonder Ansel hadn't wanted to go in there.

"A witch lived here," Ansel said.

Jesine was so startled, her eyes flew to his face. Ansel caught her gaze, ensnaring her. She could not look away.

"I almost died here." His voice was quiet.

I know, she wanted to say. *I know, I know. I was here too, don't you remember?* But of course he didn't.

Her father had seen to that.

"Poison," Ansel said, startling her again. He went on, clarifying, "That was what almost killed me. It was how the witch Henrietta lured me here."

He sighed, the ugliness of the memory evident on his face, in the pained furrow of his brow. "She offered me poisoned candy. Poisoned with her magic. I wasn't stupid," he added. "Well, not *that* stupid. I wouldn't have just taken it from her. I found the first piece on the ground. And it was—it had an addictive quality to it. When she offered me more, I couldn't say no. Then again, maybe that's even more stupid, eating candy off the ground..."

Jesine watched him, her heart straining in her chest. She didn't want to listen to this. She didn't want to relive how close he'd come to death, didn't want to hear him recount it all as though she didn't know. She didn't want to watch him rambling, so much the Ansel she remembered. The awkward but brash little boy who'd made her such promises. Promises he didn't remember.

"When my sister came to rescue me, the witch caught her too. But Isabelle was smarter than me. Always has been," he muttered. "She didn't eat the candy. She managed to slip out of her bindings when the witch was distracted, building up the fire. She got me free, and we killed Henrietta together. Pushed her in there..." His eyes shifted to the ruined oven they'd just sheltered in.

Then he lifted his gaze to her face. "But the fire got out of hand. We couldn't stop it. Everything was burning, there was so much smoke...and the poison was still in me. I could feel it. I couldn't breathe from the smoke...thought I was going to die—"

"Ansel," Jesine broke in, trying to stop him.

But Ansel didn't seem to hear her. "Isabelle tried to drag me out, but she collapsed. And I passed out, and..."

She couldn't bear this. She couldn't *bear* it. What she would give to get back what he'd been to her. What they'd been to each other. Her father's words echoed in her mind, the warning he'd given her all those years ago. It was her fault, he'd told her, what happened to Ansel, and she knew he was right. All she could do was put Ansel in danger. She knew that more than ever now.

But standing here, listening to him...after being so close, only minutes before—

Maybe it didn't matter. After all, could she really keep Ansel from this anymore? He'd said it himself, these witches were after him. Would keeping him in the dark keep him safe?

Was she just being selfish, trying to convince herself?

Stones, she didn't know anymore.

"I don't remember how we got out." A small frown creased Ansel's face. "Neither does Isabelle. She says she must have dragged me out. Once, she said she thought someone else was there, someone who helped her, but she doesn't remember. Or she couldn't see who it was. The smoke—"

"*Ansel*." Jesine surged towards him, and this time, Ansel fell silent. He looked startled, as though he'd forgotten she was there, as though he'd been recounting his story to the trees and not to her. "Please." Jesine stopped before him, barely aware of the distance she'd closed between them. "Please, stop."

"Why?" Ansel whispered. She stood so close now, he had to tilt his head down to look at her. As children, they had been of a height, but now he had to bend his head to look her in the eye. "What's wrong?"

"Nothing's wrong." But Jesine felt breathless, as though she'd just run a long distance to get to him. Trembling, she reached up and slid her hand behind his neck.

Ansel stood rooted to the spot. Like he knew, somehow, that if he moved, he would break this spell between them.

"Ansel," Jesine murmured. "Would you like to kiss me?"

It was a silly question. Silly, because he had just tried to do so when they'd sheltered in the ruins. But it was an important one too, even if he didn't remember why.

Ansel didn't speak. But she read his answer in his eyes.

Jesine leaned in, stretching towards him, all her frantic, pent-up desperation surging inside her, ready to spill free. What she would give to make him remember, she just wanted him to *remember her*—

Jesine pressed her lips to his and kissed him.

For a moment, that old fear tried to work through her again. She thought of the darkness in the glade yesterday, how it had called to Ansel as well as her. But the darkness was not here with them now.

It was a soft kiss. Sweet. As though they were still children, exchanging an innocent kiss. But it was so much more than that. Because as Jesine clutched at his arm to steady herself, she poured her magic into the kiss, reaching into his mind.

It was easy, in the end. The broken fragments were still there, just separated. She pieced everything back together.

She kissed Ansel. And with her kiss, she restored the memories that had been stolen from him.

And then, Ansel pulled away with a gasp.

It was a horrible, tearing sound. Jesine stumbled back, nearly tripping over a half-buried brick in the ground. She felt cold without Ansel's lips on hers, without the warmth of him against her.

Ansel.

She looked at him. His eyes were wide, staring, but not at her. He seemed to look through her, as though she wasn't even there, as though she were a ghost. With another rattling breath, he fell to his knees.

"Oh, stones." Jesine whispered. *Oh, stars and stones, what have I done?* The enormity of it crashed over her, and she wondered what madness had possessed her to do this. She watched in horror as his hands flew to his head.

As all his memories of her came rushing back to him.

"Oh, no," she moaned. "Oh, *no*—"

She had really done it. She hadn't meant to, exactly. Or maybe she just hadn't thought it would work. But now it was done, and his memories were back, and—

And he was going to hate her.

"Jesine," Ansel gasped, but she didn't think he was talking to her. Not to *her*, Jesine, in the here and now. He was responding to a memory. "Jesine—"

"I'm sorry," she cried. "Ansel, I'm so sorry!"

Fear and shame driving all thought from her head, she turned and ran, fleeing into the darkening woods.

15

REMINISCENCE

A NSEL REMEMBERED.

He knelt in the hollowed-out ruins that had once been the cottage he'd nearly died in, and he remembered.

He knelt in the ruins, but he wasn't really there. He was in his mind. In his memories. In the past.

He remembered.

Ansel ran in a sun-dappled glade, surrounded by soaring pine trees and brilliant aspens. The trees cast long shadows across the clearing, and the light flitted over him in snatches.

Ansel ran, and beside him ran Jesine. His friend. Ansel had not had many friends over the course of his eleven years in this world. That wasn't all his fault. Part of the reason was his family never stuck around anyplace long enough to make friends.

But there had been no moving in a while. Not since Ansel's father took off several weeks ago for a job, with orders that Ansel and Isabelle stay put near the cluster of villages here in the southern wood. They had not expected him to be gone so long, especially without any word, and that was troubling. But Ansel tried not to think about it.

And it was easy not to think about. Not when he had one very bright spot in his life.

Jesine.

His friendship with Jesine was the most wonderful thing. They were an unlikely pair in many ways. And yet, in those same ways, they just...fit. Jesine didn't talk much. Ansel didn't either, especially in large groups. That was why he usually got picked on when he tried to join groups of boys playing games. He wasn't shy, exactly. He just didn't always know the "right" thing to say, so often, he said nothing.

But Jesine didn't talk much at all. Which left Ansel plenty of room to talk about whatever he liked. This might have put some people off, his babbling on about anything and everything, but Jesine didn't seem to mind. She—who had never been anywhere except this small patch of wood—loved to listen to his tales about all the places he had traveled to, all the things he'd seen.

It was one sunny afternoon, as they ran across that golden glade and collapsed, bright-eyed and giggling, in the grass, that Jesine said to him, "Ansel. Can I tell you a secret?"

Ansel, lying flat on his back, rolled his head aside to look at her. She pushed herself up on one elbow and gazed down at him. Her freckly face and long, tumbling hair were framed by the patchy sunlight peeking through the trees, giving her coppery tresses a lus-

trous sheen, like a fountain of pennies. But she looked very serious, her lips pursed together.

"Of course," said Ansel. "You can tell me anything."

She smoothed her stiff skirt over her knees, then clutched at the edge of her pinafore. "You can't tell anyone. Not even your sister."

Ansel scoffed. "I keep plenty of secrets from Isabelle." Isabelle thought she was so smart. And, well, she was, but. Ansel was smart too, in his own way.

"All right." Jesine took a deep breath. "The truth is...I'm a witch."

Ansel burst out laughing. "What?"

"Or I will be. Someday." Something dark passed through Jesine's hazel eyes—a strange, deep look that seemed too old for her young face. It was almost frightening, but it was there and gone so quickly, Ansel soon forgot it. "Once I'm old enough."

"You could never be a witch."

"Why not?"

"Because witches are evil, Jesine. They're wicked, abominable creatures. You could never be like that."

Jesine smiled tolerantly. "Most witches are like that, yes. But I wouldn't be. I'll be a good witch, like my father."

"Your father's a witch?"

"Yes. But he's a good one. He's not wicked, he—" She broke off, her head snapping up like a wolf on alert. A second later, Ansel realized why. There was a voice in the woods, calling out. Calling for Jesine.

"Jesine? Jesine!"

Jesine's eyes widened. "That's my father. I have to go."

Before Ansel could stop her, she scrambled to her feet. Ansel had never met Jesine's father, and she claimed he was a good man.

Well, now she claimed he was a good witch. But Ansel couldn't help but notice that every time she heard him calling or found herself running late to get home, she seemed afraid. Afraid of her father's reaction. And she was dead-set against the idea of Ansel meeting him.

"Wait." Ansel dusted himself off as he rolled to his feet. "Can we meet again tomorrow? Here?"

Jesine bit her lip. "Not here. It's too close." She tossed a glance over her shoulder. "How about that shallow spot in the creek bed, west of here? You know, where we found those river stones, the black ones?"

"All right." Ansel grinned. "Tomorrow, then."

And he met her there tomorrow. And the next day, and the next. Every day that she could get away, which was most days. They passed the rest of the summer that way, until the long, sun-filled days began to grow shorter, colder, and grayer. Ansel's father had soon been away for three months, but Ansel hardly noticed. Sometimes, his mornings were a bit lonely—Jesine often couldn't get away until later in the day—and in those times, he sought out Isabelle. She spent most of her time in one of the villages, Ingstold, where she helped to care for some old woman. They were running out of money, as Isabelle often reminded him, and she worried what was keeping their father so long, and when he would be back.

Deep down—so deep that he couldn't quite admit it to himself—Ansel hoped their father would never come back. He was happy here, spending his days with Jesine. And it wasn't hard to convince Isabelle to let it be, because in addition to payment for her services, the old woman was teaching Isabelle how to read, keeping her happily plied with books. So the days passed on, summer into fall, Isabelle reading her books in the village and Ansel exploring the woods with Jesine...

Jesine seemed to enjoy their days together as much as he did, but she was not always happy. There were days where she didn't laugh at Ansel's stories, days where she barely seemed to listen to him. Days where dark moods took her, making a glum picture of her freckled face.

Ansel always knew the reason: her father.

Once, he asked if her father ever hurt her. She looked at him with wide eyes and said, "Oh, no. No, Ansel, he's not like that. I swear." She leaned against the massive trunk of an oak tree growing near the creek's edge and fiddled with the cuff of her sleeve. "There was a family who used to live near here, two boys and one girl—she was a bit younger than me. Their father beat them something awful, especially the boys. Even their mother wasn't safe from him. When my father learned of it, he put a stop to it."

Ansel, standing over her, frowned. "How?"

The look Jesine snuck at him from beneath her lashes was almost coy. "Let's just say," she whispered, as though someone might be listening, "that even good witches can do bad things. If it's for the right reasons."

Ansel eyed her skeptically. He still wasn't sure he believed her, about her father being a witch. He'd never heard of a good witch.

"Anyway," she went on, "he would never hurt me like that, Ansel. He never has." She twisted her fingers in her hair, fiddling with the fine, frizzy strands. "He's just very stern. I've only been able to spend so much time with you because he's been busy with something."

"Something like what?"

"I'm not sure." Her gaze grew distant, fixed on the thin, gurgling stream before them. "Earlier this year, there was trouble with some bad witches. A whole coven of them. I think he's been dealing with

them. *Most of them are gone now."* She looked up at him, and that dark, frightening look passed through her eyes again. *"But not all of them."*

Ansel shivered. He hadn't heard anything about witches in the area. Ansel had never told Jesine so, but witches terrified him. Not that he had ever met one.

Ansel leaned a hand against the oak tree. "Well, I don't know what your father has to be stern about. You don't seem the rebellious type."

Jesine seemed offended. "I can be plenty rebellious."

Ansel smirked down at her. "Sure."

"I can." Jesine laughed at his expression, but then grew sober. "I've been rebellious before," she said, and she was not bragging or joking now. "You have no idea. The things I've done." Her bottom lip trembled like the leaves on the branches above him, rustling in the gentle wind.

Ansel crouched down, making himself level with her. "It can't have been anything so bad."

"You don't know."

"Then tell me." Ansel tugged gently at her shoulder, urging her to look at him.

"I can't." Jesine squeezed her eyes shut. "You would—you would hate me, Ansel. You would think me so terrible. Anyway, you don't have to take my word for it," she added, her voice raw. "Just ask my father. He tells me all the time how awful I am."

"You're not awful! You could never be!" Ansel gave a hoarse laugh. "Trust me, Jesine. You want to talk terrible, you can't do worse than me. Just ask my father." He rocked back, sitting on the ground at the base of the tree. His shoulder rested easily against Jesine's. "According to my father, I'm the reason for every move *we've had to make. It's always my mistakes, my ineptitude. Getting us into trouble—"*

"Ansel!" Jesine finally turned to look at him. "That can't be true."

"Well, it is."

"I don't believe it," she said fiercely.

"Well, nor do I believe you're so bad as your father says," Ansel retorted.

Jesine didn't respond to that. She was silent for a long time as the daylight faded around them, twilight settling in. The shadows cast by the sun earlier in the day stretched now, covering the woods and the creek. Covering Ansel and Jesine.

"Look," Ansel said, "let's make a pact. Anytime I start talking about how terrible I am, or how terrible my father thinks I am, you'll tell me I'm not. And anytime you start talking that way about yourself, I'll tell you you're not. I'll tell you all the good and wonderful things about you. All right?"

Jesine's conflicted expression gave way to something different. Sort of shy. But also pleased.

"You think I'm good and wonderful?" she asked softly.

Ansel laughed. Then he realized she wasn't joking.

"Of course I do," he said, bewildered. "Jesine, don't you know that?"

And she smiled then, in a way that was so bright and beautiful, it made him blush. "Anyway," he blustered, suddenly self-conscious, "shall we promise? To tell each other we aren't terrible?"

"Yes." Jesine's eyes shone. "I'll promise you, Ansel."

"Good. And I'll promise you."

Jesine ducked her head, her tousled red hair falling forward to curtain her face. "Ansel," she said, and her voice was very serious, "would you like to kiss me?"

Ansel's cheeks began to burn. He stared at Jesine, tongue-tied, all thought vanishing from his head.

Jesine peeked at him through her hair, and on her face was an impish smile. She giggled and pushed her hair back, then leaned into him.

And placed a quick kiss on his cheek.

She'd departed for home smiling, happier than he had ever seen her. But it wasn't a week later that he found her in their meeting spot, crying. Tears dripped down her face one by one.

"Jesine, what's wrong?" Ansel scrabbled down the creek bed to join her. She crouched at the water's edge, digging up pebbles as she cried, flinging them into the brook. "Jesine?" He took her muddy hand in his. "What happened?"

Jesine shook her head. She gazed down at her hand in his for a long time. Then she said, "It's my father. He knows what I've been doing." Lifting her tear-streaked face to his, she clarified, "He doesn't know about you. He would have said so if he did. But he knows I've been shirking my studies, he knows I haven't been learning herbs while I've been out here. He said whatever I've been up to, it's at an end."

"But you said he doesn't know about me. So—"

"He said he's going to start accompanying me out here, seeing to my studies himself." Jesine's voice was so thick with tears, she didn't sound like herself. "I won't be on my own ever. I won't be able to get away, Ansel." She fell back on her heels, tears streaming down her face more quickly now.

Ansel's heart raced, dread making it beat overtime. "So you'll be busy," he said, trying to assure her it would not be so bad. Trying to assure himself it would not be so bad. "We won't have all day together—but we can still have some time—"

"I don't know," Jesine wept. "I don't think so."

Ansel leaned into her, hating to see her so distressed. "Can't you just tell him we're friends? You're allowed to have friends, aren't you?"

"No," said Jesine. And her tone was so stark and matter-of-fact, so simple, that Ansel's heart ached for her.

"That's ridiculous. Everyone's allowed to have friends."

"Not me. I have responsibilities. I have to be ready to take up my father's craft. I have to protect the woods."

"Protect it from what?"

"Bad witches," she whispered. "They want something around here. I don't know what."

Her voice had become so dead and hopeless. Ansel didn't know what to say, how to make it better. His own heart wrenched at the thought of never seeing her again, or seeing her so little. It was such a big emotion, unlike any Ansel had ever felt in his eleven years of life. Scooting closer to her, he hugged an arm around her shaking shoulders, hoping it would help.

"It will be all right, Jesine," he said quietly. "Somehow, it will."

"But how?"

"Well..." He'd had this thought before, when he'd considered what would happen when his father returned. If his father returned. Ansel knew Isabelle was afraid he wasn't coming back, even if she didn't dare say it out loud. She'd started talking about other jobs she could take on, some that weren't local.

"Jesine," Ansel said, "you could come with us."

"What? What do you mean?"

"I think Isabelle and I might leave soon. With or without my father," he added. "And when we go—Jesine, you could come with us! It might be difficult to convince my father if he returns, but if he doesn't, Isabelle wants to go someplace new. A big city, maybe, like Glen City. Or somewhere in the Mariner Kingdom. You could come with us, Jesine."

Jesine looked doubtful. "But I'm supposed to protect the woods..."

"You said it yourself, your father does that! You don't have to stay, Jesine. You can choose your own life. If you come with us—"

"Jesine!"

Jesine gasped. Tearing free of Ansel, she spun around. Ansel, too, snapped around to look.

A man stood atop the rise above them, overlooking the creek. He had fiery red hair like Jesine, only a shade or two darker. Ansel realized—the thought like a cold blade sliding into his gut—that this must be Jesine's father. He had found their meeting spot.

He had found them.

The man did not shout. He didn't charge down. Perhaps that would have been less frightening. Instead, he descended upon them slowly, every line in his face etched with anger and scorn. His blue eyes were cold. Ansel found himself motionless, unable to flee. Jesine's terrified expression was much the same.

"What is this, Jesine?" her father asked, his words dreadfully hushed.

Jesine didn't seem able to speak. Her wide eyes flew from her father to Ansel.

"Is this what you've been up to for all this time?" Now her father's voice, infused with fury, grew louder. "Spending time with this boy?"

Ansel, as the boy in question, felt he should say something. They hadn't done anything wrong, after all. Not really. "Please, sir—" he began, but Jesine's father whirled on him.

"You don't speak!" Now he was shouting, a hand leveled at Ansel. "You stay away from my daughter, do you understand? Stay away from her!"

"Father—" Jesine tried.

"Have you learned nothing, Jesine?" Now her father turned on her. "Nothing from your past mistakes? Or don't you remember what happened the last time you let your fancies run away with you? Don't you remember what you did?"

Jesine's face went absolutely white. "It's not like that. Ansel's not like that. He would never—"

"We are going home." Her father's voice dropped again, resuming that dreadful hush. It was frightening, the way he wheeled so quickly from one to the other. "I thought you had learned better, Jesine. I thought—after what happened to your brother—that I could trust you. Clearly, I was wrong." He turned on his heel. "Now, come. Let's go."

Ansel knew he shouldn't, but he took a step towards Jesine, his arm outstretched. This couldn't be the end. She couldn't go, not like this. He had to see her again, he would see her again—

But Jesine shot him one last, stricken look. Then she turned and followed her father up the rise.

They vanished into the woods.

This isn't the end, Ansel thought desperately, staring at the spot where they'd disappeared. It can't be.

No. He would come back tomorrow, here, to their meeting place. He would wait all day if he had to. And if Jesine didn't turn up, he would ask around, figure out where she lived. He would find her.

He would talk to her father, make him see reason. Or he would convince Jesine to leave with him. He could sneak her out...

This would not be the end.

But it was. Ansel never saw Jesine again.

For that night, as he traipsed through the woods back to his sister, the witch took him.

16

CRACKED

G ARRETT PEERED THROUGH THE shop window, trying to
see through the fogged-up glass. The morning had been
damp, though it seemed to be drying out now, the air turning
crisp beneath the hazy sky. "Let's go in this one," he said.

Demetri sighed. "I hadn't realized this was going to be a shopping excursion as well as an investigation."

"Gifts, Demetri! Shopping for gifts. I haven't done any yet,"
Garrett confessed, "though that's nothing unusual, I'm always
waiting to the last minute."

They were in Ingsberg, the town east of Lise. It was a proper
town, at least twice the size of Lise. The streets were broader and
cleaner, lined with tall townhouses and freshly painted store-
fronts. Their business here was twofold: visit the laboratory and
drop off the sample they'd taken from the quarry, and pay a visit
to the town morgue. Apparently, another mangled corpse had
been found in the woods, and Garrett wanted to see if the demon
had struck again.

So while Sabine went to the lab, Garrett and Demetri headed to the morgue. It was just the three of them today. Garrett's guards had not been happy about that, but it couldn't be helped. Gemma was recovering well from her injury, but she needed one more day of rest before traveling. And Klaus could not be on duty all the time; he'd already done more than his fair share. Garrett had insisted he take time off today, pointing out that Sabine and Demetri would suffice as protection.

If he needed protection. So far, this quaint little town didn't seem all that dangerous. Certainly not now, as they moseyed down the street and paused outside a shop.

"C'mon," Garrett said to Demetri, "you said you wanted to exchange gifts with Sabine. Maybe you can find her something."

"Here?" Demetri eyed the shop dubiously as Garrett pulled open the door. "Doubtful. Unless they sell ogre teeth or something."

Garrett waved a hand. "If that's all you're after, I can get you one of those. Huge things, you know." Sabine had gone off to the lab with the package containing their sample from the quarry. Unbeknownst to her, Garrett had slipped a sample of his own in the package—a sample of his own blood. Perhaps he could discover, once and for all, what Delphine had done to him.

If she had really cured him.

Shaking out of these thoughts, Garrett stepped into the little shop. A bell *tinkled* as the door swung shut behind them. It wasn't a terribly large place, but it was packed with long counters and floor-to-ceiling shelves, and every surface was filled with popular gifts. Delicate jewelry and ornate belts, painted boxes and etched porcelain. Garrett perused the items with growing anxiety. He had no idea what to get Briar, and that disturbed him. It shouldn't have been so difficult to think of a good gift for her.

Perhaps the trouble was, every time he thought of Briar, his mind went to depressing places.

"What, by the Gift, are *these* things?"

Garrett turned. Demetri was examining a row of merchandise along the front window of the store. Garrett joined him and discovered a row of bizarre dolls, built from wood and of various sizes. They all had vaguely disturbing expressions, and it was a moment before Garrett realized it was because of their teeth. Their teeth were lavishly painted, quite large in proportion to the rest of them, taking up half their faces. And sticking out from the back of each doll was some kind of...some kind of lever...?

"Nutcrackers!" Garrett and Demetri turned as the short, balding shopkeeper hurried their way. "My latest invention! Quite ingenious, you'll find!"

"Nutcrackers?" Demetri repeated. "Never heard of them. What do they do, crack nuts?" He snorted.

"But of course!" the shopkeeper cried, and Demetri quickly turned his snort into a cough. "See, watch, watch!"

He pulled a large walnut out from his pocket, still encased in its shell. Using the lever to open one doll's mouth—this one, Garrett noticed, bore a gold crown and fanciful garb—the shopkeeper placed the nut inside, then snapped the mouth shut with a loud *crack!*

"Wow." Garrett blinked as splinters of the nut's shell leaked from the doll's—nutcracker's—mouth. "It actually works."

The shopkeeper beamed. "But of course!"

"I see you have different—er—designs," Garrett said. "Different figures, I mean."

"Yes." The shopkeeper indicated the one he'd just used. "This one is the king! A wonderful gift, don't you think, to have King Victor cracking your nuts for you?" He chuckled.

Garrett struggled to contain his expression. "Oh, yes. Just...wonderful."

"Perhaps I'll buy it after all," Demetri said blandly. Garrett shot him a furtive glare, and Demetri had to turn away to hide his laughter.

"Actually, come to think of it, Briar might like one of these," Garrett said. "She'd get a kick out of it, at least. Not the king, though, maybe a different one..." He perused the line of nutcrackers, noting each one. A soldier, complete with the blue uniforms that actual Glen soldiers wore. A lady decked out in a lavish gown. A sorcerer in a robe, straight out of some fanciful tale. Garrett was considering that one when a figure at the end of the row caught his eye. It was even more macabre than the others, its buck-tooth grin ghastly, its eyes painted red. That part didn't seem quite right, but otherwise...

Picking up the nutcracker with tender hands, he turned to the shopkeeper. "Is this...?"

"Ah! One of my more gruesome creations, I will admit." The shopkeeper bustled over to him. "You have read, I'm sure, the tales in the penny press? About the princes who fought the corpse monsters up north in the mountains?"

A grin stole over Garrett's face. He hadn't *read* about it, of course... "So this is a corpse monster?"

The shopkeeper chuckled again. "Exactly."

"I'll take it," said Garrett.

Demetri shook his head as they exited the shop a few minutes later, Garrett with his wrapped parcel in hand. "I can't believe you actually bought that thing."

"You don't think Briar will like it?" Garrett fretted, as they crossed the street to the secluded spot where they'd tied off their horses.

"Oh, I'm sure she will. You'd know better than me, anyway."

"I suppose," Garrett said, his tone subdued. He sighed as he bent to secure his package to the saddle.

"Okay," Demetri said flatly. "Spit it out, already."

"What?" Garrett started, the package nearly slipping from his fingers. "What do you mean?"

"Garrett, every time I've mentioned Briar, you go all gloomy and secretive." Demetri waved a vague hand. "That's about the third time."

"I'm not gloomy," Garrett said defensively. "I just don't like being away from her. Is all."

Demetri unwound his horse's reins from the low fence. "Then you should have telegrammed her when I told you to."

"Well, I didn't want—I mean, this is dangerous, what we're doing—"

"Far more dangerous for you or me than for Briar. Which you know very well. Try again."

"Why are you being so rude?" Garrett fumbled with the ties on his saddle as he secured the package. "You used to be much more diplomatic."

"*Used to* being the key phrase, Garrett. Diplomacy wastes time, and if there's one thing I've learned, it's not to waste time. So. Are you going to tell me what's going on with you or not?"

Garrett sighed. He forced himself to turn and face Demetri. "Look, if you must know...before I left, Briar and I...well, we had a bit of a falling-out."

"Over what?"

Garrett grabbed hold of his horse's stirrup strap, steadying himself. He clenched his fingers around the strap, the cold leather digging into his palm. "So. The thing is. I'm dying."

Whatever Demetri had expected Garrett to say, this clearly was not it. He dropped his horse's reins. "You're what?"

"Dying. Or I was, anyway. Have been. I might not be anymore." Garrett looked into Demetri's puzzled face. "The corpse monster bite, Demetri. The venom. Remember?"

"I thought Thatcher was going to find a cure."

"Yes, well, he hasn't. And his supply from the Mountain Kingdom is running low, so..." Garrett scrubbed his free hand through his hair. "Anyway. I sort of got into it with my father the day before I left. To come down here. He didn't want me to go, you see. Of course, he's been pretending everything will be fine, just like Thatcher, just like—" He stopped short.

"Like Briar does?" Demetri filled in.

Garrett scuffed the toe of his boot against the cobbled street. "They all have. And yet my father threw a fit when he found out I was coming down here to hunt witches. He *is* worried about finding a cure in time, he just won't say so. So we argued, and he said something like—'I thought you were done trying to get yourself killed! Don't you have Briar to live for now?' And I said—" Garrett swallowed. "Maybe not."

A weighted silence fell. Garrett did not look at Demetri as his friend repeated, "Maybe not."

"I didn't mean anything by it," Garrett blustered. "I was just—I mean, it was galling for my father to bring Briar into it when only a few months ago he was going on about how she wouldn't make a suitable wife for me. He just made me angry. The way he does sometimes." Garrett cleared his throat. "But what I didn't know at the time was that Briar was standing right outside. And she heard, er, that last bit."

"Garrett." Demetri sounded incredulous. "Surely you told her you didn't mean it?"

"Well—" Garrett chanced a quick, abashed glance at his friend.

"Oh, Garrett." Demetri sighed. "What did you do?"

Garrett didn't answer right away. How could he explain? How could he explain the hollow crevice in his chest, the cavity in his heart? It was smaller than it used to be, but it had never wholly gone away. And there were times, like now, when he felt the emptiness there. The lack.

It was that emptiness—what *wasn't* there—that hurt so much.

He untangled his fingers from the stirrup strap and straightened. "I know what it's like to lose someone, Demetri." He spoke in a quiet voice. "To lose *the* person, the one person. The person you love. And I can't bear the thought of doing that to Briar. Of hurting her like that."

"Garrett," Demetri said roughly, and Garrett remembered that Demetri, too, knew a bit about what that felt like. To lose someone important. "You don't know that will happen."

Garrett strove for a lighter tone. "Well, it was looking very likely before I left. And I just thought...oh, I wasn't thinking. Briar confronted me about what she'd heard, and I—I told her maybe it wasn't enough. I told her *she* wasn't enough." His throat grew tight. "I told her maybe too much of me still loved Snow."

There was another silence. Then—

"You're an idiot," Demetri said.

Garrett looked up, startled. "What?"

"An idiot." Demetri's voice was thick with exasperation. "A much bigger idiot than I ever thought you were."

"Look, I didn't mean it—"

"I know, Garrett." Demetri didn't sound reassured by that fact. "I know what you were doing. You pushed her away. You thought if you die, it would make things easier for her."

"Well." Garrett floundered. "When you put it that way—"

"—it sounds idiotic?"

Garrett squinted. "I feel like we've had this conversation before. Do you feel like we've had this conversation before? Only I was on the other side of it last time."

"Yes, well, that should only convince you how stupid you've been, then."

"You're really upset with me, aren't you?"

"Of course I am!" Demetri burst out. "Garrett, you and Briar are the two people I care most about in this world. I'm very much invested in your happiness, and you've just gone and mucked it up, and for what? For some stupid, noble reason that doesn't even make sense. You can push Briar away, but she's still going to love you—stones know why, at this point. So it won't hurt her any less if you die." Demetri paused in his tirade. "What did you mean when you said you might not be dying anymore?"

"It's a long story."

"Right." Demetri reached up to pinch the bridge of his nose. "Look. You do realize you've been stupid, don't you?"

"Well, I certainly do now."

"Good. Then all you have to do, when you go back home, is say you're sorry, that you were an idiot, and plead for her to forgive you."

Garrett gnawed his lip. "Do you think she will?"

"*I* think," said an unexpected voice, "that you've mucked things up nearly as bad as I have."

Demetri spun around as Garrett snapped up straight, stepping around his horse.

A man stood down the road where the cobbled street became a dirt path in the shade of a mammoth southern oak. The man was dressed very stylishly. Absurdly, this was the first thing Garrett noticed about him—his tailored overcoat, which looked even more expensive than Garrett's, and his deep-green scarf, spun from the finest wool. He even wore a fur-lined hat, jauntily perched atop his head. Garrett couldn't decide if it looked ridiculous or admirable. He certainly pulled it off.

Demetri took in a sharp breath. "*Castel*."

"Castel?" Garrett echoed. "You mean, the one who—" Where to start. The one who had worked for the mad sea witch, Sohalia. The one who had betrayed, then saved, Kinsley, Briar's bodyguard.

The one who'd broken Kinsley's heart.

"Yes." Demetri had a pistol in his hand in an instant. Garrett was still fixated on the stupid hat. "I should have known. When Jesine said one of the witches was here to summon that demon—I should have known it was you."

Castel smiled. On him, it was a particularly deceptive expression. "Oh, please, Demetri." He gestured towards the pistol in Demetri's hand. "You know very well how useless that is against someone like me."

"I know," Demetri said tightly. "It just...makes me feel better."

"If you say so, darling." Castel arched an eyebrow, looking Demetri up and down. "You're looking...not bad. These days."

"Wish I could say the same," Demetri said, "but *bad* is exactly what you are, isn't it?"

Garrett looked at him sidelong, sensing there was more to his friend's tense tone than he'd first thought. Demetri wasn't uncomfortable because he was afraid of Castel, Garrett realized. Demetri was uncomfortable because the sight of Castel caused him pain. Because the last time Demetri had seen Castel was in the Mariner Kingdom.

Just after Perpetua died.

"That's not entirely fair." Castel's eyes darkened. "Or maybe it is. I'm not exactly objective." He flicked his gaze from Demetri to Garrett. "Your Highness. We haven't had the pleasure yet, have we?"

"We haven't been introduced, if that's what you mean," Garrett said calmly. "But I'm not sure an introduction will bring me much pleasure."

Castel let out an oddly genuine laugh. "That's because you don't know me yet, prince."

"What do you want, Castel?" Demetri demanded. "Is this a prelude to another attack? Or a distraction, maybe, while your fellow witches wreak some more havoc?"

"Oh, no," Castel said casually. He spread his hands wide. "Nothing so sinister as all that. I'm quite alone. And I'm here on your behalf. I'm here to deliver a warning."

"Why would you want to do that?" Garrett asked.

Demetri narrowed his eyes. "Playing both sides, Castel?"

"Don't I always?"

"And we're just meant to trust you," Garrett said. "Is that it?"

Castel dropped his smile. "I'm here on behalf of the only two people in the world I care about," he said. "The fact that one of them is deceased doesn't mean I stopped caring."

Demetri took a step forward, his grip visibly tightening around his pistol. He seemed to move without realizing it. If Castel wasn't careful, Demetri really was going to shoot him. Castel could have taken the pistol from him, Garrett realized, with a flick of his hand. Yet he hadn't.

"You claim you cared about Perpetua?" Demetri retorted. "Are you joking? You could have saved her."

"She didn't want me to." Castel's voice turned stiff. "I chose to respect that. I will always make that choice." He broke off, his expression twisting. As though he'd said more than he wanted to. He turned his gaze on Garrett. "I *did* save Kinsley. So you decide if you can trust me. But I think when you hear what I have to say, you'll want to get back to Lise to see if I'm right."

"What are you talking about?" Garrett asked, suspicious. "Get back to Lise? Why?" They hadn't even stopped to look over the remains in the village morgue yet.

As though reading his mind, Castel said, "You don't need to visit the morgue here. The corpse they have wasn't killed by the demon. Judging by its mangled state, it was probably a wolf attack. Which makes sense, since the demon shouldn't be anywhere near here. It's supposed to stay close to Ansel."

"Ansel?" Garrett echoed. He and Demetri exchanged a sharp look. "Why would the demon be after Ansel? Or rather, since you lot control the creature, why is your coven after Ansel?"

"Well, for one thing, Adela really wants him dead," Castel said flippantly. "She was just going on about it this morning."

"But Adela isn't in charge, is she?" Garrett asked, watching Castel closely. "I mean, so far, she's done the queen's bidding. Delphine, I mean." Garrett cursed his slip of the tongue. Delphine would always be *the queen* to him, even though she'd never deserved the title.

"Because Ansel's fate isn't her call," Castel said coolly.

"That's what I just said." Garrett's words betrayed his exasperation.

"No, what you said was that Adela is doing Delphine's bidding. You assume Delphine is in charge." Castel clasped his hands together in front of him. "I suppose you think all of this is about you, don't you, prince? You and Delphine. You think this is some revenge scheme on Delphine's part? That you were deliberately lured here for her?"

Garrett hesitated. That *was* what they'd thought...

"Well, you were lured here," Castel admitted, "and Delphine does want revenge. But you're wrong to think she's in charge."

"Who else would be in charge?" Demetri asked. "You? Is this a confession? You're the mastermind behind your coven's grand plan?"

"Hardly. I was the last witch brought into this little coven." Castel shook his head. "Don't you understand? No one is in charge. We are each here for our own reasons—revenge, mostly. And Adela isn't the only witch Ansel has run afoul of."

Garrett exchanged another look with Demetri, this time in confusion. Was Castel talking about Delphine? Ansel had worked as a guard for Delphine when she was still queen—and he'd disobeyed her when she ordered him to hunt down Snow. But Castel had also just said this wasn't all about Delphine...

"You might remember," Castel went on, "that about—oh, six years ago—Ansel and his sister killed a witch. Right in this part of the kingdom, in fact. They stuffed her in her own oven."

"And? She's dead, isn't she?"

"She is," Castel confirmed. "Her brother isn't."

Garrett's stomach flipped.

"He's actually lived in this area his whole life," Castel continued, "even these past six years. He just never knew how to find Ansel. Not until Ansel became a famous witch hunter. Then it was just a matter of asking around, locating Adela, and, well, there you are."

Garrett said, "So this is as much about Ansel as it is about me."

"Quite," Castel said nonchalantly. "So should we head back to Lise now, or would you like to chat some more first?"

17

TRAPPED

*A*NSEL WAS DYING.

He lay on the cold, exposed brick floor of the witch's cottage, curled on his side. Billows of black smoke filled the cottage, making it difficult to breathe. Just ahead, he could see the prone form of his sister, Isabelle, one arm pinned beneath her unconscious body, the other stretched towards him.

After they had managed to shove the witch in her own oven, Ansel had collapsed. "Poison," he'd croaked to a stricken Isabelle, for the witch had told him the candy he'd eaten was a magical poison. It spread through his body like a thousand stabbing knives, twisting up his insides. Then a great, fiery explosion had issued from the oven, flames catching all over the cottage. As the fire spread, Isabelle had reached for him, trying to drag him from the cottage. But she'd collapsed, hacking in the smoke.

Now she lay unconscious, so near him. Ansel tried to reach for her. His fingers inched over the floor, reaching for his sister, scrab-

bling for her hand. It seemed so important that he take her hand in his. He didn't know why. So he could wake her, perhaps?

No. So they could die together.

His fingertips touched hers. But he couldn't reach any further.

As another wave of pain shattered through him, Ansel's eyes fluttered shut.

He was dead. He thought he was dead. He remembered a darkness so deep, blacker than the greatest depths of the sea, blacker than a new moon's night. And then...

He woke.

He opened his eyes. He was still in the witch's cottage, lying on the floor. But he lay on his back now, facing the ceiling. And the spasms of pain wracking his body were receding. Perhaps he was still dying, perhaps this was what it felt like, all the pain leaving him...but...smoke still clouded the room. Worse than ever. The pain was going, but Ansel was choking, choking on the smoke, just as Isabelle had—

And then, through the smoke, a hazy figure. A hazy face.

A familiar face.

"Ansel," whispered a voice. And Ansel knew the voice. It was the voice of someone dear to him, someone he feared he'd never see again.

Jesine.

"Ansel." Her words were pleading. "Come back to me, Ansel."

Ansel tried to speak, but his throat felt raw and swollen. He managed a cough, his head rolling from one shoulder to the other. He felt the touch of Jesine's hand upon his cheek, sweaty and shaking.

"You're going to be all right," she whispered. "I'll get you out—"

Ansel coughed again, trying to speak. Isabelle, *he wanted to say,* get Isabelle out first— *But the words wouldn't make it past his lips. And as his eyes stung and his chest burned, he saw one last thing before passing out again.*

A raven. Its black wings fluttering over Jesine's shoulder.

Then the darkness pulled him under again.

And when he woke for the second time, he was outside the smoldering cottage. Isabelle, coughing, sat by his side. And Jesine was gone.

Not that Ansel noticed. He never remembered her being there in the first place.

He never remembered the altercation between them and her father on the muddy bank of the creek.

He never remembered asking her to leave with him.

He never remembered the promise they made each other.

He never remembered her kiss on his cheek.

He never remembered confessing how he felt about her, that she was wonderful and good.

He never remembered feeling that way about her at all.

He remembered this: Isabelle, as clueless as he was as to how they'd escaped the cottage. When she'd woken outside, she thought she might've seen someone fleeing into the woods, vanishing into the darkness. But who it was, what they looked like, she couldn't say. Nor could she say how Ansel had survived the poison from the witch's candy. Perhaps, they'd theorized, that magic had died with her.

He remembered this: Isabelle crying because she'd thought Ansel was dead in the witch's cottage, taking him by both hands and imploring him to leave these woods with her. Because their father, she said, was not coming back. He'd never taken so long on a job before. And it wasn't safe anymore. They had to go.

He remembered this: Leaving Isabelle early the next morning, before they took to the road. Setting out with a nagging feeling in the back of his mind. Like he was supposed to do something. Like he was supposed to go somewhere. Like he was supposed to meet someone.

His feet took him, not to the meeting spot at the creek, but to that sun-dappled glade in the woods where he and Jesine had first played. Before they'd made a new meeting place, further from her father. Vaguely, he remembered running with her in that glade.

But she wasn't in the glade now. And there was no reason she should be, he mused, standing at the edge of the clearing. He'd made no plans to meet her. He would have remembered. Anyway, she was just some girl he'd run around with a bit. But he didn't know where she was now, and, well, no matter, really. This was why Ansel never made friends. He was always leaving, taking to the road.

There was no need to say goodbye. He never did.

So he left the glade. Went back to join Isabelle for a hasty break-fast. And then they'd set out together, heading east. Ready to make a new life. One without their father. Without anyone, just the two of them.

And that was all he remembered.

Until now.

Ansel gasped as the memories flooded through him. Did they come slowly, or all at once, sliding back into place? He could not say. He had no idea how long he slumped there, in the crumbling ruin of the witch's cottage, barely holding himself up. He had no idea how much time passed as he remembered *everything*.

Everything he had forgotten. About Jesine. About what they shared, about that summer. About how he'd felt for her.

How could he have forgotten?

It wasn't until the memories finally passed, settling into him—becoming a part of him—that the answer came.

How could he have forgotten? There was only one possible explanation.

Magic.

But what kind of magic? How? Had the poison from the witch's candy done permanent damage to him? No, that didn't make sense. Why would the witch's candy have robbed him of his memories of Jesine, *only* of Jesine? How could it have been so precise, to take memories of how he felt about her—but not every memory of her. He remembered meeting her, after all. He remembered spending time with her.

He just hadn't remembered what that time meant to him.

Ansel sank back onto his knees. The memories must have taken some time coming back, he realized, for it had grown dark out. Full dark. Dusk had come and gone, all while he'd been here, lost in his own memory. And Jesine—

Jesine was gone.

Panic rushed through Ansel, constricting his chest. Not just because it was dark, not just because he was worried about Jesine. But because of how close that memory was. Waking up outside the witch's cottage without her. He hadn't remembered how wrong that was then.

But he did now.

Ansel scrambled to his feet. His head rang as though he'd been dealt a blow. Another sliver of panic slipped through him when he turned and found himself amidst the ruins, caught in the clutches of the memory of that night. The witch. The candy. The fire.

Dying.

He had to get out of here, he had to get away. Ansel started to run, tripping through bramble and over upturned roots, but he didn't care. He just wanted to get away.

He wanted to find Jesine.

But he truly ran blindly. There wasn't much moonlight to see by; no doubt the clouds that had veiled the sky all day were still there, somewhere above the trees. Masking the moon and the stars. He should have looked for footprints, for traces of Jesine, before he'd started running, but now it was too late, and he had no idea which way she'd gone. And no lantern to lead him. Ansel peered up at the sky, looking for a sliver of moonlight. Enough to find a path, enough to—

The sound of hoofbeats interrupted his thoughts.

Ansel whirled around. The hoofbeats, he thought, were not particularly close, but he could hear them clearly. Honing in on the sound, he hurried through the brush, branches snagging on his clothing—

And for the second time that day, he stumbled out onto a road. The same road, he thought dimly, where he'd found Jesine earlier. Stones, that felt like a lifetime ago. But it couldn't have been much more than an hour past.

"Jesine!" he called, wondering if she'd come this way too. "Jes!"

In hindsight, perhaps he should have been more cautious. Perhaps he should have stayed quiet. Perhaps he should have wondered whom those hoofbeats belonged to. But despite how bereft he felt, Ansel was not afraid in that moment. It was dark, yes, but it wasn't late. It wasn't so strange to think people were still on the road at this hour.

So Ansel stood there, peering down the road, not as wary as he should have been. He glanced up at the sky as he took a step forward, trying to discern whether the road headed east or west this way. He took another step, and another—

And then he could not move at all.

At first, Ansel didn't understand what had happened. Even as primal fear stole over him, entangling his breath, he did not understand. It was as if his feet were stuck in boggy mud. But it wasn't just his legs, it was his arms too, rigid at his sides, it was his neck, taut and stiff, paralyzed—

Paralyzed.

Ansel's heart surged up his throat. He found his eyes could still move, and his gaze snagged on a small, smooth stone at the edge of the road. It was pale gray; if it had been any darker in color, he probably wouldn't have seen it.

He was caught in a hex-trap. But this one had not blinded him. This one had paralyzed him.

Ansel tried to breathe past the lump in his throat. A hex-trap. Which must have been set by a witch. Which meant there was a witch, here, somewhere close by. He thought of the hoofbeats on the road. That had probably been the witch in question, luring him to this spot.

His gaze darted left and right as far as he could see. There was no one, no one in his limited field of vision. But anything could be lurking beyond that, perhaps only paces away, in the thick of the woods—perhaps right here on the road, *right behind him—*

Because Ansel had not forgotten what happened the last time he'd been caught in a hex-trap.

He'd been left as perfect bait for Adela's "otherworldly friend."

The demon.

Ansel managed a breath through his nostrils, trying to think. The hex-marker, he just had to find the hex-marker. But immediately he realized how hopeless that was when he couldn't even move. He lowered his gaze as far as he could. The road in front of him was blanketed in a layer of pine needles. Aside from that, he didn't see much else, nothing that looked like a hex-marker...

A loud *snap* sounded out on the right, back in the woods.

"Hello?" Ansel tried to call. But he couldn't open his lips, so what came out was an unintelligible noise. A small, tinny sound in the darkness.

No one called back to him.

He tried to clench his fists, to wriggle a toe, anything, but he was stuck fast. All but his eyes. He tried to call out again, but he felt like a bleating goat, waiting to be slaughtered. He waited for someone to appear—*Jesine, are you still out there somewhere?* But all he heard was his own breath, loud in his ears.

There was no one out there. No one who would help him.

He was alone in the woods, paralyzed in the dark. Lost. Helpless.

And then, suddenly, a burst of wind. A sharp gust, cutting past him. But Ansel knew at once that this was no natural wind. This wind carried a particular stench. Sickeningly sweet, like the carcass of a rotted fruit.

The fear simmering in Ansel's gut burst into flame, setting his lungs on fire. He had caught that scent before. In the cottage, where they'd found the gutted corpse of that woman.

The demon.

Another gust of air zipped past him.

And before Ansel could react, a searing pain exploded across his middle.

It was a weird sensation. Pain without form, hot and then cold and then *burning* hot. For a few seconds, Ansel was too stunned to realize he'd been hurt. Then he felt cold air upon his skin, and he realized his coat and shirt had been torn, and a second after that, the *pain*—stones, it hurt—and his exposed skin was not cold anymore, but warm. Warm and wet.

He was bleeding.

Ansel's breath came short. A wordless whimper escaped his lips. He was on his own, and he had no way to fight this thing, no way at all—

And then, Ansel's legs were knocked out from beneath him. With no way to brace himself, he landed with a bruising *thump*, flat on his back, one arm twisted beneath him. His head banged into the paved road so hard, his neck gave a sharp jolt. For a moment, Ansel saw stars, the pain and trauma stealing his vision. He still couldn't move, lying there, and now he couldn't breathe, his lungs spasming as they sought air—

Slowly, his vision returned, everything coming into focus. The knotted tree branches, twined together above him, hanging over the road. Glimpses of cloudy night sky between them.

Then something else slid into his line of sight.

A face, stark in the jet-black darkness.

A ghastly, bone-white, mask-like face.

Ansel felt like he had the night of the fire. When the witch's poison stole through him, twisting his insides. Only this time, it was his own fear, tearing him apart. It was a thing too big for his body, and it scrabbled at him, trying to rip free—

And then, pain. Pain rending his flesh.

But it wasn't the fear ripping through him.

It was the demon, burrowing long, slender fingers into his middle. Cleaving him in two.

Ansel couldn't open his mouth to scream. But one issued forth from his clamped lips anyway. A thin, agonizing scream, slicing through the night.

18

BEWITCHED

JESINE RAN UNTIL SHE didn't know where she was. Dusk had fallen. Night reigned over the woods, and she'd dropped her lantern on the road when the blood-rain had started. She ran without thought, not in any particular direction. She had no idea where she was. She didn't care.

Something flew at her in the darkness, flapping wings blinding her.

Jesine's cry was a wordless puff of air, and she raised her hands to protect her face, to smack the creature away. Her first thought was of bats, remembering the attack on Lise. But then she realized the wings brushing against her neck were not leathery, but feathered.

"Bastian!" A raven, not a bat. Bastian, her brother. He arced over her head, then wheeled about, screeching and coming at her face again. Jesine couldn't help it; she batted him away. "Stop! What are you doing?"

The raven cawed and flapped his wings in agitation, flying round and round above her head.

"What's wrong?" Jesine demanded.

The raven screeched again, landing on her shoulder. His talons dug painfully into her, stabbing through her coat, and then he pushed off, soaring away to land on a tree branch. Not the way she'd been going, but in the opposite direction. Jesine lifted her eyes to the sky, trying to get her bearings. North and west. That was the direction Bastian flew.

"You want me to follow you?" she asked.

In answer, Bastian soared onto another tree in the same direction. Any further and he would be beyond her line of sight. Jesine followed. The raven swooped and soared from tree to tree, leading her back through the woods. Much as he had probably done earlier today when he'd led Ansel to her.

Ansel.

Dread coiled around Jesine's heart like a serpent. She'd left him alone in the forest, and now it was dark out, black as pitch. Why, oh why had she run like that? Her feelings had overrun her, sent her fleeing like a frightened animal. Where was Ansel now? What if something had happened to him?

Jesine quickened her pace, stumbling over shallow roots. Bastian, too, flew more quickly, as though he knew of some danger. After a few minutes, Jesine realized he was leading her towards the main road. If he didn't change direction, if he didn't stop, they were going to hit it any minute now—

The raven let out a cry and swooped out of sight. Jesine darted after him and emerged from the trees out onto the paved, open road. She stifled a curse as she tripped over something hard, something that clattered and rolled in the road. She glanced down.

It was, amazingly, her lantern. The one she'd dropped earlier. Jesine bent to retrieve it. Part of the glass casing had shattered, and the gear-bulb within had come a bit loose, but when she wound it up, it flickered on, perhaps a little less brightly than it should have. Wrapping her fingers around the cast-iron handle, Jesine straightened, looking around.

"Bastian?" She didn't see the raven anywhere. "Bastian, where are you?"

The raven called no answer. Jesine stared down the long, dark road, but it was deserted. The shadows seemed to swallow it whole in the distance, like a pathway to some netherworld. The night had turned silent, even the wind dying down, and Jesine lifted her lantern as though its light could pierce the silence. But all she saw was a misty layer of thin fog, coalescing over the road as the night grew damp and chilly.

Heart racing, she turned to peer in the other direction. South-ward, the way that lead into Lise. It seemed even darker that way, the wood lining the road thick with pines, shading out the moon's dampened light. Jesine raised her lantern higher, the weak gear-bulb casting a fuzzy glimmer before her—

A dark lump lay in the road, motionless.

Jesine dashed forward. Long before she was close enough to make out any distinguishing features, she knew what she would find. She knew who it was.

Ansel.

He lay half on his back, half on his side, one arm thrown over his face and the other crumpled beneath him. He was uncon-scious, his eyes closed as though in sleep. But in the dim light of her lantern, something slick glinted over his torso, coating his shredded coat.

Blood. A lot of it.

Jesine glanced up, swinging her gaze left and right until she saw Bastian perched on a branch nearby, ruffling his feathers as he stalked up and down. "Bastian, what did this? What happened to him?"

Bastian squawked dolefully.

Fear stole through Jesine like a thief in the night. She remembered what Ansel had told her, the warning he'd given her. *They have some kind of fell creature working for them—some call it a demon. It kills quite gruesomely.*

Was that what had done this? What had attacked him? But why hadn't it killed him?

She caught a whiff of something sooty, something that brought to mind ashes and smoke. It took her a few moments to locate the source, lying in the pine needles just off the road. The charred, smoldering remains of something small. Jesine snatched at it, then dropped it almost just as fast. The remains were still hot enough to sting her fingers. But in the split-second she held it, she recognized the remains. It was a human bone, tiny and blackened. Likely a baby's bone, a finger or something similar.

A hex-marker. Only, someone had already destroyed it. And set Ansel free from whatever hex he'd been trapped in.

Jesine shot Bastian another look. "Have you seen anyone else nearby?"

The raven only cocked a questioning eye at her.

Frustrated, Jesine turned back to Ansel. Someone had burnt the hex-marker, but whatever had happened to Ansel had done plenty damage. Jesine tried not to look too closely at him because she knew the panic simmering in her gut would bubble over and incapacitate her. She distracted herself by feeling for his pulse, making sure he was still alive. Then she rose to her feet, looking up and down the road.

Her house was not far, but she despaired at the thought of getting him there on her own. Jesine hurried behind him and bent over, getting her arms under his, but she could barely lift his torso on her own. There would be no carrying him to her house, she realized helplessly. She would have to use her magic—she would have to hope she had enough.

Closing her eyes, she reached for that delicate chain inside her. It seemed more fragile than ever, and Jesine trembled as she felt along the length of that chain, reaching for magic from the other end.

She needn't have worried. It came easily, flowing along the chain. Jesine let out a breath. Stretching her arms out, she directed the magic towards Ansel.

And he rose slowly from the ground, hovering in the air.

Maintaining the levitation spell was tricky as she navigated the woods. It took all Jesine's concentration to wind a clear path through the trees, to keep Ansel from bumping into anything in the darkness. It took even more of her concentration to keep herself steady. Even tripping over one stone or root might have broken her focus long enough to drop Ansel to the ground.

Luckily, Jesine's house was less than a mile from the road. Still, by the time it came into sight, fatigue tugged at her, and she swayed as she mounted the steps of her porch, Ansel floating eerily before her.

Once they were inside, Jesine continued up to her loft, Ansel still drifting before her. The steps were even more cumbersome than the woods; the staircase running along the wall was narrow, and Jesine had to turn Ansel several times to keep from knocking his head against the wall.

She didn't release her spell until Ansel was gently laid upon her bed. When she let the magic go, she nearly collapsed, her knees buckling as her energy drained out of her, leaving her as boneless as an earthworm. But she couldn't rest yet. Jesine switched on the gear-bulb lamp at her bedside table and bent to see to Ansel.

He really did look awful. Dried blood from the rain crusted his clothes and coated his head, and raised welts marked his face where he'd been burned. But more concerning, he was still unconscious. His face was as gray as cold ash, but he didn't feel cold. His forehead burned, shining with sweat. She took his hand and squeezed it, hoping he might stir. But he didn't wake, didn't move.

Jesine dropped her head into her hands, flinching as her fingers made contact with the tender welts left by the blood-rain. Then she raised her head, pushing her bloody hair back from her face. With it, she pushed back the tide of distress and dismay threatening to overtake her, and then she got to work. She removed Ansel's coat, rolling him from one side to the other to get it off him. Then she peeled his tattered shirt away, cringing where it stuck to his wounds. She cut the rest of the shirt away, leaving him bare-chested.

He'd been gouged by something, that was clear. Large puncture wounds marred his torso, just below his breastbone. Jesine shuddered at the sight. She placed her hands on either side of the ugly wounds, laying her palms flat over the planes of his ribcage. She could just barely feel the labor of his breaths, in and out, in and out.

One of the reasons she hadn't wanted to use magic to bring him here was because she knew she needed to save it for this. For healing him. Closing her eyes, she reached again for that delicate silver chain.

Come on, she begged, *please, please, just a little more—*

It came in a trickle, but it came. She called for magic, and magic was returned to her, flowing along the chain. Power flooded through her, and she directed it all into Ansel, stitching his insides, staunching the blood flow, patching up his skin. When it was over, the exhaustion that swept over her was like a ton of bricks, piled high upon her shoulders. She slouched over Ansel, bowing her head into his shoulder. His skin was still warm beneath her, his body shifting slowly with each breath he took.

Jesine longed to remain there with him. But there was still work to be done. She longed for a bath to wash the blood from her, but she didn't have the energy for that. Instead, she scrubbed her hands clean over the basin in the washroom, trying to get every fleck of blood out of the cracks in her palms. Then she took a wet cloth to her face and used a pitcher to rinse her hair. Lastly, she stripped out of her bloodstained clothes and changed into a fresh shift.

Then she returned to Ansel. She took a damp cloth to his hands and face too, and to his hair. There wasn't really anything she could do for his trousers, she thought. Her cheeks burned at the thought of removing them. But they were not too grimy; his coat had sopped up most of the blood. He was fine for now. Wearily, she adjusted the lumpy pillow beneath his head, then pulled up the extra quilt, laying it over him.

There was nothing else she could do. As Jesine let herself relax for the first time that night, another wave of exhaustion washed over her, pulling her down. She sank onto the bed beside Ansel, her limbs weak and unsteady. *I shouldn't sleep here*, she thought, *not so close to him*. But it was so easy to just sag into the mattress and pillow her head against his shoulder. It was so easy to wrap her arms around his, entwining them together. Ansel's skin felt less clammy to the touch now, his breathing deep and even.

It was so easy. So familiar. Just the two of them together, like they had been all those years ago. When they were children.

That was the danger of it. It was so easy to slip back into old ways with him. Like they had never been parted. Like they'd been together all this time.

But if she'd done the spell right and restored his memories, then it might not be easy at all.

And it was still dangerous. For him. Jesine slid her gaze down, opening her hand to look at the black splotch there. When she'd scrubbed the blood off her palms earlier, the mark had remained, a permanent stain. A reminder of the danger she represented.

Beside her, Ansel let out a soft exhale. As though he knew she was there beside him and took comfort in her.

Jesine allowed herself to forget the danger. She closed her eyes and gave into sleep.

***

When Jesine woke hours later, she woke in complete darkness.

She wasn't sure, at first, what had woken her. She wasn't even sure where she was. It felt like her bed, Jesine thought, the thin, well-worn mattress, the soft, scratchy quilt. But it was completely dark, and the air briskly cold. Her toes felt frozen.

And there was something different. Something wrong...

Ansel. Of course. Asleep in the bed beside her. That was why her pillow felt so warm and oddly shaped. It was Ansel. But also...

She'd left the candles burning. Two candles, one on her bedside table and the other on the bookshelf by the stairs. They had both burned out. But they were new candles, only just lit; they shouldn't have burned out completely. Not unless they'd slept until morning, and they couldn't have. It wouldn't be so dark in here.

Jesine lay very still.

Something was wrong.

The gear-bulb lamp on her bedside table. She just needed to reach over, she told herself, and wind it on.

But she was afraid to move. She lay in the darkness, and she listened.

There was a strange sound. A sort of...*scritch-scritch*. A soft, shuffling noise. So soft, she probably wouldn't have heard it had it not been the dead of night, when everything else was quiet and still.

Jesine let out a slow, silent breath through her nostrils.

Turn on the light, she told herself. *Just turn on the light.*

Nearly shaking—afraid what she might touch in the darkness—Jesine groped for her bedside table. Her fingers found the gear-bulb lamp and quested alongside it until she felt the knob to wind it up.

The light flickered on. A bright, pulsing white light.

At first, nothing seemed amiss. The lamplight filled her bedroom loft, but there was nothing there. Everything was as it should be. Ansel lay beside her, eyes shut, still breathing deeply in sleep.

She could still hear that sound. That soft shuffling. That dreadful *scritch-scritch*.

Slowly—stomach clenched tight—Jesine sat up.

Something was moving along the floor.

Jesine leaned forward to get a better look. When she still couldn't see properly, she inched all the way to the foot of her bed and leaned out to look.

The floor of the loft was covered in spiders.

Jesine caught her breath. She was not afraid of spiders, but there were *hundreds* of them, perhaps thousands. They were small, but they completely covered the floor, their long, thin legs skittering over the wooden boards, slipping beneath them, creeping over each other.

Jesine forced herself to breathe, trying to reason her way out of the fear that had come over her. *Another hex*, she told herself, *like the blood-rain, like the bats*—it had to be another hex. And like the blood-rain and the bats, it would burn itself out. The spiders would disappear—

But when Jesine forced herself to release another breath, it misted the air before her. The loft plunged into an icy cold as glacial as a frozen lake. The unnatural cold settled around her, solidifying in the air.

And Jesine's heart froze inside her chest.

No, she thought, *no, not again...not here, not now...*

Without thinking, she reached for Ansel. Her fingers closed around his arm in a reassuring grip, though she didn't know if she was reassuring him or herself. She waited for the darkness to appear, swooping over her like a cloak or choking her from the inside.

But the darkness did not appear. The gear-bulb lamp flickered and sputtered, threatening to go out, but it did not. It faded, the light dimming. But it stayed on.

Before Jesine could take comfort in this, a deep rumbling built through the loft, like thunder closing in around them.

No, Jesine thought, squeezing her eyes shut, *no, no, no—*

The rumbling formed words, the voice of the darkness filling the loft.

Jesine...

Terrified, Jesine peeked one eye open. She could still see her breaths misting the gelid air. The lamplight flickered again, threatening to go out.

But still, the darkness did not appear.

Jesine...you...are...MINE.

Jesine still clutched Ansel's arm. Perhaps he gave her strength, she thought. It was ridiculous, romantic, but the idea lent her some hope. Hope that she could fight back.

She would not let the darkness reach Ansel.

"I am not yours." Jesine spoke in a harsh whisper.

The rumbling intensified, blocking out all sound. Jesine could no longer hear the shuffling of the spiders, nor Ansel's sleeping breaths. She couldn't even hear her own breath. The rumbling encased Jesine, taking hold of her. Taking her for itself.

I will have you, my child...

The voice filled her. So potent, so powerful, like the force of it would shatter her bones. Jesine fought for her own voice. She fought to speak. But her blood pumped in her body, and it was for him. Air filled her lungs, yet it was for him. She could not move. She could not speak.

But her hand was still wrapped around Ansel's arm. His skin was warm to the touch.

"I—will—never—be—*yours!*"

The words tore from Jesine's lips, and with it, she expelled the voice, *his* voice, from her body. Exhausted, she collapsed onto the bed beside Ansel. She had wrested back control of herself, but the dark presence wasn't gone. She sensed it still in the loft, lingering in the air. Lurking. Waiting.

Jesine trembled from head to toe. She clung to Ansel, pressing her face into his shoulder. Breathing him in.

Then a long, unsettling *hissss* cut through the shuffling of the spiders. Jesine lifted her head.

A slender black snake slithered up her bed. It coiled around a bedpost until its flat-nosed head appeared over the mattress at the foot of the bed. Jesine watched, holding her breath, as the serpent's forked tongue darted out from between its teeth, emitting another sharp *hiss.*

Jesine didn't dare move. She was afraid if she did, the serpent would strike. At her. At Ansel. So she lay very still, her jaw clamped shut, clasping Ansel by the arm. She didn't even lift her head as she watched the black serpent slither onto the bed. She stifled a flinch as its scaled, reptilian body brushed the side of her calf. It slid alongside her, up her body, raising its head, rearing back—

A loud *bang* sounded out from somewhere in the house, somewhere below. Jesine heard shouts. Footsteps pounded up the stairs.

The serpent hissed again, turning away from Jesine. To face the group of people suddenly gathered at the top of the stairs.

The serpent hissed at the intruders.

Then the lamplight went out, and the room fell into darkness.

19

Corrupted

J ESINE HELD HER BREATH in the darkness, squeezing Ansel's arm tighter than ever. Somewhere in the room, someone cursed. Another voice emitted a high-pitched yelp, followed by a scuffling sound. Someone else groaned, and then—

Light. A bright orb of light appeared, hovering above cupped hands. By the orb's light, Jesine identified Castel, one of the witches she'd spied on a few nights ago. The light was just large enough to show his face, but not large enough to penetrate the shadows in the furthest corners of the room. But Castel held his arm out, and the light flitted away from him. It sank into the gear-bulb lamp at Jesine's bedside, long enough to light the bulb. Then it flitted to the candle beside it and touched the wick, and a flickering flame flared to life. The orb flew across the room, lit the second candle on the bookshelf, and then winked out.

In the silence that followed, Prince Garrett spoke first. "Pretty." He stood at the top of the staircase beside Castel.

"Why, thank you." Castel gave him a breezy smile. "I can do some nice things with my magic. Without, you know, losing years off my life."

"Or messing up your hair," Demetri said acidly. Demetri, Jesine noticed, stood on her small, wobbling chair in the corner of the loft.

Castel gave Demetri a quizzical look. "What are you doing?"

"I don't like spiders," Demetri muttered.

"They can't really hurt you."

"We've seen things," said the short girl beside Demetri. Jesine had met her briefly before; her name was Sabine.

Gingerly, Demetri stepped down from the chair, and it was only then Jesine realized the spiders had vanished as though they'd never been there. The serpent, too, was gone.

"What the hell is going on?" a mumbling voice groused.

Jesine flinched, dropping Ansel's arm as though it had burned her. She hadn't even noticed him stirring, no doubt roused by the commotion. His eyes were groggy as he sat up, his mouth turned down in a grumpy scowl. He was still shirtless, of course, and Jesine herself wore only a shift. She felt her cheeks warm, realizing how compromising this looked.

Perhaps Prince Garrett thought so too, for he did not quite look at her as he said, in answer to Ansel's question, "Well, I'm not sure. You seem to have slept through all the excitement though."

Demetri added, "There were spiders. All over the floor. And a snake."

"And did anyone else feel how cold it was?" Sabine asked.

"I was a little distracted by the way the entire house was shaking," said Prince Garrett. "Another hex, I take it."

Jesine's stomach flipped uncomfortably. She squeezed her hand shut so tightly, her nails bit into the soft flesh of her marked palm.

"Jesine," said Prince Garrett. "Are you all right?"

Jesine gave a sharp nod. She really should cover herself, she thought, but the thought of reaching for the quilt covering Ansel and pulling it over—the thought of *sharing* it with him before all these people—was mortifying. She couldn't even look at Ansel, though they were mere inches apart. She hadn't looked at him once since he woke.

So instead, she stood and reached for her wool dressing gown, hanging in the back corner. Once she'd pulled it on, securing it at her waist, she turned back. She darted a quick look at the bed and immediately regretted it when she found Ansel's eyes on her. The look on his face was wary. Conflicted. Tangled with a million different emotions.

Jesine turned away, folding her arms across her chest.

"All right, Castel." This came from Demetri, who still eyed the floor apprehensively. As though he expected the horde of spiders to reappear any minute. "I think it's high time you explain what's going on."

"I thought I already did."

"You said Ansel was in danger," Garrett said mildly. "From the demon. Not from spiders and snakes."

"The demon." Ansel's hand flew to his bare chest. He winced, caving in on himself, but when he looked down, his eyes went wide. As though he couldn't believe what he was seeing. "How..." His gaze traveled over to Jesine. She tried not to cower beneath that gaze—*oh, stars, stars, what does he remember?* she thought wildly—but she tightened her arms around herself.

"Did you...?" Ansel asked.

Jesine nodded mutely.

Prince Garrett cleared his throat. "Ansel? What's wrong?"

"Nothing. That is, not anymore. I suppose." Ansel ran another hand over his face. "I was attacked by the demon. In the woods. I got stuck in a hex-trap—"

"Another one?" Sabine asked, holstering her pistol.

"A hex-trap." Demetri eyed Castel pointedly. "I wonder who might've left that lying around."

Castel looked unimpressed by Demetri's hostile tone. He flicked something miniscule off the cuff of his overcoat. "Well, it obviously wasn't me. I was with you two. What, am I meant to be keeper for every witch around here?"

"When you're working with them? Yes."

"I was paralyzed," Ansel muttered. "I couldn't move. And there was no one around. And then..." He swallowed visibly. "The demon came. The pain was like—I thought I was dead." He shot Jesine a quick glance. "But Jesine must have healed me."

"Yes," Jesine said. It was the first word she'd spoken, she realized, since everyone had arrived.

"It's just a little sore." Ansel rubbed a tender hand over his ribcage.

"Fantastic," Castel remarked, sounding remarkably bored. "Perhaps you could put a shirt on, then, because this is all awkward enough as it is."

Ansel glowered at him. Then he turned his glare on Prince Garrett and Demetri. "This is another one of the witches? A bad witch?"

"Ansel, Castel," Demetri said tersely. "Castel, Ansel."

"Demetri's met him before," Garrett added.

"So, what exactly are you doing with him?" Ansel demanded.

"We ran into him in Ingsberg," Garrett said with an apologetic air.

"And? You invited him home for tea?"

"Don't be silly," Castel blustered. "It's far too late for tea. Wouldn't say no to a brandy, though."

"He said you were in danger." Demetri joined Ansel in glaring at Castel, turning to face the witch head-on. "He said we were wrong thinking Delphine is the one to worry about."

Ansel looked nonplussed. "If not Delphine, then who?"

"Harper," Castel answered.

"Apparently, he really wants you dead," Prince Garrett added.

"He's the brother of the witch you and your sister killed," Demetri explained.

Jesine felt as though someone had dumped a bucket of water over her head. Cold shock washed over her, dripping down her sides. *Harper. The brother of Henrietta.* How had she never known this? But though Harper had often spoken of his family, he'd never named them.

Ansel gawked at Demetri and Garrett. "The brother...Harper is Henrietta's *brother?*"

Castel gave a huge sigh. "Yes. He's her brother. What's so difficult to comprehend?"

"Nothing." Ansel tugged the shabby quilt up over his lap, then slung his arms over his knees. "In fact, it makes a weird kind of sense. Given everything he said..." His brow furrowed. "But if he wants me dead, he's had plenty opportunity. What is he waiting for?"

"All I know is, he wants revenge, and that's why he agreed to help free Delphine in the first place." Castel shook his head as he began to remove his overcoat, shrugging his arms free of it. "That man talks a good game, all charming smiles and easy laughs—rather attractive too, I must say—but beneath it all, he is dead inside." He lay his coat over the foot of Jesine's bed and flicked a glance in Ansel's direction. "Except when it comes to you, dear hunter. On the subject of you, he comes alive."

"He said something weird, though," Ansel murmured. "Like—that he wouldn't have to do anything. That he could just sit back and watch..." He trailed off, twisting around to look at Jesine. Jesine forced herself not to look away. But when he met her gaze, Ansel's expression shuttered. As though the sight of her reminded him of something unpleasant.

Like the fact that his memories had been stolen from him. And it was all her fault. Jesine felt her heart constrict.

"So what about these hexes, then?" Demetri pressed.

Castel turned a puzzled look on him. "Pardon?"

"The burning man." Sabine, leaning back against the staircase railing, straightened, folding her arms across her chest. "The snakes, the spiders, the bats. What are they all for?"

Castel looked even more mystified. "Still not following."

"The winter solstice?" Prince Garrett prompted. "Aren't you lot planning to use it for something nefarious? To get more power, or—isn't that what the hexes have been for, seven of them, or twelve or whatever..."

"Is that what you all think?" Castel snorted, slouching back into the corner. "The hexes were just to lure you here. We figured between the demon and Adela, it would get you here, princeling. And you too." He spared a nod for Ansel.

"And the blood-rain?" Ansel asked.

"The what?"

243

"It rained blood on us!" Ansel gestured between him and Jesine. "Blood! And it burned!"

Castel looked vaguely impressed. "I don't know anything about that. But I'm guessing it was either Harper's or Adela's doing. Adela certainly has been getting impatient for some retribution." When Ansel continued to stare at him suspiciously, Castel went on, "Don't you understand? There is no grand plan. No plans to grab power or take over the world. Delphine is just here for revenge. Harper and Adela too." He tipped his head at Demetri. "The others think I'm here for revenge on you. Of course, if any of them knew what a lunatic Sohalia became in the end, they'd realize they were wrong. I'm well rid of her. Thanks for that."

"I need a drink," Demetri muttered.

"See, it's not just me." Still leaning into the wall, Castel turned on his heel, giving Jesine a winning smile. "I don't suppose you keep any liquor in the house, do you, darling?"

"Don't talk to her," Ansel growled.

Castel looked quite amused. "Because she can't handle me talking to her? I've a feeling she's made of sterner stuff than you are. Anyway, I need to talk to her. That's why I'm here."

Jesine blinked. This witch, Castel, wanted to talk to *her*?

"Why?" Prince Garrett asked bluntly.

Castel said, "Because I want to help her."

"Why?" Garrett repeated.

"Yes," Demetri said in an accusing tone. "She's a good witch, isn't she? Doesn't that make her, I don't know, your mortal enemy or something?"

"Goodness. Mortal enemy." Castel rolled his eyes. "The way you lot think." He stood up straight and leveled a very direct gaze at Demetri. "I want to help Jesine for the same reason I wanted to help Perpetua."

Demetri sucked in a breath, looking stricken.

"Who's Perpetua?" asked Ansel.

Castel ignored him. "I have reason to believe Jesine is in danger. I have reason to believe someone wishes to manipulate her." He took a deep breath. "We witches all have a choice, one way or another. But it should be our choice and no one else's. So. Jesine." Castel turned to face her, steepling his fingers together. "What do you say? Shall we have a private chat, you and I?"

———◆○◆———

Jesine set her lantern down on an old pinewood trunk as Castel entered the dim attic behind her. The attic was the only room in the house with a proper door that could be shut, which accounted for the stale, dusty smell and frigid chill. Once, it had been Jesine's bedroom. *No*, she thought, her eyes sweeping over the cobwebs in the corners, the long shadows cast by the light of her lantern. *It was mine and Bastian's.*

But ever since Jesine had returned to the house—since her father's death—she'd taken his old space in the loft, leaving the attic abandoned. It was filled with her father's old things. Ancient trunks littered the floor and rickety wooden shelves lined the walls, all full of old books, magical artifacts, and even some of her father's clothes. Castel ran a critical eye over the room, from the hexagonal window in the far wall to the low eaves and grimy floorboards, coated with years of dust. "Charming," he remarked.

Jesine eyed him flatly. She hadn't brought him up here so he could insult her, standing there in his fine, stylish clothes. He wore tailored trousers and a double-breasted waistcoat, not to mention square-toed shoes so polished, they gleamed.

Castel flashed her a careless smile. "Don't mind me, love. I grew up a pampered little rich boy. I suppose I'm still spoiled, all these years later."

Jesine eyed him some more, wondering just how many years he was talking about.

"So." Stepping further into the room, out from beneath the low curve of the eaves, Castel clapped his hands together. "Jesine. I think we both know that what happened down there—the spiders, the serpent—was no hex."

Jesine took a step back. Castel had to know about the mark on her palm, didn't he? And how it was connected to the darkness? But Jesine was not as sure as she might have been before. It seemed these witches had come together out of convenience, not because they were united in any common goal. So why had the golden-haired witch—Malina—marked her as she did? And what she'd said—*it's not time for you yet*—what had that meant?

Perhaps Castel knew.

But she said none of this aloud. She didn't know what Castel wanted with her yet. She didn't know if she could trust him, no matter how he claimed to want to help her.

If Castel was unnerved by her lack of response, he didn't show it. "Harper told me you were a woman of few words. Honestly, I like that in a person. The world is too full of people who love the sound of their own voice."

Jesine could not keep quiet at that. "You don't say?"

Castel tipped his head as though to acknowledge a point to her. "Look, everything I said down there to the wonder brigade was true. The witches here all came for revenge, nothing more. Unfortunately—" He eased himself onto the edge of a wooden stool "—since she arrived here, Delphine has taken another interest. In you."

"Delphine? The queen? The one you all summoned?"

"Yes. Sorry about that, by the way. I never dreamed she would catch you spying on us. That's not supposed to be possible."

Jesine frowned down at the floor. Delphine was interested in her? Not Malina? Unless they were working together—but Malina had marked her before they'd summoned Delphine. And Castel had just said...

Jesine snapped her head up, his words sinking in. *I never dreamed she would catch you spying on us.* "It was you. That sent me the note, the eavesdropping spell."

Castel spread his hands. "Yes, that was me. See, unlike Delphine, I'd heard of you. Not you specifically, but I knew there'd always been a family of good witches in this area. I thought it best you were kept apprised of what was going on." Dropping his gaze, he tugged at the sleeve of his sack coat. "But once Delphine found you out—and learned more of your history from Harper—she became very interested in you."

"But why?"

"There's an old story among witches," said Castel. "Honestly, I always thought it a silly bedtime story. But the way it goes is, if a bad witch can steal the soul of a good witch, she can bargain for all sorts of things. More power, more youth—or even a way out of her deal. A way to escape the eternal torment that awaits us in death."

A chill took hold of Jesine. *Steal the soul of a good witch.* "You mean...what, turn a good witch bad?"

"Essentially." Castel's careless tone was gone. His dark eyes were uncanny in the glow of the gear-bulb lantern, reflecting the light back at her.

"But I'm already a good witch." Jesine couldn't suppress the desperate catch in her voice. A part of her was inclined to agree with Castel that this was nothing more than a silly story. But if it wasn't... "I have a fairy familiar. How could anyone turn me bad?"

"I really couldn't tell you, love," Castel admitted. "From the little I've gathered, there's some kind of ritual. The point is, whatever Delphine means to do, she will do it soon. Before the week is out. So I wanted to warn you, Jesine. Because I think she will come for you." He pointed a finger at the ceiling and twirled it around. "I suggest strengthening your wards on the house. You might have noticed they didn't keep me out."

Jesine blinked, startled. She hadn't even thought about her protective wards, or how Castel had gotten past them.

"Quite a clever little spell," Castel noted. "Confuses the hell out of the locals, I'm sure. So they can't find your house on their own? Unfortunately, it's not powerful enough to keep out a witch. I'd recommend strengthening the spell."

Jesine ran her tongue over her lips. She could worry about her wards tomorrow. "I just don't see how she could force me to turn bad. From what I've always been told, there must be a choice."

"Look," said Castel. "There is a reason Delphine thinks you a particularly good target. Not just because you're a good witch—which is rare enough—but because of your history."

Jesine gazed back at him. That was the second time he'd mentioned her "history." History learned from Harper, no doubt. Which meant...

"You've tasted darkness, Jesine." Castel dropped his hands into his lap. "Quite literally."

Jesine flinched.

"And that darkness still has a hold on you. It calls to you. Haunts you. That's what really happened down in your loft, isn't it?" He paused, then added, "I didn't know if your friends down there knew. That's why I asked for privacy."

Jesine dropped her gaze. "Ansel knows some of it. But not everything." After a moment, she seated herself on the trunk before her. "There's always been this...presence. Just a feeling, really. The feeling of being watched. Sometimes, I heard things. Voices." She chanced a quick glance at Castel. "*His* voice."

Now Castel was the one who flinched. That surprised Jesine, though perhaps it shouldn't have. Not if he knew what she was talking about. But when he spoke, Castel's voice was very level. "And does this presence make you do things?"

"It hasn't so far. But it feels like it could. Like it wants to. It's been happening more often lately. More intensely. It's not just a feeling, but...a coldness. When it comes to me, I am covered in darkness. It takes a hold of me. As though I don't have control over my own body."

"And when did this start? This darkness?"

Jesine began tracing designs into the thick layer of dust on the trunk. Creating whorls and spirals, a veritable mural. Then she took a deep breath, lifted her hand, and held it palm-up. "Since the night of the bat attacks. Since that witch Malina marked me."

Castel stared at the dark blotch on her palm for a long, long moment without saying anything. Jesine watched his face very closely for a reaction, but there was none.

Finally, he said, "I didn't know about this." It was said quietly, almost more to himself than to her.

"You don't know what it is?" Jesine pressed him. "What it means?"

"Not exactly," Castel said, "though I can guess. I think that—whatever it is—that mark has opened the door further. Made you more susceptible to this presence."

"I don't understand."

Castel slipped off the stool and dropped to his feet. "Your situation is rather unique, Jesine. So this is all speculation. But I think, when you drank fairy blood six years ago, you opened a door. Between you. And the darkness." His eyes narrowed. "Perhaps that door would have closed if you had continued your life as any other mortal. But instead, you became a good witch from a long line of witches. Your link to magic also links you to the land in ways other humans are not.

"That's why I wanted to warn you, love. Because I never credited this story, I never thought it possible to turn a good witch bad. But Delphine—and maybe Malina—" Castel grimaced "—seem to know more than I do."

He turned away then, as though to leave. Jesine rose to her feet. She still had so many questions. What should she do, how could she stop Delphine, wasn't there anything he could do to help?

But she kept those questions to herself. She sensed Castel had said all he would. He didn't seem a bad sort, but he *was* a bad witch. That meant there was only so much he could do to help, even if he cared to. And she had no reason to think he cared to.

But there was one question she had to ask. "Castel," she said, her lips forming his name uncertainly, "before—I was out at the cottage where that woman was killed. I was there with Ansel, and Harper turned up. And then the darkness appeared."

Castel turned to face her. "And?"

"It spoke to me as usual," she said, "but it also spoke to Ansel. Well, he said he heard a voice calling to him. But how could that be? How could *he* have a hold on Ansel?"

"I don't think it could, unless Ansel's been dabbling in the dark arts," Castel drawled. "Which seems unlikely." He seemed to think it over. "Perhaps, in that moment, the darkness was able to reach Ansel through you."

Jesine shivered. She had feared as much. But— "Earlier. Down in the loft, before you all turned up. It almost felt like Ansel—his presence—helped keep the darkness away. Kept it from manifesting fully."

Castel shrugged. "Maybe he did, love. The darkness isn't the only one who has a hold on you, after all." His eyes took on a strange, distant cast. "Maybe that can help you, in the end. Against Delphine."

And with that enigmatic answer, he was gone.

20

REFUGE

J ESINE'S HOUSE DIDN'T HAVE much space for guests, but she did her best to accommodate Prince Garrett, Demetri, and Sabine for the night, as it was far too late for them to safely head back to Lise. Castel left, of course, but then, he had nothing to fear from the demon. Since he was the one who'd summoned it.

So Demetri and Prince Garrett slept down in her sitting space, and Sabine in the alcove behind the hearth. Ansel remained in her loft. Jesine slept upstairs in the attic, in her childhood cot bed. Or at least, she was meant to sleep. Instead she lay awake, fitful and restless, watching her candle cast dancing shadows across the wooden beams on the ceiling.

She finally knew more about what was happening to her. What Malina had done to her. What the darkness wanted with her. But Castel's warning had been far from reassuring. *She will come for you*, he'd said. Delphine. Before the week was out.

But he'd said nothing about what she could do. How she could stop Delphine. How she could escape the darkness.

If she could escape the darkness.

Jesine's stomach churned, a cold clamminess settling over her. She'd opened a door, Castel said, between her and the darkness. She'd let him in.

What she'd told Ansel was right. What her father had always said about her was right.

She was tainted. Weak. Wrong.

Holding her arm up before her, she stared at the black mark on her palm. She felt suddenly that it was something dirty, but not something Malina had sullied her with. Rather, it was something that had already been inside her. A stain on her soul that Malina had pulled forth, making it visible. She remembered the way the darkness had manifested in the glade. The way it had poured from inside her. Shuddering, she dropped her arm to her side.

She had to do something. She couldn't just lie here worrying. She couldn't just wait for Delphine to come take her. She needed to find out more about this. Find out if there was a way to stop it.

So she scrambled out of her cot, pulling her dressing gown back on. It was still freezing in the attic, her tallow candles, spaced out around her, the only warmth she had. Shivering, she popped open the brass latch on one of her father's old trunks and began sifting through it. Jesine piled a stack of thick, ancient books beside her cot, then crawled back into it. Pulling her blankets around her, she lifted the first ancient book into her lap.

Hours passed in that attic, the night whittling away as her candles burned low, pools of wax gathering on their iron plates. Soon, Jesine barely registered the cold, as she flipped through pages and pages of worn, crinkled parchment, some of it eaten away at the edges. Even a few scorch marks marred a page here and there. These books had been in her family for generations, or so her father had said, and they contained some of the most ancient knowledge ever writ on magic, on witches, on their beginnings.

"Why is *he* here?"

Jesine barely stifled a scream. Leaping to her feet—dropping the ancient book in the process—she spun around.

The single window in the attic stood ajar, cold air whistling in. A shadow sat perched on the sill, a shadow that loomed like an overgrown bat.

It was a fairy.

It was Jesine's fairy.

"*Kel.*" Jesine gaped in astonishment. "What are you doing here?"

The fairy gave an audible sniff. She shifted on the windowsill, and the light of a flickering candle fell over her. Her tatty little dress, bearing her arms and most of her legs, would have made anyone blue with cold. But Kel's skin, like all fairies, was mint-green, the green of the wood, the green of the land. And she didn't seem the least bit cold.

Her massive wings were the same burnished yellow as her hair, but Jesine couldn't see those feathered wings now. They were outside the window, swallowed up in shadow, only the dark outline of them visible as they beat in time with the fairy's heart.

"I asked my question first," the fairy said. She assumed an indolent pose, slinging one arm over her knee. "So you should answer first."

Jesine sighed. Part of her was still grappling with this—that after their argument, after Kel's refusal to come south with her, after all these months, *now* she was here—but the larger part of her slipped into the familiarity of the situation. She had lived much more of her life with Kel than not; it felt only natural to see her here, perched at the window. She cast her mind back, having already forgotten what the fairy had asked. *Why is he here?*

"He who?" Jesine asked. Currently, there were three young men in her house. Though she had a feeling she knew which one Kel referred to.

"The boy. From before."

"You mean Ansel?"

Kel shrugged a tiny shoulder, as though names were inconsequential. "Yes. That one. The one you loved."

Jesine sputtered at that. "What makes you think I loved him?" *Well, don't you*, said a snide little voice in her head.

Kel cocked her head to one side. "You were always running around with him. When you were smaller."

"Yes, because he was my friend."

"You never ran around with anyone else your age. Boy or girl."

"Yes, because my father didn't allow me to have friends."

"Well, he shouldn't be here." Kel sniffed again. "Your father never liked him."

"He's here because he's injured." Jesine bent to pick up the book she'd dropped, cringing when a few of its thin, ancient pages fell out. "He was attacked out in the woods. There are witches after him. Including Harper."

"Harper?" Kel echoed idly. "Oh. The other boy you loved?"

Jesine chose not to respond to that.

"I thought his coven were all dead." For the first time, the fairy sounded concerned. And well she should, Jesine thought. Since bad witches were the bane of any fairy's existence. "Dead or gone."

"Well, he's got a new coven." Carefully placing the fallen pages within the book, Jesine snapped it shut. "So thank you very much for finally turning up, Kel. It's not like I haven't needed you these past several days. Going up against bad witches. Including one who's after me in particular."

"Who?" Kel asked sharply.

"Her name is Delphine."

Kel hissed, curling in on herself. "The heart-eater?"

"I suppose."

"Every fairy alive knows of Delphine." Kel's black eyes glittered with contempt. "She is the most vicious of witches. The most evil."

"Well, she's here. And Ansel is the only person I've had to help me."

"He still shouldn't be here." Kel, it seemed, would not budge on this point. For some absurd reason. Probably, quite simply, because Jesine's father had thought so. Kel practically worshipped Jesine's father. Even though he was dead. "You said he was injured."

"Yes."

"So when he recovers, will he leave?" Kel pressed.

Jesine's heart gave a painful pulse. She thought of Ansel, falling to his knees as his restored memories came flooding back. Then she thought of his shuttered face earlier. The way he'd *looked* at her. "Yes," she said, and it was a miracle she could speak past the lump in her throat. It was the size of a walnut. "Then he'll leave."

At that moment, something shot through the window, diving in through the narrow space between Kel's right wing and the crook of her elbow. That something let out a shrill *squawk*, circling the attic in a flurry of wings. Jesine watched as her brother, the raven, settled on one of the dark wooden beams overhead.

"Of course," said Jesine. "I have had one other person to help me." She settled a cold look on Kel. "Bastian."

Kel was not quelled by Jesine's hard gaze. "He isn't a person, Jesine. He is a raven."

Jesine threw her hands in the air. "If you've just come so we can have the same argument—"

"And so?" Kel asked. The fairy shifted on the windowsill, her movements almost agitated. As though she wanted to come inside. But she couldn't; her wings were too large to fit through the window. "You've been here nearly half a year, Jesine. Have you found anything?"

"No. But—"

"Because you have no idea where to look. Or even what you're looking for."

"I'm mapping out the most ancient landmarks." *Or I was*, she thought, *before all this.* Jesine's cheeks felt hot. "All the oldest trees—" Even as she said it aloud, she realized how ridiculous it sounded.

Kel barked a laugh. "It has nothing to do with age, child. It is a weakness in the land. A thinness in the world. There will be no ancient tree or rocky mass to mark it. It could be under this very house, for all you know. It could be in the middle of the road, not one mile from here."

"Well, if you would help me!" Jesine cried. "If you would just tell me what to look for—"

"It won't matter."

"It matters to me!" Jesine pointed a finger up at the rafters. "It matters to Bastian!"

"Does it?" Kel twisted around in a way that would have been most unnatural for a human. Swiveling her head to peer up at the raven. He cocked his head similarly to stare back at her, as though to accentuate Kel's point. That he looked more like *her*, a creature of the woods, than a human. "Jesine. He has been a raven for six years. Nearly half of his life. Soon he will have been a raven longer than he was a human."

"Not if I save him first. Not if I can find a way—"

"You have searched all these years. In places as high as the moon and as far off as the sun. Yet you found nothing. What makes you think there is still a chance?"

Jesine turned away, wrapping her arms around herself. One arm around her middle, the other clutching at her own shoulder. Yes, she'd searched everywhere. For a way to help her brother, for magic to undo his hex. And yes, she'd found nothing. That was why she'd come back here. After all these years. That was why she'd returned to the southern woods. There was power in the land here. Harper's old coven had known it, searched for it. But only her father knew where it was.

If only he'd told Jesine before he'd died.

As though reading her thoughts, Kel said, "Don't you think, if your father had believed the land here could save your brother—don't you think he would have used it to undo the hex?"

No, Jesine thought bitterly. *Not in a million years.*

Her father had cared far more for protecting that power than he had ever cared for his children.

Without turning around, Jesine said, her voice stiff, "If you're not going to help me, then you should just leave. You won't change my mind, Kel. You just won't. So if that's the only reason you're here..."

She let her voice trail off. Silence followed in its wake, a long, weighted silence.

Then Bastian let out another *squawk*. Jesine turned around.

The window was empty. Kel was gone.

———————— ◆ ————————

The next morning, Prince Garrett, Demetri, and Sabine set out at first light. He wouldn't be in such a hurry, Prince Garrett said, except his guards would have expected him back last night. They were probably out searching for him, he said.

But Ansel, Jesine determined, was not well enough to travel. She had healed him, yes, but only on the surface. She'd staunched the bleeding and knit him back together, but there was still healing to be done, healing his body would need to do on its own.

So Prince Garrett and his friends set out, leaving Ansel behind to rest.

They left him behind with Jesine. Alone. With Jesine.

She felt the reality of this very acutely, as soon as the three of them turned their horses away and rode out from her front lawn. As she stood in the doorway, watching them go, she was very aware of Ansel's presence behind her. She was startled out of her anxious abstraction by a soft mewling sound, and she glanced down. A black cat had intruded onto her porch, weaving through the wooden railing.

"Shoo," Jesine told the creature. She couldn't have cats hanging around her house, not with Bastian around. And she couldn't stand here, letting the cold in, no matter how much she didn't want to face her houseguest. So, reluctantly, she stepped back into the house and shut the door.

Then she turned. Ansel sat in her armchair before the hearth, staring into the crackling fire. The house was mostly dark, shadows clinging to the corners like cobwebs. But here before the hearth, the fire cast a warm glow over Ansel, ensconcing him in the cozy space. Jesine really wished he had stayed in bed, but when she rose this morning, she'd found him already up, seated in that chair.

Now, as Jesine inched towards the hearth, Ansel looked up. He looked at her. For a moment, his gaze was faraway, both looking at her and somehow not looking at her.

Jesine swallowed. "You really should be in bed."

Ansel's eyes focused. On her. "Jesine."

"I know you hate being cooped up," she babbled, "but the more you rest, the quicker you'll heal." And leave here. "I can help you up the stairs if you—"

"Jesine." Ansel's voice was soft and serious. "We need to talk."

"You need to rest." Jesine peeled back the thin blanket covering Ansel's lap; then, mortified by the intrusive gesture, she dropped the blanket at Ansel's feet and reached for his teacup instead. There were only dregs left, sodden tea leaves clumped together at the bottom. "I can make you another cup if—"

"Jesine, stop." Ansel grasped her by the wrist. "Just stop."

Jesine went still as a statue. Ansel's touch was gentle, but his tone was almost stern. Slowly, Jesine opened her hand, releasing her grip on his teacup, and Ansel, in turn, released her. Then, grunting at the effort, he climbed to his feet. Jesine hurried back a step; she'd been leaning over for the cup, so now that he stood, she was practically right up against him.

But before she could back up further, Ansel reached for her again. This time, it was a warm hand upon her shoulder, another loosely taking her by the opposite arm. For a moment, Jesine wondered if he just needed support to keep from falling over. But then he guided her back a step—gently, so gently—and a little to the right. Closer to the fire. Putting herself, she realized, within its light.

Taking in a shaky breath, Jesine looked up into Ansel's face.

He was smiling.

He was...*smiling?*

"Jesine," he said, and something about the way his mouth formed her name, the sound of it, was so achingly familiar. So like the boy she used to know, the boy she had fallen in love with. "I never thought I would see you again!"

Jesine blinked. Did he mean because he'd been attacked by the demon? He had thought he was going to die last night? No, that wasn't it. His dark eyes gleamed in the firelight with unshed tears. But he was still smiling.

He was happy to see her. And when he said he thought he'd never see her again, he didn't mean since last night.

He meant since that summer. Six years ago.

She was startled when he leaned forward and wrapped her in a hug. "I went back and looked for you," he told her, his words thick and shaky. "I didn't know what I was looking for, but it was like some part of me remembered. The glade where we first met." He released her, leaning back. "I went back there one last time before Isabelle and I left. But I didn't know what I was looking for."

Jesine stared at him, feeling oddly bereft without his arms around her. As though she'd lived more of her life with those arms enclosing her rather than the other way around. At the same time, as she listened to his words, something strange and terrible rose inside her. No, not terrible. Wonderful? She didn't know. She couldn't name the feeling. It filled her lungs, filled her chest. Squeezed her heart so tightly, it was almost painful.

Ansel startled her again with a short laugh. He pinched at the corners of his eyes, staunching his tears. "But I think even after I'd gone, some part of me was still looking for you. Some part of me was always looking for you. No matter where I went. I just didn't know it." His smile broadened. "Until I found you."

"What are you talking about?"

"I'm talking about you, of course! About us. I remember now. I remember everything." He gave her an odd look, tilting his head. "Do you remember?"

"I—yes, of course." Jesine's voice sounded strange to her own ears. Fuzzy. Thick, like Ansel's had been. Stones, was she going to cry too? "I always remembered. You didn't because your memories were taken from you. Your memories of me."

For the first time, the happiness on Ansel's face wavered. "By you? Did you take my memories?"

"No. It was my father."

"But why? Just to keep us apart?"

"It was more than that. To keep you safe, really. Safe from me and the bad witches after us. And..." Her words turned bitter. "To punish me."

"Punish you! For what?"

"Because it was all my fault, Ansel." The words tumbled from Jesine. "That witch who took you—trying to kill you and your sister—"

"Jesine, no." Ansel took her hands in his and gave them a squeeze. "It had nothing to do with you. She was just a mad witch, and I was just unlucky to run across her."

"You don't know that," Jesine protested. "She was Harper's sister, their whole coven was after my father and me. After the power we protected. They'd already tried to get to me through my brother, they might have been trying to get to me through you."

"Jesine, if that was her plan, she did rather a poor job of it. She was ready to cook me and Isabelle long before you got there. Why would she kill us if we were meant to be leverage?" Ansel frowned down at her. "You were there, weren't you? That night. The fire. I thought I was dead and Isabelle too. But then I saw you..."

"Yes, my father saved you. He healed you and your sister. And then he took your memories. He said it was for the best, that I would only ruin you—"

"Ruin me?" Ansel sounded incredulous. Of course he did, oh, of course he did, Jesine thought miserably. Because he couldn't see it. How she'd ruined her brother, getting him hexed, getting caught up with Harper. How she'd let Harper ruin her, persuading her to drink that fairy blood. Opening that door between her and the darkness.

He couldn't see it. What her father had always known.

She ruined everything she touched.

Ansel slid a hand up her arm, rubbing it back and forth. A comforting gesture. His eyes glimmered in the light of the fire—not because he was crying again, but just because they were lovely and dark and beautiful. "Jesine. You could never ruin me. Don't you understand? You saved me, Jesine. Not from the fire, just—" He gestured vaguely, as though he couldn't find the right words. "Before I met you, I had no friends. Precious little family too, and only one of them truly loved me. I failed at everything, got into trouble wherever I went. I was convinced there was something wrong with me. But then I met you. And you were like...this light. The only bright thing in the darkness."

That strange, wonderful feeling expanded inside Jesine, pushing out all her air. Only, it wasn't so wonderful. She'd been right the first time. It was terrible, *terrible*, because she couldn't stand this. Hearing him call her a light, when she knew the truth.

"I never knew how to talk to people." Ansel let out a laugh, and it was such a beautiful sound. So boyish and genuine. "I mean, I talked, but anything I said just put people off. I didn't know how to connect to people. Honestly, I still don't. But with you, it was never like that. You always seemed to know the thoughts in my head before I said them." He smoothed a hand over her hair. "You were my safe place. You were *everything*."

"Stop," Jesine blurted out. She didn't mean to. But she was choking on it, that strange, terrible, wonderful feeling. "Don't, Ansel. Please don't."

"Don't what?" Ansel rubbed a finger across her jaw. "Why are you crying?"

She hadn't realized she was. But he was right; her cheeks were damp beneath his touch. She disentangled herself from him, stepped back, turned away.

How could she explain? Oh, what an idiot she was. Not twenty-four hours ago, she had been so desperate for him to remember everything that was between them. And now he did, and she couldn't stand it. She couldn't stand to hear him say these things about her. How to explain that she had dreamed, all these years, of this very moment? That she had dreamed he would come back and remember her, and say all these wonderful things...

But it wasn't wonderful. She wished she'd never restored his memories.

"Jesine." Ansel sounded worried. "What's wrong?"

Jesine fought to speak past her tears. "You were angry at me before," she found herself saying. "You acted like I'd betrayed you. When you found out I was a witch. You were angry, and you didn't really know why, did you?" She spun back to face him. "But now you know, now you know everything, and you're not angry!"

Ansel looked bewildered. "You want me to be angry at you?"

"Why aren't you? Your mind was violated, your memories stolen—"

"You said your father did that. Why should I be angry at you?"

Jesine dashed away more tears, then said, "What if I said I agreed with what he did?"

"Do you?"

"Not back then, I didn't. But now, maybe now, I do."

"Why?"

Jesine forced herself to meet his gaze. "Ansel. I can't put you in danger. I can't be the reason you're in danger."

"You're not! Didn't you hear what Castel said? Harper and Adela are after me because of what *I* did to them. I'm a bloody witch hunter, Jesine, I've made plenty of enemies among witch-es. So I don't see how you could put me in danger. These witches are after me, and it has nothing to do with you."

Jesine bit her lip. *Just tell him,* a voice inside her head urged her. But she couldn't. She couldn't bring herself to explain about the darkness and Malina's mark and Delphine's plans for her.

Instead, she said, "Don't you remember what Harper said? Back in the glade? When he said, 'I don't have to do anything, just sit back and watch.' Remember?"

"Jesine, I have no idea what he meant by that. Do you?"

"Not exactly," she admitted. "But, Ansel, if there's even a chance I'm putting you in danger—"

"Jes, Jes." Ansel stepped forward. Hesitantly, he reached for her, sweeping her hair back from her damp cheek. "Haven't you heard a word I've said? I'm willing to take that chance." *To be with you*, his eyes said. His dark, lovely eyes.

He still didn't understand. She had heard him, yes. Every word. Every word of what she meant to him. Every word of how he felt.

She felt the same. He meant the same. To her.

"I'm not." Gently, she removed his hand from her face. "Ansel, I'm not willing to take that chance."

She wondered if he could read what her eyes said.

Because I love you.

21

ENDGAME

G ARRETT ROSE, DRESSED, AND went down to breakfast
with the most peculiar feeling nagging at him.

He couldn't say what it was. It felt a bit like when he'd forgotten something but didn't know what. And it was a stronger,
more persistent feeling than that. Darker. Like a cold hand at
his back, prodding him along. Like a spider crawling around the
nape of his neck, tickling, itching, putting him on edge.

"Morning, sire," Gemma greeted him as they crossed at the
top of the stairs.

"Hmm? Oh. Morning."

Gemma stopped. "Are you all right, Your Highness?"

"Fine." Garrett looked out over the top of the stairs. The common room below was a little emptier than usual this morning,
and the light filtering in through the windows even dimmer. He
drummed his fingers against the wooden stair railing. "You ever
have a feeling like you've forgotten something, Gemma?"

"Of course. Everyone does."

"It's driving me mad."

It wasn't until Garrett was down in the common room that he realized, belatedly, that he hadn't asked Gemma how she was feeling. She seemed fully recovered, but even so, Garrett thought, he usually would have asked. It hadn't even occurred to him.

With a shrug, he went to place his breakfast order at the bar. He'd only just seated himself at a small table when the side door blew open, and Demetri rushed in. That was enough to break through Garrett's abstraction, if only for a second or two. It was a rare day when Demetri rose before he did. Demetri's cheeks were flushed red with cold, and his tall boots were damp. But he brightened when he saw Garrett, hurrying over to him.

"You won't believe this," Demetri said, pulling out the chair opposite Garrett. "It's snowing."

"Snowing?" Garrett echoed.

"Yes. Snowing."

"Huh."

Demetri frowned. "I thought you'd be more excited."

"I thought you wouldn't be," Garrett said vaguely. "Didn't you tell me once you hate snow?"

"I'm excited on your behalf," Demetri said. "Which, apparently, was a waste of my efforts."

"Sorry." Garrett rubbed a hand over his face. "I've forgotten something."

"Forgotten what?"

"If I knew, I wouldn't have forgotten it," Garrett fretted.

They ate breakfast together. A full spread for Demetri with ham, eggs, mushrooms, tomatoes, and buttered toast. Garrett had only a bowl of porridge, which he didn't quite finish. As they ate, Demetri talked about the snow, how the watchmen in the village thought it might become a full whiteout. "It seems unlikely to me," Demetri scoffed. Politely. "From what I recall, it doesn't snow much this far south. Or has the climate changed that much in eighty years, Garrett?"

"Hmm," Garrett murmured. "No, not really. Sounds about right."

"That's what I thought. Usually, the snow melts almost as soon as it touches the ground. Certainly it doesn't pile up more than an inch or so—"

Dropping his spoon, Garrett stood up. So suddenly, he rattled the whole table, knocking it with his knee.

"Garrett!" Demetri clutched at his teacup to keep it from spilling over. "Is something wrong? Garrett?" Demetri peered up at him. "Did you remember? What you'd forgotten?"

"What? Oh. Yes." It came to Garrett at once. "We have to go. Out. Now."

"Out?" Demetri echoed. "Out where? It's snowing, remember?"

Garrett waved a negligent hand. "You said yourself, it never snows much down here. We'll be fine."

"Well, I know," Demetri said. A tad grumpily. "I just don't like going out in the snow. Er, where exactly are we going?"

"We have to go..." Garrett frowned, trying to pinpoint the thought. "South. South of here. There's a clearing..." He shook his head. "I'll know it once we get going."

Demetri's eyes narrowed. "And why are we going to this clearing? What's there? Another hex?"

Garrett grasped at this. "Yes. A hex. Something to do with...some animals. Mutated animals. I think. So if you're coming, we should go. I just need to get my coat." He pushed back his chair and turned, heading for the stairs.

"Garrett, wait!" Demetri called after him. Before Garrett could start up the stairs, Demetri stopped him with a hand on his arm. Garrett bit back the urge to snap at Demetri, then immediately chastised himself.

He would never snap at Demetri. Not for something so stupid, anyway.

"Garrett, you never said where you heard about this hex," Demetri said carefully. "Are you sure you're feeling all right?"

"One of the people staying here mentioned it this morning," Garrett babbled, the answer coming to him easily. It felt like a lie, somehow, or something he had made up. But that was rubbish. He wasn't making anything up; he knew the answers, that was all. Everything had a rational explanation. "And yes, I'm fine. Just eager to get ahead of these witches. You know."

"All right." Demetri still eyed him shrewdly. "But what's the rush?"

"Oh." Garrett turned away, starting up the stairs. "We have to pick up Ansel first."

"So," Ansel said as they rode through the woods, "where are we going, exactly?"

"Garrett heard about another possible hex. Somewhere near here, I think," said Demetri.

They had not stopped at Jesine's house long. Ansel had been only too eager to leave, and evidently, Jesine had permitted Ansel was well enough to travel by horse—which Garrett and Demetri had brought for him. So they soon left Jesine's house behind.

The snow continued to fall, flurries light but swift, streaming to the ground. It was positively glacial, as though the air itself would turn to ice, freezing the landscape in an eternal moment. An eternal, beautiful moment. The naked branches of the aspens looked as though they had been iced like a pastry, and the evergreen branches like they had been dusted with powdered sugar.

But the beauty was lost on Garrett. He only wanted to continue on their way.

Ansel said in a dubious voice, "But didn't that witch, Castel, say the hexes didn't mean anything?"

"Well, he said they weren't in preparation for some big spell," Demetri answered. "Doesn't mean they won't help us track these witches." He lowered his voice a bit. "I think Garrett just wants to get something on these witches for once. He's a bit testy this morning."

Garrett wasn't supposed to hear that part, he thought absently. That's why Demetri had lowered his voice. But he had heard him, and nothing Demetri said bothered him. In fact, it barely registered.

As they continued through the forest, the snow began to pile up beneath them. Demetri made a few noises about it, worrying that it might worsen and make their travel difficult. Ansel was his usual quiet self, only making a few responses here and there to show he was listening to Demetri.

Garrett didn't listen. He tuned it all out, distracted by that nagging in his mind, that cold touch spurring him on. The clearing, he thought, was a couple of leagues west of Jesine's house, and he eyed their surroundings anxiously, trying to gauge how close they were. The woods began to thin, even more snow falling through the gaps between the trees. Yes, they were almost there, Garrett thought, nudging his horse to go a little faster. Almost there, almost there—

He urged his horse into a gallop.

"Garrett!" Demetri called after him, but Garrett hardly heard him. The itch at the nape of his neck had increased tenfold, not spiders crawling on his skin but beetles, burrowing beneath it. He was desperate to be rid of his agitation as he rode on, his horse bursting through the last trees, out into a clearing layered with snow a foot deep.

There was nothing there, of course. No mutated animals or anything strange. There never had been.

"Garrett." Demetri sounded breathless as he and Ansel caught up, their horses slowing on either side of him. "What's going on? I don't see anything out here—"

"That's not why we're here." Garrett spoke with a trace of impatience.

"Then why are we?"

"Because Delphine wanted it," Garrett said unthinkingly.

Demetri gawped at him, incredulous. Garrett stared back, and as he did, the nagging in his head seemed to fade away. But that cold touch remained, seeping through him. Sinking into his bones.

Reason slowly returned to him. And with it, utter horror.

"What did I just say?" he whispered.

"She put a hex on you." This grim declaration came from Ansel, who whirled his horse around to face them. His gloves creased as he clenched his reins, and he pinned Demetri with a glare. "You couldn't tell he was hexed?"

"You couldn't tell either!" Demetri shot back. "Aren't you supposed to be the expert?"

"When could she have put a hex on me?" Garrett's voice was a coarse whisper. But the answer came to him before anyone else could supply it. "That night. When she supposedly cured me. That night—"

"That lovely night we spent together in that secluded cabin, Gallant," came her voice. "Yes."

Demetri and Ansel wheeled their horses around. Garrett followed a few seconds later, more slowly. Steeling himself before he faced her.

She emerged from the trees like a shadow detaching from the darkness. Garbed in a black, fur-lined gown, she sat astride her own horse, its mane and coat coal-black to match her. She circled around them into the snowy clearing and stopped there, looking for all the world like a cut of onyx in a pile of opals. "I delved into your bloodstream that night, dear Gallant," she said, "which allowed me to create a rather special hex just for you. A hex built from twigs and twine, linked together by your blood."

Ansel drew in a sharp breath. "A poppet."

"What is that?" Demetri muttered.

"A sort of doll," Ansel explained in a low voice. "Built in a person's image. If she's linked it with Garrett, then she can control him. Exert her influence over him, even from a distance."

Garrett's stomach churned, making him feel sick.

Ansel raised his voice, his tone hardening. "Where have you stashed it, Delphine?"

Delphine gave a light laugh. "As though I would bring it with me. I don't need it now. I have other weapons at my disposal here."

"What is that supposed to mean?" Demetri demanded.

"Hush," Delphine rebuked him, and with a flick of her wrist, Demetri's mouth clamped shut. Garrett watched helplessly as thick, black stitches appeared across his mouth, sewing his lips shut. Demetri's eyes bulged wide, darting between Ansel and Garrett in a silent cry for help.

"Stop!" Garrett snapped around to look the witch in the eye. "Leave him alone! He's got nothing to do with this."

"Exactly, so why did you bring him?" Delphine asked with a bored air. "He's only going to get in the way. Better to leave him like this so he won't interrupt us. Sorry." She turned to look at Ansel, and she made a negligent gesture, encircling him and Garrett. "I meant *us*. The three of us."

The look Ansel directed at her was full of contempt. Garrett did not understand how he could look so unafraid. "I want nothing to do with you," Ansel said evenly.

Delphine pouted. "No, you never did, did you. Dear Ansel. I have longed to see you again, even if you haven't longed for me. Gallant and his father might have put me away, but you had the gall to disobey me. I don't think any of my other soldiers ever dared do that. It hurt me," she said in a careless tone, one that didn't sound hurt at all, "but it impressed me, too."

"I don't care what you think of me," Ansel said, and Garrett realized that the hunter's steely tone didn't come easily to him. There was a tension in his voice. He *was* frightened, but in a way that was different from Garrett's fear. He was frightened of something else, perhaps, other than what the queen might do to him.

Garrett could not think what else he could be afraid of right now.

"No." Delphine's bloodred lips pursed in a thin line. "You care for nothing, isn't that right, Ansel? Harper tells me you care for that little good witch, but we know better, don't we? You aren't capable of it, are you?"

A chill ran down Garrett's spine. It was a moment before he realized why, why the cold inside him seemed to intensify, unsettling him deeply. It was what Ansel had said. Ansel had said the exact same thing to him only just a few days ago. When they had spoken about love, about romance. *I'm not capable of it*, Ansel had said bitterly.

Ansel's face went gray. "You don't know anything."

"Oh, but I do," she breathed. "That's what you're afraid of, isn't it? How much I know? What my dear stepdaughter might have confided in me before she took a bite of my apple? What I might have glimpsed of her through my bespelled mirror?"

If possible, Ansel went even grayer. Something seemed to go out of him, some battle he'd been fighting. Garrett *saw* him give it up, the hunter's shoulders sagging, a light going out of his eyes.

Ansel turned in his saddle to face Garrett. His expression was shattering.

"I'm sorry," he said. "I'm so, so sorry."

"What?" Garrett whispered. "What is it?"

"Dear Garrett," Delphine said, and the use of his real name from her startled him, drawing his attention back to her. "Haven't you ever wondered, sweet prince, why your kiss failed to wake darling Snow from her endless sleep? True love's kiss, after all, should have broken the hex." She patted her carefully curated hair with one hand. "Back in the day, it was all the rage. I just couldn't help but work it into my little spell."

"You're lying," Garrett said in a baleful voice. "I tried it. More than once. It wasn't part of the spell—"

"Oh, but it was," Delphine said. All the laughter had gone from her. Her voice was thick with undisguised rancor. "Just like the dark fairy's curse, the one she cast on your new love. Only, I'm much more skilled at such things than Tenalabralilah ever was. She was only a fairy, after all, and a warped one at that. What did she know of love, true or otherwise? That's why you managed to wake Princess Briar. Anyone could have. The dark fairy didn't understand enough of love to make it work for her."

Garrett exchanged a sidelong glance with Demetri, whose lips were still stitched together. They had figured as much already; Delphine wasn't telling him anything new.

"But I knew better," Delphine went on. "I understand the intricacies of the human heart. Perhaps better than any witch who has ever lived. So you see, Garrett, my hex could only be broken—unfortunately for you and dear Snow—by true love's kiss. A kiss from someone who loved her—"

"I did love her," Garrett said through gritted teeth.

"—and whom she loved in return." Delphine smiled, and this time, her smile was a victorious one.

For a moment, Garrett looked at her, befuddled. Waiting for her to make her point. Then he realized she had, or thought she had. "What, you're saying Snow didn't love me? That's ridiculous. What would you know about it?"

"Well, not everything, I'll admit." Delphine swept her arm aside, making a broad gesture. "Ansel, I'm sure, can tell you much more."

Garrett stared at her a moment longer. Then he looked at Ansel.

Ansel, who wore regret and consternation stitched into every part of his face.

"What?" Garrett asked. "What is she talking about?"

"I'm sorry, Garrett. I really am. I never wanted—" Ansel shook his head. "I'm sorry."

Garrett whipped back around, looking at Delphine. "What are you saying?"

"Isn't it obvious?" Delphine's face was the picture of innocence. "My darling stepdaughter didn't love you, Garrett. Maybe she did once, but …" Her voice hardened. "In the end, she loved Ansel."

Denial and doubt warred in Garrett simultaneously. The churning in his gut increased tenfold. "No. She didn't."

"One can hardly blame her." Delphine spoke as though she was oblivious to the turmoil inside him. Though she wasn't. Of course she wasn't. "Strapping Ansel, dark and handsome, the hunter sent to kill her but who saved her instead. Saved her from the clutches of the evil queen and delivered her to safety. But first, he had to get her through the perilous Mariner swampland, the pitfalls of the dark forest—"

"You make her sound like some helpless damsel," Ansel scoffed. "She wasn't. She didn't even need me—"

"Well, then it must have been something else about you that made her fall in love with you," Delphine suggested.

But Garrett barely heard this last part. He was reeling. The queen's words hit him like a battering ram, sending him tumbling over the edge of a deep abyss. He was falling with no end in sight, his devastation growing, expanding, engulfing him. He reached a hand out for something to stop his fall, some scrap of truth that didn't fit with this version of events.

But it *did* fit. It all fit. Too well.

Memories swirled around him like a treacherous fog. Snow, during the summer they'd spent together at her castle. Courting each other, laughing together, sneaking off whenever they could. She had loved him then, he knew it. Not just because she'd told him so, but because he'd seen it in her dancing eyes, he'd felt it in the whisper of her touch, the warmth of her kiss...

The way she'd said his name. *Garrett*, or sometimes, teasingly, *Prince Gallant*—

But then came the other memories. The memories of after. When she'd arrived at Glen Castle, having fled Delphine in the Mariner Kingdom. He remembered how distant she'd been. How the way she'd looked at him changed. It had been inexplicable, indefinable. Just a feeling, deep inside him, that something wasn't right. Garrett had chalked it up to her mourning her father's death, her worry over her vanished sister.

And then...the sleeping hex. The kiss.

Why hadn't it worked?

Delphine was speaking again. "But I'm surprised to hear you speak so admirably of her, Ansel."

Feeling dazed, Garrett looked up at her.

The queen folded her hands over the pommel of her saddle. "Since, tragically, you didn't love Snow back. Did you?"

Garrett turned his numb gaze on Ansel. The hunter closed his eyes.

"Did you try?" Garrett asked hoarsely. "Did you try to wake her?"

Ansel's eyes flew open, and they were raw with pain. "Garrett. I'm—"

"Don't tell me you're sorry!" Garrett exploded. "Why didn't you wake her?"

"I tried! Don't you think I tried? I did, but it didn't—" He squeezed his eyes shut again. "It didn't work. All I had to do was love her. And I couldn't."

"Like I said," the queen said in a nasty voice. "Not capable. Utterly heartless."

"That's not true," Ansel snapped. "You don't know what you're talking about."

"Oh?" Delphine placed a hand over her heart. "Is it the little witch, then? Is that why you couldn't wake Snow? All these years, and your heart still belongs to her? Well, how lovely for you, Ansel. Too bad my stepdaughter had to bear the bad end of that deal."

"The deal was yours," Ansel said. "You're the one who made it. *You're* responsible, not me, not Garrett—"

"You go on telling yourself that, dear," said the queen. "All I did was set the play in motion and watch how it fell out. And I must say, I found the results *much* to my liking."

Garrett felt physically ill now, clammy and dizzy. His surroundings had become a white blur. He wanted to fall off his horse and vomit into the snow, but he wouldn't do it, not again. Not in front of her. Instead, he forced words through his mouth, words he needed to speak. "Why didn't you just kill her?" he asked in a broken voice. "Why do all this, why—why didn't you just *put a knife through her heart?*"

Delphine gave a husky laugh. "Because this was so much more fun. A long game, if you will. And thanks to my new friends, I've finally had the chance to play my last move. Not that all the fun is over." Delphine looked smugly at Ansel. "You're still in the game, aren't you, Ansel? Oh, yes, you absolutely must stick around. If you try to bow out early, well—it'll be a messy end for you, won't it? Positively *demonic.*"

She laughed, a forbidding sound that filled the air in a whirl-wind of snow—

And then she was gone.

22

RUINED

ANSEL TREMBLED ALL OVER, but not from the cold. In the wake of Delphine's departure, all he could do was stare at the vast field before him, the snow growing thicker and higher with every passing minute. He stared at it until the bright white began to blind him, searing his vision. He squeezed his eyes shut against it, turning his head.

Away from Garrett. He could not look at Garrett.

He couldn't bear to see the pain on his face.

But Garrett didn't spare him. He didn't wait for Ansel to meet his gaze. He spoke, and Ansel heard the pain in his voice instead. "Why didn't you tell me?"

"I—" Ansel dared to open his eyes, but still, he didn't turn. He couldn't face the prince. Even the words stuck in Ansel's throat. "Garrett, I—"

"*Why didn't you tell me?*"

"What good would it have done?" Ansel's hands were clenched so tightly around his reins, he thought his fingers had frozen in place. "I didn't want to—and she's *dead*, Garrett, I mean—oh, stones, I'm sorry—"

"Stop saying that." This command from Garrett was spoken in hushed tones. It would have been better if he'd shouted at him, Ansel thought. "Stop saying you're sorry."

"Garrett," said Demetri.

Ansel finally raised his eyes long enough to look for Demetri. He was ashamed to admit he'd forgotten about him entirely. Garrett must have as well, for the prince whirled his horse around. "Are you all right?" he demanded of Demetri.

"Fine." Demetri looked shaken, but otherwise unharmed. He touched a quivering hand to his mouth. "Like they were never there. She didn't hurt me."

"Good," said Garrett, but he did not sound good. His tone was brusque. "Then let's get out of here. Let's go." He wheeled his horse around without looking at Ansel.

"Garrett," Ansel croaked, urging his horse forward a step. Now that the prince had turned his back on him, he found he did not want him to go. Not like this. They couldn't leave things like this. "Wait. Please. I never wanted any of it to happen. Like this. I never wanted—"

"Do you mean you never wanted me to find out?" Garrett stopped his horse but still sat turned away from Ansel. His back was ramrod straight beneath his long overcoat, the set of his shoulders stiff. "Or that you never wanted her to fall in love with you?"

Ansel bit his lip. "Both. I certainly never wanted you to find out like this."

"You didn't want me to find out at all," Garrett said bitterly. "That's what you just said, wasn't it? No point, after all, when she's dead and gone. What does it matter?"

Ansel slumped in his saddle. "I didn't want to cause you unnecessary pain."

"See, it does matter, though," Garrett went on, as though Ansel hadn't spoken. The snow tumbled down between them, falling harder and faster now, beginning to obscure Ansel's vision. Garrett was almost a blur on the other side of it. "Maybe she is dead, maybe she's gone, but she didn't have to be. You could have prevented it—"

"How?" A spark of defiance rose in Ansel. He tried to remind himself that Garrett was grieving, that he was not thinking straight, but then, Ansel wasn't sure he was either. Perhaps he had not been in love with Snow, but he had cared for her. He had admired her. Snow was the kind of person who was impossible not to like—fearless and lovely and so authentically herself. The kind of person Ansel would love to be, the kind of person he never *could* be. Perhaps that was why Ansel liked and trusted Prince Garrett so implicitly—he was so like Snow, in so many ways.

Losing Snow to the queen—knowing he had failed her—had weighed on Ansel more heavily than any other loss in his life. Knowing, too, that he had failed Garrett by extension only made it worse.

"How could I have prevented any of it?" Ansel demanded now. "By loving her back? By, what, somehow stopping her from falling in love with me in the first place?"

"Both," Garrett said heartlessly. "Either."

Ansel took these two, simple words like successive hits to the gut. Oh, if only the prince knew. If only he knew how desperate Ansel had been to fix it. To feel something, *anything*, for Snow, even if just for a moment, long enough to wake her. To feel something for her, if only to prove to himself that he could. That he wasn't just built wrong, unable to love. Unable to feel that way for another person.

The irony was, he finally knew now that he *could* feel that way for another person. He did feel that way for another person.

"Garrett," Demetri broke in, tentative, "that's not really fair—"

"What would you know about it?" Garrett wheeled his horse again, putting Demetri in his line of sight.

"Which part?" Demetri's tone was mild but firm. "The part about loving someone who doesn't love me back or the part about losing someone I love? Because I know a bit about both of those things."

"Losing someone you love," Garrett echoed. His tone had become hollow, as though he was only the ghost of Garrett and not Garrett himself. An imprint of the real prince. "Only, you didn't love Perpetua, did you? Isn't that why you torture yourself so much? Because she loved you, but you couldn't get over Briar in time to love her back?"

Ansel winced. He looked at Demetri and saw the young man had gone as white as the snow. He looked as though Garrett had struck him. "Now *you* don't know what you're talking about," Demetri shot back. "I know you're hurting, Garrett, and that's the only reason you're saying these things—"

"Oh, really?" Garrett interjected.

"Stop it." Ansel tried to move his horse forward, but the creature whinnied and stamped a foot, as though sensing the hostility around him. "Both of you, please—"

"Don't tell us what to do," Garrett snapped.

Ansel tightened his jaw, falling back. "I'm sorry. I forgot I wasn't a prince, like you two. I'll just stay out of it, then."

"I'm not a prince," Demetri said tersely.

"Right, of course." Ansel felt his ire rising, spurred on by an eddy of emotions, overwhelming him. "Because you just woke up one day and decided to be a commoner like the rest of us. I keep forgetting."

"You know what you should have done, Ansel?" Garrett's voice shook with barely suppressed emotion. "You know how you could have prevented her death? You could have stayed out of it completely. Ignored the queen's orders to kill her, or better yet, you could have never taken a job as a Mariner guard. Then, not only would Snow be alive, but you'd never have abandoned Isabelle either."

Ansel, finally, looked at Garrett head-on. The prince's face was bloodless, as cold as crystallized ice. He had never, ever seen Garrett like this. So brimming with pain that it had turned him rancorous and brutal.

The queen had planned this treachery for Garrett well. With only words, she had unmade him.

Ansel said quietly, "None of us can know what might have happened, Garrett."

"No." Garrett took in a deep, shuddering breath. "None of us can."

Then he wheeled his horse one final time and galloped out of the clearing, plunging into the frosted forest.

"Damn it!" Demetri threw one last look Ansel's way, not quite meeting his gaze. "Ansel—"

"Just go," Ansel said. He was full of misery and full of resentment. "Go after him. He'll get lost in these woods, in this blizzard."

To his credit, Demetri hesitated, turning his snorting horse one way, then another. "And you?"

"I'll be fine. Just go!"

Demetri hesitated no more. He lashed his reins and took off, vanishing into the snowy woods.

Ansel did not move for a long time. He knew he should. He knew he was vulnerable out here, alone, with the demon on the loose, and Delphine, for all he knew, still lurking nearby. She might have hoped for just this, to break them apart and get them on their own. And the snow was still coming down, thick and relentless, with no sign of letting up. The villagers were right; this would be a whiteout. Already, Ansel could only see about ten paces in front of him.

He needed to go. But for a long, long time, he didn't move.

When he did turn back, delving beneath the trees, it was with no knowledge of where he was going, no awareness of his surroundings. Everything looked the same. The pines were no longer green but white, and the thinner, barren trees had become as thick and full as they would be in springtime, only their branches were weighed down with snow instead of new leaves. The snowfall blurred Ansel's vision until he was dizzy with it, until he didn't know up from down, right from left.

He rode for a long time before the urgency of the situation overpowered all the other things he was feeling, and then he realized, worried, that he should try and find shelter. He didn't know how long he'd been riding for or how late it was. Dusk would be upon him soon, and then he would be in real trouble.

When he did find shelter, he and his horse nearly stumbled over it. A stump of brick, sticking out of the snow. Wiping a gloved hand across his face, Ansel leaned down from his saddle, squinting. These were some ruins, he thought, here in the woods, half-buried in the snow. Hastily, Ansel dismounted. He was so stiff from riding, from the cold, that he nearly tumbled down instead. Wincing, he caught himself between his horse and the ruins, laying a ginger hand over his middle. Jesine was right; she might have healed him, but there was still a soreness deep inside him that needed time and rest to properly heal.

Jesine. Ansel's chest tightened at the thought of her. He had tried not to think of her all day today. At first, because he didn't want to dwell on the conversation they'd had yesterday, because he didn't want to dwell on the way she'd rejected him. Not that he didn't understand. Not that he didn't know what she was doing. He had done it himself, after all, to Isabelle. Jesine thought she could protect him by pushing him away.

He knew that, but it still hurt. To hear her say she didn't want to be with him. Because all he wanted was to be with her. Now more than ever. After that horrible scene with Prince Garrett. After hearing Delphine lay Snow's death at *his*, Ansel's, feet—

Ansel had blamed himself for Snow's death for years. He hadn't known for sure what Delphine had just confirmed—the intricate way she'd worked *true love's kiss* into her hex—but he had suspected. When he'd heard what had happened to Snow, when he'd heard that her betrothed, Prince Garrett, hadn't been able to wake her—he had suspected the reason why. Snow had confessed her feelings to him, after all.

Ansel hadn't been able to return those feelings. He simply couldn't. And he'd lived knowing Snow was dead because he, Ansel, was broken inside. Because there was something wrong with him.

That's what he'd always believed. Until two days ago. When his memories of Jesine came flooding back.

That was the crux of it. Perhaps Ansel had forgotten Jesine, forgotten his love for her. But that didn't mean he'd *stopped* loving her. All this time, some piece of him had carried that love, tucked away inside him. Hidden from himself, buried deep beneath a heap of magic.

But now that love had been unearthed. Now Ansel could see it for what it was. That brokenness inside him wasn't brokenness at all—it was just a missing piece.

He didn't have a heart of stone. He'd given his heart away. Six years ago.

He clung to that now. As he stood there in the snow, before these ruins, thinking of Jesine. Because as much as it had hurt to hear Delphine confirm what he'd suspected—as much as it had hurt to hear Garrett condemn him for Snow's death—Ansel knew they were wrong. For the first time since Snow had died, he knew they were wrong.

It wasn't his fault Snow was gone. It wasn't anyone's fault, really. And he didn't want to dwell in guilt and regret anymore. He just wanted to move forward.

He wanted to move forward with Jesine.

But he couldn't get back to her right now, in this blizzard. He had no idea where he was. Leading his horse, Ansel ventured forward. He dusted snow off a stump of bricks, passing into the center of the ruins. On his right, he could just make out the skeleton of half an archway, part of it curving into the air above him. And most of a wall, it looked like. In one part of the wall, some of the brick jutted towards him, forming something like a tunnel. Ansel lay a hand against the brick.

And as though his touch had awakened some memory—his or the house's—he knew.

He had been here before. Just a couple of days ago, with Jesine. He hadn't recognized the ruins in the blizzard, covered in snow. He hadn't recognized the tunnel where he and Jesine had sheltered from the blood-rain.

It was not a tunnel. It was an oven.

The memory ripped through him vividly and violently. Fear rancid in his mouth. The stench of burning flesh. Thick smoke choking him. Flames so bright and hot, flames he nearly hadn't escaped—

Ansel's hand shook, hovering over the brick. He gazed into that cavernous tunnel, so cold now, so barren. Its last fire lit long ago. And Ansel let out a horrid, empty laugh. Filled with the old fear Ansel still couldn't escape to this day.

"It's funny to you, is it?"

The laughter died in Ansel's throat, and he spun around. But when he saw the witch before him, he almost wanted to laugh again.

Of course he was here. Harper.

"What happened here." Harper stood in what remained of the arched doorway, his form blurred by the flurries rushing down from the sky. He wore a tan topcoat, his hands shoved into its pockets. When he spoke, his tone was as casual as ever, yet there was an edge lining his voice. Something felt and tamped down. "It's funny to you?"

"Not at all," said Ansel. "I nearly died here. My sister too."

"My sister did die here."

"Yes. I know."

It hung there between them. Ansel felt weirdly detached from this scene. After what he'd endured from the queen, after the way Garrett had spoken to him, Harper didn't seem such a threat. That was probably a mistake, but Ansel could not bring himself to care.

After a moment, Harper said, "So you know."

"Yes."

In one swift, sudden movement, Harper raised a hand and flicked his fingers at the sky. Ansel had no time to react. But all that happened—all that Ansel saw—was a burst of power flaring outwards. It was visible, the air rippling above them, over Ansel's head and the whole of the brick ruin.

And abruptly, the snow stopped falling.

Ansel blinked. No—the snow was still falling. But Harper had erected some kind of invisible dome over them, shielding them from the blizzard. Ansel watched, fascinated, as snow fell above them and landed upon the barrier, a small pile forming, seemingly frozen in mid-air.

Harper slapped a gloved hand against the half-broken arch over his head, drawing Ansel's attention back to him. The witch gripped the arch for a second, then let his arm drop. "You know the funny part about all this, Ansel?" Harper's tone was more conversational than ever. "The really funny part? I never cared about any of this. The witchcraft, the coven, making deals and hunting fairies. Back when I knew Jes, I didn't want anything to do with it."

90

Ansel did not bother to hide his skepticism. "Then why become a witch at all?"

Harper gave a diffident shrug. "It was the done thing in my family. I wasn't really given a choice. Made my deal with the devil at the ripe age of fourteen."

"I thought you couldn't be forced into it."

"I didn't say I was forced," Harper corrected him. "I just didn't know any other way."

"And I'm supposed to feel sorry for you?"

"Not at all. I don't care enough about you to want your pity. All I'm saying is, I didn't care about it. I cared about...oh, the things most sixteen-year-old boys care about. Meeting women. Having fun. Making trouble, and not the witchy sort. Just typical trouble." Harper stepped forward beneath the arch. His topcoat was buttoned up tight, and he reached up to adjust the thick gray scarf at his neck, stuffing the ends beneath his collar. "But like I said, it was a family thing, the witchcraft. And back then, my family was involved with a coven who was very interested in the land around here."

Ansel felt as though he was sliding back into himself, coming to his senses. He shook his head. "But why? What's so special about the land? What does it have to do with witchcraft?"

Harper ran a finger along one snow-crusted, half-crumbled line of brick, what had once been part of the wall. "The land around here runs thick with elarium. And you know what elarium is, Ansel? Elarium is magic. It's the lifeblood of this whole world."

"You're not making sense."

Harper rolled his eyes, as though Ansel was being deliberately obtuse. "Suffice it to say, any piece of land rife with elarium is of value to witches. The trouble is getting to it. You can dig up elarium easily enough, but getting to the magic in it isn't so simple. That requires a connection. Usually a connection made through fairies, one way or another."

Ansel frowned, trying to follow this explanation. *One way or another*. Such as killing a fairy and drinking its blood...or bonding with one as Jesine had.

Harper tucked his hands back into his pockets. "But there are some places in the earth where there's a weakness in the land. A weakness witches can breach to make a direct connection with that power. And if that weakness happens to lie where there is a massive pocket of elarium, where there are great stores of magic...well. The rewards of power would be far beyond anything, say, a solstice event could provide." He tipped his head at Ansel. "That's what my coven was after. The kind of power they could feast on for centuries, without any need of fairy blood."

For the first time since he'd laid eyes on Harper, here in these ruins, Ansel felt a stab of fear. He shrugged a shoulder, trying to feel for his fairy-wood stake up his sleeve. But he was bundled up so tightly, he couldn't budge it. "And that's what you're after now?"

"No," Harper scoffed. "Aren't you listening? That weakness *was* here somewhere. Now it's out of anyone's reach. It's sealed away."

"How?"

"All thanks to a mad witch—the sea witch, they called her—named Sohalia. This past summer, she performed some fairly powerful magic out near the ocean. Magic that was meant to open a portal deep in the earth. She didn't finish her spell, but the damage was done. That kind of thing can cause some rather large ripple effects all across the world."

"I don't understand."

"I finally found it, Ansel." A funny little smiled played around Harper's lips. "That weakness in the land my family was so obsessed with. I found it when the earth shifted and sealed it away. I *felt* it go—I was only a few miles away when it happened."

"And I'm just supposed to take your word for this?"

"Ask the locals." Harper sounded indifferent, as though he did not care whether Ansel believed him or not. "The whole thing caused a sizable quake. It didn't cause too much damage, but I'm sure everyone around here remembers it."

"So you're just here for me then," Ansel said in a numb voice. "To have your fun with me."

"I'm here for vengeance, Ansel," Harper said quietly. "There's no joy in vengeance."

"We were children, my sister and I." Ansel felt outrage stirring inside him. He fought the urge to take a step forward, fought to remember the danger. "You can't possibly mean to defend what your sister wanted to do with us!"

"Defend it? Of course not. But that doesn't matter. She was my family." Harper's gaze fixed on Ansel. Against the backdrop of the white winter woods, his eyes were darker than ever, gleaming like glass in a black night. "What if it was your sister, Ansel? What would you do?"

Ansel said nothing, curling his fingers into his palms. He couldn't even begin to answer that.

"Don't worry." Harper turned aside, standing in profile. "I'm not going after her. Your sister. I thought I would. I thought to take her from you like Henrietta was taken from me. But if what

Adela says is true, she's too hard to get to now, and too hard to kill." He turned back to Ansel. "It's better this way. It never felt right, going after her. She minded her business, after all. She was only trying to save you. And she minds her business now. But you, Ansel. You decided to make a name for yourself, killing witches. Built on the back of my sister's death."

Ansel bit his tongue on a reply. What was the point in arguing with this witch? It was clear Ansel would never convince him he didn't deserve his revenge. He glanced up instead, surreptitiously, looking for a way out of Harper's magical dome. The invisible surface above them was thickly covered in snow now, blocking out what little light was left in the day. Washing them both in a spectral blue glow.

"Family is a funny thing," Harper mused in a faraway tone. "You can spend years hating them. Wishing them dead. But they have a hold on you that you can't escape."

"So you want me dead."

"I want you to suffer. And that's where Jesine comes in."

Ansel's fear sharpened inside him like a knife. He dropped his gaze, thoughts of escape flying out of his head. "What do you mean? You can't kill my sister, so you'll kill Jesine instead?"

"Oh, Jesine's fate will be much worse than that, Ansel." For the first time, something real entered Harper's eyes, some kind of feeling. Something bright and cruel. "And the best part is, I don't have to do anything to make it happen."

These words had a ring of familiarity to them. The kind of familiarity that made Ansel's stomach turn. It was a moment before he placed the memory—Harper in the glade that day, with him and Jesine. *I don't have to do anything. All I have to do is sit back and watch.*

"The darkness," Ansel said. "You know what it is, don't you?"

"The darkness," said Harper, "is Jesine's fate. It's *my* fate. It's the fate of all bad witches. The one we promise our souls to for all eternity."

Ansel was nonplussed. "But Jesine is a good witch."

"She is now. But I told you before, didn't I? She wasn't always so good. She flirted with the dark, and it haunts her even now. All it will take is one good push—something simple, but devastating—to send her over the edge. To convince her to embrace the dark."

"No. She would never do that."

Harper said, "Not even when she realizes she can't save her brother?"

Ansel fell silent for a moment, befuddled. *Her brother.* The raven. "I think she already knows that. She said she's tried everything—"

"Not everything." Harper shook his head. "See, Jesine wasn't here, Ansel. When the weakness in the land sealed away. She didn't feel it like I did. She doesn't know that power is gone for good." Harper let out a hollow laugh at the continued confusion on Ansel's face. "Don't you know? That's why she came back. Not to protect the weakness in the land, like her father did, but to search for it. To use that power to undo her brother's hex."

Ansel went cold all over.

"You forget, Ansel," Harper said. "I knew Jesine too. I know what she's like. Saving her brother is the only thing that matters to her. But when she realizes her last chance of doing that is gone—well, she won't have anywhere else to turn. Except to the darkness."

23

REQUIEM

G ARRETT SAT ALONE IN the tiny, cramped room that
served as a bar in this backwater little village. He and
Demetri had quickly lost their bearings in the blizzard outside;
there was no way they could get back to Lise through it. Luckily,
they'd stumbled upon a village, though it was so small, it wasn't
on any of their maps. It was only a few houses clumped together
on one side of the road, but thankfully, it boasted a very small
inn with two rooms.

The taproom, if it could be called that, was an L-shaped bar in
the corner with all of four seats. There was also a small, rickety
table by the single window, and a narrow armchair next to the
fireplace. That was it, and hardly any room to walk at all.

They didn't need the space, though. Garrett was the only one
in the room. Well, there was also a black cat, stalking the shadowy
corners. Looking for mice, no doubt. Even the bartender appeared sparsely, only long enough to refill Garrett's mug. Then
he vanished into a back room.

Garrett didn't know how long he'd been sitting there. Outside the dirty little window was a swirling white vortex in the darkness, snow continuing to pile up around them. They'd be stuck here overnight, that was for sure.

Garrett didn't care. He could barely remember what he was doing here to begin with. The thought sparked a pang in his chest, reverberating through him.

What he was doing here.

He wanted to go home.

Everything hurt. It hurt so badly, he'd just stopped feeling at all. Like the stinging bite of a frozen river, so cold and so strong it rendered its victims completely numb. He'd forgotten what it felt like *not* to hurt this much. He felt as though he'd never stopped hurting, not since he'd first seen Delphine in that cabin.

He was sick with shame, eaten up by despair. And he wanted so much to leave it all behind, to just *let it go*, but. He didn't know how.

Dusk had come and gone by the time thumping footsteps sounded out on the stairs, someone else coming to join Garrett in his misery. He didn't have to look up to see who it was. There was only one other person staying at the inn besides himself, and that was Demetri. So Garrett didn't lift his eyes from his mug, not even when Demetri slid onto the barstool beside him. He merely sat there, slumped over his drink. Silent.

Demetri didn't say anything either. Not until the bartender appeared, and then he said, "I'll have whatever he's got." Indicating Garrett.

The bartender—also silent, which suited Garrett—slapped a mug down for Demetri. Then he disappeared again, leaving the two of them alone.

Garrett heard the scraping whisper of the mug against the bar as Demetri slid it towards himself. "I thought I'd find you here," he remarked.

"Really?" said Garrett. "Weird, since there's nowhere else to go."

Demetri made no verbal response. Instead, he reached out, and his hand closed around Garrett's mug. Garrett spluttered as his friend yanked the drink away from him.

"What are you doing?" Garrett demanded, finally lifting his head.

"Taking this away from you." Demetri slid the mug further down the bar. "Since it seems to be making you meaner." He lifted his own mug and downed a long sip. When he set the mug down again, he was coughing and spluttering. "What is this?"

"It's just cider," Garrett confessed. If there was any alcohol in it, it was so little as not to matter.

"But...why?"

Garrett shrugged, trying to hide his embarrassment. He didn't want to admit that he had first ordered something stronger, taken one sip, and realized his stomach couldn't handle it. Not right now.

Demetri gave a resigned sigh. He wore only his shirt and waistcoat, leaving off his riding coat and scarf. Dingy as the little inn was, it was very warm, the roaring fire giving plenty heat to the small space. Garrett watched out of the corner of his eye as Demetri took another sip from his mug, then grimaced. "Well. It'll do, I suppose." He wiped an arm across his mouth, then fixed Garrett with a direct look. "Do you want to talk about it?"

Garrett hastily averted his gaze. "No."

"Well, too bad, because you're going to."

Resentment sprang up inside Garrett, striking hot, and it felt better than the pain. "You can't possibly imagine what I'm feeling right now, Demetri."

"No, I suppose not. I mean, I could try to put myself in your shoes. Try to imagine what it might feel like to discover Perpetua didn't love me after all. But I guess I still couldn't sympathize, since I never loved her. Or so I hear."

Another wave of shame slid through Garrett, undercutting the resentment. He clasped his hands tightly before him. "I should never have said that."

"No, you shouldn't have." Demetri's tone was dry, calm. Unemotional. "Because you have no idea what I felt for Perpetua."

The shame dug in deeper. "I'm sorry."

"Let me tell you a bit about what I felt, Garrett," Demetri went on, as though he had not heard the apology. "When Perpetua died, I felt—with quite a lot of conviction—that I didn't want to live anymore. And I almost didn't."

"Didn't what?"

"Didn't live anymore."

Frowning, Garrett turned to look at Demetri. Demetri wrapped both of his hands around his mug of cider and continued, "After Perpetua died, I went to the cave she used to live in, on a rather desolate part of the coast. I lay down in the dark and the damp there, and I didn't get up for a long time. For hours. It got very wet, and very cold, and I think I passed out for a bit. But I didn't care." Demetri shook his head. "I would have frozen to death in that cave. I knew it, and I didn't care. I just wanted to stay there."

Garrett's throat felt very full. "But you didn't. Stay there, I mean."

"No." Demetri took a deep breath. "Because I saw Perpetua. And she told me to get up."

Garrett blinked.

Demetri said wryly, "I know it sounds mad."

"Admittedly, I'm not really in a position to judge anyone when it comes to mad things."

"I don't know if it was real or not. It doesn't matter." Demetri flicked a hand over his shoulder, as though a gnat was buzzing around his head. "What matters is, I got up. It was the hardest thing I've ever done. And that's what you've got to do now."

"Get up from this barstool, you mean?"

Demetri gave him a faint smile. "You have to move on, Garrett."

They were only words. Yet Garrett felt each one like a bullet. He hunched his shoulders. "You make it sound so easy."

"It's not," Demetri admitted. "But if there is one thing I learned from Perpetua, it's that life is fleeting. Perpetua lived on this earth—really lived, I mean, as an actual human with feelings—for only a few weeks. But she *lived*. Sometimes I feel she lived more in those few weeks than I have in my entire life. And she didn't shy away from any of it, the good or the bad. And sometimes it *is* bad. But you can't dwell in those parts. You have to leave it behind."

Garrett slid a hand over his face. "The thing is," he said, "I thought I had. I thought I'd confronted all of this when I first met Briar. At the time, I struggled with my feelings for her because I didn't know how to leave behind my feelings for Snow. I didn't know how to reconcile that I still loved Snow, yet also loved Briar. But I did. Or. I thought I did."

"I think you did," Demetri said gently. "Garrett, I think you have moved on. Only here is Delphine, stirring up all these old feelings, and making it worse with this news about Ansel. And you're right that I can't imagine how it feels. To realize her feelings were not what you thought they were. To realize that doomed her."

"I think that's the worst of it." Garrett struggled to get the words past the lump in his throat. "Because I can't stop thinking how I could have changed it or stopped it—"

"But you couldn't have. I mean, if anything, the whole thing was even more out of your control than you realized, wasn't it? You could never have broken the hex. And I know that hurts, Garrett. But you had no control over the things Snow felt. No one did, not even Snow herself. You know that better than anyone, I think."

Slowly, Garrett nodded.

"And in the end," said Demetri, "it's in the past, Garrett. Whether you could have changed something or done something differently...whether Ansel could have, or Snow...you didn't. They didn't. And there is no changing it now." For the first time, Garrett heard the hint of something lurking beyond Demetri's calm composure. The smallest measure of grief. "So there is nothing to do but move on. And you're lucky. You already have someone to move on with."

Yes. Garrett did have someone, and in that moment, he wanted nothing more than to see her. Be with her. That was why he wanted to go home. Because Briar was there. Briar was his home.

Coming here, seeing Delphine—and even Ansel—had dredged up all those old feelings. Perhaps, even, his feelings for Snow. What he'd said to Briar, in haste and idiocy, about still having feelings for Snow—yes, that had been a foolish attempt to push Briar away. But he had felt, too, the tug of his old feelings. Because he'd been so close to death then, close enough that Snow, in her grave, felt nearer to him than Briar did.

But he might not be dying anymore. And even if he was, he wasn't dead yet. He was still here. And so was Briar. Well, if she forgave him for being an idiot. At that thought, a glimmer of hope awoke inside him like a tiny, guttering candle flame. Small but warm. Uncertain but comforting.

Garrett looked over at Demetri. "You're very wise, you know?"

"Course I am," scoffed Demetri. "I'm about a hundred years old."

"Can I have my cider back?"

"I suppose so. We won't be going anywhere until the morning."

But in the morning—before they had time to see how much the snow had cleared—they found a familiar face waiting for them in the taproom. A lean, dark-haired figure sat on one of the barstools, clad in his stylish overcoat and fur-lined hat, drilling his fingers impatiently against the counter.

"There you are," said Castel, as Garrett and Demetri stopped short at the sight of him. He swung around to face them, his expression unusually sober. "No time for a hot breakfast, I'm afraid. You need to come with me."

"Why?" Demetri demanded.

"Because Ansel is in trouble." Castel sighed. "Again. And this time, Jesine might not be able to save him."

24

DARKENING

JESINE WOKE SLOWLY. THE first thing she noticed was a dull ache in her neck. She'd fallen asleep on the floor in the attic, half-draped over one of the trunks. A bit of drool stained the crinkly page of the open book she'd used as a pillow. Groggily, she lifted her head, looking out the single window.

It was morning.

Stones. Morning. When had she fallen asleep? She remembered noting the growing dark through the window. She remembered remaining in the attic, pouring through her father's books. The attic had become a veritable library, books everywhere, left open and sprawling, stacked precariously on trunks and stools or just on the floor. Jesine sat in the midst of this chaos of whispery parchment, fragile binding, and fading ink.

She remembered sitting here for a long time after it had grown dark, the cold seeping through her wool dress. Despite the chill, she must have fallen asleep. And now it was morning.

Pushing her hair back from her face, Jesine looked down at the book she'd been sleeping on. It was one of the oldest books in her father's collection, and Jesine recalled that most of it had seemed like pure gibberish.

The land is magick, and magick is in the land, she read from it now. *Humans shall not divine these magicks unless a conduit is made.*

Jesine frowned, but before she could try to decipher this, she heard a distinctive *squeal* from somewhere down below. It sounded like a door—specifically, it sounded like the front door. She'd lived in this house long enough to recognize that. Pushing herself to her feet, she stepped out onto the landing, peering around the corner of the staircase. From here, she could see the loft below, but it was empty, the bed neatly made.

"Ansel?" she called uncertainly. But she couldn't see the front door from here. All she could see was the stone hearth below her and something of the kitchen table. She'd left her boots on the landing here and now slipped them on before padding down the stairs, past the loft, all the way to the ground floor.

Ansel, she recalled, had left sometime yesterday with Garrett and Demetri. She'd assumed he was coming back, but now she thought of it, he hadn't said anything to indicate that. They'd hardly spoken since they'd argued two days ago. Jesine had spent most of that time closeted in the attic. When Ansel stuck his head in long enough to tell her he was leaving, she'd clenched her jaw but only replied to let him know she'd heard. She didn't like him leaving—she wasn't sure if he was fully recovered—but she didn't have much leg to stand on, telling him what to do. Not after the way they'd left things. Not after what she'd said to him.

If he'd returned last night, he must have returned quite late, after dusk. But she knew Prince Garrett and his people had avoided traveling in the dark with the demon out there. Perhaps that was Ansel returning now, she thought, perhaps they'd stayed the night somewhere. She didn't even know where he'd gone yesterday. Rounding the bottom of the stairs, Jesine raised her voice and said, "Is that you, Ansel? Where—"

She stopped dead.

It was not Ansel who stood there, just inside the open door.

It was two women. Two women Jesine recognized. Two witches.

Adela, the witch in the midnight-blue cloak...and *Delphine*.

Delphine. The one who, according to Castel, had taken a special interest in her. The one who wanted to steal Jesine's soul.

She was a small woman. That was the first thing Jesine had noticed about her, she remembered, when she'd spied on the witches. And yet she was terrifying. Not even despite her smallness, but *because* of it, somehow. She wore no cloak like Adela, but instead a rich, ermine-trimmed coat that flared from the waist to accommodate her voluminous bustled gown. Her long hair, dark and lustrous, was swept up and pinned at the nape of her neck beneath a stylish hat adorned with lace.

"Good morning, Jesine." Delphine smiled at her, revealing a set of white teeth. "I believe we have an appointment, dear. I've come to collect you."

Jesine stood still as a statue. Should she feign ignorance? Pretend she didn't know who Delphine was or what she was talking about? But she couldn't see what good that would do. She had no idea if there was anyone nearby, anyone who could help her.

And she had no idea how to help herself. Not against this powerful witch.

She opened her mouth and asked the question she hadn't realized was in her head. "How did you get in here?" Her voice was a soft rasp, barely audible.

Delphine cocked her head. "What now?"

"I've a warding." Jesine licked her lips, trying to moisten her throat. Her whole mouth had gone dry with fear. "It should have kept you out. No one can enter unless—"

"Unless you've already showed them in?" Delphine gave a deep chuckle. "But you did show one of us in, dear."

Castel, Jesine thought. She felt a bitter stab at his betrayal. She'd strengthened the ward after he'd been to her house, just like he'd instructed, but she hadn't reset it. Which meant he could still find her house. He'd led the other witches here—

But the third person who walked into Jesine's house was not Castel. It was a young woman. She was short like Delphine, but there the similarities ended. She had a head of curly hair and blue eyes in a round, freckled face. Jesine recognized her.

It was Saskia. The barmaid.

Jesine's friend.

Saskia laughed as though Jesine had spoken out loud. As though she'd heard that thought. *Friend.* "Oh, Jesine, your face!" She laughed some more, as though this was all a childish prank. Girls teasing girls. "That right there. That makes all of this so worth it. Not that it wasn't already." She tossed a smug look at Delphine.

"Yes, becoming a witch has its perks," Delphine murmured. "Eternal youth, for one."

Jesine barely heard her. She stared at Saskia, trying to process this. So not only had Saskia betrayed her, but she was a witch too? A bad witch, obviously. How long had she been one? For as long as Jesine had known her? Or was it new? Had Delphine convinced her to make a deal with the promise of eternal youth?

Saskia looked at Jesine with a pitying gaze. "Honestly, Jesine, you should never have trusted me with your home's location. You thought just because we knew each other when we were five, that meant I was your friend?"

Jesine found her voice. "I never knew you at all."

"No, you didn't." Saskia shook her head. "Though honestly, your previous warding wasn't so strong. I thought any witch could get in here even without my help. But then you strengthened the spell. So it worked out, in the end."

"Yes," Delphine said, tenting her fingers together. "Everything's worked out. So, my dear Jesine. Will you come with us freely? Or must we take you by force?"

"We can, you know." Adela sounded contemptuous, but her eyes were bright. As though the prospect of using force excited her. "Quite easily. Your feeble fairy doesn't grant you as much power as we three have together."

"And," Delphine added, "we also have *this*."

She snapped her fingers, and a fourth person appeared in the doorway.

It was Ansel.

Jesine's breath stuck in her throat. *Ansel*. His arms had been bound to his sides with thick black ribbon, wrapped around his torso several times, and another piece was wadded up in his mouth, gagging him. And as Delphine crooked her finger at him, he slid forward, his boots dragging over the wooden floor.

Delphine snapped her fingers again and Ansel stumbled to a halt beside the witch.

"We're happy to leave him here," Delphine said lightly. "Leave him out of this mess."

Adela shot her a venomous look. Delphine noticed it. "But you see, Adela here would really like to rid herself of Ansel." Delphine pursed her lips in a mock-pout. "She tried once already, a few nights ago. Set her pet demon on him. If I hadn't gotten there in time, well—but I knew we still needed him."

A few nights ago. "The hex-trap," Jesine said hoarsely. "The one that paralyzed him. That night on the road. That was—"

"My doing," Adela said. She sounded almost sulky.

"And I chased off the demon and burned the hex-marker." Delphine smiled beatifically. "You're welcome." The smile vanished from her face. "But Adela, you see, wasn't too pleased. She's ready to be rid of the dear little witch hunter. So if you won't come with us—if you try to fight us—then she would only be too happy to..."

Delphine trailed off.

A wrenching gasp tore from Ansel's throat. His eyes bulged. His fingers twitched down by his sides as though he was desperate to get his hands free. As Jesine watched, panic and horror shredding her heart, Ansel's face began to turn purple. That was when she noticed Adela, a look of triumph on her face as she clenched her fist tighter and tighter. Her gaze was bent on Ansel, her eyes alight with fervor.

"Stop." Jesine's plea was little more than a whisper. Drawing a breath, she raised her voice. "Stop. Please! I'll come with you, I will, please—just stop—"

"You know," Adela breathed, "I don't think I will."

She clenched her fist even tighter.

"Adela." Delphine's voice held a warning note. She was no longer smiling.

"Oh, come now," Adela snapped. "You said yourself we can take her by force. And I was promised this hunter's life. I was promised him dead—"

She was interrupted by a flutter of black wings as something flew in through the open door. It dove at the witches, all three of whom ducked instinctively. "*Caw!*" the feathered devil cried, flapping its wings. "*Caw!*"

Another jolt of terror arced through Jesine. "Bastian."

Yes, it was the raven. Her brother. Saskia screamed as he swooped over the witches again, his talons tangling in her curly hair. He twisted in the air, yanking at her, and she shrieked and shrieked, reaching up to bat him away. Jesine saw blood flying as he pecked at her with his beak. Saskia finally got free of him and ran, still screaming, out of the house.

"Bastian!" Jesine cried, but the raven paid her no heed. He wheeled in the air, a blur of beating black wings, and dove straight at Adela. Adela raised an arm to shield herself and cursed when Bastian raked her with his talons, ripping through her cloak. With relief, Jesine saw the witch had lost her hold on Ansel, who slumped to the ground, spitting the bunched-up ribbon from his mouth and wheezing.

Adela muttered another curse—a literal one, this time—and a burst of sparks exploded from her fingertips, aimed at the raven. Bastian took flight again, spinning free of her. He was magnificent in flight, whirling and gliding, even in the confines of the cottage. He spun again, preparing to dive—

Delphine barked a word and flung her hands out at the raven. A jet of pure power burst from her fingers, black like the darkest night but flashing bright like lightning.

The bolt of power hit Bastian in his tiny chest, engulfing him in crackling darkness.

And the raven fell, limp and lifeless, to the floor.

Everything...stopped. That was how Jesine felt. In that moment. Everything. Just. Stopped.

The world froze. The witches before her, Ansel on the floor. The sun in the sky outside, hiding behind a haze of clouds, the wind in the woods, sighing through the trees.

The birds in the sky. Soaring through the air.

Just as Bastian had only seconds ago.

Someone was laughing. Someone else spoke. But the sounds were muffled, as though Jesine heard them through thickly paned glass. She gazed at the crumple of feathers on the ground, on the raven's tiny feet, sticking up into the air. She zeroed in on its eye. On *his* eye. Bastian's.

Her brother lay motionless on the floor. Trapped in the same form he'd been in for the last six years.

And he was dead.

Something welled up inside Jesine. An unbearable, heavy darkness. Not *the* darkness. Not *him*. No, strangely, unbelievably, *he* was nowhere to be found now, in this most dreadful of moments. The darkness that rose inside her was one of her own making. A mass of writhing shadows, full of unspeakable things. Grief, and anger. Fear and pain. And worst of all, guilt.

It was too big for her. She could not contain it, this darkness.

She opened her mouth and screamed out raw power.

A wave of magic exploded from her. It must have come from her link with Kel, though she had not consciously reached for the delicate chain connecting them. She had never summoned this much magic, this kind of unrefined, undiluted power. It burst from her, rippling over the cottage, bowling over everyone in it. Ansel, on his knees, tumbled onto his side. Delphine and Adela both flew back, Delphine slamming into the wall, Adela catching herself on the kitchen counter.

Jesine raised her eyes and looked at Delphine. The witch was *smiling*.

"Jesine." Ansel's voice, tiny and wretched, pierced through the darkness. "Don't."

Jesine ignored him. Still bristling with magic, she flung her arms out at the witch. But Delphine was too quick for her. Her smile never faltered as black plumes appeared, wrapping her in shadow. When the shadows dissipated, like so much smoke, she was gone. Completely gone.

No. Fueled by her own darkness, by the agonizing gnawing inside her, Jesine staggered forward, looking left and right. But Delphine was nowhere. The witch had truly gone.

Then, a flicker of movement. A flash of blue near the door.

Adela. Jesine had nearly forgotten her. The witch who had nearly killed Ansel just moments ago. Before Bastian stopped her. Adela was at the door, about to slip outside. She snuck a glance over her shoulder, as though to see if her departure had been noticed.

It had.

"Jesine—" Ansel croaked, reaching up for her.

Jesine flung another wave of power at Adela, swift and true.

It seemed Adela didn't know Delphine's trick with the shadows. Or perhaps she just wasn't as quick.

The jolt of power hit her right in the chest, stopping her heart. Jesine *felt* it stop. She felt the magic seep into Adela, felt it sink through flesh and sinew. She felt it coil around her heart. Felt it squeeze until it stopped.

It was all over in a few seconds.

And then Adela, too, dropped to the floor. Just like Bastian. She was dead.

A horrible silence followed. Jesine could only hear her own breath, heavy in her ears. She waited for the new darkness to abate, even a little. She waited for that black mass inside her to shrink.

But it didn't. Because Delphine had escaped. And her brother was still dead.

"Jesine." Ansel's voice was even lower than before, hoarse in his throat. His tone was pleading. He knew what she was going to do. "Jesine, please. Don't go. Just don't—"

For the first time, Jesine looked down at him. She hadn't wanted to look at him, she realized. She had ignored his pleas on purpose, tuned his voice out. She was afraid the sight of him would sway her. Turn her from what she knew she had to do. But now she looked at him. And her heart clenched somewhere beneath the darkness.

"Jesine," Ansel begged. "You don't have to do this. It's what they want. Please, just stay here with me. We'll wait for Prince Garrett. We'll go after the witches together—"

But Jesine turned and looked at the dead raven, still crumpled on the floor. "I'm sorry, Ansel." Her voice felt very faraway, as though it didn't belong to her anymore. She knelt and stretched a hand out, placing three fingers against Ansel's forehead. Muttering a single word, she drew on her magic.

Ansel slumped to the ground again. Peacefully asleep.

She hadn't taken her eyes off her brother. Off his tiny, broken body. That agonizing darkness rose in her again, barreling up her throat, pressing against the confines of her chest.

She couldn't look away from him. From Bastian. So instead, she closed her eyes.

Then she left the house, stepping over Adela's lifeless body, out into the cold, crisp morning air.

25

CHOICES

ANSEL SAT ALONE IN Jesine's kitchen, arms folded on the wooden countertop, his head bowed. On the other side of the counter was a dark, rustic table, and that's where most of the others were gathered.

Sometime after Jesine put him to sleep, Ansel was roused by Prince Garrett's soldiers and Sabine. They'd come looking for Demetri and Garrett since they'd never returned to the village yesterday. And it was a good thing, because they were the ones who discovered Ansel, asleep on the floor of the cottage. The door had been left ajar, letting in all the cold. When Ansel had fallen unconscious, Adela had been sprawled over the threshold. Dead.

But when the soldiers arrived and he woke, Adela's corpse was gone.

Bastian was not. Ansel had scooped up the raven's broken body, cradling him to his chest. Then he'd wrapped him in a thick cloth and laid him in the alcove behind the hearth.

He hoped Jesine would be back before they needed to bury him.

Prince Garrett, Demetri, and Castel turned up shortly after that. Ansel had related what had happened to them. He'd been frantic, desperate to set out after Jesine. But once the others pointed out that nearly an hour had passed since she'd left, he'd slouched grudgingly onto the wobbly barstool in the kitchen. Now he sat there, head buried in his arms, listening to the endless debates and discussion on the other side of the counter.

"So Saskia is a witch?" This came from Demetri, who sounded dismayed.

Sabine gave a cough. "You certainly can pick them."

"Yes," Prince Garrett said delicately. "This makes, what? The third supernatural girl you've fallen for?"

"Fourth," Sabine corrected. "There was a, er—spider-girl?"

Demetri spluttered at that. "I didn't fall for her! Noticing a lady is attractive isn't the same as falling for her. And Briar wasn't supernatural when I met her."

Someone loudly cleared their throat. Klaus. He was the only other person who wasn't gathered at the table, but instead stood leaning against the far wall. "Getting back to the matter at hand. It sounds like Jesine wants to take out the other witches. Shouldn't we just let her?"

"The problem is, that is exactly what Delphine wants," Prince Garrett replied. "She wants Jesine to give in to darkness. To a need for revenge. I'm guessing that would play right into her plan to steal Jesine's soul. Wouldn't you agree, Castel?"

But it was not Castel who spoke next. It was Demetri. "I don't mean to be, er—but hasn't she already gone bad? She did kill someone, after all. With her magic. Doesn't that make her a bad witch?"

Now Castel spoke. Ansel could practically hear him rolling his eyes. "No. That's not how it works."

"Well," Prince Garrett said, his voice deceptively mild. Ansel knew Garrett well enough by now to realize that his always-pleasant demeanor was sometimes a front to mask his displeasure. "Would you care to fill us in then, Castel? How does it work?"

Castel sighed. He'd seated himself at the foot of the table, opposite Garrett. "Look, the terms 'good' and 'bad' witch are gross oversimplifications. And they're terms that don't have much to do with the kind of magic a witch does. What makes someone a good or bad witch is how they get their magic."

"Bad witches kill fairies," Demetri said. "Good witches use a fairy familiar."

"Yes." There was a creaking sound. Castel, shifting around in his chair. "Magic, you see, is in the earth."

"Elarium," Ansel mumbled into his sleeve.

There was a short pause. "What was that, Ansel?" Prince Garrett asked.

Ansel lifted his head. He meant to lift it all the way, sit up straight, but he didn't quite manage it. Instead, he rested his chin on his arms so everyone could see and hear him. "Elarium." His voice sounded dull. "Harper said elarium is magic."

Castel squinted. "That's...also an oversimplification. But, essentially, sure. The point is, magic is in the earth, literally. Fairies are the only creatures in this world with a direct connection to that magic. It has to do with their connection to the trees and the way the trees root in the earth. What matters is, a human can only do magic by gaining access through a fairy in one of two ways, like Demetri said. That's the difference between a good witch and a bad witch."

"But bad witches do have limits on the kind of magic they can do," Demetri interjected. "That's why it cost you when you healed Kinsley."

"Yes." Castel lounged back in his chair. Ansel noted the lock of white hair at his temple—the mark of that "cost" he'd endured. "But that's because of the...forces...we make our deals with."

"Why make a deal at all?" Klaus demanded. "If it's the fairies with magic, why not just take magic from them when you kill them?"

"We do," Castel said coolly. "The deal isn't for the magic. It's for our soul."

"A human can't kill a fairy without losing their soul," Garrett said.

Castel pointed at him. "Exactly. The deal protects our souls. Keeps us from losing them."

"I still don't get it," Klaus persisted. "You're evil anyway. What does it matter if you keep your soul?"

"I realize it may sound a rather academic difference," Castel said, not bothering to hide his frustration, "but believe me. It isn't."

"It's a bit confusing," Demetri said to Klaus, "but a person without a soul isn't really a person anymore. They're just a body. A shell. They can live, but it's not really life."

"And trust me," Castel said, "we witches like to live."

"Even Delphine scoffed at losing her soul," Demetri admitted, "and I would consider her quite soulless to begin with."

Ansel listened to all of this without really hearing it. The back-and-forth prattling was driving him mad. He'd agreed to sit and formulate a plan, but from what Ansel could see, that wasn't what they were doing. It was all taking too long. And with every passing minute, Jesine was getting further and further away. He glanced anxiously out the small window above the sink, but he couldn't get any idea about what time it was. The day outside was too overcast, and all he could see through the window was the tangle of trees encroaching on the house.

Thankfully, Garrett cleared his throat. "We're getting rather far afield here."

"Yes," Castel agreed. "The point is, a good witch has no limitations on the kind of magic they can do. The only thing that makes them 'good' is that they don't murder fairies or make deals with devils. But they can do any magic they want. Including killing other people."

Demetri frowned. "So the fairy familiar can't put any kind of limitation on the magic their witch does?"

"I imagine they could," Castel admitted, "but that doesn't mean much, does it? Have you ever met a fairy that cared much what one human did to another?"

"Oh."

It doesn't matter, Ansel thought, as they all continued to natter back and forth. His hands formed fists, his nails digging into the sleeve of his shirt. Didn't they understand that it didn't matter? Just because Jesine's magic allowed her to go around killing people didn't mean it wasn't dangerous for her. Because of *her*, because of who she was.

She wasn't a killer. And Ansel was afraid what might happen if she forgot that.

"We may be idiots," Prince Garrett was saying, "but we're all here to help Jesine. Why are you here, Castel? I don't suppose you're going to help us?"

Castel folded his arms atop the table. "I thought we just established that there is only so much I can do."

"I still don't see why we don't just help her take down the coven," Klaus said dismissively. "We've all killed people here. Especially people who are part monster."

"Monster?" Castel twisted around to look at him. "*Monster?*"

"Well, what else would you call a person who murders fairies and drinks their blood for—"

But Ansel had heard enough. He pushed himself off his stool so violently, it clattered to the floor. Gripping the counter, he burst out, "None of this is helping anyone! Least of all Jesine. If you lot had just helped me track her down the minute you arrived, we might've found her by now! Well, I'm not waiting any longer. I'm going, and I don't care what the rest of you do."

Silence met his words. Snatching up his coat, Ansel marched out the front door. He heard voices behind him, but he didn't stop, didn't wait.

Out on the porch, he passed Gemma, who stood guarding the house, her rifle slung over her shoulder. She didn't say a word as Ansel thundered down the front steps, clomping out into the slushy snow. But when he came to the edge of the small, scrubby yard, Ansel stopped.

He didn't know where to go. He didn't know where to look. His lungs grew tight, as though he couldn't get enough air. For a moment, Ansel thought his legs would give out beneath him, so heavy and crushing was his despair. He ran a hand over his face, clutching at his forehead.

He didn't know what to do.

He stood like that for perhaps a minute before he heard crunching footsteps behind him, boots pushing through the sodden snow. He was a little surprised when he raised his head and saw, not Prince Garrett, but Demetri coming to stand beside him. Demetri gazed out in the same direction as Ansel, out into the woods.

For a moment, neither of them spoke. Perhaps this silence should have infuriated Ansel, increased his impatience, but as he stood there beside Demetri, staring out into the woods, he found he could breathe again. He found he could think.

"I'm sorry we left you yesterday," Demetri said softly. "Perhaps if we'd stayed together—"

"The witches still would have come for her." Ansel's voice came out scratchy. "It's not your fault, what happened. Or Prince Garrett's."

"Well. I'm sorry anyway," said Demetri. "And I'm sorry about—" He blew out a huge breath. "About everything. Shooting you, that first day we met, with the bats—and I'm sorry I didn't tell you I used to a be a prince—"

"It wasn't my business."

"Perhaps, but. I know I must seem very privileged. I *am* very privileged."

Ansel slanted a glance his way. "Yes. You are. But you also seem like a good person, so. I didn't have to be an ass about it."

"You weren't—"

"I was," Ansel cut in. "And I'm apologizing."

"Well. Apology accepted."

"Likewise." Ansel flexed his fingers. They were stiff with cold, he realized. Because he hadn't taken the time to put on gloves.

He pulled them out of his pockets now and began slipping his fingers into them. Demetri went quiet again, giving Ansel room to speak. And he did, once he finished putting on his gloves.

"She's a good person too," Ansel said quietly. The words tried to stick in his throat, but he forced them out. "Jesine."

"Which is why you don't want her to kill Delphine. Or the rest of them."

"Klaus doesn't get it. It's not that the witches don't deserve to die. Especially Delphine."

"It's that, if Jesine does this," Demetri said gravely, "because she's angry and grieving—because she wants revenge—it could turn her."

"It could destroy her," Ansel corrected. "Forever."

They fell silent again. Ansel thought of the way Jesine had looked when Delphine killed her brother. When the raven fell to the floor, wings splayed, black feathers crumpled. He thought of Jesine in the seconds that followed. The cry that tore from her lips. The helpless way her hands had fluttered when she'd looked at her fallen brother, as though she'd wanted to reach for him but couldn't bring herself to.

He thought of the hunched set of her shoulders. The way all the breath in her body seemed to leave her.

He thought of the same thing happening to Isabelle, and the mere thought made his heart hurt.

He didn't know what to do. He didn't know how to save Jesine from this.

His own words came floating back. Words he'd spoken six years ago to Jesine. *Look. Let's make a pact. Anytime I start talking about how terrible I am, or how terrible my father thinks I am, you'll tell me I'm not. And anytime you start talking that way about yourself, I'll tell you you're not. I'll tell you all the good and wonderful things about you. All right?*

They had promised each other. In their own childish way, they had promised only to see the good in each other. And to remind one another of that good. That was what Ansel had to do now. He had to help her.

He didn't realize he'd said that last bit out loud until Demetri said, "Ansel, I know you have to try. But you need to be prepared—you need to know—you may not be able to stop her. Because it's her choice, in the end. You can't make it for her. And frankly, you shouldn't."

Ansel looked at the former prince. There was a look of inexplicable sadness in him, sadness that seemed far beyond the young man's years. Ansel remembered what Garrett had told him. That Demetri had lost someone. A girl he cared about.

"I know," Ansel said. "I don't want to make her choices for her. She's had enough of that. I just want to be there for her. Do what I can."

"All right, then." Demetri seemed to shake off the darkness that had come over him. "I'm coming with you."

Ansel hesitated. "Look, I'm not very good at, er. Working with people. I don't make friends well."

"I am shocked to hear that, Ansel. Just shocked."

Ansel managed a rueful smile. "But, well, I just wanted to say—thank you. For sticking with me."

"Of course. Shall we be off, then?"

Ansel hedged a glance back at the house. "Well, shouldn't we—"

"We don't need to wait. Garrett is coming up with a plan as we speak. He's very good at last-minute plans—and inserting himself into the most danger possible," Demetri added sourly. "But once he's got things set, he and everyone else can catch up to us."

"But I don't even know where to look. Where Jesine will go—"

"The quarry." Demetri jerked a thumb back at the house. "Castel said, right after you left. That's where Delphine intends to do her ritual. So Jesine will probably find her way there eventually." He glanced up at the sky. "I estimate it'll take us a couple of hours to ride out there. So. Shall we go be hunters, and take on some witches and monsters?"

26

QUARRY

JESINE AMBLED THROUGH THE woods for what felt like
hours. Alone, save for her darkness, pulsating inside her. It
was her constant companion, and the only good that came of it
was it kept that *other* darkness away. It kept *him* away.

Perhaps he couldn't stand the feelings in it. Jesine could hardly
stand them herself.

At times, she almost managed to forget it. She'd focus on
her surroundings, on the physical sensations. The way the cold
shivered through her, making her teeth chatter. The sound of
the wind in the trees, whispering through the pine needles. The
heavy drag of her boots as she tramped through the slushy, melting snow. Snow. When had it snowed? Last night, as she'd lost
herself in her books up in the attic? She hadn't even noticed.

She focused on these things. And the darkness retreated a
little, growing small inside her. But then she'd catch sight of a
bird, casting itself into the air, and a memory would surface. She

and Bastian, laughing and playing as children. And the darkness would return, swift and brutal, rising inside her.

It was unbearable. It was *alive*, the darkness. A thousand shadowy wraiths, grown from her grief and her anger. Her pain made manifest. The wraiths tangled together, a mass of bodies, squirming, pressing, bruising, pushing.

She could not escape it. She feared she never would.

Unless, maybe, she could kill Delphine.

The problem was, she didn't know where Delphine was. The witch had wanted her, but now she was nowhere to be found. And Jesine knew she was trampling aimlessly through the forest.

But when a witch finally appeared, materializing in the frozen winter wood, it was not Delphine.

It was the beautiful one. Malina.

The one who had marked her.

She really seemed to just appear. Jesine spotted her beside a gnarled yew tree, silent, watching Jesine. Jesine was startled, but she didn't let that slow her. She raised her arms, gathering her magic, and aimed a bolt of power at the witch.

But Malina was unfazed. The golden-haired witch merely raised a gloved hand. She pushed away Jesine's burst of power with little effort, as though it was a buzzing fly. The magic struck a tree instead, severing a stout branch that snapped and fell, thundering, to the forest floor.

"Don't waste your magic, child." Malina's voice was as cool and calm as a freshly thawed stream in new spring. "You will never overcome me."

It was not a boast. It was a simple statement of fact. Distantly, Jesine recognized this. It was as though in that moment, she could see the years Malina had lived, stretching back over the centuries. She was simply far too old, far too powerful, for Jesine to defeat.

"Fine." Jesine didn't care about Malina anymore. A week ago, she'd been the one Jesine wanted to find. She'd wanted to know what Malina had done to her, why she had marked her. But that didn't matter anymore. She knew enough. All that mattered was that Malina worked for Delphine. "Take me to Delphine, then."

"That is why I've come." Malina stepped forward. "Here. You're going to freeze to death." She held out a cream-colored garment. Jesine realized it was the cloak Malina had worn the first night Jesine saw her. She glanced down and realized she herself wore no coat, only the belted, moss-green wool dress she'd been wearing since yesterday. No wonder her teeth were chattering.

Jesine took the cloak from Malina and pulled it on, slipping her arms through the wide sleeves beneath the cloak's outer folds. Malina nodded once, then turned, starting back through the woods. She moved gracefully, her steps light but sure over the slippery snow, even though she wore boots with thin, delicate heels. Her hooded coat was beautiful too, blending into the snowy landscape. Her golden tresses escaped the confines of her hood, perfectly arranged over one shoulder. It was strange, Jesine thought, her mind still weirdly distant. It was strange that she was so beautiful. Jesine had the oddest impression this woman did not care about something so prosaic as physical beauty.

Jesine followed the witch through the woods, her own steps dogged, stumbling and tired, not anywhere near graceful. If Malina noticed, she said nothing. They must have walked for another hour, Jesine thought. She wasn't really sure. She'd lost all sense of time. When they finally stopped walking, Jesine looked up and found herself at the edge of the forest.

A vast quarry stretched out before her. A pit carved from dark-gray rock.

Malina led Jesine down into the quarry, traversing back and forth along the ledges. At the bottom, along the far side, was a cluster of rubble, rock cut from the quarry but not yet harvested. The rock was piled high enough to form a kind of shelter, and Malina brought her into this, a room with no ceiling and three walls made of roughly cut stone.

No, not a room. A cell.

For once they stopped, Malina turned and snapped a pair of shackles around Jesine's wrists. They clicked shut before she could process what they were. As soon as they closed, the chain connecting each shackle vanished, leaving her with only two heavy cuffs, enclosing each wrist.

"I know it must seem barbaric," Malina told her, as Jesine stared at the iron bands on her wrists. "They're spelled. They'll keep you from doing magic."

Jesine gazed at her wrists a moment longer. She would need magic to kill Delphine. Her mouth settled in a firm line.

"Don't worry." Malina herself did not sound concerned. Or smug. Or anything, really. She was like ice itself. "You'll get your chance."

"Where is Delphine?" Jesine asked evenly.

"She'll be here soon. She has preparations to make. For the ritual." Malina took a step back, her eyes intent as she studied Jesine. "Your fairy is very old, you know. Frail. Her tree is infected with rot. Her tree is dying."

These words startled Jesine, bringing her mind back from that distant place it had fled to. "What?" When Malina didn't elaborate or repeat herself, Jesine said, "It can take a tree a long time to die."

"Even so." Malina tilted her head. "That fairy is your greatest weakness. She holds you back from discovering real power. You should remember that when the time comes. When you face Delphine."

Jesine snarled, "I will never deal with your devil."

"We'll see." Malina took another step back, then turned, vanishing around the piled rubble.

As soon as she was alone, Jesine sagged to the ground. She felt suddenly exhausted, the weight of her grief and her trek through the woods crushing her. The quarry floor had been cleared of snow, but the rock was damp beneath her, the cold bleeding through her dress and borrowed cloak. Still, she was too tired to notice much.

Her eyes fell shut and she slept.

When she woke, she woke suddenly. Alert at once, her exhaustion vanquished. Yet she had the distinct impression that she hadn't slept long. She glanced up at the sky. It was still shrouded in a thick layer of clouds, but even so, it couldn't be that late. There was too much daylight pressing through that gray haze.

Pressing. Pushing.

The darkness flooded her again. The tangle of wraiths, subdued by sleep no more.

She hadn't dreamed, Jesine thought dully. At least, she didn't think she had. Her sleep had been as deep and dark as death.

"Ah, you're awake."

Jesine whipped around.

Delphine stood at the entrance to her rocky cell.

Jesine surged to her feet, just as Delphine tossed something at her. Instinctively, Jesine raised her hands—her wrists still encased in those iron bands—and caught a whispery, ivory-colored garment.

"You'll need to put that on," Delphine said, "for the ritual."

Jesine stared down at the dress in her hands. It was yellowed with age, made from smooth linen and corseted around the waist. The skirt was relatively loose, but the rest of the dress looked as confining as the magical shackles she wore. The corset, the long, cuffed sleeves, the high neck layered around the throat. Ready to choke the life out of her.

Several different questions sprang to mind, the foremost of which was, *What's wrong with what I'm wearing now?* But Jesine looked at Delphine, her lips clamped together, her darkness swelling inside her. For the first time, she welcomed that darkness. She let herself sink into it. And when she spoke, her question had nothing to do with the dress.

"So you're actually going to face me?" Jesine's voice was low and grating.

"Oh, yes. That's the culmination of the ritual, you see. We face each other and channel as much power as we can. Attempt to overcome each other. If you defeat me—which you won't—you're free to go." A trace of contempt touched Delphine's face. "And free to kill me, as I imagine you very much desire. But if I defeat you..."

"What? You deliver my soul to your master? Buy yourself some favor? A few more years before you face eternal torment?"

"Not just a few more years." Delphine spoke with fanatical relish. "A way out. A way to something better. True immortality. And why not? I've no desire to escape my 'master,' as you call him. I'm happy to work dark magic for him until the end of days. Why ignore such a request? Especially if he gets you in return." She let out a nasty little laugh.

Jesine had almost forgotten about that *other* darkness. The reason she was here. Castel's words came to her, unbidden. *"You've tasted darkness, Jesine. And that darkness still has a hold on you. It calls to you. Haunts you."*

But Delphine was the first witch Jesine had ever heard speak of *him*. Other witches, like Castel, alluded to him. But it was always "that darkness" or "dark forces." Perhaps "devil" but in a colloquial sense. Even when Jesine had said *him*, Castel had responded with "darkness."

But not Delphine. Delphine spoke of *him*.

"Who is he?" Jesine asked.

Delphine's laughter died off. Still, it echoed in the cavern around them, eerie in the surrounding silence. Then Delphine said, looking thoughtful, "Who is he. No one really knows, child. Where he comes from. How ancient he is. Even what he is." She reached up and touched her hair, the gesture oddly self-conscious. "Do you know the old religion? The Church of the Saints?"

Jesine gave her an odd look. She had never heard the Church of the Saints referred to as the "old" religion. People still practiced it, after all, especially in the Mariner Kingdom. Still, she supposed it was not as prolific as it once was. And it was very old.

"The ancient stories about the Saints speak of a great evil they fought," Delphine continued. "A being so old and powerful, it took the combined strength of thousands of Saints to subdue it. A vast darkness. Church lore says this darkness was banished but not destroyed. It was too powerful for that."

"And you think *he* is that darkness?"

"Who can say? At least half of Saint lore is a bunch of non-sense. Stories made up to comfort frightened peasants. But even nonsensical stories sometimes have a grain of truth in them." Delphine inhaled, her nostrils flaring. "I know this, Jesine. I know you and he are connected. I know you traipsed through his darkness six years ago, and even though you foolishly bound yourself to a fairy, you also stored up some darkness inside you. And you will not escape it, in the end. You cannot."

Jesine lifted her chin. Her own darkness expanded inside her, the grasping hands of a thousand wraiths pressing at her from the inside. But this time, the pain and grief cradled her. Lent her its strength. It, too, was vast. It was endless. She had no room inside her for any other darkness, no matter how powerful or ancient.

"He will never have me," she said quietly.

"Why?" Delphine clasped her hands together in a gesture of mock-piety. "Because good triumphs over evil? I'm afraid that is also nonsense, Jesine. I'll let you in on a little secret." She dropped her hands by her sides and leaned forward. "Evil always wins. Again and again. Because it's always there. It's everywhere. All it has to do is outlast good. There is no defeating it."

And though Jesine took comfort in her own darkness, she feared Delphine was right.

27

POSSESSED

G ARRETT STARED GLUMLY OUT the front window of Jesine's cottage. Gemma stood on the porch outside, bundled in her hunter's coat, her dark hair bound in a thick braid
pinned behind her head, rifle in hand. Standing guard.

Everyone has something to do, Garrett thought, *except me.* He
turned away from the window. "I still don't see why I had to stay
here."

Castel rolled his eyes at him. The witch sat on the floor before
the hearth on a threadbare rug. His legs were folded beneath him,
and a large, shallow stone bowl was set before him. "For the last
time," he said, "so far as we know, Delphine still has the poppet
she made to control you. If you go anywhere near that quarry,
you very well might find yourself doing things you don't want to
do. Perhaps even fighting against your own people. At the very
least, they might use it to incapacitate you. So. You wouldn't be
much help there, would you."

"And I'm so much help here," Garrett drawled.

"No, not really." A devious smirk tugged at Castel's lips as he removed his sack coat and set it aside, folding it neatly. "But you can watch me be helpful."

Garrett rapped an impatient knuckle against the wooden countertop. "And you're sure you can banish the demon?"

That was why Castel had stayed here while the others went to the quarry. Well. That, and Castel had flatly refused to go to the quarry. He wouldn't be able to fight against the other witches anyway, he claimed, and he didn't want to be anywhere near Delphine in case this all went wrong.

"Oh, certainly I can banish it." Castel poured a tiny vial of black powder into the bowl before him, then added a pinch of something that looked suspiciously like bone ground into a fine grit. "I'm the one who summoned it, after all."

"Don't remind me," Garrett muttered.

"Banishing it will be easy." Castel furrowed his brow as he bundled a pile of crow's feet together with a thin strip of moss. "The difficult part is wresting control from Harper first. But once I've done that, well. With any luck, the demon will be gone before your people get there."

"Hmm. And what makes you so sure Harper is the one controlling it?"

"Well, Delphine won't be. She'll need all her magical energy focused on her ritual with Jesine. And I doubt Saskia, little whelp that she is, has the power to control a demon. That leaves Harper."

"Wasn't there another witch? Jesine mentioned her. Er—"

"Malina."

"Yes. How do you know she's not controlling the demon?"

"Dear princeling, I've not seen Malina for days. After she helped us summon Delphine, she disappeared. I assume she's gone. She did her part, after all."

"But I thought you were all getting something out of this deal. So what did Malina get?"

"I've no idea." Castel lifted his gaze long enough to catch Garrett's skeptical look. "Truly. Malina isn't one for sharing. All I know is, she said she was here for revenge just like the rest of the lot."

"Well, who did she want revenge on?"

"Again, no idea. Perhaps the people of Lise. Maybe the man who burned up did her some great wrong years ago. How should I know?"

Garrett pinched the bridge of his nose. "Castel. It sounds to me like, for all *you* know, Malina very well could have control of the demon now."

"Well, I suppose it's possible."

"And? If she is, will you still be able to banish it?"

"Considering she's about a thousand years older than me and much more powerful, probably not. But let's cross that bridge if we come to it, all right?" Castel held up a small, writhing garter snake over his bowl. As Garrett watched, the witch raised his other hand, in which he held a black knife. With one swift motion, he beheaded the snake, angling the body so its blood trickled down into his bowl.

Garrett turned away. "You're a horrid person."

"I know," Castel said blandly. "Keeps me up at night."

Still with his back turned, Garrett gazed through the front window again, looking for Gemma. She was just visible through the smudgy paned glass, her outline hazy. She'd paced to the other end of the porch and now bent her head, checking something on her rifle.

"What is the demon, anyway?" Garrett asked.

"What?"

"The demon. As I understand it, it was one of the naiads—in the Mariner Kingdom—who called it a demon. But Briar said it was just a word she used for it. She didn't really know what it was. So what exactly is it?"

"Hmm." Castel's tone was pensive. "Well, demon is as good a word as any. It's a creature from a dark dimension, driven by insatiable hunger. Especially when it is brought into this world."

"So there's no other name for it?"

"Not that I know of." Castel fell silent, and for a moment, all Garrett heard was a strange whispering sound, followed by a sizzling *spark*. As a noxious smell filled the room, Castel said, "They were witches."

"What?" Startled, Garrett turned to face Castel.

"These demons." A tendril of black smoke rose from the bowl, and Castel closed his eyes, inhaling deeply. When he opened his eyes again, they were pale, like the filmy eyes of an old man. His dark irises and pupils blended together, fading to gray. But he looked right at Garrett. "They were witches once. Bad witches. Or their souls, anyway."

Garrett stared at him.

"It's what will become of us all, eventually. We witches who make deals for our magic." Castel spoke lightly, but it was clearly a forced nonchalance. "After centuries of living on this earth, doing evil. After an eon of torment in death. What's left of us is chipped away until only the monster remains. The only bit that's capable of living in that dark place." Castel smiled a bleak smile.

Garrett didn't know what to say. Bad witches were hardly deserving of sympathy, and yet...did anyone deserve that fate? Especially a witch like Castel who, despite being *evil*, had healed Kinsley, helped Perpetua and Jesine, and even now, helped them still?

Something of this conflict must have shown on his face, for Castel laughed quietly and said, "No need to mourn me yet, dear prince. Or ever." He looked unearthly through the gauzy curtain of smoke hovering before him, his eyes wide and milky. "I'll be alive long after you're dead. I've a great many years ahead of me before I meet that fate." He closed his eyes again. "Now. Either stop pestering me or go outside. I need to concentrate." As the smoke spiraled up out of the stone bowl, Castel drew in another deep breath.

When he opened his eyes again, they were completely white from eyelid to eyelid. He inhaled once more, then began to chant in a low voice.

"Castel?" Garrett ventured.

Castel didn't respond. He didn't seem to have heard. He only continued to chant.

Garrett sighed. *This is it*, he thought. And now he had nothing to do but sit here and wait. He realized with some consternation that he'd been chatting up Castel because he wanted a distraction. He was so bored and desperate to forget how useless he was that he'd preferred conversation with an evil witch.

He paced the front of the house for a bit, floorboards squeaking beneath him. He tossed a few glances Castel's way, but the witch didn't move, chanting, caught up in his spell. Garrett tried not to think about his friends, his people, out there now, racing to the quarry to help Jesine. He tried not to think about them going up against the demon—for he was not convinced Castel could banish it before they arrived—and he tried not to think about Jesine herself, alone, grieving her brother, targeted by Delphine.

He tried not to think about any of it, and he tried not to think about how he was stuck here, unable to help.

The light was low inside the cottage, only a few tallow candles casting flickering shadows over the hearth and the kitchen. Garrett moved closer to the front door; the smoke drifting up from Castel's bowl was making his nose and throat itch. The day should have been growing brighter as it neared midday, but there was no sun today. It was sunk behind a solid wall of clouds.

Garrett wheeled around to peer out the window, looking for Gemma. She'd moved again; the corner of the porch he'd last seen her on was empty. He looked closer, at the other end of the porch, but she wasn't there either.

She wasn't anywhere.

Garrett's heart flipped. She'd probably just gone to scout around a bit, he reasoned, just to check there was nothing out there—she was probably as bored as he was, after all—

Still. He'd better check in with her. Glancing over his shoulder at the white-eyed Castel, Garrett pushed open the door and stepped outside.

It was bitterly cold, though not so cold as it had been. The snow that had fallen so quickly last night was melting just as quickly, leaving a sludgy layer over the leaf-strewn ground. Ice dripped from the branches of the trees as though the forest was weeping. Garrett scanned those trees, looking for any sign of

Gemma, but the wood was still and quiet. He opened his mouth to call out, but before he could, he heard a sound.

A disturbing sound. A low moan.

Garrett looked around sharply, stepping up to the edge of the porch.

Gemma lay in the snow before him.

"Gemma!" Garrett nearly slipped in his haste to get down the porch stairs. He rushed to Gemma's side, falling to his knees. Her eyes were shut, her breathing erratic and labored. When he saw blood staining the slushy snow, he looked for a wound but found none. It wasn't until he took her head in his hands that he realized the blood was coming from one of her ears—thick, black blood, oozing down her neck.

"Gemma." Frantic, Garrett leaned in close to her. "Gemma, can you hear me?"

Gemma did not respond. But a ringing peal of laughter did.

Garrett whirled around.

A figure emerged from the forest. A figure cloaked in midnight blue. For a moment, Garrett thought it was Adela, risen from the grave. But the figure was too short to be Adela, and as she came closer, he saw the mousy curls spilling out from the hood pulled over her head.

Then she thrust the hood back, and Garrett recognized Saskia the barmaid. Garbed in Adela's cloak.

Garrett straightened, reaching for one of his pistols, but Saskia laughed again and said, "I wouldn't, if I were you." The menace in her voice was totally at odds with her doe-like blue eyes. "You know I can take it away from you. I can even make you turn it on yourself."

"Can you?" Garrett spoke in a level voice, but he didn't draw his pistol. "I understand you're new at all this."

Saskia ignored his jibe. "Or I could have you turn it on your friend there. Might be a mercy. Put her out of her misery."

Gemma. "What have you done to her?"

"Oh, nothing, really. The damage was already done, you see. By Adela." Saskia gripped the edge of the midnight-blue cloak and gave it a little twirl. "What do you think, by the way? Does her cloak suit me?" She giggled and then, just as quickly, sobered. "No, what happened to your friend is Adela's doing. She's had a bit of swelling in her brain ever since Adela incapacitated her. The night she took you to Delphine. That swelling would have burst on its own eventually. I just helped it along."

Garrett took all this in with quiet horror. *Damage. Swelling in the brain. Burst.* "Fix her," he grated. "Stop this."

"No, I don't think I will. I have better plans, you see." Saskia reached into the folds of her cloak and removed something small. A crude doll, built from jagged twigs and bundled twine.

The poppet.

A chill slid down Garrett's spine. But he clenched his teeth, refusing to let any fear show. "And again I ask: do you really think you're powerful enough to work that?"

"No, you're right." Saskia gave a mock-sigh, tapping a finger to her chin. "The way Delphine used this to torment you—the way she manipulated you, leading you around where she wanted, putting fear and doubt into your head—I'm not sure I could manage such sophisticated magic. But maybe..."

She caught Garrett's eye and smirked.

Then she took hold of one of the poppet's branch-like arms and *snapped* it.

Garrett screamed as his own arm snapped. Pain exploded above his elbow and shot upwards as bone fractured inside him. He collapsed to his knees, the pain so overwhelming, he almost blacked out. The world swayed around him, and for a moment, he saw nothing—

He blinked hard, barely holding onto consciousness. Gritting his teeth, he tried to get a leg under him, tried to stand again—

But Saskia wasn't finished. Too late, Garrett saw she'd taken something else out from beneath her cloak—a long, thin needle. Holding it up, as though to see it in a better light, she said, "Now I wonder what will happen if I do *this*."

She jabbed the needle into the middle of the poppet.

Garrett grunted, doubling over as another flash of pain ricocheted through him. He clutched at his side, a few inches above his hip, and ripped his coat back. Breathing shallow breaths, he watched in disbelief as a dark stain appeared through his waistcoat, blossoming out, wetting his clothes.

Blood.

Garrett's knees buckled beneath him, and he slumped over, falling onto his face. Saskia was laughing. It was very different from Delphine's deep-throated laugh, bright and girlish, but it haunted him even so, bringing him back to the night he'd first seen Delphine in that cabin in the woods. "You see, Prince Garrett," Saskia sang, "you don't need much power to use this thing. Just a little concentration, a little imagination—and an intent to hurt."

Breathing heavily, Garrett rolled onto his back. *Get up*, he told himself furiously, *you have to get up*. But he could feel blood pooling past his fingers, no matter how hard he tried to staunch the wound, and the pain in his arm was so bad, he couldn't see straight, couldn't think—

"That," said a new voice, "is quite enough of that."

There was a gasp. From Saskia, Garrett thought, but he couldn't see anything, lying on his back. Even the thought of turning his head was difficult. Still, panting, he forced himself to try, twisting his neck, letting his head droop to the side—

His vision was blurry. Someone stood before Saskia, someone in a light-colored coat. Whoever it was stretched an arm out towards Saskia, and the barmaid gave a little shriek as a blast of light hit her. The shriek cut off abruptly, and Saskia fell, boneless, to the ground.

Garrett blinked again, trying to clear his vision. But the stranger, whoever they were, remained blurry as they stepped forward, reaching down to take something from Saskia's fallen form. There was a flash of sparks, a smokey stench, and then the stranger dropped whatever they'd taken into the snow.

Then the stranger turned and approached Garrett. His eyes fluttered, and suddenly the stranger was there, leaning over him, her golden hair spilling around her.

"I can save your friend's life," the stranger said, "but I want something in return. Something from you, Prince Garrett."

Sweating in the snow, Garrett stared as the face before him came into focus. It was a woman. A very beautiful woman, an *impossibly* beautiful woman. "The—poppet—" he croaked.

"Destroyed," the beautiful woman said. "Unfortunately, that won't heal you, but your wounds aren't life-threatening. But your friend here—" She glanced aside. At Gemma, Garrett thought. Gemma, who was bleeding in her brain. "She will be dead very soon. I can take steps to stop that, but I want your word first, Prince Garrett. That you'll give me what I want."

"And what's—that?" Garrett demanded, barely getting the words out.

"Something I've wanted for a long time now." She reached up and swept a strand of hair from her face. "I want your blood, Prince Garrett."

Something I've wanted for a long time...

"I know who you are," Garrett said.

Then he passed out.

28

SEVERED

ANSEL EDGED ALONG THE face of a boulder, trying to peek around it. A quick glimpse showed him the top of the quarry and the vast drop below, but not much else. "This is no good," he muttered. "I can't see anything from here."

Beside him, Demetri shifted. "All right. But let's move through the trees, see if we can find a closer vantage point. I don't think we should move out in the open, not unless we have no choice—"

"We have no choice!" Ansel shot back. The long ride through the twisted woods had been slow, reigniting Ansel's desperate impatience. Now he just wanted to see Jesine, he wanted to know if she was all right. "I'm going out to take a look."

"No, Ansel, wait—"

But Ansel did not wait. He darted out from the trees. The land cleared and sloped down slightly between the woods and the quarry edge, which wasn't far—about twenty paces. But Ansel had crossed less than ten when something crashed into him, sending him sprawling. His knees *banged* into the ground, pain reverberating up and down his legs, and all the breath in his body left his lungs, jamming at the base of his throat.

The demon, Ansel thought, gasping for air, but the force that hauled him to his feet was nothing so tangible as a demon. It was an invisible force, like the one that had taken ahold of him earlier that morning, in Jesine's house. When Adela had controlled him.

But it was not Adela controlling him now. Adela was dead.

Against his will, Ansel jerked upright and saw Harper facing him with a small smile playing at his lips.

"Ansel!" Demetri cried, but Harper gave a sharp flick of his wrist and Ansel went flying, spinning around as he surged through the air. He didn't stop until he was right beside Harper, facing the evergreen tree line, facing Demetri, who skidded to a halt about ten paces from them.

"Not another step," Harper called to him. "Or I'll snap his neck."

Ansel believed it. His neck felt rigid, caught in a vicelike grip. As though someone held him by the sides of his head, ready to twist it off. His whole body was frozen, still as a statue. He couldn't move except to speak. "You won't kill me," he said to Harper. "You told me yourself. You need your vengeance."

"And it would be a shame to cut it short," Harper admitted, "but though I don't want your death, it would serve. So." He raised his voice again. "Not another step."

Reluctantly, Demetri held up both hands in a placating gesture.

"Good," said Harper. "Thing is, I can't trust you'll stay like that long enough for Ansel to see what I want him to. So."

He gave an indifferent shrug. "I'll have to leave someone else to watch you."

Something moved at the tree line, something bone-white, starkly visible through the greens and browns of the wood. Ansel's gaze snagged on it, and his mouth went dry with fear.

"Demetri," he croaked, trying to get a warning out. "Demetri!"

Demetri turned.

There, at the edge of the tree line, was the demon. For once, it stood still, terrifying in its silence, in its inhuman visage. Ansel had not forgotten that masklike face with its barely formed features—the empty sockets where eyes should have been, the nub of a nose and sunken-in cheeks. But worse than its face were its long, slender fingers, hanging down by its sides like bizarre knives made of bone.

Demetri's face went as white as the demon. He immediately reached for the pistol at his waist, but as soon as he had it, Harper waved a hand and the pistol went flying, soaring back into the trees. Demetri cursed.

"Leave him be," Ansel growled. "You don't have to do this. Call that thing off—"

A shot rang out, interrupting him. The bullet didn't hit the demon—at least, Ansel didn't think it did—but the creature vanished, zipping away. A second later, Sabine ran out of the trees.

"Sabine." Demetri's voice was ragged with relief. "Thank the stars."

"Klaus is here too. That was his shot." Sabine stopped at Demetri's side. "Surely three of us are enough to take that thing down?"

Harper let out a low chuckle. "I wouldn't count on it."

"Look out!" Ansel cried.

The demon appeared in another pale streak, moving so fast, Ansel didn't see it until it knocked into Sabine, bowling her over. Demetri shouted and ran for her, yanking his rapier out of its sheath. Another shot rang out from the woods, but Ansel didn't get to see if it hit. With another flick of his wrist, Harper spun Ansel, and he found himself drifting away, the toes of his boots sifting through pebbly ground until he reached the edge of the quarry. He came to an abrupt halt beneath a young, stubby maple tree. A roaring wind whipped at him and the tree alike, so cold and powerful that Ansel had to blink into it, his eyes watering.

"Let me go," Ansel spat. "Call that thing off!" He tried to twist around to look for the demon and his friends, but his neck went even more rigid. He couldn't turn it more than an inch in either direction.

"Forget them," Harper said shortly. "They're not why we're here, remember?"

Ansel caught his breath. Now that he stood, unwillingly, at the edge of the quarry, he had a clear view of it, stretched out below him. The bottom was about a hundred paces across. Multiple ledges lined the stone walls of the quarry, like vast platforms carved out of the rock. Directly below Ansel, on a ledge about halfway up the quarry, stood Delphine.

And Jesine.

Absurdly, relief flooded Ansel at the sight of her. She was all right. She was unharmed. She wore a strange, old-fashioned ivory dress, and her long red hair hung down her back, wild and tangled. But Ansel's relief was short-lived, because Jesine was not alone. Delphine was with her. The witch stood across from Jesine, garbed in her own strange dress—strange because it was so lavish, a dark gown encrusted with black sapphires and black pearls. The two of them stood at either end of the ledge, circling each other, two predators preparing to strike.

"Jesine," Ansel cried. "Jesine!"

"She can't hear you." Harper sounded almost bored. "Besides, you're not here to talk. You're here to watch." He brought his hand down sharply, and Ansel crashed to his knees for the second time, bruising the bone, it felt like.

If only, *if only* he could get to his fairy-wood stake. He'd started to slide it free of his sleeve before Harper grabbed him but hadn't quite gotten it into his hand. He was sure it would slide free with a twist of his arm, but he couldn't even do that much. Harper's power held him tight.

"It's starting." Out of the corner of his eye, Ansel saw a slow smile spread across Harper's face.

"Jesine will never go bad," Ansel swore. "She'll never make a deal."

"I think she will if it's the only way she can kill Delphine and take her revenge." Harper laughed. "It worked out even better than I said it would, didn't it, Ansel? It never occurred to me to kill her brother. But that worked even better than dooming him."

Ansel strained his arms, trying to get free, trying to move an inch. He tried for another glance over his shoulder to check on Demetri, but he still couldn't twist his head far enough. He could hear them, though. Demetri and the others were still alive, still fighting. He heard shouts and screams, the occasional gunshot—and—

And something whimpering?

No. Not whimpering. *Meowing.*

Ansel tilted his head back as far as Harper's power would allow. It was just far enough to see into the lower boughs of the maple tree above him, creaking and rocking in the wind. Just far enough to see the swish of a long, black tail.

There was a cat in the tree.

"Are you paying attention, Ansel?" Harper asked. "Are you watching, little hunter?"

Ansel dropped his gaze. Jesine and Delphine had raised their arms, staring each other down. "They're gathering their power," Harper said. "Watch closely, Ansel. I don't want you to miss this."

"Even if Jesine kills her," Ansel said through gritted teeth, "that doesn't mean she'll go bad. She can kill her without going bad." Like Castel said, there were no limits on the kind of magic a good witch could do. Ansel didn't want her to do it, but even if she did, that didn't mean she would turn. That didn't mean she would make a deal.

"Can she?" Harper asked. "Even if—argh!"

Ansel whipped his head around. Ansel *could* whip his head around. Something had broken Harper's concentration just long enough for him to lose his grip on Ansel. Just long enough for Ansel to move.

It was the cat. The black cat in the tree. It had jumped down and landed on Harper's shoulder, digging its claws into the back of the witch's neck.

Ansel didn't hesitate. He twisted his arm.

The fairy-wood stake slid into his palm.

Ansel didn't even bother to stand. He stabbed the stake into the fleshy part of Harper's calf.

Harper let out another cry. As he staggered and fell, slumping forward, the cat let out a distressed *meow* and leapt free of him, dashing off into the trees. Blood oozed down Harper's pant leg as he fell onto his side, groaning. That stake wouldn't kill him, Ansel thought, as he scrambled to his feet, but it didn't need to. So long as it was stuck inside him, he wouldn't be able to use magic. In fact, any magic he was using would have been severed the moment Ansel stabbed him. Which meant—

"The demon!" someone shouted. Klaus, Ansel thought. "It's gone!"

Ansel spun around. Sabine was on the ground but climbing to her feet. Demetri, too, looked unharmed, swinging from left to right with his rapier drawn. Klaus was on his knees, wincing, but otherwise looked all right—

The sound of pounding hooves drew Ansel's attention. He gaped as a horse cantered around the top of the quarry, carrying Prince Garrett.

"Ansel! Demetri!" The prince drew his horse to a halt. He breathed heavily, leaning over with a pained expression. His arm was in a sling.

Before Ansel could ask what had happened, Harper let out another groan, stirring on the ground. Ansel glanced down and realized the witch wasn't groaning, but laughing. Harper lifted a hand, pointing out across the quarry.

"Can she still kill Delphine," he rasped, "if her access to magic is broken?"

Ansel jerked around. His gaze instinctively sought out Jesine on the ledge below, facing Delphine. But that wasn't where

Harper pointed. Harper pointed along the top of the quarry, some thirty paces from them.

Where a golden-haired woman stood, garbed in a cream-colored coat. And she wasn't alone.

A fairy stood before her. A green-skinned fairy in a tatty little dress. Ansel knew at once what she was, even though he'd never seen a fairy before. The massive wings were a dead giveaway, beating gently back and forth. They were the only part of the fairy that was moving. Otherwise, the creature stood motionless, as rigid as Ansel had been under Harper's power.

Still down on the ground, Harper said, "I don't know if you've met Malina. The final member of our coven. And Kel, of course." Harper's voice was honed with malice. "Jesine's fairy."

Ansel's eyes widened. He looked down and saw Jesine, on the ledge below, turn to look at the fairy too.

Ansel lifted his gaze just in time to see Malina raise one arm. She made a swift gesture, slicing through the air like a blade. Even from this distance, Ansel saw the witch's lips form a word. An incantation.

And a thousand cuts opened all over the fairy's delicate elfin body, staining her mint-green skin red with blood.

29

CONDUIT

J ESINE WATCHED AS MALINA'S spell engulfed Kel, opening a thousand wounds all over her body. As though she'd
been sliced by a thousand blades, the cuts small but deep. Blood
poured from the wounds, soiling Kel's brown tunic, running
down her arms and legs. The fairy swayed, once, in half a circle.

Then she fell off the top of the quarry, tumbling onto a ledge
below. Like a puppet with its strings cut.

The fragile chain inside Jesine gave a violent quiver. It was
still there, but more fragile than ever, ready to snap. The magic
Jesine had built up inside her vanished; it could not be sustained
through so tenuous a connection.

Kel, her fairy, her link to the land, was bleeding out.

Soon she would be dead, and that connection severed.

"*Yes.*" Delphine spoke the word like a prayer of worship.
"Now what will you do, Jesine? Your fairy is dying. You've no
hope of killing me and taking your revenge."

351

Jesine began to run, dashing across the ledge, making straight for Kel. As she ran, Malina's words floated through her mind, a forbidding premonition. *"That fairy is your greatest weakness. She holds you back from discovering real power. You should remember that when the time comes. When you face Delphine."*

Not a premonition, Jesine thought swiftly. It wasn't a premonition if you knew it was going to happen. Malina had planned this. Her and Delphine. There was no ritual. No spell to claim her soul. No one could make that choice for her, but she could be influenced.

Is that what I am? Jesine thought. *Influenced?* Inside her, the darkness that had sprung into being when Bastian died grew larger and more terrible than ever before. She could see no way through that darkness, no way to put it to rest. There was nothing else. Nothing but grief and guilt. Writhing shadows, consuming her from the inside.

She couldn't stand it. She couldn't *stand* it. This pain was like nothing she had ever felt before, and it would go on and on and on without an end. She could not live like this. She could not *live* like this. She just wanted to sink into that writhing mass, let it become her.

She just wanted to disappear into the darkness. Feel nothing. Take her revenge.

As Jesine clambered up the next ledge, Delphine called after her. "It's not too late, Jesine. Let him in. Allow yourself his protection. Take your fairy's blood before she dies. Then you will have all the power you need."

Jesine pulled herself onto the next ledge. The wind funneling through the quarry buffeted her, whipping her hair across her face. She crawled to her fairy's side. The ledge was not large, and one of Kel's arms dangled over the side of it. Her blood soaked into the ground, pooling beneath her. That pool spread quickly, reaching Jesine, staining her ivory dress.

"Jesine." Kel wasn't dead yet. The fairy locked eyes with Jesine and spoke, her voice weak and broken. "Listen to me...Jesine. I am dying, girl."

Jesine didn't try to deny it. She only reached out to cover the fairy's cold hand with her own. Trying to offer some comfort.

"Y-you cannot save me," Kel croaked. "I will die. Your connection to magic will be s-severed forever. Unless...you take my blood."

"No. I won't."

"Not like that. Not as the heart-eater intends. You will not consume it. You must...*take*...it. Use it. Find...a source."

Jesine shook her head. "I don't understand."

"It's all in the taking." Kel's voice was softer than ever, barely audible. Jesine had to lean down to hear her, so close that the ends of her hair dipped into the pool of Kel's blood. "Bad witches...steal power. But I *gift* mine to you. Use it...as a conduit...delve deep..."

"I don't know what you mean, Kel."

"I can show you," Kel breathed. "My—gift to you. The ancient ones...called it forbidden...but it can be done." She let out a long, rattling breath. "My—blood. *Feel* the blood."

Jesine felt dazed. As though she was half in a dream and half in the waking world. Slowly, she placed her hand into the pool of blood between her and Kel. She closed her eyes.

There was a tug inside Jesine, a tug at one end of that delicate chain, the end Jesine couldn't see. The end that was connected to Kel. There was another tug, harder this time, and the chain snapped.

Jesine cried out, or some part of her did. She felt as though some vital organ had been ripped from her body, the sudden *punch* of it physically painful. She flailed, reaching for the broken chain as it vanished, but it was gone. She felt weak, as though she was the one bleeding out. Her eyes flew open, landing on Kel, but the fairy wasn't dead yet. She blinked her black eyes slowly, her chin dipping in the barest of nods.

Kel was alive, but their connection was gone. Jesine had become unmoored. Untethered. A raft adrift in an ocean, useless and helpless without her magic—

"Here," Kel whispered. "The blood. Right here. Feel it."

The blood. Kel's blood. Jesine closed her eyes again, and she could feel it now. Not just physically, beneath her hands, but the power in it. It *burned* with power. The urge to take it was strong, but Kel's words guided her away from that. "Follow the blood. Follow its path. See...how it delves into the earth. How it feeds the land."

Jesine struggled. She could somehow see, *sense*, what Kel wanted her to do, but it felt just out of reach.

"Open yourself to it," said Kel. "Open yourself to the land."

Jesine struggled a moment more. She pressed her fingertips into the blood, into the stone beneath it—

And then she was falling.

It was as though a trapdoor had opened beneath her, leading deep down into the pits of the earth beneath the base of the quarry. She wasn't physically falling—some part of herself was still in her body, kneeling beside Kel, fairy blood staining her hands and face. But her mind, her spirit, was falling, delving deep as Kel had said, deep into the earth.

Magic. The land, the rocky earth beneath the quarry, teemed with it. It burned hot and bright like magma, beds of magic waiting to be harvested. It wove through the earth like the roots of a tree, plumbing the ground for life. And Kel's blood was part of those roots. The blood of every fairy was, and Jesine could feel them all, every one in the world. Connected to the land. Connected to magic.

"Go deeper," Kel urged. "Tap into...a source."

A source, a source. Jesine still didn't know what that meant. But she did as Kel said and went deeper. She wasn't falling anymore. She was in control. But the deeper she went, the more difficult it became. The earth hardened, and even the roots of magic struggled here, slithering along ledges and winding through tiny crevices, deep into the earth's core.

There was a darkness here. Jesine stopped and found herself in a network of caves, buried deep. The roots here turned black and damp, a venomous rot slowly claiming them, poisoning the earth.

Jesine...

A deep shiver worked through Jesine. She knew that voice. *His* voice. The darkness. That fell creature who ruled over every bad witch, taking their souls for his own.

Jesine...at last, you are here...

No, Jesine thought desperately, *no, I'm not—I won't—* Had she delved too far into the land? There had to be a way out—a way to escape him—

The darkness around her intensified. Black shadows crawled over the cave walls like millions of spiders, converging on her.

Cold crept through Jesine, not one icy hand but hundreds, grasping at her, squeezing, stealing all her warmth and life—

There has to be a way out, she thought, *there has to be—*

And then she saw it.

A door.

What was it Castel had said? *You opened a door. Between you. And the darkness.*

"Follow the blood, Jesine." Kel's voice again, piercing through the shadows. "Turn away from the darkness."

Yes, Jesine realized. It really was that easy.

She turned and gazed down the cavernous corridor, watching the creeping darkness encroach upon her. It was vast. Ancient. Powerful.

But the darkness inside Jesine was more powerful. Her own grief was more powerful. She let it surge inside her, a thousand wraiths crying out, pushing at her, hands splayed, ready to burst free.

Then she reached out and shut the door, closing it forever.

Nooooo! The screech was long and terrible, echoing throughout the caves, but Jesine heard it distantly. She turned her back on that door and took another path instead, tracing the roots as they branched off in a different direction.

As they led her to their source, teeming with life and light.

Magic immersed her as she dove into it. She let it swallow her whole.

And when she surfaced a moment later, she exploded with power.

She *exploded* with power. Just as she had in her cottage that morning when Bastian died. Only this time, the wave of magic that rippled from her was far stronger, washing over the entire quarry and the woods beyond, knocking down everyone in its path.

She was connected. To *everything*. The dark, pitted stone beneath her, rife with elarium. The vast stretch of forest atop the ridge, shadowed and deep, yet bursting with life. The babbling brook gushing through a nearby ravine, carving its path into the earth. The birds in the sky, calling to each other as they tumbled and soared through the air.

The birds in the sky. The ravens. Black as the night but oh, so bright.

And—most importantly of all—she was connected to *them*. All the other witches. She could feel them. She could feel their stolen magic, pulsating, stored up in rot-stained wells.

"What—!" The exclamation centered Jesine, tethering her back to the here and now. To this physical world. "How—"

Still perched on the narrow ledge, kneeling in her fairy's blood, Jesine rose. Kel's tattered body lay before her. Jesine couldn't feel her anymore. The fairy was gone. Grief speared her, but it was just one more painful jab. Grief already had its hooks in her. She acknowledged the pain and pushed past it.

She could grieve later. Now, she had business to take care of. Jesine turned her back on the fairy and faced the witch awaiting her.

On the wider ledge below, Delphine climbed to her feet, her movements hasty and much less graceful than Jesine's. Her dark hair was askew, half-fallen from her intricate coiffure, and she clutched her bejeweled black skirt in one hand so she wouldn't trip on it. When she spoke, her voice was hushed and hoarse, as though Jesine's blast of magic had scarred her throat. "Where did that come from? That magic—that power—" Even from this distance, Jesine could see the hand Delphine put to her own neck was trembling. "*No one* has that much power."

"You're wrong, Delphine." Jesine's skirt trailed in her fairy's blood as she began to descend to Delphine's level, navigating the curve of the ledge. The slope was steep and treacherous, but Jesine walked it with ease, every step surefooted. "Because that power came from me."

"But—" Delphine's piercing blue eyes flicked briefly over Jesine's head. At Kel's limp, lifeless body.

Jesine ignored her, taking a moment to steady herself as she joined Delphine on the broad ledge where they had begun their match. She felt different, somehow. Physically, she felt different. Her new connection to the land had altered her from the inside. She had been rebuilt. She felt dizzy, but also strong. Disoriented, but clearer than ever. She took a step forward, acclimatizing to this new reality.

"You made a deal." Delphine licked her lips. Almost unconsciously, she backed away as Jesine circled closer. "You must have. I didn't see—but you're one of us now. Aren't you?"

"No, Delphine. I'm not."

"Then how—" Delphine's eyes widened as she reached the edge of the platform, the thin heel of her boot slipping off the ledge. Her arms windmilled wildly, and she narrowly caught her balance before she could fall back.

"Careful there, Delphine." Jesine did not slow her pace as she circled nearer, closing the distance between her and the bad witch. "That fall could kill you. And we both know what happens when you die." Jesine cocked her head to one side. "In fact, I know better than you. I know exactly where you'll go, Delphine.

I've seen it. I've been there." She recalled that black rot deep beneath the earth, the cold as deep and impenetrable as a grave.

But Delphine didn't seem concerned with her ultimate fate. As always, she was still fixated on power. "You can't have magic!" she rasped. "It's impossible! Without a deal, without a fairy—"

"I found a new way, Delphine. A different path. A *source*." Jesine stalked forward, coming close enough that Delphine flinched back. But she had nowhere to go. "You see, Delphine, you are a thief. You steal magic. It's a violent taking, and you warp it with your violence. As for me—and my father, and all my ancestors—we borrowed magic. With a fairy's permission, we tapped into it." Jesine furrowed her brow. "I didn't understand at first. But I do now. My fairy made a gift to me, a gift of her blood. Not to take for my own. The blood was only my guide. To help me trace a path through the land itself."

A harsh breath gurgled deep in Delphine's throat. "You're talking about a conduit," she breathed. "But that's im-pos—how? *How* did you do it?" The fear in her eyes gave way, a fevered, hungry light taking its place. "You found it? The one beneath this quarry? But Harper said it had been sealed—"

"It was sealed. You misunderstand, Delphine. I didn't find a conduit. I made one." Jesine snapped her fingers, and Delphine flew towards her. A shrill yelp escaped the witch as she hurtled through the air, coming to an abrupt stop inches from Jesine. She hovered there, a stricken look on her face, as Jesine leaned forward, trapping Delphine with her gaze. "I am the conduit, Delphine."

Delphine's eyes bulged in shock. In utter incomprehension. No, she wouldn't be able to comprehend it, Jesine thought. She could never. "The power I can access is stronger than you could possibly imagine." Jesine's voice fell to a whisper. "You were right, Delphine. Good doesn't triumph over evil. But it beats it back. Again and again. For every new assault, it beats it back. And so long as there is a single person left to do that, evil does not win."

Jesine leaned back, standing up straight. But she kept her magical grip on Delphine, and her eyes never left the witch's face. "Now. It's time we see what such a beating looks like."

A slow anguish crossed Delphine's face as—for the first time, Jesine thought—she considered that fate awaiting her. That horrific fate that awaited all bad witches. "Please," Delphine whimpered. "I can help you. All this power you have, I can show you how to use it! I will be your creature, Jesine, I swear it. Just please—*please* don't kill me."

"Oh, I'm not going to kill you, Delphine." Jesine raised a hand. "That's not my burden to bear. I'm just going to send you where you belong. You've had, what? Nearly five hundred years on this earth?"

"No. Please—"

"That is more time than you deserve," Jesine said.

And with a flick of her wrist, she drew on her power and gave Delphine a shove.

Delphine flew backwards off the edge of the platform. Her scream floated away from her as she plummeted down, down, down the cavernous quarry. And just before she reached the bottom, the rocky floor beneath her crumbled, cracking open into a great yawning pit. Delphine plunged into the pit, deep into the bowels of the earth. Damp, rotting roots coiled up to wrap themselves around her, and Delphine managed one last scream as the roots dragged her down to meet the darkness.

And then she was gone. The ground trembled, the rubble in the quarry floor rolling back into place, reknitting itself together. Sealing over the yawning pit, and sealing over Delphine. Forever.

30

FORGOTTEN

"J ESINE! *JESINE!*"

Jesine turned from the edge of the platform and looked up. She was almost startled to see that it was still daytime, the sun struggling to break through a shield of gray clouds. It felt like so much time had passed since she'd first stood to face Delphine in their "ritual," and it felt like so much had changed. But her surroundings looked the same. Cold winds broke upon the northern wall of the quarry, and it was to this wall that Jesine turned.

She turned just in time to see Ansel lose his footing as he scrambled down onto her ledge. He landed in a heap at the base of the rocky wall. Behind him, Prince Garrett and Demetri descended into the quarry as well, though very slowly and carefully, as Garrett's right arm was in a sling and Demetri was helping him, making sure he didn't fall too. Jesine had a feeling they needn't have worried, though. Because behind them came a fourth person—Malina, clad in her cashmere coat. The witch had her eye on Prince Garrett, as though ready to catch him if need be.

"Jesine." Ansel clambered to his feet. "We saw—from up there—everything. What happened, Jesine? What did you do?"

"Yes," said Prince Garrett as he reached the bottom. His face was pale, and Jesine wasn't sure if that was because of what he'd witnessed or because of his wounded arm. He stumbled and winced, putting his left hand to his side, and Jesine realized he bore more than one injury. "What did you do to Delphine? Did you kill her?"

"Not quite." Jesine spoke calmly, and it was a strange thing. Was she calm? Was that how she felt? It was difficult to say. She didn't quite feel like herself with all this power rushing through her. Ebbing and flowing, cycling back into the earth. A never-ending stream.

It would take some time to get used to, she imagined.

"I sent Delphine to her master," Jesine said. "Body and soul. She isn't dead, but she may as well be." She smiled at him. "Certainly as far as you are concerned. She can't hurt you anymore, Prince Garrett."

Garrett's eyes were haunted. "Are you sure?"

"Yes. Very sure. There is no coming back for her."

"Jesine." Ansel made a strange motion with his arm, as though he meant to reach out and touch her but thought better of it. "I don't understand. What happened. Did you—have you turned? Become bad, I mean?"

"No, she hasn't."

The three boys turned to stare at the person who'd answered: Malina.

"Jesine used her fairy's blood to gain access to magic." Malina stepped forward, coming to join them near the edge. "But not by consuming her blood. Not through any dark rite. Instead, Kelavandriana made a Gift of her blood to Jesine. Allowing Jesine to trace its connection deep into the land, to the source of all magic. And form her own connection with it there."

She placed a special emphasis on the word *Gift*, somehow giving it a different meaning. And something clicked into place for Jesine.

"It was like the Gift the old fairies made for the first royals, wasn't it?" she asked. "When they made their pact of peace, the 'Gift.' They Gifted their blood, didn't they?"

"Well, we already knew that," said Demetri, resting a hand on the hilt of his rapier. When Jesine looked at him, he blushed, dropping his gaze. "I'm sorry. I realize not everyone knows. But we did." He gestured between himself and Garrett. "A fairy told us last year. When we were in the Mountain Kingdom."

"But it can't be the same." Garrett scratched at the edge of his sling, where the cloth met his sleeve. "I mean, the royals—from the original families, I mean—don't have access to magic, do they?"

"I hope not," Demetri muttered.

"No, it's not the same," Malina said. "The details are a little intricate. For one thing, it's not just the Gift itself that allows access to magic. It takes a witch to use that Gift the way Jesine did, to forge a connection to the land. The original royals do have a special connection to the land, but not one that grants them access to magic."

"Even still," said Garrett, "Jesine's fairy had to die for her to claim this power. Whether she Gifted it or Jesine took it, what does that matter? Seems a bit of a philosophical difference."

"It makes all the difference." Malina turned cool gray eyes on the prince. "You of all people should know by now, Prince Garrett. Magic is about intention." She turned back to Jesine. "And it very much was, you know. It was your fairy's intent to make this Gift to you. She agreed to this plan with me ahead of time."

"When?" Jesine whispered. "When did you—"

"I found her. Just before I came to the southern woods. I didn't lie when I told you she was dying, Jesine. That her tree was dying. I explained to her about the connection between you and the darkness."

"A connection you created!"

"A connection I enhanced," Malina corrected. "I didn't create it. It has existed since Harper first manipulated you all those years ago. And because of that connection, you were vulnerable. I explained this to Kel, and I explained that when she died, you would become more vulnerable than ever. Easy prey for the darkness. But if she *allowed* herself to die—if she controlled the circumstances so she could Gift you her blood—then she could save you from that. She could give you another option."

Jesine wanted to argue. Though she felt a stab of grief for Kel, grief mingled with gratitude. That she had made this sacrifice for Jesine—a fairy, a creature known for their caprice and dearth of empathy. Kel had proved herself a fairy like no other.

But Jesine didn't like being manipulated, and whether Malina admitted it or not, Harper wasn't the only one who had done so. But she bit back a retort, glancing down at her palm instead. The black splotch that had marred her skin was gone, as she knew it would be.

It had probably disappeared the minute she'd shut that door.

She looked up at Malina. "You could have just told me all this. Spoken to me as well as Kel—"

"No, I couldn't." Malina raised an eyebrow. "Even if I thought you would have agreed to your fairy's death, I couldn't have come to you. You may not be a bad witch, child, but I am. So I had to work this very carefully. I don't have the option to help people directly when magic is involved."

Jesine twisted her mouth bitterly.

"So you're not really a good witch or bad witch," Demetri mused. "I mean, perhaps that was true before—the way Castel explained it, 'good' witches have always been capable of any kind of magic—but it sounds like you truly have no limitations now, Jesine. That is, assuming it doesn't go away. The power you've found."

"It won't," Jesine murmured. The magic rushing through her was part of her now.

"Could other witches do this?" Garrett asked. "Access magic this way, I mean?"

Malina pursed her lips. "Technically it would be possible, but, I think, very unlikely. For one thing, a fairy already bonded to a witch would have to be willing to spill blood for them. They would have to be willing to die. Which, as I'm sure you all know, would be a very rare thing." She shook her head. "Besides, some of Jesine's...unique experiences on her path to becoming a witch also made this possible. The chance that another person could replicate what she's done—yes, I'd say it's extremely unlikely."

Garrett and Demetri still looked thoughtful, and a bit confused, but Ansel, Jesine realized, was looking at her. His arms were folded tightly over his chest, his eyes tearing a little against the wind. He looked troubled as he took Jesine in, studying her face.

"I'm all right," she assured him.

"Yes." He managed a brief smile, but there was something troubled about that too. "I know."

"Are you all right? All of you?" She looked from Ansel to the other boys. Prince Garrett bowed before the wind, his tall form hunched over. Demetri stood up straight, though he, too, winced as the wind grew stronger and more cutting. "What happened? What about the other witches? Castel, Harper—Saskia?" Her stomach clenched.

Prince Garrett grimaced. "Unfortunately, Saskia got away. Malina stopped her before she could use the poppet to do me in." He gestured vaguely at his sling. "But Gemma was hurt, and we had to help her. Once we'd finished, Saskia had gone."

"Ah, well." Ansel sighed. "I suppose there's always one more to hunt down."

"Castel's been helping us," Demetri continued. "He was back at your house, doing a spell to banish the demon. Which seemed to have succeeded. As for Harper—well." He half-turned, tossing a nod up at the top of the quarry. "You'd better come see."

Demetri, Prince Garrett, and Malina turned to climb back up the quarry, but before Jesine could follow, Ansel stopped her, taking her by the arm. "Jesine," he said in a low voice, "are you really all right?"

"Yes, Ansel. I really am. Why?"

Ansel hesitated. "It's your eyes."

"What about them?"

"Well, they're the same color." Ansel peered at her, leaning in close. "But they're sort of glowing."

"What?" she asked, half-reaching for her face.

"Yes, the green in them—it's like they're glowing." Ansel leaned even closer. Then—as though he'd realized how close he was, his face inches from hers—he dropped her arm and stepped back hastily. "Sorry."

"That's all right."

"But also..." Ansel snuck another glance at her. "The last time I saw you—well, you seemed devastated, Jesine. Understandably so. Your brother..."

Your brother.

The hook that dug into her middle this time dug deep, painful and cruel. It wasn't that Jesine had forgotten about Bastian, exactly. About his death. It was just that she'd had other things on her mind—Kel's death and Gift to her, discovering a new source of magic, dealing with Delphine—

And banishing *him*, the darkness, from her forever.

But there was still her own darkness to contend with. Her grief. It was not gone, she realized, it was still there. Inside her. But the writhing mass had calmed, no longer pressing at her, stealing all her breath. It was simply there, waiting. Waiting for what, she wondered. For her to deal with it? Accept it? Allow it to become a part of her?

She wasn't sure she was ready for that yet. Her heart gave a wrench when she thought about Bastian's broken little body. Even now, as powerful as she was, there was nothing she could do for him. There was no bringing back the dead. The power inside her recoiled at the very idea. If he had lived, perhaps she could have saved him—perhaps, with the power she had now, she could have found a way to return him to his human form.

But it was too late for that now.

Jesine met Ansel's gaze. "Perhaps I'm not entirely all right. But I think I will be." She took him by the hand. "Come. This business is not finished yet."

When Jesine reached the top of the quarry, she found the others waiting for her, some twenty paces back at the tree line. Sabine had a pistol drawn in hand, and it was leveled at a man slouched at the base of a sprawling southern oak, its canopy drooping around him.

Harper.

The reason for his lack of resistance became apparent as Jesine stepped closer: Harper wore the same cuffs Malina had put on her earlier, the shackles spelled to keep a witch from doing magic. Malina, Jesine thought, glancing back at the golden-haired witch, was full of help for them. And she still didn't really know why.

But that could wait. First, there was another witch to deal with.

"Harper," Jesine said evenly. The others all stepped back as Jesine approached, giving her room to face the witch. All except Ansel, who remained close to her.

Harper looked at them both, his gaze flicking from one to the other. There was absolutely nothing telling in his gaze. It was the same dead-eyed stare he always wore. Blood stained the leg of his trousers, just above his ankle. He held his bowler hat in his shackled hands, fiddling with it as he asked, "And will you kill me now, Jesine? Or perhaps Ansel will do it?" He half-lifted his cuffed wrists. "Should be easy enough while I'm in these. You don't even need your fairy-wood stake. A regular old bullet should do it."

Ansel spoke, not to Harper, but to Jesine. "He deserves it, Jesine." His voice was hard yet brittle. "He deserves to die. For what he did to your brother, if nothing else. He was seven years old."

"That wasn't my doing," Harper said.

"You may not have cast the hex," Ansel retorted, "but you were part of it. It was your coven. It was all part of their plan to get to Jesine."

But Jesine swept her gaze over Harper. Did he deserve to die? She wasn't so sure. For one thing, she didn't want to be the arbiter of who lived and who died. And for another...

She remembered him as a youth, handsome and grinning and playful. He had been her first friend. No matter his intentions, no matter what became of them later, he had been her first friend. She remembered passing the time with him, confiding in him, just as she had with Ansel. And he had confided in her too, she recalled. He had confided about his stifling and controlling family. He didn't dwell on it much. Back then, he had believed in living for the good things and forgetting the bad. But in some ways, he had been as lonely as her. She believed that.

"He never really chose this, Ansel," Jesine said in a soft voice. "He became a witch out of obligation to his family. Because he knew no other way. He was younger than we are now. Even what he did to me was on the orders of his family. And they're all gone.

He has nothing left. Nothing except…" Jesine's voice hardened to match Ansel's. "His vengeance. And I fear he will never stop trying to take it. Even if he had no power, I don't think he could stop."

"Could you do that?" Ansel sounded startled. "Take his power? Could you undo his deal?"

Harper gave a humorless laugh. "No one can do that."

"I'm not sure you realize how powerful she's become," Ansel said sharply.

"No, he's right." Jesine shook her head. "Even I can't do that. It's possible I could bind his power…" Harper's eyes widened, and Jesine could not help the surge of satisfaction she felt at that "…but I could never undo his deal. And as I said, I'm not sure what good binding his magic will do."

From behind, Prince Garrett spoke up. "Well, if he has no magic, we can lock him up. In a regular old jail cell. That should keep him from trying to hurt Ansel."

But Jesine had thought of something else. Even a powerless Harper might someday escape a jail cell. Delphine had, after all. "I have a better idea. A more fitting idea. One that will help all of us. Even you, Harper."

Harper eyed her warily. "What are you going to do?"

In answer, Jesine placed a hand atop his head and drew on the magic inside her. There was no delicate chain anymore, linking her to Kel. She simply opened herself up. The magic *was* her, and she was the magic. Muttering an incantation, she directed tendrils of magic into Harper's mind, delicate roots searching for specific pieces. Specific memories.

She knew how it was done. She'd healed Ansel's mind. She knew what to do.

When she finished, she lifted her hand from Harper. A shudder ran through the witch, and he raised his head, looking disoriented. There was something missing in his face. Jesine could see that right away. "What was that?" Harper's eyes alighted on Jesine.

There was recognition in his gaze. But that dead-eyed look. That hollow, mirthless expression.

That was gone.

"Jesine?" Harper looked more confused than ever. "What did you..." His eyes slid over her, onto Ansel.

There was no recognition in his gaze this time.

"Who's this?" he asked. He studied Ansel a moment, then looked over all the others. "Who are these people? Jesine?"

"Come on." Jesine took Ansel by the arm and turned away. Ansel stared at Harper in amazement, but he followed her, leaving Harper behind.

"What did you do?" he asked. "What did you do to him?"

"I made him forget," she said simply.

"Forget what? He recognized you—"

"I made him forget you, Ansel. And anyone he's ever met in pursuit of you and his vengeance." They stepped out from beneath the thick, twisting branches of the oak tree, coming out beneath the open sky. "Anything that happened as a result of it, he won't remember. I took away his vengeance." Jesine sighed sadly. "He's free of it now. Forever."

31

GIFTED

G ARRETT SAT IN ONE of the hardbacked wooden chairs in
his room at the inn. His arm rested on the table, his sleeve
rolled up above his elbow. "You know," he said, "I would've
thought you'd use magic for this sort of thing."

"Why?" Malina bent to insert the needle into the crook of his
elbow, and Garrett looked away. He didn't have a problem with
needles, but he didn't need to watch a thousand-year-old witch
draw his blood for nefarious purposes. "When there's such an
efficient way without magic?"

"I don't know. Because you're a witch."

"Once upon a time," Malina murmured, "drawing someone's
blood was a rather messy affair. But nowadays, it is very easy."
She looked up at him. "You haven't asked."

"Asked what?"

"What I intend to use it for."

Garrett snorted. "Would you tell me the truth? You didn't tell
Gryphon."

When Malina had saved his life two days ago—and saved Gemma's life as well—Garrett had finally realized who she was. She was the witch who had caused so much trouble for his brother, Gryphon—the witch who had befriended Gryphon and persuaded him to give her his blood. Only, she'd wanted Garrett's blood as well, and when they'd tried to get it, everything went wrong. The entire incident had led to Gryphon's exile.

She had never gotten Garrett's blood. Now she finally was. In exchange for saving Gemma. Though really, Garrett thought sourly, Jesine had done most of that.

Malina looked amused. "What makes you think I didn't tell Gryphon the truth?"

Garrett gave her an incredulous look. "You said you wanted it for a protection spell."

"And? That can't be true?"

"Doesn't sound like something a bad witch would do," Garrett muttered.

"That depends on who the protection is for." Deftly, Malina capped off a tube of blood, then bent to remove the needle from his arm. "And who—or what—it's protecting *from*."

"And will you tell me those things?"

"No. I don't think so."

"So why would I bother asking," he grumbled. Though he did wonder. Malina had specifically told Gryphon their blood was meant for a protection spell for the Glen Kingdom. But that seemed unlikely. He'd wondered if maybe she wanted blood from the original royal families—Gryphon was descended from the last Forest king, and he wouldn't be surprised if Malina knew that. But he, Garrett, was *not* descended from the original Glen line, and she had to know that too. It wasn't exactly a secret.

So there was no telling, really, what she was about. He just had to hope it was nothing too terrible. She hadn't done anything very terrible here, after all. Mostly, she had helped them.

"So all of this," Garrett said, as Malina pressed a strip of gauze over his arm and secured it there, "was just to get my blood? I mean, that's why you helped us?"

"More or less."

"Because Castel said you were here for the same reason as the rest of the witches."

"Which was...?"

Garrett leaned back, rolling his sleeve down. Awkwardly. His other arm, which had been properly set by a real doctor, was still in a sling. He had to sort of hold his good arm up so his immobile fingers could tug the sleeve down. "Revenge."

Malina looked up from her black leather medicine bag, where she'd packed her supplies away. The smile that came over her face was chilling. Perhaps because it was first time Garrett had seen her smile.

"Oh," she said, "I came for that as well. And I got it."

"You did?" Garrett twisted back to shrug his arm into his sack coat. "Who did you want revenge on?"

"Delphine."

"*What?*"

"I knew she wouldn't be able to resist the idea of stealing a good witch's soul. Turning her in exchange for true immortality. She always was a vain, selfish creature." The contempt in Malina's voice was shocking—again, perhaps because it was the first emotion Garrett had heard from her. Thus far, Malina had been cool and calm, displaying little feeling. But she wasn't hiding her feelings now.

"So you engineered this whole thing." Garrett wiped a hand over his face as the enormity of it dawned on him. "Turning Jesine—it was your idea? You brought it to Delphine?"

Malina nodded.

A sudden suspicion occurred to Garrett. "Just how much of this did you engineer? I haven't heard anyone say whose idea all this was in the first place. Whose idea it was to free Delphine and draw us here. Was it yours?"

But Malina's voice was cool again when she said, "Wouldn't you like to know."

"You must really have hated her."

Malina snapped her medicine bag shut. "Let's just say, I owed her. I very much owed her. For something she did so long ago, she probably didn't even remember it." Straightening, she added, "Just like Castel owed me."

"What?"

"Castel. I don't suppose he ever told you why he was involved in this?"

"No." Garrett thought back. Well, Castel had implied he'd helped them because of Kinsley and Perpetua. But that didn't explain why he'd gotten involved in the first place and agreed to free Delphine.

"He owed me a debt. One he couldn't ignore." Malina shrugged. "We needed a fourth witch for the spell to free Delphine. I thought of him. But he didn't get anything out of the deal except freedom from his debt to me."

Garrett shook his head, befuddled. "You witches. I suppose you must all have crossed each other one time or another, as long as you've lived."

"It is one of the pitfalls of such longevity." Primly, Malina tugged on her white satin gloves. She didn't look a thousand years old, Garrett thought, nor like a witch. She was the picture of a well-to-do young lady of society, her hair swept up behind her head, garbed in the richest of garments. A bustled dress, high-heeled shoes. Not to mention that cashmere coat. Really, he couldn't blame Gryphon for falling for her. If Garrett had known her then, he probably would have fallen for her too.

Malina turned to go, but then paused, turning back. Even in the dull daylight filtering in through the window, her hair gleamed like burnished gold. "By the way. I noticed something. About your blood."

"You noticed something? How?"

"Well, I suppose there was a little magic involved in that blood draw."

"Of course there was."

"It's about that poison in your blood."

Garrett's heart sank. They had received the results of their samples from the lab a couple of days ago. The sample from the quarry had showed nothing but rocky earth filled with elarium, no blood at all. The geyser the workers saw, Malina had explained, was the result of a spell Delphine had done at the quarry. She'd wanted to ensure Harper was telling the truth about the weakness in the land sealing itself.

As for Garrett's blood sample, he hadn't looked at the results yet. He couldn't bring himself to. And now, it seemed, he didn't need to. "Delphine said she cured me," he told Malina.

"I know."

"But she didn't," Garrett said heavily, "did she?"

"Actually, she did. Sort of. But," Malina added, and the fleeting hope rising inside Garrett died, "it's only temporary."

"I don't understand."

"She couldn't cure you. Not because she's a bad witch—magic is about intention, and her intent in curing you was to have more time to torment you. The forces we answer to would have allowed such a thing. No, the reason she couldn't cure you is because that poison is rooted in fairy magic, Prince Garrett. And we can't undo such a thing. Not even Jesine could."

Garrett said evenly, "I see."

"But she did burn it out of you for now. I'd say she's bought you a little more time. Six months to a year, perhaps."

"Well, that's something," said Garrett. And it was. When he'd embarked on this venture, he'd thought he was using up the last of his time on this earth. He'd thought he'd return home with weeks to live, at best.

Now he had another six months. Perhaps more.

He would take it.

Malina left, sweeping from the room with all the regal grace of a queen. Garrett did not rise from his chair until she was gone, the door shut behind her. It was time for him to be gone too, and he still had packing to do.

They were heading home today. All of them. At least, Garrett thought, everyone had survived this venture. Even Gemma, though it had been a near miss for her. Before they'd set out for the quarry—while Garrett had patched up his own wounds—Malina had seen to Gemma. She couldn't heal her, but she was able to freeze Gemma with a spell that put her in a kind of stasis. That would hold, Malina had explained, and keep her from dying until Jesine could return and heal her. Which she had.

Still, the cost had been steep. For Gemma. Jesine had healed the tracker; she'd stopped the bleeding in her brain. But there was injury she couldn't fix. Gemma's sight in her right eye had been damaged, and there was no telling, Jesine said, if it would fully heal. She might get some sight back, Jesine said. But it would take time.

Gemma was one of Garrett's best sharpshooters, but she wouldn't be anymore. Garrett didn't care about that, though. All he cared was that she was alive. And that she would be all right.

Once he finished packing, Garrett slung on his fur-lined over-coat, slipping his good arm into it and leaving the other sleeve hanging over his shoulder. Then he headed downstairs, leaving his bags in his room. The innkeeper had offered to send some-one to fetch them. He had obviously known, Garrett thought ruefully, who Garrett was since the night they'd arrived. Still, he was grateful for the assistance. He couldn't carry much with one working arm.

Downstairs, everyone was bidding farewell. Garrett and his soldiers were making the two-day journey up to the train sta-tion just north of here, but Ansel, Demetri, and Sabine were not headed that way. Demetri and Sabine already had another job, something they had heard about out west, just beyond the borders of the Glen Kingdom. Ansel, meanwhile, was planning to stay here. He didn't say so exactly, but Garrett knew Ansel was staying for Jesine. Whether or not he'd had that conversation with Jesine yet was unclear.

So Garrett bid goodbye to Ansel. It was an awkward goodbye, and Garrett hated that. He and Ansel had apologized to each other—Garrett for the things he'd said, Ansel for keeping the truth from him. Ansel had nothing to apologize for, Garrett thought. But even so, it was hard to speak to the hunter now, knowing the truth about Snow. Perhaps things would always be awkward between them, Garrett concluded sadly. Perhaps there was no help for it.

Garrett stepped out of the inn, onto the street. He found Demetri at the end of the block, rubbing his hands together as he waited for Sabine to fetch their horses.

"You know," Garrett said as he approached him, "I meant for Sabine to be your partner in all of this. Not your servant."

Demetri's eyes widened. "She's not! She offered to go get the horses, both of them—oh, stones, I don't treat her like a servant, do I?" He groaned.

Garrett grinned. "I'm only joking. If she has any complaints, she hasn't mentioned them to me."

"It's just," Demetri muttered, "I've recently realized that maybe it isn't as easy as I thought. To stop acting the prince."

"Well, of course not. You've had all that privilege and snobbery primed into you from birth. I'm newer to it," Garrett said modestly.

"Right," Demetri said sagely. "And I suppose you didn't even notice the innkeeper gave you a room three times as large as anyone else's. With a fireplace, and your own private tub—"

"I knew he knew who I was," Garrett mumbled.

Demetri clapped Garrett on the shoulder. "Well, then. I suppose this is farewell. I'll let you know if anything interesting turns up."

"Of course. Always happy to help." Garrett tried for another smile, but it faltered. "Are you really all right, Demetri?" He thought of what Demetri had confided in him back in that little hole-in-the-wall inn, the night of the blizzard. And he remembered how changed he'd thought Demetri was, the first night he arrived here. *We all grieve in different ways*, Sabine had said. "I mean, really?"

Demetri didn't answer right away. Then he smiled, but there was something bitter in his expression. "Oh, I'm all right."

"Really," Garrett said.

"Really."

"Is this the part where I tell you diplomacy wastes time, and to just tell me what's going on with you?"

The look Demetri shot him was wry. "Yes. Well. I *am* all right, Garrett. It's just that my definition of 'all right' has shifted a bit after—well—everything." His eyes took on a faraway cast. "Look, I told you before what happened to me. How I went to that cave. How I didn't want to get up and leave, but I did anyway." He shrugged. "That's what I do now. I wake up in the morning. And I get up. And then I do it again the next day. Some days, I don't want to get up. Some days, it's very hard. But I figure, so long as I keep doing it...well, then I'm all right."

Garrett nodded. It sounded a bleak existence, not altogether reassuring. But he knew a little something of what it was to live that way. And eventually, he had found a way through it.

Demetri would too. In time. He had to believe that.

Sabine returned with the horses then. Garrett watched as she and Demetri mounted up, and he waved his last goodbye as they set off down the street, heading out of Lise.

"Shall I make my teary farewell too, dear prince?"

Garrett turned around.

Castel stood behind him, in the exact same spot Demetri had been in a moment before. Garrett was not surprised, somehow, to see him. He didn't think he would ever be surprised to see Castel pop up. Even if he woke one morning in his bedroom in Glen Castle and found Castel there, he didn't think he would be surprised. Disturbed, yes. But not surprised. The witch had a knack for turning up out of nowhere.

Garrett gestured over his shoulder. "You've just missed Demetri."

"Yes, that was on purpose. I don't think he likes me very much."

"Any reason he should?"

"No." Castel sighed, and it seemed a very genuine sigh. "I suppose not. I don't think he's forgiven me for not saving Perpetua."

"As I understand, she didn't want that."

"No, she didn't."

"I think Demetri accepts that," Garrett told the witch. "But you're right. That doesn't mean he's forgiven you. Perhaps he can't."

"And you, dear prince?" Castel put on a winning smile as he adjusted his festive red scarf, knotted and smartly tucked into his topcoat. It was a very fine, double-breasted coat, the collar lined in luxurious velvet. "Have I won you over?"

Garrett folded his good arm across his chest, tucking it within his overcoat. "Won me over how? I suppose you think warning us about Harper's revenge and Delphine's intentions earned you some good will. Telling us where the witches were taking Jesine and banishing the demon, the demon *you* summoned in the first place, I might add—"

"My, did I really do all that?" Castel's dark eyes sparkled.

"The thing is," Garrett said flatly, "Malina told me the only reason you were here was for her. Because you owed her a favor."

Something flickered over Castel's face—surprise, perhaps?—but all he was said, "That was why I was here, prince. That's not why I helped you."

"So why did you, then?"

Castel didn't answer. He only looked at Garrett, a little smile playing over his lips.

"Because it seems to me," Garrett continued, "that I'm not the one you want to win over. Certainly, I'm not the one you want forgiveness from. Nor's Demetri."

"I'm not looking for forgiveness from anyone, Prince Garrett. That, I'm afraid, is a waste of time. I learned that long ago."

Garrett looked into the witch's eyes, looking for a glimpse of...well, anything, he supposed. Regret. Loneliness. Hope. But he saw nothing like that. He remembered, then, what Castel had told him about the demon and what it truly was. "When you healed Kinsley, you told Briar you lost a fifth of your life."

"Unfortunately." Castel made a sour face as he brushed back the lock of white hair at his brow. Almost unconsciously, it seemed.

"And you knew it was going to happen."

"That, or something worse." Castel smiled breezily when Garrett turned a startled look on him. He smiled like that, Garrett noticed, when he was trying to act as though he didn't care about something. "I didn't know exactly what the punishment would be. It could have been a lot worse. Suffice it to say, I got off easy."

"But you healed him anyway," Garrett said quietly. Given the long lives these witches had, Garrett hadn't really considered a fifth of one's life to mean all that much. Four-fifths of a thousand years, after all, still left a witch a long time to live. But when he considered the fate awaiting them.... Garrett repressed a shudder, thinking of the gutted corpses those demons left behind. To think those demons had once been human...no matter how evil a human...

Well, that fifth of Castel's life suddenly meant a bit more.

Castel was still smiling, but there was something tense about his mouth. He said, "Well, we all do stupid things sometimes, don't we? For the people we love. You certainly have."

"I know," Garrett said ruefully. Perhaps it should have been shocking. To hear Castel admit he loved Kinsley, to hear him *claim* to love Kinsley. Given who he was and what he'd done. But Garrett believed it.

He just wasn't sure that it mattered, in the end. Given that Kinsley might not ever forgive Castel. Justifiably.

And given Castel's fate.

"Farewell then, dear prince," Castel said lightly. "I feel certain we shall meet again someday. Perhaps I'll pop around for high tea some time."

"And in the meantime, there aren't any messages you want me to convey? To...anyone?"

Castel seemed to think about this a moment. Then he flashed a grin. "You can give Briar my love. I'm sure she's missed me terribly."

Then—with a little wave of his fingers—he rounded the corner and was gone.

It was a nearly a two-day ride to the train station, and they pushed it to the very end of two days because, thanks to Garrett's and Gemma's injuries, they rode more slowly than usual, taking breaks more often as well. So it was after dusk by the time they arrived, and they found the train waiting for them. The station sat in the midst of the woods, the platform shaded by broad evergreen boughs as well as its own steel covering. The train itself sat rumbling on the tracks, smoke curling up from its chimney and vanishing into the darkening sky. But bright lights shone through every window, giving it a welcoming air.

Garrett felt heavy as he boarded the train. Heavy with exhaustion. Heavy in his heart. Someone had decorated the train with bunches of holly hung on all the compartment doors and glimmering ribbons tied about the gear-bulb fixtures on the walls. But Garrett looked at the decorations and felt no sense of holiday cheer. Stones, the winter solstice had already come and gone, and he hadn't even thought about it.

Holiday celebrations felt very far away. Garrett was just tired. So, so tired. He usually wrapped up a venture feeling more fulfilled. Tired, yes, that was not unusual. But there was a sense of satisfaction to a successful venture, a satisfaction that Garrett didn't feel this time. Delphine was gone for good. None of his people had died. They'd even helped a young woman escape a terrible fate, though really, Garrett thought, Jesine had done most of that herself.

But perhaps it had all taken a bit of a toll. Facing Delphine again. The argument with Ansel. Worrying about Demetri. Yes, it had all been resolved. But everything still hurt a little.

He just wanted to go home. He'd told Demetri he was free to contact him if any more adventures turned up, but truthfully, Garrett hoped he wouldn't. Not anytime soon. For the first time in a long time, Garrett wanted to stay home. For a good long while.

He just wanted to be with Briar. Even though he'd left things horribly with her, even though seeing her would mean facing their argument and the stupid things he'd said. But even if she was angry with him, he wanted to see her.

Well, it would be another night and day before they were home. Garrett found an empty train compartment and slumped onto a cushioned seat. He had a sleeper compartment booked somewhere, but he could find that later, after his things had been loaded onto the train and they were underway. Right now, he just wanted to sit. He let his head fall back against the seat. His arm throbbed and his stomach grumbled—they had not stopped for lunch in order to make the train; he'd need to find the dining car as well—but despite those discomforts, he felt settled and sleepy, the train engine purring beneath him as it idled there, readying to depart.

He thought he dozed off for a bit, because the next thing he knew, the train *was* underway, jerking as it slid into motion, rolling down the tracks. Garrett's eyes flew open just as someone appeared in the doorway of the compartment. "Well. Fancy meeting you here."

Garrett gaped in astonishment. The person who had spoken, the person standing before him, framed by the dim, warm glow of the shaded gear-bulb lamp, was—

Briar.

"I went to your compartment," said Briar, "but you weren't there. Got lost, did you?"

"What are you doing here?" Garrett blurted out. He ran a hand over his tired eyes, wondering if he was dreaming. Or hallucinating.

"Well, I took the train down, of course." Briar slid into the compartment, seating herself across from him. Her knee bumped his—there never seemed enough room for his long legs in these cramped compartments—and it seemed a sign that she was real. "I meant to greet you all on the platform, but it took you forever to get here, and then I got distracted talking with some of the engine boys—well, working, actually, with some of the engine boys, there was an axle that needed greasing—and then I had to wash up, and by the time I finished, they said you'd boarded already. And you weren't in your compartment, so—"

"But I mean..." Garrett ran another hand over his face. "Why did you come?"

Briar looked him in the eye. There was a small smile on her pale face, one that said she worried for his state of mind. But there was also affection in that smile. "Because I wanted to see you, of course. What, did you think I would make the train ride down because I missed Klaus so much?" She wrinkled her nose. "I don't suppose you lost him somewhere, did you?"

"You wanted to see me," Garrett echoed, his voice hollow. Hope rose inside him, but it was tempered by shame. Because as much as he'd wanted to see Briar, he *was* ashamed, facing her now. "Even after what I said? The way I left things?"

Briar gave him a very level look. "Garrett. I'm not an idiot. I know very well you only said that to push me away. Because you thought you were dying."

"Well, I was dying—but I'm not anymore," he hastened. "Not yet, anyway. And even if I was, that's no excuse. Briar, there is no excuse for what I said to you. You're not an idiot, but I am. I'm so sorry for what I said. I didn't mean it, you are enough to live for, you're everything—"

"Garrett." Briar's gaze softened. "I know."

"But that doesn't mean I shouldn't say it."

Briar leaned forward and placed her hands on his knees, bracing herself against him. "That's true. You can say it again, if you like."

"You're everything to me," he said with an air of confession. "Everything. And I love you."

"I love you too," she said in a low voice, and she leaned in further and kissed him.

A bit later, Garrett found himself dozing off again, this time with Briar ensconced beside him, leaning into his shoulder. "So you really just decided to come down and meet me? Just because?" he asked her sleepily.

"Well." Briar wove her arms around his. "It's possible Demetri sent me a telegram a couple of days ago. Letting me know you'd wrapped everything up, but that you were in quite a bad state and perhaps could use an extra special holiday present—"

"Of course he did." Garrett smiled down at the top of her white-blonde head. "So you're my present? From Demetri? Isn't that a bit weird, given the history between the three of us—"

Briar poked his chest with a bruising finger. "I'm your present from *me*, you dolt."

"Well, that's a bit disappointing."

"What! Why?"

"Because it means Demetri didn't get me anything."

Briar laughed quietly, burying her head in his arm.

"Briar?" Garrett said. His throat felt very full, for some reason. But it wasn't a bad feeling.

"Yes?" she said, her voice muffled by his sleeve.

"I love my present."

32

FOUND

ANSEL APPROACHED THE GROVE of poplar trees near Jesine's cottage, his steps slow and quiet. For the first time since he'd arrived in the southern wood, it was a clear, if cold, day. This late in the afternoon, the sun dipped below the forest canopy, its rays shedding light over the grove, bathing the naked trees in gold.

In the center of the grove, Jesine knelt upon the faded, stubby winter grass. Half of her red hair was gathered in a knot behind her head, the other half spilling over her shoulder. She was clad in her olive-green coat and wore supple gloves over her hands, hands that painstakingly piled smooth river stones together as a marker.

A marker for a grave.

Ansel stopped at the edge of the grove. He stared at the river stones, remembering how he and Jesine had delighted in gathering such stones when they were children. He was still stuck in those memories when Jesine rose and turned.

"Oh." Ansel blinked. "I'm sorry. I hope I didn't startle you."

"You didn't," Jesine said softly. "I knew you were there."

Ansel tried not to feel unsettled by that. He wondered if she had heard him, or if she had sensed him somehow. With her newfound magic. With her connection to the land.

"I am surprised you're still here, though." Jesine picked at a strand of her hair, absently running it through her fingers. "I heard Prince Garrett and his guards left yesterday. Demetri and Sabine too."

"Yes. Well. They all left." Ansel stuffed his hands into the pockets of his baggy coat. "I'm, er...well, I haven't got anything on at the moment. No other job lined up. So I thought I'd stick around for a bit. Through the holidays, at least."

Jesine nodded. Silence fell between them, punctuated only by the chirping chatter of songbirds. But the longer the silence stretched on, the more Ansel felt the awkwardness fading. It really was absurd to think there could be any awkwardness between them. Not after everything they'd shared together. Not considering what they'd been to each other.

What Ansel was hoping they still were.

Ansel dipped his head to indicate the tiny cairn Jesine had built. Before the carefully curated pile of river stones was a small mound of freshly turned earth. Bastian's grave. "I didn't mean to interrupt," he said quietly.

"Oh. Not at all."

"If you want some time alone with him—"

"No, that's all right." Jesine gestured halfheartedly. "This is just temporary. There's a mason in the village who's working on a proper stone to mark his grave. Properly engraved for him, you know. Once it's ready, I'll hold a service for him." Her mouth made a sad little smile. "Course, it'll just be me. No one else knew him."

"I knew him," Ansel offered.

Jesine looked startled at that. "Yes. You did." She paused, then added, "Perhaps you could be here with us. If you're still here, I mean. When the stone is ready."

"I'd like that."

"Good." Jesine gave a soft sigh. She perched on an upturned boulder, facing the grove and the grave. Ansel went to join her, leaning against the rock. Just close enough for their shoulders to touch.

They stood that way for a long moment. The wind soughing through the grove, rustling Jesine's hair. At some point, Ansel became aware that Jesine was crying, silent tears streaming down her face. He wrapped his arm in hers and took her gloved hand, giving it a squeeze.

"It hurts," Jesine admitted. "I miss him so much. I know that sounds—I don't know, obvious—but it wasn't like this for me before."

"When your father died, you mean."

"Yes. I know that sounds horrible. He was my father. He was my parent. But he wasn't really my *family*. Not in the way Bastian was." She shook her head. "I wasn't glad he was dead or anything. He wasn't cruel. I just...didn't feel anything. He was gone. And it didn't mean anything to me. It didn't hurt like this."

They fell into silence again. Ansel wished he could think of something to say, something that would make Jesine feel better. But he had never been through this before. He had mourned the loss of his father, but in a different way. His father hadn't died, he just left. Ansel's mourning had been a long, slow process, a gradual acceptance that his father wasn't coming back.

No, he didn't know what to say. He had no wisdom, no experience. So he simply said, "You know, he saved my life. Twice."

Jesine turned a surprised gaze on him. "Bastian?"

"Mm-hmm." Ansel took in a breath. "That day in your house. When the witches came." *The day he died.* "And he was there before, wasn't he? The night Isabelle and I killed Henrietta. When her cottage burned."

"Yes. He was there." Jesine squeezed his hands in hers, turning towards him. Ansel wasn't sure if she sought comfort in him, or just wanted to shield her face from the wind. "In fact, he showed me the way to her cottage. Then he went to get my father. And he did the same thing the night the demon attacked you. He led me through the woods. And before that, when you were blind and stuck in that hex-trap—"

"So that's at least four times that I owe him my life."

"Yes."

"He must have liked me," Ansel joked. A bit lamely.

Jesine was quiet for a moment. Then she said, "I think maybe he knew."

"Knew what?"

"That he wouldn't always be here." Her voice went softer than usual. "I don't mean he knew he was going to die. But—Kel, my fairy. She thought Bastian had been a raven for so long, he'd forgotten how to be a boy. And maybe he was forgetting. Forgetting who he was." She leaned into Ansel even further, turning her back on the grove. "I think he wanted to make sure I wasn't alone. Once he was gone."

"You're not alone, Jesine." Ansel gazed into her eyes. Her beautiful hazel eyes. Ever since she'd assumed her new power in the confrontation with Delphine, the green in her eyes gleamed with the teeming life of the land. Like the emerald boughs of a tree, glittering in the light of the setting sun.

She looked at him for a long moment. Then she dropped her gaze.

But she didn't move away.

"Where are you staying?" she asked him.

"Oh. Just at the inn. In Lise. For now."

"Would you...like to come in?" She tilted her head, indicating her house, set back from the grove.

"I—of course." Ansel's voice turned hoarse. "Just for dinner, you mean?"

Jesine lifted her eyes to meet his. "Or you could just. Stay."

Ansel's breath caught in his throat.

"Will you?" she pressed.

He could barely get any words past his lips. "Are you sure you want that?"

"Yes." Jesine reached out and took his other hand in hers. Joining them together more closely. "You said you were always looking for me, even when you didn't know it. Well. I was looking for you too. Even if I couldn't admit it. Because I knew it was impossible, I knew you didn't remember me. But all those years, I still hoped you would. I hoped you would turn up one day. And then you did."

Ansel raised both of her hands in his and pressed them to his lips.

"Does that mean you'll come in with me?" Jesine asked, as another gust of wind broke past them, blowing her hair into his face.

"Yes," said Ansel, "it does."

They left the grove and walked up the porch steps, hand in hand. Then, together, they went inside.

Sometime later, Ansel slipped out of the house. He and Jesine had sat in front of the fire for hours, talking—and doing a bit more than talking—until they'd both fallen asleep. That was where Ansel had left her, curled up in her armchair in front of the hearth. He left her and stepped out onto the porch.

He wasn't leaving. He just wanted to stand beneath the dark-blue sky. To breathe in the deep, resinous scent of the woods. To feel the icy air burn his throat. The night was as clear as the day had been, and through the gaps in the trees, Ansel glimpsed the distant light of stars, winking above him.

It was clear, and it was cold, and it was quiet. Ansel had never been happier.

He hadn't been outside for more than a few minutes when the door squeaked open and Jesine stepped outside, bundled in her coat. "You must be freezing," she said.

"It's all right. I like it."

Jesine slipped up behind him and wrapped her arms around him, resting her head against him. She didn't say anything for a while, and Ansel shivered, enjoying the warmth of her. They were so alone out here. Lise wasn't more than a few miles away, but at this hour, swallowed up by the woods and the night, it felt much further. It felt like they were the only two people in the world.

"Ansel," Jesine murmured into his back.

"Hmm?"

"You once promised to tell me all the good and wonderful things about me."

Smiling, Ansel turned within the circle of her arms to face her. "And you want me to do that now?" He linked his hands behind her back.

But the look in Jesine's bright eyes was serious. "No." She pressed her fingertips into his back, exerting the smallest pressure. "Because I'm not only good and wonderful, Ansel. There is a darkness in me that is entirely my own." She pursed her lips. "I'm not a good witch anymore. I'm both now. I always will be." Her gaze met his. "Can you accept that?"

"Of course I can." Ansel tipped his head back, indicating the black night sky. "I love the darkness, Jesine. It's my home. I know some people are afraid of the dark, but it's only frightening if you're alone in it." He pulled her closer to him. "And I'm not alone."

Jesine smiled. "No. You're not." She slid a hand up his chest. "Ansel."

"Yes?"

"Would you like to kiss me?"

That was not the first time she'd asked him tonight. And it would not be the last, Ansel thought, as he lowered his lips to hers. He would never be alone again. He'd been lost in the woods and hadn't even realized it.

But Jesine had found him. And he would never be lost again.

Don't Miss the Next Book in the Series!

GHOUL GIRL

In this sinister retelling of "The Goose Girl," Gemma and Klaus are assigned as bodyguards to a princess visiting Glen Castle. But when strange things start happening in the castle, they begin to suspect this princess isn't who – or *what* – she seems...

———◆O◆———

COMING SPRING 2026

Turn the page for a sneak peek!

The princess ran and didn't stop running. She tore through the forest, branches snagging at her shirt and slicing through her skin. But she didn't slow down, didn't flinch. Because if she did, it would mean the end for her.

Not just death. Not that kind of end.

It would mean being devoured.

It would mean annihilation. Mind, body, and soul.

So she ran and didn't stop running.

The moon was fat overhead, bursting with luminous brilliance. The princess cursed that misfortune. On the one hand, it gave her some light to see by. On the other hand, it gave her pursuers—and there would be pursuers—light to see by as well.

She should have fled days ago under the cover of a darker night, but she would have had too far to run. She knew, she had always known, that she wouldn't get far. She wasn't fast enough, strong enough, or clever enough to make it on her own. That had been drilled into her from the moment she was old enough to listen and understand.

Her only chance was reaching Glen City before anyone caught up to her.

Catching herself around the middle of a stout oak tree, the princess stopped, heaving a breath. Her chest burned as though her lungs had caught fire, her legs screamed in pain as the muscles began to stiffen. Her stomach roiled. She was going to be sick, she thought. She'd never run so fast in her entire life.

The woods were still and ominous, the thick darkness suffocating, a manifestation of her fear. It wasn't the darkness itself that scared her—it was what could be lurking in the dark. What might be hiding in the shadows, just out of sight.

A light wind blew through the forest, and something *creaked* overhead. The princess jumped, but it was only a nearby tree, its branches swaying in the breeze. Gulping for breath, heart thumping wildly, the princess staggered away from her oak tree, its rough bark scraping the palm of her hand as she pushed off it.

She stumbled through the trees, more carefully now, looking for the road. It shouldn't be far, unless she'd veered off in the wrong direction somewhere. Her frazzled hair tangled on a thorny bush and she cursed, wincing as she pulled it free. She'd thought to change into practical clothing before sneaking away from her retinue, but she hadn't thought to tie her back. She was so stupid.

But you don't have to get far, she reminded herself. *Just to Glen City. Then the king and his son will help you.* Or so she hoped. Not only had she never met King Victor and his son, the crown prince, but she knew very little about them. Still, she wasn't coming to the king empty-handed. She was going to warn him. There was danger coming to the Glen Kingdom, and King Victor had no idea. Surely he would be grateful for the information the princess had.

Or perhaps he would be so angry, he would throw her in a dungeon. Or have her killed. That was entirely possible.

But the king was her only chance at safety. She had nowhere else to turn.

The wooded land rose sharply just ahead. Cringing, the princess forced her legs to move faster, breaking into a jog as she crested the hill. The road should be visible over the rise. But she stumbled again as her shirt caught on a low-hanging branch. The princess gave a mighty tug, ripping the fabric, and tumbled free of the forest, out onto the road.

It was right there. She hadn't realized it was *right there*. She was so startled, she nearly darted back into the thorny bushes. But then she saw it, just up ahead.

It was a carriage. No, a cart. A simple cart carrying a load she couldn't make out from here. It had already passed her by. The princess hesitated. But her legs were so tired, and her chest and throat still felt like they was on fire.

She made the decision in a split-second, hurrying down the road after the cart. "Wait!" she called. "You there! Cart driver! Wait!"

Slowly, the cart jangled to a halt. Relief flooded through the princess so strongly that it gave her a jolt of energy, and she picked up her pace, dashing forward to make up the distance.

She slowed as she approached the back of the cart, caution tempering her enthusiasm. The cart was not large, its bed filled with wooden crates. And at the very back, legs swinging off the edge, was a boy. The only light from the cart was a lantern hung on a pole up front with the driver, so the boy was cast in shadow, his features obscured. The princess eyed him warily as she circled the cart, coming around to the front.

The driver had not climbed down from his seat, but he peered at the princess. "Are you all right there, miss?" he asked, casting a puzzled look back down the road. "Where've you come from? Is something wrong? Do you need help?"

The princess licked her lips. "I'm all right," she said, trying to make her squeaking voice sound calm and assured. "I just—I wondered whether—I might have a ride? Are you going to Glen City?"

"That I am." The driver smiled at her, and she tried to smile back. "It's not much further up the road here, but I don't blame you wanting a ride so late at night. Have you got a name?"

The princess hesitated. "I'm—Lena. My name is Lena."

"Well, Miss Lena, hop into the back with the lad there. Won't be the most comfortable seat, but as I say, we've only a few miles to go."

The princess—Lena, now—managed another smile. "Thank you," she said, very proud that her voice didn't shake. She walked around to the back of the cart, trying not to feel apprehensive of this boy. There was nothing particularly ominous about him, aside from the fact that she couldn't see him all that well. That, and he was utterly silent. Now, as she struggled to climb into the cart bed, the boy still did not say anything. He certainly made no move to help her. Finally, she hoisted herself up into the cart, none too gracefully, nearly sprawling into the stacked crates. "*Oof*," she muttered.

"Ready to go?" the driver called cheerfully.

Lena cleared her throat. "Ready," she called back.

A moment later, the horses pulling the cart started up again, and the cart jolted down the road. Flushing, Lena righted herself so that she sat like the boy, her legs dangling off the edge of the cart. She tried not to sit too close to him.

Running her fingers through her matted hair, Lena eyed the boy sidelong. Now that her eyes had adjusted to the dim light, she could seem him a little better. Though the brim of the cap pulled over his head still obscured his face.

"Hello," Lena ventured, wondering if the boy would ignore her outright.

But the boy gave a start before turning to look at her, and Lena wondered if he'd been asleep all this time. Or perhaps he was just shy. "Hello," he said. "Going to the city, too?"

"If you mean Glen City, then yes."

The boy shrugged. "No other cities 'round these parts."

Lena dug her nails into her palms, trying to think of a follow-up question, but before she could, there was a terrible *clank* and the cart gave a great, uncontrolled lurch. Lena gasped, flinging out a hand to keep herself from pitching forward off the cart. She grabbed hold of a crate at the last minute, and luckily, it held her weight.

"What was that?" she demanded.

The boy, who had also managed to keep his seat, peered around. "Jammed axle, it looks like."

"You two all right back there?" the driver called.

"Yes." Lena half-slipped, half-jumped off the cart, coming around to approach the driver. "What happened?"

The driver smoothed a hand down the neck of one of the horses, patting it gently. Trying to calm it, Lena guessed, for both horses were a little wild-eyed, stamping their hooves and whinnying softly. "Not sure," said the driver. "Some damage to the wheel, sounded like. You sure you're all right? And the boy?"

"I'm fine." Lena turned to look for the boy. Coming around the back of the cart again, she asked, "You're all right, aren't—"

But she broke off.

Because the boy was gone.

Lena swallowed, unsettled. A nasty feeling grew in the pit of her stomach, a deep feeling of disquiet. Turning back to the driver, she said, "Erm—he's gone."

"Sorry?" the driver called back. He had left the horses and now bent beside the wheel, fiddling with it. "What's that?"

"He's gone." Lena stepped forward, pitching her voice a little louder. "Your boy. He just—"

"My boy?" The driver straightened, looking at Lena in puzzlement. "Oh—you mean the boy back there. He's not my boy. Just another young 'un needing a lift into the city, like yourself."

Lena's mouth went dry. "He doesn't work for you?" The unease inside her grew into a yawning pit of alarm. "But—"

She didn't get a chance to finish.

A shadow appeared—just *appeared*—behind the driver, wrapped its arms around his neck, and twisted.

There was a sickening snap, and the driver fell to the road, limp and lifeless at Lena's feet.

Lena screamed.

The shadow grinned at her. White teeth in the darkness, bodiless and maniacal. "Hello, princess."

Lena spun and ran, plunging into the forest.

She tore through the woods. There was no thought in her head, not a single one. Only mindless fear drove her on, like a deer fleeing a hunter. Her boot skidded over a mossy stone and she tripped, her ankle twisting, but she lurched to her feet and kept running, ignoring the throbbing pain. She had to get away, had to keep moving, *keep running*, until—

Something tackled her from the side, a solid, heavy weight, and she crashed down to the forest floor. Pain registered dimly as Lena's temple banged against a hard, knobby root. But the fear surmounted the pain, driving it out. The fear raced through her bloodstream, squeezed her heart until she was sure it was burst, turned her bones to jelly. Lena scrabbled blindly against the ground, but that heavy weight was on her, pinning her down. Then it flipped her over.

It was the shadow. The one who had snapped that poor driver's neck. And in the depths of the shadow's darkness was a face, a face Lena could barely make out. Gray and skeletal.

It was the face of the boy, the one who had ridden in the cart beside her.

The shadow straddled her, putting so much pressure on her chest, she could barely breathe. It grasped her by the wrists. "Dear, sweet Lena," the shadow breathed into her face. The princess clenched her lips, trying to turn away from the shadow's dreadful grimace. "Did you really think you could escape us?"

The shadow's grip tightened. Lena tried to scream, but she couldn't draw a breath, couldn't make a sound. The shadow lowered its head towards her.

Then the pain came, and it was suddenly, searingly brighter than any fear the princess had felt tonight. She found her voice.

She screamed and didn't stop screaming.

———— ◆O◆ ————

Gemma was almost halfway home when she heard the scream. It was a thin, distant sound, faint enough that, had Gemma been another person—a person living a different kind of life—she might have wondered if she'd just imagined it. But Gemma was a hunter and a tracker. Gemma was a soldier. Gemma served a prince who regularly went out looking for monsters.

Gemma knew a scream when she heard one, no matter how faint it was.

She stopped dead in her tracks. She'd been making her way along a winding path that led out of Glen City proper and back to the castle. It was not the most direct route, but it was the shortest. It led through a stretch of dense woodland—a large copse, really, not a proper forest—that most people would avoid this late at night.

Which was why Gemma was so startled to hear that scream.

Gemma let out a long, low breath. Closing her eyes, she went loose and alert at the same time. Relaxing her body, letting go of any distracting fears or worries or irrelevant tension. Honing in on what she could hear. Listening for another sound, another scream.

She didn't hear another scream. Instead, she heard the barest *scrape* on the path behind her.

Gemma let out another breath, silent and controlled. Then, in a single, fluid movement, she drew her pistol and spun.

"Whoa." The young man on the path before her raised his hands. He didn't look alarmed, though. In fact, he raised a quizzical eyebrow and said, "I would say 'Don't shoot,' but you really can't, can you?"

Gemma repressed a flinch at these words, hiding their impact behind a glare. "Klaus," she growled.

"I'm just saying." Klaus—fellow soldier and fellow woods-man—lowered his arms. "Why even carry that thing? You should be reaching for your knife."

Gemma seethed. Because Klaus was right. It was still her instinct to reach for a firearm, when her hunting knife was the better bet. Because while Gemma certainly could still shoot, hitting her target with any kind of accuracy was another matter.

That had been the way of things, ever since an evil witch caused a bleed in her brain that had ruined the sight in her right eye.

Gemma displayed none of her consternation, though. She only said in a flat voice, "Even I wouldn't miss at five paces."

"But a kill shot? You'd hit me, maybe."

"Maybe I don't want to kill you," Gemma said lightly. "Maybe I just want you screaming and bleeding."

"Ah, Gemma. That you want me at all touches my heart."

Gemma holstered her pistol, rolling her eyes. Then she stiffened as another scream tore through the air.

Klaus and Gemma both went silent. This scream was different than the one Gemma had heard before. It went on and on, an animalistic shriek, pain and terror clear in its raw, wretched tones.

Finally, it stopped. Klaus swore softly. "That sounded like—"

"Someone being tortured," Gemma said grimly.

"Yes." Klaus exhaled. "Check it out?"

"I think we'd better."

They left the path, crossing the scrubby field that separated the city's outskirts from the forest to the east. The main road that led out from the city here diverged a few miles into the woods, forming three separate routes. It was a well-traveled road; even at this time of night, it was not unheard of for travelers and merchants to make their way into Glen City.

"That delegation from the Desert Kingdom," Klaus said, as they approached the edge of the forest, "they weren't arriving yet, were they?"

"No." Gemma slowed to a halt, peering through the towering trees. "Prince Garrett said they aren't expected for another couple of days." Still, there was no telling how close they were. If they had made better time than expected. Which was one of the reasons Gemma thought they needed to investigate this disturbance. King Victor wouldn't be pleased if something attacked this foreign princess and her entourage, just miles outside the city.

They entered the forest at a northeast angle, but they reached the road quickly. The road was smoothly paved here and continued that way towards the east. Here, their footsteps were relatively silent as they walked, looking for tracks or disturbances. Klaus lifted his rifle and clicked on the light attached to it. The light was a recent addition, thanks to Princess Briar's genius. "You know," Klaus said, slowly sweeping the rifle's light through the trees ahead, "I can check this out on my own. You can go back to the castle. Get reinforcements."

"Do we need reinforcements?" Gemma asked coolly.

"Kind of hard to say, since we don't know who was screaming or why. I'm just saying, you could at least fetch a lantern or something."

"I can see just fine, Klaus. I grew up in the woods same as you." Even with only one good eye, Gemma was trained to see in the dark better than the average person.

"It's just," Klaus said, dropping his rifle as he turned to face her, "I think we'd better split up here."

Gemma looked at him. His face was carefully blank, no trace of concern on his features. Though they both belonged to the same army, they could not have looked more different. They wore the same navy-blue uniform coat, but where Gemma's was pressed neatly and fastened to the neck, Klaus's was rumpled and unbuttoned, revealing his plain vest beneath and the scarf wrapped around his neck to ward off the cold. His boots were scuffed, his leather belt worn, and a day's worth of stubby growth covered his chin.

Still, he was a good soldier, though Gemma would never tell him so. And right now, he *was* concerned about Gemma, though she knew he would never tell her so.

"So let's split up," she said. "No need to have a teary goodbye about it."

Now Klaus rolled his eyes. "Fine. You stick to the road, keep heading east. I'll scope out the woods on this side." He tossed a nod towards the north side of the road.

They parted ways, Klaus vanishing into the woods. Gemma went about a quarter of a mile up the road and stopped, her eyes scanning her surroundings. One of her hands rested on her holstered pistol, and the other she flexed constantly. This was to keep her hand warm, keep the blood moving, so her fingers wouldn't stiffen up in the cold. It was really, really cold. Far colder than it had any right to be. The spring equinox was next week, and yet, the chill of winter persisted. Just this morning, Gemma had seen a melting icicle dripping off the edge of the roof on one of the barracks.

The road was still and dark. The woods were quiet too. Gemma cocked her head to listen for a few minutes—not just for another scream, but for anyone on the road. Hoofbeats, carriage wheels. She scanned the skies as well, looking for smoke, signs of campfires. But she saw nothing. Heard nothing. Nothing out of the ordinary, anyway.

Gemma blew out a breath. Klaus had told her to stay on the road. But there was nothing to find here. And she wasn't going to stand around waiting for him. He said he'd search the north end of the woods.

So Gemma turned right, heading south through the trees.

Amazingly, she didn't have to go far before she heard it. Not another scream, but a faint mewling sound. Not very human-like—more like a wounded animal. Nevertheless, Gemma followed the noise through the darkness, until she came around a cluster of three gnarled oak trees, twisted together. Beyond the trees, standing out in the pitch black of the wood, was a blot of white and red.

A person, kneeling on the ground. A person garbed in white, clutching a bloodied arm to their chest.

Gemma sucked in a breath. The person, hunched over on the ground, was just far enough in the distance that she couldn't make out any discernible features. She thought, maybe, it was a girl—the person's hair was long and tangled, shielding their face. Her good eye focused on the red, on the bright blood staining the girl's white clothing. It was her arm that was bleeding, only—Gemma took a step closer—

It was the *stump* of her arm that was bleeding.

Because this girl was missing a hand.

Suddenly, the girl's head snapped up. Gemma glimpsed huge eyes in the darkness, but before she could say anything, a *shot* rang out, cracking through the woods like a bolt of lightning.

Gemma whipped around. "Klaus?"

There was no answer. Cursing under her breath, Gemma turned back to the bleeding girl.

But there was no girl.

She was gone.

In this Rapunzel-inspired novella, Demetri and Sabine get more than they bargained for when they investigate a ghost story in a dark forest. Sign up for the author's newsletter and download your copy of *Don't Go Into the Woods* for FREE!

WWW.ELIZABETHKKING.COM

Scan the QR code to sign up now:

GLOSSARY OF TERMS

THE FIVE KINGDOMS

The Mountain Kingdom
Princess Briar's home kingdom. Currently ruled by Briar's cousin.
The Glen Kingdom
Originally ruled by Demetri's family, the Georgas, until their fall. Currently ruled by King Victor and his son, Prince Garrett.
The Mariner Kingdom
Princess Snow's kingdom. Currently ruled by a council of lords.
The Forest Kingdom
A fallen kingdom. The last king vacated the throne 150 years ago.
The Desert Kingdom
Located far to the south. Little is known about this kingdom.

MAGICAL ELEMENTS

Fairies
These woodland creatures have green skin, petite statures, black eyes, and enormous wings. They mostly live in the north. Though at peace with humans, they retain the ability to curse them. They are forbidden to kill humans, and humans cannot kill fairies without dire consequences.

Djinn
Mortal enemies of the fairies, the djinn are confined to a shadow world. Theirs is the ability to grant wishes. They gain strength and freedom from their confinement by feeding off the life force of descendants of the original royal families. They can be identified by the blue markings on their faces; however, they can shapeshift into other forms.

Witches
Witches can only access magic through fairies, usually by spilling and consuming fairy blood. Witches also must make a deal with dark forces to access magic. This deal grants them long life, but guarantees an eternity of torment once they die.

Were-wolves
The were-wolves were created when a witch cursed the last king of the Forest Kingdom to become a beast. The curse is tied to the moon and continues to affect the descendants of the last Forest king. While in some cases, the bite of a were-wolf can pass along the curse, most who are bitten go mad and die.

Naiads
Also known as mermaids, the naiads once had to hunt and eat humans to survive. Now free of that curse, they live in the sea but can assume a human form when they wish to.

Demons
Little is known about these terrifying creatures, other than they kill quite gruesomely. They are believed to hail from a dark realm and can only appear in the world when summoned by a witch.

The Gift
This term commonly refers to the pact that ended the ancient war between fairies and humans. Specifically, the Gift was a gift of fairy blood, bestowed upon the five original royal families.

Elarium
A mineral unique to the Five Kingdoms, which is capable of powering various devices, including bulbs, mechanical devices, vehicle engines, and more.

CAST OF CHARACTERS

MEMBERS OF THE ROYAL FAMILIES

Princess Briar – a princess of the Mountain Kingdom. Abdicated her throne and currently lives in the Glen Kingdom. A "corpse creature," blessed with supernatural strength and speed.

Prince Garrett – crown prince of the Glen Kingdom and heir to the throne. Romantically involved with Princess Briar.

Demetri *(formerly prince)* – Was crown prince of the Glen Kingdom until his family was deposed. Now works as a monster hunter for the current Glen royals.

King Victor – the king of the Glen Kingdom and Prince Garrett's father.

Princess Snow – a princess of the Mariner Kingdom. Once betrothed to Prince Garrett. Hexed and killed by her evil stepmother, the witch Delphine.

Queen Laurel – the queen of the Mountain Kingdom and Briar's cousin.

Gryphon *(formerly prince)* – older half-brother of Prince Garrett. Was the crown prince of the Glen Kingdom until his exile. Also a descendant of the last Forest king.

WITCHES

Jesine – a good witch from a long line of good witches.

Adela – a bad witch hunted by Ansel. Assisted in an attempt to control and kill Prince Garrett's brother, Gryphon.

Castel – a bad witch who likes to play both sides. Used to work for the sea witch, Sohalia.

Malina – an ancient bad witch with a mysterious background.

Delphine – a bad witch who was once queen of the Mariner Kingdom. Was imprisoned when she murdered her husband and stepdaughters.

Harper – a bad witch who has a history with Jesine.

Sohalia – known as the "sea witch," a naiad who operated in the Mariner Kingdom. Was killed attempting to open a portal to a shadow world.

GLEN KINGDOM SOLDIERS

Gemma – a tracker and sharpshooter.

Klaus – a tracker, new to Prince Garrett's company. Served Garrett's exiled brother, Gryphon, until they had a falling-out.

Sabine – served as a guard for Princess Briar. Left her service to work with Demetri as a monster hunter.

Kinsley – personal bodyguard to Princess Briar. Was once romantically involved with the witch Castel.

Roy – an archer and sometimes Prince Garrett's medic.

Thatcher – Prince Garrett's medic.

OTHER FAIRYTALE CHARACTERS

Ansel – a witch hunter and brother to Isabelle. Killed a cannibalistic witch with Isabelle when they were kids. Worked as a guardsman in the Mariner Kingdom for the evil witch, Queen Delphine. Saved Princess Snow when she escaped Delphine. Has been hunting the witch Adela since she tried to kill Gryphon.

Isabelle – sister to Ansel and romantically involved with Gryphon. Was turned into a beta were-wolf when bitten by Gryphon.

Kel *(full name: Kelavandriana)* – a fairy bonded to the good witch Jesine.

Bastian – a raven with personal ties to the good witch Jesine.

The Dark Fairy *(full name: Tenalabralilah)* – the fairy who cursed Princess Briar and her kingdom to sleep and rot for a hundred years. Killed when Briar took her wings and made her mortal.

Perpetua – a naiad who lived in the Mariner Kingdom. Was romantically involved with Demetri. Sacrificed her life to save the rest of the naiads.

ACKNOWLEDGEMENTS

I will begin by thanking my main beta reader on this story, Emilie, who not only continues to provide enormously helpful feedback but also tireless enthusiasm and support for this entire series. Whenever I receive a manuscript back from her, I look forward to the suggestions as well as the fun guesses for what might happen in future books. Thank you so much.

I also want to thank the entire team at Miblart, who illustrated and delivered another gorgeous cover. Thank you for continuing to inspire me with your brilliant artwork. Credit also to Saumya Singh, who created the wonderful map for this book.

And as always, thank you so much to my family. I can't imagine anyone anywhere has such an amazing family. They are like my built-in team of fans and cheerleaders. Thank you all so much for your support.

About the Author

ELIZABETH K. KING is a fantasy and horror writer. Over the years, she has nurtured her love of monsters through TV shows like *Buffy the Vampire Slayer, Supernatural,* and *Grimm.* She spends her time writing in her gothic study and roaming the Shire (her backyard) with her cocker spaniel, Blue. She lives in Houston, Texas.

You can find Elizabeth online at www.elizabethkking.com, on Instagram @elizabeth_k_king, and on her Facebook page, Elizabeth K. King, Author.